a DEAL with the ELF KING

a MARRIED TO MAGIC novel

ELISE KOVA

Silver Wing Press

a DEAL with the ELF KING

a MARRIED TO MAGIC novel

ELISE KOVA

Published by Silver Wing Press
Copyright © 2020 by Elise Kova

Cover Artwork by Marcela Medeiros
Developmental Editing by Rebecca Faith Editorial
Line Editing and Proofreading by Melissa Frain

ISBN (paperback): 978-1-949694-28-4
ISBN (hardcover): 978-1-949694-27-7
eISBN: 978-1-949694-26-0

Also by Elise Kova

Married to Magic

A Deal with the Elf King
A Dance with the Fae Prince

Air Awakens Universe

AIR AWAKENS SERIES
Air Awakens
Fire Falling
Earth's End
Water's Wrath
Crystal Crowned

GOLDEN GUARD TRILOGY
The Crown's Dog
The Prince's Rogue
The Farmer's War

VORTEX CHRONICLES
Vortex Visions
Chosen Champion
Failed Future
Sovereign Sacrifice
Crystal Caged

A TRIAL OF SORCERERS
A Trial of Sorcerers

Loom Saga

The Alchemists of Loom
The Dragons of Nova
The Rebels of Gold

See all books and learn more at:
http://www.EliseKova.com

for those who need a break
and a second glass of wine

Table of Contents

one 1
two 10
three 21
four 27
five 33
six 40
seven 46
eight 55
nine 64
ten 72
eleven 77
twelve 84
thirteen 90
fourteen 98
fifteen 107
sixteen 118
seventeen 126
eighteen 132
nineteen 142
twenty 146
twenty-one 154
twenty-two 165
twenty-three 176
twenty-four 185
twenty-five 191
twenty-six 199
twenty-seven 208
twenty-eight 215
twenty-nine 228
thirty 236
thirty-one 245
thirty-two 253
thirty-three 265
thirty-four 275
thirty-five 281
thirty-six 288
thirty-seven 295
thirty-eight 302
thirty-nine 312

Quinnar

Midscape

one

THERE ARE ONLY TWO REASONS WHY THE ELVES COME TO OUR WORLD: WAR OR WIVES. In either case, they come for death. They come today.

My hands shake as I reach for the next jar. My solace and calm are hidden somewhere among the herb-filled containers that line the shelves of my shop. If I dig deep enough within them, keep looking between them, and continue mixing their contents, I might find some semblance of peace. There are two more poultices to make, one more sleeping draught, a strengthening potion, several healing salves…about five hours of work and only two hours to do it all.

If the Human Queen isn't found among the women of Capton, war will befall us. War would lead to all of humanity's destruction under the might of the elves' wild magic. Finding her would fulfill the treaty and secure the safety of humanity for another century. But if you *are her*, you might as well be dead.

It's the lack of queen that has the whole town on edge, myself included.

The chime of the bell above the door to my shop steals my attention from the meditation of my work.

"I'm sorry; I'm only open for emergencies tod—" I still as I settle the heavy jar of dried valerian root on my counter. There's a familiar reflection on its surface—a man with light brown hair and doe eyes, carrying a large bag. I look up quickly, affirming my suspicion. "Luke! What're you doing here so early?"

Luke stands in more traditional garb than he usually wears as a Keeper of the Fade. His dark trousers are freshly pressed and his bright blue tunic doesn't have a trace of dirt. The Keepers of the Fade look after the temple and forest at the edge of town, at the foot of the great mountain. They're the ones who traditionally deal with the elves, and keep anyone in Capton from accidently crossing over the Fade—the barrier that splits our world from the land of the elves and wild magic.

My work is quickly forgotten. I pop up the counter and step over to the other side. Luke drops the bag with a heavy thud and sweeps me up in his arms. The embrace goes on a little longer than typical for merely friends greeting each other.

His grip loosens, but he doesn't fully release me. His slack arms rest around my waist and I don't know what to do with my hands. They finally settle on his shoulders. Though what I want to touch is his chest.

"I had to come to see you." He runs his knuckles over my cheek. I tilt my head upward and swallow thickly.

I want to kiss him.

I've wanted to kiss him for at least six months now, likely more. I knew it when he came with me on my excursion to find winter root deep in the frigid marshes. I knew when he told me that the lack of Human Queen meant his duties as one of the Keepers of the Fade would triple, preventing him from spending as much time with me.

I likely wanted to kiss him before I really even understood what kissing *was*—back when we were small children playing games in the woods at the start of our lifelong friendship. But realizing you have a *want* to kiss someone makes everything agonizing. If I still thought we were *just* friends, I could've kissed him several times over on a dare, or a whim, or if he asked. I could've kept his company without my stomach doing flips.

But this *wanting* makes every movement between us unbearable. Especially because I can't kiss him. Doing so would be cruel...to both of us.

"Well, you've seen me now." I finally break away, smoothing

out my apron. I'm at war with myself around him. Every second hurts. I want him to sweep me up in his arms again. But I *can't* want that. I know I can't deep in my marrow. I don't have time for him; duty calls me. He's already too distracting as a friend. "I'm sure you're busy with the Keepers today, preparing for the arrival of the elf delegation this evening. We can go out to the forest tomorrow." Assuming there is a tomorrow.

"I want to take you this morning," he says in a tone I thought was reserved only for my dreams. "But I want to go farther than the forest."

"What're you talking about?" I ask, returning to the other side of the counter, where I continue adding various dried herbs into one of my most prized possessions—a silver kettle.

It's one of two gifts from Luke. The kettle was a gift when I graduated from my herbology studies at the academy in Lanton across the narrow strait to the mainland. The other gift, a necklace, he gave me when I was just a girl and it's never left my person since. Both are breathtaking.

But elvish goods usually are stunning. And extremely rare. I generally keep the necklace hidden to avoid drawing attention to the fact that I have two items of elvish make in my possession. I don't want to get Luke in trouble for any favoritism.

"I want to take you away." He motions to the bag at his feet. "I've prepared traveling supplies. There's a boat at the harbor ready for us to go."

I shake my head, as if I can jostle his words enough that they'll fall into an order that makes sense. "Traveling? A boat?"

"We'll start in Lanton, obviously. You still have connections from your academy days, right? Maybe we could stay with some of your old friends as we make our way," Luke suggests casually, as though we're talking about strolling up to the bluffs to the south of town. He doesn't break eye contact with me though—that's how I know he's serious. Dread tastes as metallic as fear. "And then who knows where from there? Do you want to explore the vast southern deserts? Or perhaps the Slate Mountains to the west?"

I force laughter. I wish I could pretend like he's joking. "What has gotten into you? We can't just leave. I have obligations here—and so do you, for that matter. Who will mend bones, stop fevers, and ensure the Weakness is kept at bay if I leave?" *Though there's little even I can do on that last one.* The Weakness has been a withering sickness plaguing Capton's people. It beats my attempts to combat it at every turn.

"Our work is what we do, not who we are. Nothing traps us here. We're not like the old ones in town who are only kept alive by the Fade River. We can leave. We'll make it out."

"Even if that were true, the elves are coming today. I have to get my work done before the town hall; I can't let everyone down. Mister Abbot needs his tea and Emma needs her strengthening potion or her heart—"

"Luella, we have to leave." Luke walks over and leans against the counter with both elbows. His voice drops to a hush as he glances upstairs.

"They're not awake yet," I say of my parents. Their room is above my shop and it's been quiet for the two hours I've been up working.

"The Keepers still haven't found the Human Queen. The magic in the line has been fading for some time." They say that the power of the Human Queen is passed from one queen to the next when the former queen dies. No one knows what would happen if there wasn't a Human Queen to be taken. It'd be unprecedented. "Some of my fellow Keepers think that maybe she just isn't here at all. Maybe the magic ran out. Which is all the more reason to get out while we can."

Since the treaty between the elves and humans was signed three millennia ago, there has been a Human Queen selected from Capton every hundred years like clockwork. Finding her was never hard; she's the only human with magic, after all. But this time, not one young woman of Capton has mended something with a thought, or made plants grow from barren earth, or had animals swear their allegiance to her.

Now, it's been one hundred and one years since the last Human Queen was chosen, and the town is suffering because of it.

"If she's not here then I especially can't leave. The Weakness is spreading through the town. People are dying as young as one hundred and ten. I have to do what I can to stop it." And if there is a war to come, healers will be needed more than ever. But I can't bring myself to say that. I can hardly think it.

"If there is no queen, you can do nothing to stop it. The town's connection with the Fade is dying and people will die with it. Their lifespans reduced to nothing more than those beyond our island." Luke grabs my hands. "The elves are coming, and I had a terrible dream about it. Please, let's leave *now*."

"Luke," I say gently, reaching forward to caress the shadow of gold across his chin. The constant stubble is new. I can't tell if he's growing a beard, or just keeping it closely cropped. Either way, I think I like it. "You look like you haven't slept. And you've been under a tremendous amount of stress with a long day ahead. Let me make a strengthening brew for you and then something for you to take tonight to help you sleep."

"I haven't slept because I have been preparing for us to leave before war breaks out." Luke pushes away from the counter and ducks underneath the thoroughfare. I'm cornered—counter on one side, shelves of herbs on the other, Luke before me, no exit behind. "I want to take you away. I want to keep you safe."

"Luke," I say gingerly, pleading. I want to pretend like he's joking but I can tell he's deathly serious. "I can't just leave."

"Yes you can, of course you can." The tone of his voice gives me pause. The way he's looking at me now leaves me breathless. I have to remind myself to breathe. "I want to take you away and spend time with you, and only you, Luella. Surely, you know…I've loved you for a long time."

I open and close my mouth, several times. Yes, I knew. And I love him too. I love him enough that I dreamed of this moment. But in my dreams I was wearing something nicer than my work smock and I didn't stink of lavender oil.

His expression falls in the wake of my silence. "Oh, I see… And here I thought that you might—"

"I love you too." As soon as I get the words out, sensation returns. Tingling vanishes from my toes. My whole body bursts with laughter. "I've loved you since I was a child."

"Then run away with me, Luella." Luke grabs my hands. His thumbs run over my knuckles.

My soul is soaring over the roof. Yet my feet are rooted deep in the land of the people I've vowed to serve.

"You know I can't," I whisper.

"But you love me."

"I do."

"Then let's go." He tugs at my hands.

"I *can't*." I'm unbudging. His expression falls into something I don't recognize. "I want to, Luke. I wish I could go with you. But I can't just leave. This town has invested so much in me; I must be here when they need me."

The people of Capton paid for my years at academy when my parents could not afford them. They bought me room and board. They supported me at every turn with the hard-earned and scraped-together change at the bottoms of their pockets.

"Besides," I continue, softer. "If the Human Queen isn't found, and the council can't sort things with the elves, there's nowhere we could run. All of humanity is doomed at that point. I would rather stay here with our people and face whatever may come."

"We could find a way," he insists. I shake my head. "If you love me, truly love me, then that's all you need. Our love is enough."

"But—" I don't get to finish.

In a wide step, he closes the distance between us. One arm snakes around my waist. The other cups my cheek. He tilts my face upward and I don't fight him. I don't want to.

Luke's lips meet mine as my eyes close.

The stubble that lines his lips is rough on my face. But I hardly notice; my sole focus is kissing him. How much movement is too much, and how much is too little, when it comes to kissing?

Unexpectedly, I desperately wish I'd given in to the boys at the academy and allowed them to "teach me kissing" when they found out I'd never been kissed before. I had been waiting for this moment. I'd been waiting for these lips.

Yet…as he pulls away, I'm left awkward and unfulfilled. None of this is quite how I imagined it would happen. I'm not soaring. My heart isn't fluttering. Something in me is detached and…sad?

A soft ahem comes from the doorway behind us. Luke turns. My face is hot as I meet my mother's grinning eyes—the same shade of hazel as mine. To make embarrassing and awkward matters worse, my kettle begins to hiss and the sleeping draught I was making is now boiling over my counter.

"Oh!" I rush over, beginning to mop up the mess.

My mother crosses with a laugh, helping lift the kettle off the heat. "Luke, it's good to see you; would you like to stay for breakfast this morning?"

"I would love to." He gives a dashing smile. Hopefully the need to fill his stomach distracts him from his insane notion of leaving. And when he's full, he'll have a more level head.

"I have work to do," I needlessly remind them both.

"And doing it on an empty stomach is pointless." My mother tucks wayward strands of fiery hair—the same bright hue as mine—back into her bun. "Take a break, hardworking daughter of mine. You are not going to be saving a life in the twenty minutes it takes you to eat a scone and a boiled egg."

"One of your scones sounds lovely, Mrs. Torrnet."

"It's Hannah, Luke, you know that." My mother titters and I roll my eyes. "Now, come upstairs, both of you."

A plate of scones is in the center of the table—lavender and orange. It's incredible the number of different plants that grow on Capton's island. Too many. So many that it should be impossible. But the main water source for the island flows through the Fade itself, making the impossible possible here.

Father is seated at the head of the table. His glasses hang on the tip of his nose as he looks over paperwork—no doubt going over speeches before the town hall today.

"Good morning, Luke," he says without looking up. Luke has been coming around since we could walk and is as much a staple in this kitchen as my mother's iron pot or my potted herb garden in the back window. "Surprised to see you today." He pauses. "Though I suppose today is the usual day you escort Luella to the forest."

"I thought we could get it done with before the sun was up. That way I could get back to my duties as Keeper," Luke says cordially as he sits, helping himself to a scone. No mention of trying to steal me away, thankfully.

"What are the Keepers doing about all this?" Mother asks from where she works a skillet behind me. Our kitchen runs the length of half the brownstone—galley style, the sailors would say.

"Mother—"

"We're doing our best to find the Human Queen," Luke says calmly.

"Well, maybe there shouldn't *be* a Human Queen," Mother huffs.

"Hannah," Father cautions.

"It's true, Oliver, and you know it. The Capton Council is just as bad as the Keepers." Mother is as aggressive as the boiling water she pulls eggs from.

"Can we just have a nice breakfast, please?" I beg. I'm so tired of hearing about the Keepers pointing the finger at the Capton Council for not being more aggressive in trying to find the Human Queen by interrogating the townsfolk, and the council pointing the finger at the Keepers for not sharing more of their elvish relics or histories that could help identify the Human Queen.

Father thinks there must be something the Keepers are hiding. Luke claims otherwise and says the council doesn't share enough information with the temple. They both look to me to take their side and it takes all of my effort to remind them that all I care about is keeping the people of this island healthy—I have no horse in their race.

"If there's no Human Queen then all of humanity dies a horrible death as they use their wild magic to peel our skin from our bones, turn us into beasts of the deep woods, curdle our blood, and worse; I think it's safe to say none of us want that." Father flips through his papers.

"We're dying now." Mother situates the eggs on a platter and sets it on the table. "You've heard about the Weakness. Men and women are falling where they stand. We are dying like any regular human on the mainland."

"Once there is a Human Queen the order will be restored and the treaty will be fulfilled," Father says. "No more of this Weakness."

"Is that true? Do we know that things will return to normal for certain?" Mother turns to Luke.

"So the texts that outline the treaty say." Luke peels an egg.

She sighs and grabs a scone, tearing off a hunk and mumbling, "While I hate the notion of this Human Queen business, if it must happen then let it be done with. My heart bleeds for the family whose daughter will be taken though..." Mother squeezes my hand. I'm too old—historically the queens have displayed magic tendencies at sixteen or seventeen. I remember a few years when my parents watched me like a hawk. Thankfully, there's not a trace of magic in me. "What a grim circumstance to see your daughter get married under."

"Speaking of weddings," Luke says casually. "Has Luella told you both yet?"

My parents exchange a look with me. I glance nervously between them and Luke. I've no idea what he's talking about.

"Told us what?" Father is the one to ask.

"Luella has agreed to marry me."

two

I SPIT THE GULP OF WATER BACK INTO MY CUP WITH A SPUTTER.

"Luella, you should have told us!" Mother gasps and claps her hands together. "This is wonderful news!"

"I thought you were too busy with your shop to think of courtship?" Father arches his eyebrows. I'm still coughing up a lung. He adds, "Are you all right?"

"Well, I…" I cough. "Sorry, water in the wrong pipe."

Marry him? When did I agree to that? Oh, right, I *didn't.* I look at Luke from the corner of my eye. He's beaming from ear to ear.

I can't marry anyone. I've told him that. I've told *everyone* that just so my mother's friends would stop digging their noses into my affairs.

I don't have time for marriage. I don't have time for whatever it is Luke and I have already been doing. I've never even *thought* of marriage.

For the entirety of my nineteen years, I've known I was destined to be married to trees and herbs and duty before a man. I have been content—fulfilled, even—with that alone. But marriage? Motherhood? Wifely duties?

I have more important things to focus on…like keeping people alive.

Standing, I say, "Mother, Father, please excuse us. I have rounds to make before the town hall and I don't want to keep Luke from his duties." I catch Luke's eyes with a pointed look. "Shall we head to the forests now?"

"Yes, we'll clean up, go and enjoy yourself." Mother is beaming. Father, however, gives me a knowing, wary look.

I feel bad making my parents clean when they cooked, but I need to escape. I need to talk to him and sort this marriage thing out. I practically drag Luke back downstairs, into my shop, past his stupid bag still by the door, and out into the crisp Capton morning.

"What was that?" I whirl on him as we emerge onto the street. "*Marriage?*"

"You said you loved me."

"I may be inexperienced with all this but saying 'I love you' is *not* the same thing as 'I'll marry you.'"

He tilts his head with a gentle smile and rests his hands on my shoulders. "Isn't this what you've always wanted?"

"What?"

"You and me, together. We love each other, Luella, we have for years. There's no one more perfect out there for you than me."

"That's not the point," I mutter.

He hooks his arm with mine, beginning to lead us down the road lined by brownstones of the residential area of town. "You need to stop holding back and stop being so focused on your work."

"My work makes me happy."

"Don't I make you happy?"

"Yes, but—"

He kisses the tip of my nose, silencing me. "Then I'm all you need. Your father can perform the wedding himself..."

Luke rambles about silk and flowers and toasts the entire walk down the street, up the narrow stairs that lead into a stone path lazily wandering the cliff-tops overlooking the ocean. A river cuts across in the distance before crashing down as a waterfall to the sea foam beyond. Its stunning blue waters are under the protection of the Keepers, as is the forest we head toward.

Our island is small, just off the coast of the mainland and across from Lanton. Nestled in the only sheltered bay of the island is the lonely town of Capton. I grew up wedged on this narrow strip between mountain and sea. The thick and gnarled redwood forest runs down from the foot of the great mountain that looms over us to the town. The temple winds as a sort of bridge between the two.

Capton historians say the temple was built long ago, before the great war that resulted in the treaty. But it's hard for me to think of anything that old still standing. More likely, one of the original Keepers built it to house their order.

Slithering out from the side of the temple is an unassuming pathway of arches. I've never walked that path. I'm forbidden to, even with a Keeper escort. That is for the Human Queen and the elves. Luke tells me it stretches all the way into the darkest part of the forest at the foot of the mountain.

It is the path that leads to the Fade—the split between the human world and the magic wilds.

Capton is somewhat of a between, at least that's how I've come to think of it. It's on the "human side," the "not magic side," of the Fade. But our proximity to the Fade, and the river that flows through it, gives our island diverse wildlife and the people here extremely long lifespans. The cost of these benefits is the Human Queen. We give up one of our own every hundred years to honor the treaty. That is Capton's burden for humanity's sake.

I wonder, not for the first time, what the Fade looks like. If I were to stand before it, would I know I'm at the border of mankind and wild magic? Is the air electric, like right before a summer storm? Would it shake me like the howling wind high on the mountain ledges? Or could I stumble across the line without even knowing, like the folktales say, and get lost forever?

Those thoughts are dangerous and I shake them from my head. There's no shortage of mystery surrounding the Fade. But we know one thing for certain: the queen is the only human who can go beyond the Fade and make it back alive.

"What is it?" Luke asks.

"Nothing."

"Were you even listening to me?"

"Of course I was."

"What did I say?"

"*Uh...*"

He chuckles and leans forward. The pad of his finger brushes against my temple as he gently tucks a strand of wayward hair behind my ear. I've kissed him, I've said I loved him, I'm somehow engaged to him, and yet I still blush.

"You should grow it long again." His eyes focus on where he hooks my hair by my ear. I fight a shiver at his fingers pausing there. "I liked it better long."

"It gets caught in brambles when I'm collecting herbs," I explain apologetically. Though I don't know what I'm apologizing for. He knows why I cut it during my years at the academy.

"Maybe for our wedding."

"Right…"

"What were you thinking of, really?" he asks as we arrive at the forest's edge. I begin collecting small flowers that grow at the foot of the redwoods—morning stars, I call them, because they bloom at dawn. They're good for strengthening body and mind and I use them for Emma and Mister Abbot.

When I was a child, I imagined that they grew only for me. But the whole forest seemed more alive back then. It's still alive now, but in a dulled and quiet way. With age and time, I lost an imaginary friend.

"Luella? What were you thinking of?" he repeats with a note of agitation seeping into his tone.

I wish I could tell him outright that the idea of engagement makes me want to throw up on his shoes. That I care about him—I love him—but I made a vow to the people of Capton to always be there to serve and that will always come first. Maybe I just want him to explain what's really gotten into him.

"I was thinking of that time when we were children and we wandered too far into the woods and saw the wolf."

It had been a hulking beast of darkness and shadow, bright yellow eyes cutting through the unnatural thickness that lingered in the air of the deep forest.

I stare off between the trees, imagining those eyes now. Oddly, I hadn't felt afraid that day—though I later told Luke I was more terrified than he had been. He wouldn't have handled it well to know he was more afraid than I.

There was knowledge in that beast's eyes. Knowledge and

secrets. Secrets that I've always felt like I'm on the cusp of knowing and yet are just out of my grasp.

"Nothing, no beast or man, will ever harm you as long as I'm around." Luke crouches next to me, resting his hand on the back of my neck. He rolls the dark, glassy beads of the necklace he gave me over my flesh. "And as long as you wear this."

"I've never taken it off." I touch the pendant suspended by the beads. It is a stone that looks like a rainbow was caught in a fisher's net. Luke wears a similar stone on his wrist. It's a special stone usually reserved for the Keepers.

Yet another reason why I've always kept his gift to me hidden beneath my clothes.

"Good. Wear this and never go into the forest without me."

"I never do." I chuckle and shake my head. "You're always so afraid of me going into the forest."

"I don't like you alone in the woods," he murmurs. Luke stands, turning eastward. The horizon is hidden behind the mountain. But we can see its first rays outlining the summit in orange. "We can still leave, you know," he whispers.

"I can't," I repeat myself from earlier.

"We'll be husband and wife. It's normal to leave home."

"Not for people from Capton, and not for me." I stand, having collected the flowers I need. "You should go. The Keepers need you today."

"I'll walk you back."

I almost ask him not to. There's a strange air about him today. One that almost makes my best friend unrecognizable.

But he's tired. I believe him when he says he had a bad dream about the day's events. Given the recent requests to my shop, I think half of Capton can hardly sleep from anxiety.

He's acting rashly because he truly believes our lives are about to end.

Back at the shop, he kisses me once more in the doorway. Once more, the kiss is empty. But I try and hold on to the feelings I think I should have, to him, and the dream of us, with all my might.

"If you change your mind," he whispers. "The boat is ready. Leave with me, please."

"Luke, I—"

Before I can say anything else, he's gone. I watch him walk briskly down the street. He doesn't even look back at me. I put my back to him with a sigh and start inside.

When the sun is properly risen, I begin my rounds for the day. The elves aren't expected until nightfall. Half the brews are still warm as they clank in my basket. I have a long list in my head of all my patients, but I'm only hitting half the list this morning—the people who are too weak, wounded, or ill to make it to the town hall later.

I'll make the rest of my deliveries when the recipients are conveniently all in one place. Hopefully, by then, I'll have had enough time to finish their various medications.

First up is Douglas, a fisherman who has been laid up for two weeks following a spearfishing incident. Usually, a wound like this would've healed with just a wash in the waters of the Fade River. But it's still angry and red, dripping with pus. Today he runs a fever as well.

After that is Cal. His daughter caught a chill this winter that just won't abate. Then Amelia—her monthly bleed is agonizing, this month particularly so. Then Dan, who can't seem to find the strength to get out of bed and attend to his duties as the town carpenter.

On and on I go from door to door, checking in and making sure they have what they need or, at the very least, the best I can give them. It doesn't feel like enough. Each one seems worse than the last, as if their illnesses are clinging to them for the express purpose of making a mockery of everything I'm trying to do.

I became an herbalist to help people. But in the year I've been in Capton since finishing my studies at the academy, things have only become worse. They tell me that I'm doing a good job, that the problems lie with the lack of a Human Queen. But I can't help wondering if I couldn't be doing something more.

Kindly Mr. Abbot is the last on my list for the morning. Thankfully, he's doing all right still. I doubt I could keep my composure if he wasn't.

"Come in, come in." He waves me inside with small, trembling motions of his weathered hand.

"Mr. Abbot, I'm afraid I can't stay today. But I brought your tea so you can brew—"

"I've already put the kettle on." He shuffles about the kitchen. "The tea never tastes the same when I brew it."

"I'm sure it does." Yet I'm putting my mostly empty basket down on his counter anyway.

"It doesn't work as well," he insists, per usual.

"I think you just like having company." I smile and set to work as he eases himself into a chair at his table.

"Can you blame an old man?"

"No."

Mr. Abbot isn't the first person to claim they can't replicate my brews, salves, and poultices at home—even when I sell them the exact herbs and give them detailed instructions. I suspect it's because of my elvish kettle. The Keepers say a bit of the elves' wild magic lives in the things they make using it. If that's true, then maybe part of my skills are because of the necklace Luke gave me.

No matter what the reason, I'm glad my gifts can be of service. If my hands must be the ones to make the brews to have them work, then so be it. Yet another reason why I must stay in Capton.

"The town is so busy today." Mr. Abbot looks out the large front window of his home. He lives down by the docks, not far from the large square where town halls are held.

"The elves are coming," I remind him.

"Ah, right."

"You should stay home, you don't need that kind of excitement," I encourage.

"If ordered by my healer, I suppose I must." A frown crosses his lips before he brings the mug I hand him to his mouth. His eyes seem to be staring at a distant memory. "They'll take another young woman, won't they?"

"Unfortunately." I run my finger along the top edge of my mug, thinking of the conversation at the breakfast table. "Yet none of the women of Capton have displayed any magic tendencies."

"The Keepers are usually watching closely for any signs."

I remember when Luke was assigned to me for three years—fifteen through my eighteenth birthday. He and my parents kept an eye on everything I did whenever I was in Capton. Luke even came to Lanton a few times to observe me.

My mother once suspected even that my herbology gifts were magical manifestations. But Luke assured her it was just good training at the academy.

"They still do." I take a sip. "But they haven't found anyone who might be the Human Queen."

He sighs. "This whole business is a wound that never heals."

"What is?" I think he's talking about the treaty. I'm wrong.

"Losing your family to the elves. They take a daughter, a sister, forever."

"The Human Queen can return to Capton every midsummer," I needlessly remind him. He's lived in this town far longer than I. Mr. Abbot is pushing one hundred and twenty.

"They're never the same after; Alice wasn't."

Alice... That was the name of the last Human Queen. Surely, it couldn't just be coincidence...

"Who's Alice?"

He turns his milky eyes toward me. "My sister. And before you ask, yes, she was."

"Your sister was the last Human Queen?" I ask anyway. He nods. How did I never know this? Why was it never taught or mentioned? Mr. Abbot has been coming into my shop every other day for a year now. I was making him poultices and potions long before I had any formal training. "I had no idea," I say, feeling somewhat guilty.

"One thing you will soon learn is that the name of the bride quickly disappears off the tongues of the people. Whoever leaves will be forgotten as ever being a part of this town. She will become the 'Human Queen' for stories and nothing more."

I shudder. We learn about the Human Queens in grade school. Even before then, there's not a resident of Capton who *doesn't* know the stories. Seeing the queen leave is a rite of passage for a generation. And it isn't until this conversation—until the last Human Queen becomes someone more than just an idea to me—that I even realize Alice must've come back on midsummers and I never once saw her.

"I think people do it, consciously or not, out of kindness," Mr.

Abbot continues with a weary smile. "As if, by saying her name less, it will hurt less that she is gone. As if a person can be expunged so neatly from a family and community."

"I never thought of it that way," I whisper.

"Keeping the peace between worlds is an ugly business." His hand shakes as he raises his cup back to his mouth to take a timid sip. When he brings it back to the saucer, however, his movements are much smoother. I'm relieved to see the draught is having the intended effects.

"Did you meet with her, during midsummer?" I ask, genuinely curious. I try and imagine him with a Human Queen, sitting at this same scuffed and scratched table as we are now.

"Yes, and corresponded with letters."

"Can letters cross the Fade?" A thousand questions burn my tongue as they swirl in the scalding tea.

"No, but the elves can. They brought the messages to the temple, usually when they came for last rites or to trade with the Keepers."

"What did she say it was like beyond the Fade?"

"Not much." He shook his head. "Alice said that her role as queen was merely to exist."

I stare into my teacup.

The elves will come and they will take a woman from her family and home to fulfill a treaty that they could just as easily call off. They'll sit her on a throne to do what? Exist? To have no power or responsibility?

What is the point of the deal the elves struck if all they wanted was a puppet? Why take one of us at all?

To remind us we are nothing, my mind answers. They hold all the power. What the elves want, we are here to give them. I'm sure they would tell us to be grateful that all they take is a woman every century. That it is a kindness.

My stomach turns molten and I have to leave or risk saying something that would upset the kind old man.

The town hall is held four hours later, in the late afternoon. It's enough time that I can go home, restock my basket, and freshen up. I'm not the only one with the idea of conducting business before the meeting. Some of the fishermen have brought their hauls. I see a few townsfolk displaying needlepoint. Everyone is all too happy to have something else to focus on—or *pretend* to focus on—beyond the impending elf arrival.

Yet, rumors and theories buzz in the air around me like bees in a field. I hear the whispers and speculation. What will happen? Will the queen be found?

I ignore it all, focusing on my duties. There is no way war will break out after three thousand years of peace. That's what I've settled on to keep my hands steady as I pass out my jars and pouches.

"Hear ye, hear ye, citizenry of Capton," the town crier shouts from the stage at the far end of the square. A group of weary men and women line up behind him—my father among them. "We call to order this meeting of the Capton Council."

I stop with the rest of the townsfolk, listening to the various announcements. There are some clerical matters to get out of the way—a few disputes over fishing territories with Lanton, an agreement for tearing down an old warehouse. But everyone is just listening for the important part.

"Regarding the matter of the Human Queen," my father says. He stands with the head of the Keepers. "The council has heard your concerns and decided to—"

He doesn't get to finish.

"Look, there!" someone shouts.

All heads turn in the direction of the long stairs that head up from town to the temple. On them, a small legion marches. They're led by a man who rides a horse made of shadow, its form writhing and fading like mist with every movement.

His long, raven hair fans across his shoulders. I can see a shimmer of what looks like purple, or blue, in the withering sunlight. Bands of iron weave around each other almost organically around his temples, before jutting up into a fan of sharp points at the back of his head—almost like oversized thorns—to make a crown. His ears extend away from his face into points that match the spears of his crown. When he and his soldiers are at the edge of our square, I can see that his eyes are a brilliant cerulean, nearly the same shade as the pillars of the temple.

He is nothing like the ancient, gnarled monster I imagined or the stories made him out to be. The only thing those stories seem to have portrayed accurately is the sheer power that radiates off the man.

The Elf King's face, ethereal, handsome, youthful, as hard as diamonds, is as handsome as it is terrifying. He is like a poisonous flower—stunning and deadly. *This*, I realize as his eyes flash an even brighter blue, *is the face of death.*

three

THE ELF KING SITS ATOP HIS STEED OF SHADOW, LOOKING DOWN ON US AS THOUGH WE'RE NOTHING MORE THAN ANTS. A legion of elves, armored and armed, stand behind him. Though he is surprisingly unarmored.

As he dismounts, I realize I have never witnessed a more perfect study in contrasts. His physique is cut from marble, but his movements are as fluid as the silken fabric that drapes from his shoulders. His long-sleeved, silver tunic is tailored tightly to his body and pressed so stiff that it almost gives the illusion of hammered steel. Yet, I can imagine my fingers gliding over the silky fabric across the smooth plane of his broad chest.

I quickly stare at my toes, willing away whatever magic spell he's glamoured over himself. But my eyes are drawn back to him against my will. I can't *not* look at him. Not when he dismisses the horse as though it were nothing more than smoke on the breeze. Not when his armored knights begin to move. And certainly not when he marches up onto the platform the Head Keeper, council, and my father are standing on.

"Your Majesty." The Head Keeper's voice quivers as she bows low. "We were expecting a delegation, an ambassador, or some—"

"You have had a year," he says slowly, displeasure

dripping from every word. "I have been patient. I have sent a delegation to the Keepers' temple. Yet I do not have a queen."

"We were—"

"*Silence*." He seethes, leaning close to her. "Have you forgotten who I am? You will speak only when you are spoken to."

The elf knights move around us, circling us as though we're cattle. I see some go off in pairs down the streets of town. What're they looking for? Stragglers?

I bite my cheeks and resist the urge to say something. Surely they wouldn't rip a man from his sickbed just to terrorize him in the streets…would they?

"I will have my queen, here and now. We can afford no more delays," the king continues. He turns to face the citizenry of Capton. "I know you have hidden her, tampering with forces you do not understand."

"Your Majesty." The words sound awkward from my father's mouth. I wish he would stay silent. The last thing I want are those emotionless, elven eyes turning to him. "Perhaps there is no queen this year?"

"She is here, of that I'm certain. Merely hidden." He sweeps an arm over the crowd. "Hand her to me or I will tear through every household in search of her. Hand her to me or I will take every young woman of age and bring them back across the Fade one by one until I have my queen."

To be brought across the Fade as a normal human would spell death. He would kill every woman to find one. I clench my jaw, *hard*.

"Luella." Luke's fingers close around mine. I look at him in surprise. Where had he been hiding in the crowd? "Come on, we can still sneak out."

"Are you insane?" I hiss.

"There's still time," he insists. "Let's go. The elves will let me pass as a Keeper, the boat is still waiting and—"

A scream interrupts him.

"Emma, Emma!" Ruth shouts. "The Weakness, it's claimed her!"

I move to leave but Luke holds fast. "Let me go."

"Now is our chance, while there's a distraction."

"I said let me go!" I rip my hand from his and rush over, pushing past the people that don't part for me. Ruth—Emma's mother—kneels by her daughter, howling. Tears are already streaming down her face.

"They have brought the Fade upon us! They are here for war. We are doomed!" she shrieks.

"Ruth, Ruth, please." I quickly kneel down, dropping my satchel and basket on the ground next to me. "Let me see her."

"You said you don't know what the Weakness is. What can you do? You didn't even get her draught to her this morning." Ruth wounds me with the truth.

"You're right. I don't know what the Weakness is," I admit, keeping my voice low and even, hoping she'll match my tone and calm down. "But this isn't it. The Weakness has only claimed the oldest among us—" *so far* "—making the residents of Capton pass on when a normal human would. Emma is only nineteen." My age.

"The Weakness has her heart, her draught, she—this is because of *him*!" Ruth points toward the Elf King, clutching Emma to her breast. Their golden curls toss in all directions with Ruth's jerky motions. "*He* did this. He killed her first. She wasn't your queen so you killed her!"

"Ruth, stop," I say sternly, lunging to grab her arm. It's too late, the Elf King's attention is on us. As though it hasn't been from the moment the commotion started. "Emma is breathing, see?" I yank Ruth's hand toward Emma's mouth. She feels the slow and shallow breaths that I already saw and her face crumples with relief.

"Oh, blessed be the old gods." Ruth rocks back and forth. "What's wrong with her?"

"It's likely just the excitement. Without her draught it was too much," I say thoughtfully. I hope that's all it is. This is why I couldn't run away with Luke. Just one morning of breakfast with him and my parents and I have a patient on the ground, unconscious. "Lay her down, please."

Emma's heart is weak. It has been since we were schoolgirls. She was actually my first patient and treating her is a wash of nostalgia to this day. We would sneak off into the woods, sometimes with Luke, and sometimes not. I would make her mixtures of berries, leaves, river water, flowers, sometimes even mud, and she would take my concoctions dutifully.

Even though we were playing pretend, I always wanted to help. She always swore my potions worked, even back then.

Luckily, I never leave home without my satchel. My basket has custom-made creations—tailored to people's individual needs. But my satchel is a staple pantry of the herbalist's essentials and my personal notebook. I can never be certain what someone might ask me for on a whim, or what I might need at a moment's notice.

I pull out a series of herbs and crush them into a small wooden cup. I'm so engrossed that I don't even notice I've attracted an audience. A shadow eclipses the sunlight, casting me in darkness.

Ruth blubbers incoherently, staring up at the towering man. I turn my gaze skyward, meeting the eyes of the Elf King, who looms over me.

"Continue." His voice is the whisper of silk.

"I…"

"Don't touch her!" Luke shouts, pushing past the thick line of people who backed away from Ruth, Emma, and me. "Don't lay one finger on her."

"Luke, *stop.*" Any affection I felt for him is quickly withering. It's as though he's turned into a stranger in the past twenty-four hours. There's someone else occupying the outline of a man I once knew.

The king turns slowly to face Luke. He tilts his head, as though he were regarding a cat, or a rat, or even a fly. That's likely all we are to him.

The temperature suddenly plummets. A wintry chill has my teeth chattering and hands shaking. I'm torn between continuing to help Emma and watching what happens to Luke.

Luke touches his Keeper's bracelet, clutching it to him.

"Yes, Keeper of the Fade," the Elf King says silkily. "Reach for your labradorite. It will protect *you* from the Knowing, but it does nothing to protect the world around you."

The Knowing? I've never heard of it before. But I can't linger on the thought as the stones beneath Luke's feet suddenly come to life. They rise upward, curving unnaturally and weaving into a prison cell around where Luke stands. I stare in awe and horror at wild magic.

The Elf King looks back to me. "*Well?* Heal her," he commands, impatient.

I watch helplessly as Luke fights against his prison, but the stone bars don't move. He's as helpless as the rest of us in the face of power that defies all laws of nature. I wish I could do something for him, but I know I can't. There's nothing in my bag of herbs that can reverse wild magic.

Emma's soft whimper brings my attention back to her. She's the one who needs me most right now—and the one I can help. Regardless of the Elf King's orders, she is my duty.

With the last of the herbs in my cup, I place it carefully on the ground before me. In my bag is a small tinderbox. I light a shaving of dried redwood and drop it in the cup. It flares as it burns quickly, incinerating the crushed herbs and singeing the rim.

I say a silent prayer to the old gods that this will work. And dip my finger into the soot and ash. I smear a line underneath Emma's nose. It looks like a ridiculous mustache that we'd draw on each other as children as a joke when someone fell asleep during break between lessons.

Emma's shallow breaths catch the scent of the ash and she jolts awake.

"Emma." I hover over her so I'm the first one she sees—not the Elf King. She doesn't need any more shocks. "Emma, how do you feel?"

"Luella? I... What happened?" she murmurs.

I look to Ruth. "Take her back to your home; she needs to rest. I'll come by later with a strengthening potion."

"All right."

"I see." Two words from the Elf King freeze us all in place.

Emma's breaths are quick and shallow. She's going to make herself faint again with this much excitement. I push off the ground and stand between Emma and the Elf King.

"Go," I say to them. "Go home. No one will stop you."

They slowly rise and begin to step away when the king says, "You do not speak for me."

"Emma is not your queen." I turn to face him. My insides have liquefied. But I swore to do right by my patients. I swore to help this town. And if helping Emma means standing up to the Elf King then this is just another day at work. "She needs to rest. You must let her go."

"She is free to go." The king gives a nod to his knights and they allow Emma and Ruth to pass. "Because you are right, she is not my queen. I have found the woman I seek."

"Good, leave," I mutter under my breath. But when my gaze sweeps back I find his attention solely on me. The weight of his stare reminds me of just how bold I've been and my insides liquefy.

"You hid yourself," he says, dangerously quiet.

"I have no idea what you're talking about."

He takes a wide step forward, encroaching on my space. This close, I can smell him. The air around him is perfumed with a cologne of sandalwood, moss, and a bright fresh note like the air before a storm. It's a lovely, earthy, intoxicating aroma that is in stark contrast to the scowl of disgust he wears.

I try and step away but I am snared. He reaches forward, sliding his fingertips down my throat. I shiver, frozen in place.

The king's finger hooks on the necklace Luke gave me all those years ago. They slide down to the pendant and he makes a fist. His expression darkens to something almost sinister and I wonder if I should be begging him for my life.

His other hand has worked around the back of my throat, cradling my head. His fingers move. Is he about to snap my neck? Is this how I die?

"You will know, soon enough," he says before he yanks the necklace away.

The world goes white, then fills with screams.

four

I'M DIZZY AND BREATHLESS. Energy sizzles and cracks across my body. Inexplicable power I shouldn't possess threatens to tear me apart.

Like fireworks, magic explodes out from me in bursts. It strikes the lampposts surrounding the square. The glass shatters and falls to the ground as cherry blossom petals. Where iron once stood are now trees.

A lush carpet of moss and grass unfurls across the cobblestones of the square. Brush and vine spring from it and creep up the buildings like writhing, sentient tentacles trying to reclaim the buildings. The world around me is transformed, exchanged from constructed to natural. It is as if nature has erupted from my feet to oppose the audacity of mankind's hubris to stand against it.

I can see it now. It? Everything. I can see *everything*.

My eyes have never been more open. I see every pulse of magic—of life—in those around me. I see the raw essence of existence and it steals my breath and composure.

Bitter cold tears flow down my cheeks. I'm suddenly hot. I'm molten fire in a world that has become ice.

The king finally releases me and I stumble backward, landing on my bottom, arms back to brace myself. The moss grows over my fingers. Tiny vines spring forth, grabbing my wrists. I yank my hand away and grip my shirt over my chest, panting. My red hair curtains my face around my jaw and I use it for a brief second of privacy as I press my eyes closed.

That can't have been real. *Tell me this is all a nightmare*, I want to scream.

But as I straighten, I can't help but *see*. The square has become something out of a storybook. Plants and humans pulse with a greenish light. Inanimate objects are gray.

I blink several times, watching the auras fade in and out of my awareness. Everything around me is awash with the same color... except for *him*.

The king is a pale blue. The aura that surrounds him is unlike the still, orderly magic of life. His magic is writhing, angry, and violent. Much like the scowl on his face. Whatever vision I was granted fades as I continue to gape at him.

He stares down at me, eyes unreadable, brow furrowed.

"What..." I rasp, trying to find my voice. "How?"

He tilts his head to the side. "So you truly did not know."

"I..." My throat closes and I choke on air.

Know.

Know I am the Human Queen, he means.

"Tell me what's happening?" I manage, but am ignored.

"So the question becomes, who?" The king turns, sweeping his eyes across the square. The people I once knew, my friends and family, gaze in shock and awe. "Who hid her? Who gave her this?" the king demands, holding up the necklace he tore from my throat.

"That..." The moment I speak, the Elf King's eyes are back on me, accusatory and oppressive. Even if I had the capacity to lie, I couldn't. My eyes have already betrayed me as they dart over to my caged childhood friend. "Luke. It was a gift from Luke."

"How dare you," Luke seethes at me. His face is ugly, horrible. It is the face of hatred. The eyes I'd dreamed about—eyes that, hours ago, looked at me with admiration as he declared he would marry me—I now can't recognize. "I loved you, I wanted to protect you and now you'd condemn me?"

"It...it would've come out anyway." I defend my actions by instinct. It only makes him scowl deeper. Can't he see the best possible way forward is honesty? I'm sure this is all some kind of misunderstanding. It has to be.

"What is the meaning of this?" the Head Keeper demands.

"What did you do?" another one of the Keepers asks.

Luke says nothing. He continues to dig daggers into me with his eyes alone, holding me to the ground as if I am nothing more than dirt to him.

He said he loved me.

The king marches over and the stone prison containing him melts away. He grips Luke's face so tightly his nails dig into his chin, drawing blood. "Tell them what you did," the king growls.

"I did nothing," Luke claims.

The Elf King casts Luke into the center of the square, in a circle created by all those gathered. Luke staggers, spinning, searching for someone to take his side. We can all hear the lie in his voice. His eyes land on me. They beg for something I don't know if I can give. I might have been able to, once, but not anymore.

"Tell *her* what you did," the king commands.

"I tried to take you away," Luke breathes. I can see his eyes are red, tears welling in them. "Why didn't you leave with me?"

"How did she get this?" The Elf King shoves the necklace Luke gave me in his face.

"Someone, help me, why won't anyone help me?" Luke turns, begging the townsfolk.

No one comes forward.

"What happened?" I finally find my voice. Using what remains of my strength, I stand, collecting myself and my satchel from where it fell at my side. "Tell me," I demand.

He crumples. "I... I never meant for you to get hurt. I never meant for any of this to happen." I can see the lie in Luke's shifting eyes as he speaks. Lies, lies, *lies*. "I thought...I thought we could find another way."

"What're you saying?" I whisper. Luke's eyes come back to me.

"Do you remember the day I went with you and Emma to the forest? When we were twelve? It was the first time she had one of her attacks and you made her a potion." I do remember, exactly as he says. "I saw it then—how you wielded magic without realizing it. How tiny flowers sprouted in your footprints among the grasses behind you without you ever knowing. How the trees seemed to rustle in greeting as you passed and yet you always thought it was the wind."

The forest had seemed so alive when I was a child, like it was its own person—a friend, as much as a place. I thought it had just been something that vanished with age and maturity. But now I'm not sure.

"I knew you were the queen," he admits. The townsfolk gasp.

The Head Keeper steps forward. "How dare you." She says what everyone is thinking.

"But I couldn't give you up. I wouldn't. I loved you then as I love you now," Luke continues, speaking only for me. "So I found the necklace in the Keepers' stores and gave it to you. I thought it would keep you hidden and when we were old enough I would—"

"Take me away," I finish with a whisper. He swallows thickly and nods.

As if on command, the king throws the necklace he ripped from my throat to the stage. It lands at the feet of the Head Keeper.

"Elvish make, an old style of token. We have not traded goods of this like with Capton in centuries, so I have no doubt it was buried deep. Black obsidian to mute her powers and labradorite to protect her from the Knowing should she encounter any elves who attempted to discover her true name."

I look to the necklace and then back to Luke. "You said it would protect me."

"I was trying to spare you," Luke pleads with a high-pitched, whining voice that I've never heard from him before. "I thought I could save you from a terrible future."

Luke's actions, my abilities to heal, the fact that I always felt duty bound, it all makes sense now. Terrible, horrible sense.

"Luella." Luke staggers toward me. "I loved you, even then. I was made for you, and you were made for me."

A willowy arm blocks Luke's path, preventing him from drawing any closer to me. I never thought I'd be grateful for the Elf King. But I don't know what I'd do if Luke dared to touch me right now. It's hard enough to have him just *look* at me.

"No," I breathe to Luke. "You don't love me, you never did."

He tries to step around the Elf King. But the king continues to position himself in Luke's way, grabbing Luke's wrist.

"You must believe me. All I did was try and save you from this wretched future."

"You tried to save me at the expense of everyone I loved! You would see them all suffer and die because you wanted to keep me hidden for yourself."

"Because of love!"

"This isn't love!" I allow my voice to echo to the mountaintops. The trees shudder at my rage. Their roots quake the foundation of the earth deep below my feet. The wind howls and storms close in on the horizon. "Love is choice," I continue before he can get another word out. "You—you wanted to *own me*. You wanted to keep me for yourself regardless of how I may have felt. You never even allowed me to make the decision on my own and now our town, our people, have *suffered* because of your selfishness. I shudder to think what might have happened to our whole world if you had gotten your way."

Every funeral we attended of townsfolk, dead before their time from the Weakness, flashes before me. Luke, standing with the other Keepers, mourning for their loss as though he actually cared—as if his actions hadn't led to their deaths. His tears meant nothing then and his remorse means just as much now.

"Luella—"

"Stop," I whisper. "Never say my name again." I barely stop from wishing the earth would open up and swallow him whole. With how I feel right now...it just might heed my command. "Get rid of him. I want him gone," I ask no one in particular. I don't care who does the deed.

It's the Elf King who heeds me. He rips off Luke's Keeper bracelet without a second of hesitation. His eyes flash a bright blue, he crosses his arms before him, and then slowly pulls them apart—as though he's stretching taffy between his hands. Luke goes rigid and he hovers on his toes unnaturally. The king's fingers tense further, pulling. A pathetic, whining sound escapes Luke as he contorts. Popping fills the air. The townsfolk begin to scream.

"No! Don't hurt him!" I rush over to the Elf King and grab his arm. He looks at the contact with an air of shock and offense. "I don't want him *dead*." My heart is being torn apart; I can't bear witnessing Luke being ripped in two. The Elf King tries to shrug me off but I hold fast, digging in my heels. "He must be tried by the Capton Council. He must atone for his crimes as is fair and just."

The Elf King narrows his eyes at me in a scowl and, for a moment, I think he might ignore me. I don't release him. What more can he want to take from this town? He already has my life. If I am the Human Queen—and I am, there's no denying it after that display earlier—he should need nothing more.

"Luke doesn't matter to you," I say, my voice thin. "My people *will* see justice done. You have me, let him go."

The king releases Luke and he crumples to the ground, gasping. Two Keepers step forward and grab him underneath his arms. They begin to drag him away, Luke begging and muttering apologies the entire time.

None of the townsfolk listen. They glare openly at him, their faces cold and closed.

The Elf King turns to me. "Come, Queen, we must depart immediately. You are needed across the Fade," he says gravely.

I'm numb from the top of my head to my toes. He grabs my arm, summoning me back to reality. I glare up at him. A thousand objections live on my tongue and yet I can't muster the strength to say any of them.

Since I was a girl, I've been taught the fate of the Human Queen. If I tell him of my duties as a healer, my pleas will fall on deaf ears. If I beg him to let me stay a little longer, I know he will refuse because this is the way of things.

If I refuse to go, my world dies.

"There is no time. You and I must be wed."

five

WE ARE TO BE WED. Me. To the Elf King. I can't think
straight.

"When?" I manage to ask.

"Now. Time is of the essence," the Head Keeper says.

My attention shifts off the Head Keeper, landing on a
man beside her—my father. My ribs collapse on my lungs
and I let out a soft gasp of air that chokes into an emotion
rawer than tears.

"But—" I start.

"There is no time," the king says gruffly. "The fact that I
was able to come here and use so much wild magic on this
plane is proof enough that the Fade is wavering. The lines
between our worlds are blurring—which, let me assure you,
is something you do not want."

I seek a flicker of some kindness or resignation in the
king's eyes. But all I see is sheer determination. I wonder if
he is enduring this on strength of will alone too. I wonder
what he's hiding underneath his carefully composed surface.
Maybe he's hiding nothing and he is just a man of stone and
magic.

"We will do it now," the Keeper says.

I search in the crowd for my mother, but I can't find her.
Between the brush and the trees, magically created, and the
fact that almost all of Capton has assembled, she's nowhere

to be seen. I turn back to my father. His mouth is pressed in a hard line. He says nothing.

He knows this must be done, just as I do. There is no choice.

We march in a large group up to the Temple. I am silent, rigid, walking at the side of the Elf King. I try and keep my head high, but I am tired, so tired. One moment I was in the town square. The next, I'm in the main hall of the temple being anointed with oil, townsfolk surrounding me, the Head Keeper leafing through a giant tome on the altar.

Sunlight streams down through the stained glass behind the Head Keeper. It hits my shoulders, but fails to light up the dark hollow growing inside of me. I'm surrounded—people are packed into the neat rows of redwood pews, carved from the mighty trees surrounding the temple—yet I feel alone. I don't even have it in me to admire the organic architecture of the temple like I usually would, with all its vaulted ceilings supported by gnarled branches, as if it was grown rather than made in the shade of the great redwood at the heart of the temple.

Deafening silence rings in my ears as I stand opposite the Elf King. *I'm about to get married...to the Elf King.* That thought nearly makes me throw up.

"Can I have a moment?" I whisper.

"There is no time," the Head Keeper whispers back, not unkindly.

"For the washroom, please." I'm going to be sick. Or pass out. Maybe both, one right after the other.

"This will be over soon." She's found her page and begins reading from it. "Before the old gods, in the remnants of the keep of the once-kingdom of Alvarayal, in the shadow of the original keystone, we honor the pact made..."

Don't be sick. Don't be sick. I no longer hear the Head Keeper. All I hear in my head is that singular phrase repeating over and over.

The Elf King raises his hands. The sensation of his eyes boring into my forehead brings my eyes up to his. I swallow dryly.

"Let their hands first be joined," the Head Keeper repeats firmly and with some agitation. It must be the second time she's said it. I barely resist snapping at her that I have no idea what's going on.

Usually, the Human Queen is identified at sixteen or seventeen.

She has a year or three to study in the temple under the Keepers. She is fed food from beyond the Fade, taught the elvish ways, and studies the secret knowledge the Keepers protect.

The Elf King holds out his hands expectantly. I lift my trembling fingers and place them in his. His cool grip closes around mine. His eyes flash a bright blue just like they did before he made a prison for Luke.

I suppose I am headed to a different type of prison.

A chill breeze sweeps through me. It's brisk, bracing, but I'm not left shivering. I stand taller. The ice condenses in the back of my head, radiating cool composure down my spine and into my limbs. My eyes are locked on his as my mouth moves.

"I will honor the pact," I say. I think I'm repeating the Head Keeper, but I can't be sure. I can't be sure of anything beyond the Elf King. Have I ever laid eyes on someone—on anything—more perfect before? How could I have been afraid of this?

This is right. This is how the world should have been all along. A deep sense of unnatural calm fills me.

"I will honor the pact," he repeats.

"I will fulfill my obligation to this world and those on the other side of the Fade." We begin to repeat back and forth. "I will uphold the keystones. I will use the powers passed down through my blood by destiny for the betterment of us all—for peace. I will uphold the order that is both natural and crafted.

"I will honor my husband."

"I will honor my wife."

Yeah, right, my mind blurts treacherously. But the thought is frosted over by my resolve. I am marrying a king of ice. I will have to be a frigid queen to match.

The Head Elder says a few more words, and the deed is done.

We unclasp our hands and for the second time in one day I stare at mine. What magic was wrought here? What have I done?

I'm married, that's what I've done. Whenever I imagined myself as married—*if* I imagined myself as married—Luke was standing across from me. I return my gaze to the Elf King's, seeing his shining blue eyes still on me.

"We should make for the Fade," he says.

I nod.

The king holds out his hand for me and I take it. His skin is smooth, and cool to the touch, his grip unexpectedly gentle. He leads me by our joined palms in an awkward, rigid way. We walk out of the sanctum, around its side, and start down a side path. I know without needing to be told that this will take us toward the Fade.

The townsfolk collect behind us, moving silently to hover at the foot of the path. The forest is damp; the trees tangle their boughs in the fog like fingers in the hair of a lover. I see flowers bud up, blooming alongside me as I walk. They open to face me, as if bidding me farewell from this world.

Farewell… I shiver but the thought sticks to my mind. *Farewell, I'm leaving*. I shiver again, more violently this time, and can almost imagine invisible ice shaking from my shoulders. That cold core in the back of my mind fractures.

"Luella!" I hear my mother's voice, breaking the silence and decorum.

My fragile composure shatters.

I look over my shoulder. We've gone farther than I thought. My mother and father stand at the entrance to the path, down by the sanctum. My father holds tightly onto her, smoothing her ruby hair from her tear-streaked cheeks. He murmurs something I cannot hear. But I can see the words are physically painful for him to say.

"Luella!" she shrieks again.

"Mother!" My heart is racing once more. Heat floods my body and my cheeks. I drop my hand from the king's and begin to run.

He grabs my elbow. I spin in place. "We must go beyond the Fade. There is precious little time."

The Elf King's eyes are back to their normal color. The bright magic that shimmered in them is gone. It's then I realize what he did.

"You used magic on me," I whisper in realization. That frosty chill, his glowing eyes, both traits I'm beginning to associate with elf magic. Hatred mixes with horror in my gut and twists my face. "The ceremony—"

"You needed to comply."

"You bastard." I rip myself from his person once more. Damn his

Fade. Damn the wedding. Damn men who think they can manipulate me down an aisle.

An oath taken under magic influence shouldn't be upheld. But I know no one will take my side.

I am the Human Queen. Even if I wasn't trained for my role, I know enough from the stories that are rooted deeper in the social fabric of Capton than the trees around me that the Human Queen has no choice. By magic or circumstance...the oath I took was forced.

"How dare you," he seethes at my language.

"Let me say goodbye."

"It is not done."

"It is now," I snap at him with a glare.

He takes another step forward, closing the distance once more with his long stride. I'm reminded that I'm dealing with a dangerous creature. He may look like a man, but I know the truth.

He's nothing more than a tempest of raging magic.

"Very well." His voice drops so only I can hear. "I will indulge you in this, as my future queen. And, also, because I know you have not had the benefit of being properly educated. You have not been *trained* to be my bride. But I do hope you are a fast learner because I will not tolerate my queen speaking to me in such a way."

He wants me to cower. My knees are knocking in response to the silent demand. But I jut out my chin defiantly. I'm too tired to think sensibly—bravery and stupidity are two sides of the same coin. If he thinks he can "train" me I'm going to have to show him he has another thing coming from this queen.

"I will say goodbye."

The king glowers at me, but stays put as I step away. His eyes dim once more and his magic releases its frigid hold. He knows I'm his, now and forevermore. He can handle not being in control for five more minutes so I can embrace my parents one last time.

I rush into my mother's waiting arms. She leaps from my father to scoop me up. I hold out an arm and he joins too.

"Luella, Luella," Mother weeps, as if my name is the only thing she knows how to say. "I'm so sorry."

"I had no idea," Father says.

"I know. I didn't either." We're all in this terrible spot together, about to be ripped apart for good, and it's all Luke's fault. I might have always been destined to go. But he took a proper goodbye from me. I hope he rots in a cell forever for all he's done.

"I'm sorry we didn't ready you for this. Had we known, we would've." Mother squeezes me tighter. If she keeps holding me that firmly, she'll squeeze out the tears I'm holding back.

"I know," I repeat and pull away. "Don't cry, it's all right," I try and soothe as my own voice is cracking at the sight of my mother's tears. "I know you would've let me prepare to be the queen. You didn't know. None of us did. It wasn't any of our faults." I swallow hard, trying to drown my emotions. "But now I can go and I can make a difference. The Weakness will come to an end. It's not as I wanted, but I can still help Capton."

I squeeze both my parents tightly once more and stop trying to hold back the tears. I draw quivering breaths and weep with my family. It feels like the last thing we'll ever do together.

"Midsummer," Mother says.

"I'll try." I think of what Mister Abbot says. And about how I never heard of the Human Queen leaving the temple before. Hopefully I will be different.

"Luella." The Elf King's unfeeling voice breaks us apart. "We must leave."

I hastily turn back to my parents. "Both of you, stay safe, all right? I'll try and send letters. I love you both so very much."

"Don't go." Mother grabs my hand.

"She has to." Father wraps his arms around his wife, as if holding her back from me.

I take a step away, and then another. My mother's fingers curl around mine, grasping like the vines that grew in the square. We separate and a chord of emotion snaps in me. It will never resonate with sound again. The sight of my mother's face, the sound of her sobs, have muted whatever that happy feeling was for good.

"I'm sorry," I whisper. Sorry for more than I can possibly comprehend in this moment.

Putting my back to them and the world I knew, I slowly trudge up to the man who is king, husband, and stranger to me.

"Thank you for giving me that," I say begrudgingly.

"Let it be known I am kind," he says gruffly and reaches out for me. His eyes remain normal—no bright flashes—so I hesitantly take his hand and walk willingly with him deeper into the woods along the path that snakes toward the base of the island's tallest mountain.

The sound of my mother's sobs fades. The echo of my father's outburst of emotion as he broke down with her rings only in my ears. It's long since stopped bouncing between the trees.

The elf legion follows us into the dark shadows of the deep woods. I move into the great unknown that is the Fade as a stranger queen. The path becomes broken and more overgrown than not. Cobblestones are now stepping stones.

Soon, there's not a path at all. I have gone farther into the forest than ever before and the darkness of what I assume to be the Fade closes in around me.

The thick, shadowy mist blots out the trees. It curls around us and in the darkness I see the outlines of figures, wandering in the distance. Some look human, and others like beasts. I shudder, not entirely from the chill.

My fingers close a little more tightly around the king's.

Surely, we must be at the foot of the mountain now? I look behind me and see nothing but elves and darkness. The deep woods thrum with anxious energy. There's power here, pulled taut all around me, thrumming under the tension.

Then, in the distance, I see a glimmer of light. The inky blackness becomes tunneled. Trees are wedged so closely together that they form an almost perfect wall. Vines and branches arc overhead as the light grows.

Blinking, I emerge onto the other side of the Fade for the first time, and take my first steps into the city of the elves.

six

WE STAND AT THE TOP OF A LONG STAIRCASE—THOUGH
NOT HALF AS LONG AS THE STEEP PATH THAT LEADS UP FROM
CAPTON TO THE TEMPLE GROUNDS. Behind me, a wall is cut
into the mountainside. The only opening is the dark blemish
in the smooth stone that we just emerged from.

Below us, a gray city sprawls in a valley nestled in a
basin formed by mountains. Winter winds howl through the
buildings and barren trees, racing to nip at my skin. It looks
cold and closed, off-putting, and nothing like the warm cheer
that I always imagined hovering over Capton.

"Welcome to your new home," the king says, sounding
anything but welcoming.

"It's not what I would've expected." My voice is cracking
and tired from the rolling waves of emotion I've been sailing
on.

"What would you have expected?"

"Something more…lavish." The houses are simple, no
nicer than what we have at Capton, albeit a different style
of construction. Our homes are more pragmatic and boxy.
These buildings have thatched roofs and offset second and
third stories that make them look like teetering houses of
cards.

Even though it is different, it is…dull. I had hoped for
a world teeming with life and magic. But what I'm greeted

with looks like a dreary painting where the artist forgot they had more colors than just blue and gray.

"Why would you think that?"

"Elves seem fancy enough. Based on the goods the Keepers always kept under lock." I shrug. The sentiment reminds me of my few meager possessions in my attic bedroom—of the elvish teapot still in my shop. I clutch the satchel I took with me to the town hall this morning. At least I have *something* of home. Thank goodness I never leave without my journal and essentials.

He snorts and says nothing further on the matter, settling for a simple, "Come."

I follow him down the steps with chattering teeth. The legion marches behind us. Even though it was a balmy dusk in Capton, it is a brisk winter's dawn here. The city is waking up. The streets are still mostly empty. Everything is unnaturally quiet and covered with a frost to match the gray sky.

At the center of the city is a large lake. A river runs out from it to the mountain behind us, presumably into Capton. In the center of this lake is a sculpture of an elf man and human woman.

I pause. The king stops as well, as does the legion, several paces behind. "Is that the first Human Queen?"

He hesitates a moment, as if debating if he should answer. "It is. And one of my long ago predecessors."

"Predecessors?" I look to him. "You're not the Elf King?"

"What a strange question." He narrows his eyes at me. "How could you doubt after all that has transpired?"

"No, I…" I pinch the bridge of my nose and sigh. It has been a very long day. "I thought all the Human Queens were married to the same Elf King."

He tilts his head back and laughs. It would be a lovely sound if not for being at my expense. "You think one man has been alive for three thousand years?"

"Well…"

"The rumors of elves' life spans are greatly exaggerated in your human stories. We elves live about as long as the humans of Capton do." The king stares down at me. "Our lives became tied to each other from the moment we were wed. When you die, I will be marked for death not long after."

"Then, your father was the king married to Alice?"

He goes rigid, tense. The muscles in his jaw bulge as he fights back whatever his first instinct told him to say. "He was."

Without another word on the matter, we continue forward. Though I would've given anything to stop and probe the depths of the emotions he was trying to hide. What was Alice to him? And what was her place in this world really like?

I look back to the statue of the first Elf King and Human Queen. The king holds a large tablet in his hands, hoisting it upward. The queen is on her knees before him. Hands pressed into the ground at his feet, as if in servitude.

I study the timeworn details of the sculpture, trying to glean what information I can from it. But the appearances of the king and queen have faded and are covered in frost and snow. Still, I want to find something to feel toward her—the first woman to willingly put herself in my position for the sake of peace between humans and the creatures of magic beyond the Fade.

Her magic is in me now, if the stories are true about the magic being passed down from queen to queen.

"How could you tell I was the queen?" I ask as we approach a castle in the distance. It's wedged between two mountains, the castle spanning the entire width of the opening that connects this valley to whatever world is beyond. The king glances at me and I can't tell if he's annoyed I broke the silence yet again or not. I continue anyway, "I understand that the necklace was trying to conceal me— my magic—but how did you know before you took it off?"

"I saw you performing magic."

"But didn't the black obsidian hide my magic?"

"Some people can never be hidden; they are meant to be seen."

"You were certain," I persist, not taking his vague, poetic answer.

"I touched you," he says simply.

"You knew from a touch?"

"You heard earlier, the necklace was labradorite and black obsidian. The black obsidian was to conceal your power. Labradorite is a rare stone mined here in Midscape that can prevent me, or any other elf, from performing the Knowing. Usually, labradorite blocks both the Knowing from sight and by touch. However—"

"Wait, what *is* the Knowing?"

He sighs, as if the conversation is quickly becoming tedious. Too bad for him I don't care about being a pain. I care about answers.

"The Knowing is when an elf identifies the true name of an object, creature, or person. A true name is sound given to the raw essence of what something is—something unique to every creature and thing. Elves perform the Knowing by sight, or touch, and our innate magic," he says. "Once a true name is known, the elf can manipulate the creature or thing at will."

"An elf can do *anything* to something or someone they have a true name of?" I think of Luke, contorting painfully.

"As long as an elf has a true name, they are limited only by their own powers and imagination."

I try to suppress a shudder and fail. "And you know my true name now?"

"Yes. I could sense your true name despite the labradorite when we touched—something I shouldn't have been able to do. The labradorite should have protected you. But I could sense your true name because you are the Human Queen and were destined for me since birth. And as I've said, even if I hadn't touched you, I saw you perform rudimentary magic without realizing it." His feet slow to a stop as we near a square before a giant portcullis. "Speaking of labradorite, you will need this for your time here. Your hand, please."

I oblige. He pulls out a ring made of the same rainbow stone— what I now know as labradorite—and slips it on my left ring finger. I fight the urge to rip it off. All I see is another token of that terrible stone which a man has put on me, trying to claim me. All I can think of is Luke.

"Must I?" I whisper.

"Yes," he says firmly. Though the Elf King hesitates just before letting my hand go. "If you wish to change the finger it's on, then you may do so. I hardly care if you wear it as a symbol of our marriage. It is merely to protect you from other elves performing the Knowing on you. Should someone else learn your true name, it could be dangerous."

"Would someone hurt me?"

"No queen or king is without enemies," he answers gravely, nodding back toward the legion behind us.

"Who—" Before I can get the question out I'm silenced by what looks to be a general approaching.

Her skin is a rich brown and her long tresses are black, streaked with bright blue. Her eyes are the color of churned-up sea. A sword is attached to her hip and her movements are clipped and rigid. Three cords are attached to embellished pauldrons on her shoulders. Decorative buttons are pinned over her breast.

The buttons remind me painfully of the ornate pin my father was given when he first became a council member. I take a deep breath, trying to choke down a sudden wave of emotion. I'm struggling to find my footing in a new world. I can't have some *buttons* be the thing that has me a weeping mess in front of the Elf King and his soldiers.

"Your Majesty." She bows her head.

"Take the queen to her apartments and see her dressed as is fitting of her station. We can't wait a moment longer. It grows colder by the hour." The king's words condense into white puffs as if for emphasis.

"Yes, my liege."

The Elf King wastes no time leaving me in his dust with this woman.

"Wait!" I call after him. He pauses, glancing over his shoulder. One dark eyebrow arches. "What's your name?"

The thin line of his mouth splits into a smirk, as if he also can't believe he married someone who didn't know his name. "You may call me your king, or your majesty, or your liege."

I'm not taking that answer. No. Not for a moment.

"What would I call you if I was your friend?" My question gives him pause; his face relaxes into something I'd almost say is vulnerable.

"I don't have friends," he says faintly. Others may interpret the tone as cool indifference. But I hear a hurt I don't yet understand drifting through his words.

"Your subjects then?"

He grimaces at that, but finally relents. "King Eldas. I will see you in an hour. We will begin then."

seven

"BEGIN WHAT?" I ask. I know his tall ears can hear me. But he doesn't stop again. He turns a corner in the dark tunnel ahead of me and is gone.

I am now alone with an unfamiliar elf, who leads a legion of more unfamiliar elves, in an unfamiliar land of wild magic. *The Human Queen merely exists.* It seemed so unfair. But now that the butt that's in that throne is mine, I'd be happy to just sit and catch my breath.

It's been a long, *long* day.

However, if I'm only meant to sit…what "work" is there to do?

"Come along, Your Majesty." The way the elf general has to force the formality through gritted teeth tells me that, even if she knew the Human Queen would arrive, she's not exactly pleased to be answering to a human now. "I'll show you to your royal apartments."

As she goes to leave I notice a gash, gnarly and scabbed over, on the hand she rests on the pommel of her sword. Infection reddens its edges. "I can look at that," I say, without thinking.

The general stops, blinking several times at me. She finally asks, "Look at what?"

"Your hand." I'm already rummaging through my satchel. I used up some supplies with Emma, but I should still have—

"It's merely a training accident," she says dismissively.

"Well, it's getting infected and it won't be any trouble for me." I find the jar of salve I was looking for. It's good for minor injuries.

"We have a castle healer for such things," the general says before I can even get the jar from my satchel.

"Yes, but I have—"

"You are a queen," she interrupts me in a low and intense tone. Her eyes dart back to the knights still several paces behind. "Healing someone like me is beneath you."

Beneath me? Healing and helping is...*beneath me* now? The words grate against everything I've ever known.

Suddenly, the grays of this place are darker, more shadowed. Everything takes on a dingier and duller edge, if that were possible. I've been taken from my home, my people, my family, and now they're going to take me from the one thing I'm good at? The one thing I've worked toward?

I try and work up my courage, opening my mouth. But I don't get a word in.

"Now come this way, *please.*" She has to grit out the word "please," as if my offer was that shocking, or troublesome to her.

Only a sigh escapes my lips. I can't fight any of this. Focusing too much on that will overwhelm me with everything that's been taken from me. The best thing I can do, for now, is try and survive.

I can't pass judgment on this life until I try and live it. Hopefully it will surprise me. And, if it doesn't...I just have to remember that my presence here has put an end to the Weakness in Capton *and* has ensured another one hundred years of peace.

The castle is more of a fortress that's been built directly out of the mountainside, and I wonder what it's meant to keep out. Cut through the fortress's center is a single pathway of stone, two portcullises on either end. The cobblestone road has been smoothed with time; deep ruts from carts span the length of the path.

This is the only entrance in and out of the city, I realize. If the city is to be taken, the castle must be taken first.

A third portcullis is between the two entrances of this long tunnel. Behind it is a small underground courtyard lit by torches mounted on soot-stained walls. They illuminate two heavy doors.

"What's that way?" I point to the far end of the tunnel.

"None of your concern." The woman stops, hand on her sword. "We're going this way." She motions to the doors.

"Is it beyond the city?" I ask anyway.

"Yes. Which is *none of your concern.* Now come."

Her soldiers must've heard an unspoken command to them; the legion now surrounds us in a semi-circle as if they're guarding from invisible attackers.

Left with no other option, I follow her up to what must be the castle's entrance. The guard's eyes flash a bright blue at the doors and then she turns to me. "These doors are magicked shut. It'll do you little good to try and flee."

"Why do you think I'll have reason to flee?" I ask, as if the thought hadn't already crossed my mind...more than once.

"Hopefully you won't." That answer isn't exactly promising. She pushes on the doors and they open up to a landing at the foot of a long stairwell.

"What is your name?" I ask.

She seems to debate telling me. Perhaps forcing Eldas to admit his name is what forces her to concede. "Rinni."

"Are you a general of some kind?"

"Are you always this incessant with questions?" Her words are sharper than my pruning shears.

"Maybe." I shrug. Then repeat, "So, you lead the soldiers?"

"At times," she says finally. "I am considered King Eldas's second by many." I could almost see her weighing her options and what it would mean for her not to answer my inquiries. It makes me wonder how much sway I have here.

I may be a human in the city of elves, but I *am* their queen. I have magic that the Elf King himself and a legion of his elves came to Capton to get. I glance at the ring on my left hand. It weighs a thousand stones.

At the top of the stairs is a room with soaring ceilings weighted down by heavy iron chandeliers. Candles drip stalactites of wax toward the dark wooden floor we now stand on. Two more stairways, one on either side of the room, arch up to a landing and then out to a mezzanine balcony that circles the hall.

Between the stairs is a wall of leaded glass. Intricate designs have been painstakingly woven between the thousands of tiny shards. They cast a lacy pattern on the floor. It's the only thing that's soft, or bright, in this cold, drab place.

"Come, your chambers are in the west wing." She walks up the left stairs and I follow her up to the balcony.

"Is it always so quiet?" I whisper so I don't have to hear my voice echoing in this cavernous, empty space.

"Yes."

"What about people who care for the castle?"

"There are some servants." She doesn't look at me when she answers.

"Where?"

"Just because you do not see them, doesn't mean they're not here. It's improper for common folk to see the Human Queen before her coronation. So the staff here is kept extremely small and out of sight."

"I'm sorry for the extra work they must have to do by being short-handed." Though, they do have their wild magic, I suppose. What might take a human two days likely takes an elf an hour.

I must have exhausted the conversation, because Rinni doesn't say anything further.

Behind a doorway is a sitting area that connects with yet another sitting area. We pass through open doorway after open doorway in a seemingly endless string of rooms with no obvious purpose but to exist. After the fifth or sixth room, there's a hallway with a stairway at the end. We ascend three flights and come to a wide landing with only one door.

"These are your apartments."

Rinni opens the door and I blink into the light that floods the room. The ceilings are the height of the first and second floor of my family's brownstone, and rows of windows line the back wall. Rinni waits as I do a quick round of exploration of the main room and attached bedroom—a closet larger than the attic I made my room back home, a bathroom bigger than my shop, and a bed that could easily sleep five.

"Why is everything giant?" I ask, reemerging into the empty main room from the bedroom.

"Giant?" She arches her eyebrows.

"The doors are large, the ceilings are towering, what furniture there is takes up more space than a small carriage."

"Everything is appropriately sized for a castle. You'll grow accustomed to it. And if there's furniture you don't like, then you can procure a new piece. The queen usually furnishes her apartments with what she chooses. Eldas has decreed that you will have full access to the royal purse strings to order anything that will make your stay here more comfortable."

That's unexpectedly nice of him. Yet, at the same time, I don't want his money. It was hard enough to take Capton's charity and that was from people I spent my whole life with—from people I swore an oath to help and heal for my entire life in gratitude. Moreover, I'm wary of any gifts that might have caveats. And money from the Elf King must have a thousand strings attached.

I miss my shop already, and earning my own money…what little money it was, since I did most of my work for free to pay back the investment Capton made in me.

"That explains why it's so empty." I look around, wondering what Alice chose.

"We've delayed enough; come, we have to dress you for the king."

"Dress me?"

"You may have married King Eldas in those rags, but you will certainly not sit on the redwood throne in them." Her words ooze disgust.

"Excuse me?" I look down at what I'm wearing. "My clothes are practical."

"For a peasant, perhaps. But now you are a queen and you will dress like it, even if you do not act like it."

After an hour of being poked, prodded, and pulled at, I'm something that Rinni deems "suitable."

I stare in the mirror that leans against one of the corners of the bedroom. A strand of pearls—longer than I am tall—is wrapped around my neck. Rinni made an attempt to tame the knots and waves of my hair into submission and failed. My dress is cut from a fine silk the color of autumn leaves; the boning in its top keeps my back rail-straight. I don't usually wear warm colors because of my hair. But seeing me now, I look fierce.

At least until I look at my eyes.

Beneath them are dark shadows that have never been there before. I lean toward the mirror to get a better look. They're the same hazel color they've always been, but a hollowness has taken up residence where I imagine determination used to be.

"Who are you?" I murmur to the woman staring back at me. I don't know this woman whose dress is more put together than her life. I'm accustomed to having things under control. I've always had a plan—from childhood to academy.

Now…I've gained a castle and a crown I never asked for and lost everything I ever wanted.

Be strong, I insist to myself as I stare into the streaks of green in my hazel eyes. I have to try and make the best of this. I'll find something I can do here, some purpose. Even if I wanted to escape— *no, don't even think it, Luella.*

"Here." Rinni emerges from the closet after a long period of rummaging. I straighten away from the mirror. She holds a crown of gilded redwood leaves in her hands that she settles on my brow. "Now you at least look like a queen. You could even fool the court if you don't open your mouth."

"Excuse me?"

"I heard every last curse word as I tamed your mane. Half of them I didn't even know, and I've been in the barracks since I was seven. Come along."

"Is my entire existence going to be governed by you telling me where to go and when?" I ask, unmoving.

"I certainly hope not," Rinni calls, already in the other room. "I have more important things to do than babysit you. So please grow quickly into your new station."

"Babysit? Is that any way to speak to your queen?" I say, stealing one last look at myself in the mirror. The queen. *I* am the queen. If I tell myself it enough times, maybe I'll believe it. Maybe it'll sink in that this whole situation is my new reality.

"Start acting like a queen and I'll start speaking to you like one." Rinni's voice is more distant. I hear the door to my apartments open. "Now, unless you know your way to the throne room, I suggest you hurry up."

Hiking up my skirts to my shins, I do so.

We wind back down the stairs and through another endless series of rooms, up another set of stairs, through a library, across a hall, then up one final set of stairs into a small antechamber. Rinni presses her ear against the door.

"Eavesdropping is unbecoming for a general—or knight—what are you again?"

She shoots me a glare. "I'm making sure he's not in the middle of something important." Rinni opens the door and waves me in.

The throne room of the fortress is at its center, above the main atrium, so far as I can tell. The back wall is made of the same stained glass as the atrium below. But the careful latticework of lead branches out around wider panes here. I can see the hills and valleys beyond.

As far as the eye can see is brown and gray. The forests are as barren as the fields. The trees are just as withered as those I saw in the city. I lay eyes on a cold and cruel world.

The panorama is obscured by two large thrones. The throne to my right is made of redwood. It's organically shaped, as if a tree rooted into the stone of the room and grew into the shape of a chair.

The redwood is in sharp contrast to the cold iron throne at its side. A man, as harsh and unfeeling as the chair in which he sits—as the crown on his brow—stares down at me. Eldas drags his eyes over every inch of my body in judgment.

"You did well, Rinni. Even the roughest stone can take to polish, it'd seem," Eldas says finally. I rotate the labradorite ring around my finger. It's as though I'm standing on trial.

"I'm glad I meet your standards," I say dryly.

He purses his lips. Tension radiates from him in a tide that almost knocks me over. "I'd appreciate it if you begin to keep your remarks to yourself."

"Excuse me?"

"There is much to be done, and the most important thing for you to remember is that the queen has one duty, one job." He motions to the throne next to him. "Let's see what you can accomplish... *Sit.*"

I grip my skirts so tightly that I leave wrinkles when my fingers unfurl. But I keep in my frustrations at the notion that I am merely here to exist like a doll. I'm too tired to argue. I can keep my mouth shut and look pretty for a while as the king holds audiences, or makes decrees, or watches jesters dance on their heads, or whatever it is that Elf Kings do.

The heels of my shoes *clop* loudly on the floor as I trudge over.

"Queens should float, not walk like a horse." So he's allowed to make remarks but I'm not? I tilt my head to the side, pressing my lips shut in a firm line. He smirks, understanding my silent game. "Good, I'll take the horse. At least they're silent."

I whinny to spite him and I think I see his eye twitch.

I twirl, my skirts billowing around me as I stand before the redwood throne—my throne—and sit.

The second I am seated on the throne, I burn with invisible flames. Magic overcomes me for the second time in one day, scraping me raw. My vision tunnels, blurs, and then expands wider than I'd ever thought possible.

I see the roots of this throne—this tree—snaking down through eons of stone and mortar. They sink deep into the earth, penetrate the bedrock, and stretch into the very foundations of the land itself.

My head spins. I want to throw up. I try to scream. But I don't think I move. At least, my *body* doesn't move.

My mind continues to spread through the soil and rock. One root touches another. I'm in the trees of the city, then the barren forests far down below the castle. I feel the grasses in the fields, brittle and dry.

Dying. The world is dying.

Nurture. Life! every plant and animal cries out to me with a singular voice. *Give it to us.*

Give.

Give, give!

Their roots are in me, their wooden points pushing under my

nails, into my abdomen, snaking up my throat. The world itself is groping for me and I am helpless to stop it.

The land is thirsty, and I am the rain. The beasts are hungry, and my flesh is their food.

Take. Take.

They will consume me, all of me, far too quickly.

I'm fading.

There's not enough for me and for them. There's not enough in this world. Everything is dying and screaming to me for help—a help I don't know if I can give. I don't know *how* to give.

Two hands wrench me free. The clutches of the earth curl away and shrivel, silently screaming in protest. Light returns to me. Eyes—my eyes—I can see again. But the world is hazy. Things are too bright and moving too quickly.

The world tilts and I tilt with it. Bile rises up my throat and splatters on the floor. It's the first sound my ears can hear. Now I hear talking, cursing, feet moving.

"…get… Poppy will… No…stay…"

Stay.

Two strong arms are around me. They tighten as I shudder violently. I'm against something stable—more solid than the land itself.

"*Saraphina.*" The word is whispered to me by a familiar voice. No, it's not a word. It's a name. It's *my* name. I don't know how I know that, but nothing has ever resounded with more truth. "*Saraphina,*" the voice repeats, sinking deep into my soul. "Calm. Calm."

Calm.

The word settles on my bones with an icy chill. It spreads across my body, not unfamiliar, but also not unwelcome this time.

Freeze me, I want to beg. *Encase me in ice, in cold, in something that will make this horrible fire that burns underneath my skin vanish. Freeze me, or I may die.*

"*Saraphina,* stay with me."

I can't oblige. The world fades to a cold blackness and I slip away.

But this time, there is no pain.

eight

I CRACK MY EYES OPEN AND FACE THE DAWN BITTERLY. I'm back in my chambers on the massive bed. Feathers poke out at my cheek and eye through the pillowcase.

When I go to sit up, I find that I can't. My arms refuse to support my body. I can't even straighten my elbows.

With enough wriggling, I manage to flip onto my back and let out a monumental whine. I feel as though I've swum the wide, choppy strait between Capton and Lanton. I'm a beached whale, heaving, and begging for life.

Begging for life.

The violent echoes of the needy earth come back to me. I groan and bring my hands up to my ears. It's futile to try and block out the whispering demands; the sound is coming from *within me.* The hungry cries reverberate in my marrow.

"You're awake," a man says from my bedside.

I crack my eyes open and my hands fall limply on my pillow. At first glance, my mind deceives me and I'm back in my bed. My father sits beside me, wringing a washcloth out to put back on my forehead. I blink and the illusion is gone. Nothing more than a memory of comfort I will never know again.

"Who are you?" I rasp.

"Willow."

"The name suits you." He's all arms and legs, waif-like and as spindly as a willow tree. The man's eyes are a sad shade of blue and he looks at me with a heavy gaze. "I don't want your pity," I mutter.

"Like it or not, you have it." He wrings out a cloth in the basin at my side and returns it to my forehead.

"Am I fevered?" I ask.

"Mildly. It's breaking. The king won't tell us your true name, so we're limited in what we can do for you," he says in a way that tells me the fact is a point of contention. Anyone who stands up to King Eldas is a friend of mine, I decide. "So we have to use more traditional medicines."

"That means?"

"Potions, salves, whatever herbal remedies we can concoct."

"You say it like those things are insufficient." I glance up at him, perhaps with an expression a little sharper than I realize judging by his reaction.

"I didn't mean to offend you."

"Well, you did." I try and push myself up a second time. Willow helps situate me against the massive, carved headboard, placing one of the several hundred pillows behind my back so the intricate designs don't dig into my spine. "What are you giving me?"

"A potion."

"Obviously." I roll my eyes. "What's in it?"

"An infusion of basil, ginger, and elderberry."

"You're not even using your namesake?" I arch my eyebrows at him as I sink back, trying to find a comfortable position. It hurts to be in my skin. "White willow bark, don't even bother with cinnamon for the taste. Some bridewort, if you have it." He continues to stare at me. "Let me assure you, I know what I'm talking about; I went to academy for this. It's my job."

Was my job. The mental correction leaves me hollow. I had a life, a purpose, and now it's...gone.

"Fine." Willow barely refrains from rolling his eyes and goes back to a long table that's at the foot of the bed. I don't remember it being there when I first investigated my rooms.

"How long was I out for?"

"About twelve hours," he says as though the fact were nothing.

"Twelve hours..." I repeat. My attention drifts to the window. "What happened?" I whisper.

My bones creak and muscles scream as I turn back the heavy comforter trying to pin me down. My bare feet touch the floor, sleeping gown falling around my calves.

"Your Majesty!"

I ignore Willow's call and movement. My sole focus is the window. I stagger over to it and peer out at the land below.

The gray world that first greeted me has found its color.

Wildflowers bloom in patches along now-green fields. I see new growth in the forests beyond. Some trees already have springtime buds on their boughs. I can make out farmers beginning to till soil. Even the sky has changed from winter to spring overnight.

This is more than just twelve hours of change. It looks as if *months* passed. As far as the eye can see, the world is lush and alive.

"What?" My knees give out and Willow is at my side. He's stronger than he looks. His arm is around my shoulders and he supports me back to the bed. "What happened?"

"Do you not know?" he asks.

"I don't know anything," I reply curtly.

"My queen...*you* happened."

"What?"

Willow sighs and runs a hand over the tightly spun, black curls that are cropped nearly to his scalp. His bright eyes flick between me and the window. Eventually, he retreats, continuing to mix the concoction as I instructed. I stare out the window, resigning myself to remaining in the dark. No one here will—

"It took a year to find you...a long, cold, abnormal year. There was some kind of mistake, wasn't there?"

"Just a large one named Luke," I mutter. His eyes are on me and I think we're maybe on the cusp of an understanding. "You're right. I wasn't trained as a queen should be. I didn't know. My magic was hidden from me before I should have realized."

It wasn't my fault, I want to say. It *wasn't*. So why do I blame myself for Luke's actions? He was the one who did this to me...in the name of *love*.

I grimace and look back, more bitter than the dawn. I spent years pining over that pathetic man who did nothing but make me feel inept and weak—who tried to cage my abilities. Capton suffered and lost their only healer because of him. It's enough to make me want to scream until my throat is raw.

If I never think of love again it will be too soon. Everything Luke did because of "love" affirms every reason why I knew it was a bad idea to involve myself with him—with anyone. Love is a dangerous distraction from duty.

"It doesn't sound like you had much say in the matter. Well, not that any queen has a say in her fate. I meant to say, you didn't have much of a say in your magic being concealed. You can't blame yourself for someone else's actions." Willow pours his concoction into a glass and carries it over.

"I didn't have a say in anything. If I had, things would've been different." I brace myself and down the potion in a single gulp. I shudder at the taste. But it's exactly as it *should* taste. I think back to every remedy I made by taste alone. One drop on my tongue, and I knew what herbs were at play—magic I never saw. "So no, I don't know anything. I should have been taught whatever the heck the Keepers teach for years. But I wasn't and now I'm in the dark here." I look wearily up at the tall man. He's my only lifeline. "So any help beyond potions would be greatly appreciated."

Willow takes the cup back from me and holds it in both hands. "What do you want to know?" he asks finally. "The true natures of the king and queen are kept closely guarded…but I'll tell you what I can."

"Let's start with what in the Forgotten Gods' names happened when I sat on that throne." I motion to the window but it's hard to even lift my arm. "Then we can move on to how the seasons changed overnight. And maybe somewhere along the way you can tell me why I feel like I've fallen down several flights of stairs while running a mind-numbing fever."

"The basics, then." He puts the cup back on his table and then sees to settling me in bed. I want to wave him away and say I can do it myself. But the fact is, I can't. Moreover, there's something calming about his aura. Something I don't want to push away. "Do you know how the Fade was made?"

"I know about the peace treaty between the humans and the elves." *Know* is rather a strong word. I've heard it in folktales and songs since childhood. "I know that the elves live behind the Fade with all the other folk—non humans—who wield wild magic. And without the Fade to protect us magickless humans, our world would be ravaged."

I realize that "us" magickless humans is no longer quite accurate. I am the Human Queen and because of that station I have inherited magic. I have powers not one other human could ever dream of, and rather than feeling strong, I am…lonely. I no longer fit neatly with my people and yet I'm not quite one of the folk on the other side of the Fade. I'm trapped between, destined to never really belong to either until the end of my days.

"Somewhat true." He half sits, half leans on the edge of his bed and folds his arms. "From what I understand…there was only one world, long ago. That world was then split into two—the Realm of Mortals and the Beyond—with what we call the Veil. Then, the realm of mortals was split in two again, creating Midscape and the Natural World."

"There's three worlds total? The Beyond, Midscape, and the Natural World?" I clarify.

"Yes, and you come from the Natural World."

"And where I am now is Midscape," I reason. Willow nods. "What is the Beyond?"

"No one knows. Well…King Eldas may know. They say that the Veil that separates us from the Beyond was made by the first Elf King to give order to the living and the dead. In doing so, he severed the elves from the immortality they were given by the first gods. For this, other races bent the knee to the elves. They honored the sacrifice of all the elves to give the final rest to everyone and proclaimed the Elf King the king of kings—ruler of all mortals."

"Did people die before the Veil was made?" I ask.

"Not according to legend." He pauses. "And before you ask, I've no idea about the logistics of people living past when they should have died. The stories vary and each is more horrible than the last."

"I know what it's like to be told unbelievable tales," I murmur, thinking of all the tales of the elves—a mixed bag of truth and embellished lore. "So, in a way, the elves are guardians of the dead?"

"You can think of it like that. It's part of why we were granted the ability to find the true names of people, beasts, and things."

"Finding the names…that's the Knowing?"

"Yes, and it is the strongest power in Midscape."

"How was the Fade made? When the world split into Midscape and the Natural World?"

Willow looks out the window. "After the Veil was made, peace reigned, for a time. Eventually bickering and infighting took hold. Elves, vampir, fae, dryads, mer, and all the folk with wild magic, we draw our power from the Beyond."

Mer, vampir, fae, dryads, and more. All the magical and deadly creatures from the stories I was told as a child are *real*. They've always been real, lingering just on the other side of the Fade. I shudder at the notion.

"What about humans, then?" I ask. "Did we have wild magic and lose it?"

"No, humans were different… Long after the fae descended from the dryads, the ancient nature spirits made the humans from the earth itself. So, early humans drew their magic from nature."

I try and imagine telling my friends at the academy that the first humans were made by dryads and that we once had magic. Just imagining their expressions nearly makes me laugh. "So humans and fae are more alike?" I ask.

"No…think of fae as an evolution that happened by time and chance. Humans were designed—of the dryads' making," Willow explains. "Not long after, the dryads died off, and the early humans were quickly ostracized. Some blamed them for the death of the dryads. But I think that anything different is all too easily used as an excuse for hatred."

"So the great wars started and once more the elves stepped up to make a barrier, this time called the Fade, to separate the Natural World and the humans who came from it from the various peoples and creatures of Midscape," I logic out. My brain is only operating at half capacity. Everything is exhausted, including the mush between my ears. If I don't speak it all aloud I might not grasp the world I now find myself in.

"Exactly, Midscape is a between. But there's just one problem. Can you figure out what it is?" He glances at me. Now my eyes follow his to the window.

"If you create a world between the Natural World and the Beyond…then it's *not* natural," I realize.

"Someone had to bridge the gap," he encourages.

The truth is dawning on me brighter than the sun on the fields beyond. "The Human Queen."

"You got it!" He leans over and flicks my nose. Then pulls back, startled. "I'm sorry, Your Majesty, I shouldn't have—"

I burst out laughing and rub my nose lightly. "It's fine."

"You're my queen, I really shouldn't—"

"Willow, it's fine," I repeat, firmer. "It's nice to have someone treat me kindly, like a friend."

He looks suddenly uncomfortable and stands. When he continues speaking, his head is down and his hands are busy cleaning his tools and sorting his supplies. "In any case, yes, the Human Queen is Midscape's connection to the Natural World."

"Does everywhere in Midscape look like this? Springtime?" I ask.

He nods. "Because of the Human Queen—you—sitting on the redwood throne, nature could flow into this world."

"*Through* me," I whisper and shudder, thinking of the magic that raged through my body. The phantom pain of roots digging into me alights under my skin. The sensation of my soul, my life, being torn from my bones is searing hot. I feel a thousand needs screaming at me at once and I am just one woman; I couldn't possibly help them all.

All I want is my shop. I want *my* patients. I want a world I can understand and a small corner to look after.

I asked to take care of people, yes… But nothing prepared me for this. Not my parents, not the academy, and not the Keepers. My ineptitude may be more of a detriment than an aid.

"Does that answer your questions?" Willow interrupts my pity party.

"One more."

"Yes?"

"Why does the Human Queen have magic?" I ask. "No other human does."

"Right, magic was lost to humans when the Fade was erected."

I resist pointing out how unfair it is that the thing that keeps humans safe from wild magic—the Fade—is also what removed humans' natural magic.

"Does the queen keep her magic because she marries the Elf King?" I pause. "No, that can't be…because the magic comes to the Human Queen *before* she marries the King."

"The queen's magic is a bit of a mystery." It sounds as though he's wondered this many times before as well. "The prevailing lore is that the first Human Queen was actually, in part, an assistant builder of the Fade. Since she was, her magic can penetrate the Fade and that magic is passed down from woman to woman in the city where she came from."

"I see." I sigh.

"It's not really a satisfying answer, is it?" He misreads my disappointment.

"It's magic. I'm finding that magic only loosely makes sense." I shake my head and murmur, "I just wish it were different is all…" Then, I continue stronger, "You were alive when the last queen was, right?"

"Yes, but I was a child."

I'm reminded of what Eldas said. The stories of the elves living for hundreds of years is greatly exaggerated. I doubt Willow is much older than I am. In fact, I wouldn't be shocked if he was a year or two younger.

"What did she do after she sat on the throne?" What will the rest of my existence be like here?

"She—"

"Your Highness, I really must insist!" A burst of commotion and a shrill woman's voice interrupts Willow. "She's still far too weak."

"She what?" I press. Willow glances helplessly at me as I try and get the information from him.

The door opens and I don't get my answer. Standing in the frame are two new faces. In the background is a woman with the same dark shade of skin as Willow, her wiry, gray hair pulled in a messy bun.

In front of her is a young man with a shade of raven hair—glistening of purples and blues in its shade, like an oil slick—that's too unique to be chance. Even though I've only seen it a handful of times, that hair is seared onto my memory. Yet this man's nose is slightly more flat, eyes slightly more rounded.

Even with the differences, there's no denying my initial assumption—Eldas has a brother.

nine

"If it isn't the new Human Queen, here at last." He smiles widely at me and claps his hands. "What an honor to finally meet you. I do hope I'm not interrupting anything?"

"No, Prince Harrow." Willow stares at his toes, looking instantly uncomfortable. Willow's unease prickles the sensation up my arms. Something is wrong just because of Harrow's mere presence.

"Good. Both of you may leave." Harrow waves Willow and the woman behind him off.

"I told you, Your Highness, that she needs to be resting." The elderly elf woman places her hands on her hips as she tuts at the prince like he's a child. "You can have your fun at a later time."

Fun? I really don't like the sound of that. Prickling unease has turned into claws raking under my skin.

"I can have my fun whenever it pleases me. That's one benefit of being a prince," he says with a slow grin working its way onto his lips. "Now, shoo. Both of you away. I decree this interaction royal business."

"Eldas will hear about this." The woman still has yet to move.

"Run and tell my brother." Harrow rolls his eyes. "You always do, Poppy."

"Someone has to keep you in check. Not as if your mother does," she mutters. But instead of leaving, she crosses over to me and places her hand on my forehead. "I'm Poppy, dearie. I come from a long line of royal healers. So if you need anything you just call for me or Willow."

I nod. Something about her mannerisms reminds me of sweet old Mr. Abbot, and my heart aches. I never got to say goodbye to him or any of my other patients. The thought of all the people I've left behind—people who *needed* me—has my eyes burning. I nearly weep and beg for Poppy to stay as she pulls away and leaves. Willow follows behind, giving me one last wary glance.

"So, you're the Human Queen. We've been waiting all this time for...*you*?" Harrow assesses me the second we're alone. Even though Willow's potion is beginning to kick in, I don't even bother trying to shift straighter. It's impossible to be intimidating while lying in a bed.

"Apparently," I say dryly.

"Given your show on the redwood throne, I think the fact obvious." He walks over slowly.

"Glad we could clear that up. Is there anything else I might help you with?" I narrow my eyes up at him.

His navy eyes flash a glacial blue in response—something I have come to associate with the Knowing. He just tried to find my true name, and I shudder to think what he might have done with it. Harrow scowls and looks to the labradorite ring on my hand. I ball my fingers into a fist. I didn't expect the enemies Eldas mentioned to be *inside* the castle.

"My brother, detailed as ever and perpetually good at ruining my fun." Harrow sighs. "Well, get up."

"What?"

"I said, get up."

"You can't—"

"Can't what?" He arches his eyebrows. "Order you? What will you do about it? Do you even know how to use your magic?"

I purse my lips.

"You're not the only one who wears a crown in this castle." He taps the iron circlet on his forehead for emphasis.

"No, I'm not. Eldas does as well. And his crown is far more impressive than yours."

Anger flashes through his eyes, so fast I almost miss it. But it's quickly cooled by laughter and replaced with wicked amusement.

"Good, you're not a wet rag. It'd be boring if you were. Now get up; I've agreed to let a few honored members of your court get a sneak peek of their new queen."

"*Your* court can rot."

His eye twitches. "Get up or I will make you."

"Get out of my room."

"Or *what*?"

He's right. I have no idea how to use my magic. And even if I had a way to contact Eldas, I doubt he'd be on my side, or care about my plight. He was the one who had me sit on the throne without warning and then washed his hands of me after. I'm alone here.

"I thought so." His smile widens. He turns to my bedsheets and his eyes flash again. The sheets wrap around me like a cocoon and I am hoisted into the air. I fight against the constricting linens but they're too tight. My arms are trapped; my legs are rail straight.

The magic alight in Harrow's eyes fades as he puts me down, upright, in front of the closet. The sheets fall harmlessly in a puddle around my feet.

"Will you get dressed on your own? Or do I have to make your clothes dress you? Your call."

With one last glare at him, I try to march into my closet with as much dignity as my exhausted body will allow.

Harrow calls this place the lunch nook. Which is an inappropriate name since the room seemingly has nothing to do with lunch or nooks.

It's large. Of course it's large. Just as grand as everything else here.

Gilded mirrors line the wall to the right on entry, reflecting off the heavily curtained windows that overlook the city to the left. There are five tables spread throughout the room, four smaller ones set for four people and a large center table set for six.

This is where three people sit. All of them promptly ignore the tower of cakes and snacks in the center of the table to face me.

"Don't let me distract you." I approach ahead of Harrow and grab one of the glistening fruit pies off the top tier. "I'm not nearly as fascinating as this food."

"We wholeheartedly disagree." A woman with straight black hair to her waist leans forward, placing both elbows on the table.

"Perhaps we should take her at her word. She surely has the authority on how interesting she is." A brown-skinned man adjusts his thick spectacles and takes a sip of tea from the dainty cup before him.

The third doesn't raise his eyes from the book he's reading.

Harrow sits and kicks up his feet onto the vacant chair. "Your Majesty, meet my friends. Jalic is the fine specimen of a man with the glasses."

Jalic rolls his eyes.

"Our strong, silent type is Sirro," Harrow continues.

The man looks at me through his long lashes and waves of brown hair. He must ultimately decide I'm less interesting than his book, because he eagerly returns to it.

"And last, but certainly not least, is the loveliest acrobat in all of Lafaire, the one and only—"

"Ariamorria," she finishes with a snaggletoothed grin. "But call me Aria. Charmed to meet you, Your Majesty."

"Yes, the pleasure is mine," I lie, and stuff the small pie in my mouth. I was expecting the taste of cherry. I was not expecting it to be also laced with some kind of pepper so hot steam comes out of my ears. As quickly as the cake went in my mouth, it comes back out. I spit it on the floor and fan my tongue.

"She looks like a dog!" Aria shares in a laugh with Harrow.

"I guess she really is the true queen if Midscape's food doesn't taste like ash." Jalic tries, and fails, to hide his amusement behind the teacup. Even Sirro chuckles.

I race to pour myself a cup of tea. It's near boiling, but I'm ready to scald off my taste buds to stop the burning from the spices. The room spins and I lean against one of the chairs.

"I think you put too much," Aria says to Harrow. "She looks faint."

"If she faints again I'm sure my brother will just pull her off the floor like he did last time. Perhaps we'll begin calling her the fainting queen? We could have half the city adopt the title before the coronation if we tried."

More laughter. I grip the chair with white knuckles and struggle to find my voice.

"Why?" I look to Harrow and then swing my gaze to the rest of them. None of them have the decency to even feign guilt.

"Oh, don't look so murderous." Harrow pats my hand. "Just a little test is all, to make sure you're the real queen."

"I thought my sitting on the redwood throne was enough?" I motion to the windows keeping back a spring day. "Isn't *that* enough?"

"You brought us spring after years of winter. What do you want, a medal?" Harrow arches his eyes. "That's your job, *human.*"

The Human Queen's job is to exist. The words repeat over and over again and each time I gain another level of truth. At first, I thought that meant that the Human Queen was ignored and pushed off to the side, a pawn for the lasting peace treaty. Then, after speaking with Willow, I thought the Human Queen had to exist to "recharge" the nature of Midscape. I thought, foolishly, that it came with some amount of respect or even reverence.

No.

They don't care. I'm just a tool to them to make their flowers bloom and fields fertile. I'm a walking bag of manure in their eyes.

"Thank you for this test. I'm glad I could put your doubts to rest." I straighten away from the chair. My mouth is still on fire and my head is starting to throb. Pain splits my temples and I don't know if it's from fever or the blisteringly spicy food. "I'll be going now." I move to leave.

Harrow catches my wrist. "No, stay. We're not done with you yet."

"It's rare for people to get a preview of the queen before her coronation—a true honor!" Aria says. "We want to get to know you."

"By torturing me?"

"Stop being so dramatic." She narrows her eyes. "Really, if you can't handle a bit of dark amusement you won't survive here in Midscape."

"Just wait until she sees her first bear brawl. I bet she will faint then. Let's order several as a coronation present?" Jalic rests his chin in his palm and circles his spoon in his tea. I don't even want to know what a "bear brawl" is.

"I'm leaving," I say once more and wrench my wrist from Harrow's grasp.

"I doubt she'll survive her coronation." Aria giggles and the sound splits my head wide open.

I refuse to let them goad me. I'm going to be the bigger person and leave.

Harrow has other plans. The doors magically snap shut in front of me. "Stay. We must fill you in on the details of your coronation, and springtime rites, and before you know it, it'll be midsummer. You don't want to embarrass yourself by not knowing the staples of elven customs, do you? Especially not after you already made my brother look a fool by hiding for a year."

"I didn't make anyone look a fool." I keep my back to them and clench my fists.

"Oh, you did. Not that I minded," Harrow continues. "It was a good show to see it. Eldas is so rarely out of sorts."

"Let me leave."

"I don't think I will."

I spin, storm back over, and slam my hand on the table so hard the dishes clank loudly. One of the vases set out and filled with fresh-cut roses nearly tips over.

"Oh stop with the scary face." Aria waves her hand through the air like I am an annoying bug.

"If you don't let me go—"

"Let me reiterate what I said earlier." Harrow leans forward. "What are you going to do?"

My arm swings out before his eyes can flash. I grab one of the roses from its vase. My intent was to throw it in his face—to throw the whole tangle of thorns at him and then smack him over the head with the vase.

But the thorns cut into my own flesh first. Blood drips on the white tablecloth and there's a tug through my palm. It's subtle, like a whisper, an unseen friend who's ready to do my bidding.

Magic, I realize a second before it's too late. That pull is magic.

The roses on the table are suddenly writhing like serpents. They burst from their vase and Harrow lets me go in shock. Aria practically backflips out of her chair to avoid the water and vines. Sirro's book is on the floor.

I step back, the rose slipping from my fingers. The roses on the tables are already alive. They grow in size until the rosebuds are as big as saucers and the thorns are small daggers. The vines snake throughout the room, searching to cut deep into these cruel folk.

"What the—" Harrow curses.

"Open, Harrow!" Aria begs him. The doors open.

"Time to go!" Jalic flees the room before the vines can close over their escape route. Sirro is close behind.

"Harrow, let's leave the queen be." Aria yanks on him.

"How dare you," he whispers as he's being dragged to the door.

"How dare *you*," I repeat back, seething. "Get out and never bother me again."

Even though they retreat, my rage fuels the unruly vines even more. A thorny net spreads across the doorway and creeps over the walls and the ceiling. Roses the size of umbrellas now bloom like chandeliers.

I fall to my knees, gasping for air. I try and release the magic but it has as much of a hold on me as it does the vines.

The windows are completely covered and I am left in the darkness. I hear the sentient foliage, crunching over furniture, breaking the glass mirrors. The slithering continues, approaching me like serpents. The vines slide over my legs, leaving deep cuts in their wake. I don't even cry out; I'm too tired to care.

Death by vines. This wasn't how I expected to go. I close my eyes and sigh.

No.

No… If I die now, I'll never be able to return to Capton. If I die, another young woman will be chosen because the power passes on. She might be like me and have goals and dreams of her own.

She will be taken from people who need her. This wretched cycle continues.

If I live, I could have a chance to end it, couldn't I? The rogue thought is like a flash in the darkness. A quiet thunder that almost sounds like my parents' voices, murmuring late at night about the unfairness of this whole system, chases behind the thought. My eyes open again.

Maybe my father was right. Maybe there's a way out of this prison that's been imposed for centuries on the women of Capton. If the elves can separate worlds, can't we find a way to link the natural world with Midscape? Has it ever been tried?

Even if I fail, I can't return home if I'm dead. Capton still needs me. Somehow, I'll still find a way to help them. I swore to my friends and kin I would.

"Enough," I attempt to command the vines. "That's enough."

I try and wrangle my magic to get it back under control, but the power is as much of a thorny beast as the plants feeding off of it. I push the vines off my legs, letting out a cry of pain, and try and stand.

If my magic made them, my magic can control them. I have to believe that's true. I made it off the redwood throne somehow, didn't I? And the world had me in much deeper clutches then.

This isn't the throne that's steeped in thousands of years of magic. These are just some flowers. They only have power I gave them.

Focus, Luella.

Rather than retreating and curling in on myself, I extend my will out to the vines. Slowly, they begin to contract.

That's it. I don't know if I'm encouraging myself or the vines. *Smaller; let me see the day.* Light winks through the windows as the plants retreat, little by little.

All at once, they shudder. I watch as the magic withers, stolen from my grasp. The life within the vines vanishes. They shrivel, turn brittle, black, and then collapse to dust that fades away as smoke.

In their wake, the room is a wreck that stinks of roses, and standing in the doorway is a scowling Eldas.

ten

"CAN I NOT LEAVE YOU ALONE FOR A DAY?" he scolds.

"This wasn't my fault." I sway, exhausted. My cheeks burn, but I don't know if its from fever or embarrassment.

"Spare me."

"It wasn't!"

"Who else here could've done this?" Eldas stalks over to me. "Some *other* Human Queen with the power to manipulate and control life itself?" He continues speaking before I have a chance to answer. "Because for all my life I was told I was waiting for *just one woman*. But if I spent my years sequestered and alone for nothing, then please let me know. I'd love to know what options I have."

Sequestered and alone? The words stick out to me. But I know he'd only roll his eyes at best if I tried to ask. A question for Willow, maybe?

I take a deep breath and say as calmly as possible, "All this was Harrow's fault."

Surprise streaks across his face, chased by anger. He quickly pushes the emotions away—back under that cool and indifferent mask that I've seen him wear more often than not.

"Harrow was the one who ripped me from my bed— quite literally. I had no interest in being here." Eldas opens his mouth to speak, but I continue over him. My blood is beginning to boil at the mere memory of Harrow. I shove my finger in his face, nearly touching his nose. "And you know what? I took his goading in my stride. I could handle them having a laugh at my expense. I could even handle their little prank that they decided to pull on me. But when he tried to hold me here against my will I couldn't handle it." *I am so tired of being controlled by men like him, and Luke, and you,* I narrowly stop myself from saying.

His eyes darken in a way that I'd dare say is…protective? Surely, it must be my imagination. "What did he do?"

"Locked me in here using his wild magic."

Eldas looks to the windows. Some of the glass is shattered and a bracing wind sweeps through the room. He scowls deeper.

"I'll speak with my brother. In the meantime, I'll post Rinni at your room…at least until Harrow grows bored of you. She'll be more discouraging than Poppy or Willow."

"Poppy did try to tell him not to," I say, not wanting the kindly woman to get in trouble for something that was certainly not her fault.

"I know. Poppy was the one who fetched me and I came immediately. Believe it or not, I know my brother and his antics." His frown deepens.

"Then you should keep him under better control."

"I should keep many things in my castle under control yet they seem to delight in trying my patience." He brings his eyes back to me. "Starting with your magic." Eldas rounds me, as if I am a sculpture to be inspected for flaws. Based on what I know of him so far, I suspect he'll find many. "Magic is not that difficult. I expected you to have a *little* command."

"Really? Because I didn't expect to have magic at all." I meet his eyes again.

"The throne was hungry and you couldn't stop it from feeding off you. Your magic is weak and the fact nearly killed you. These vines would've done the same to feed on your power." His eyes drop to my shredded skirt and my still-bleeding legs. "Luella, you are a beacon of life in a world that is closer to the land of death. Midscape draws ever closer to the Veil and the Beyond than it does the Natural World." I remember what Willow said about how the elves draw their power from the land of the dead. "That makes you an easy target here—we all desire that which we cannot have, even magic itself. And you are the embodiment of all that has been taken from this world."

"I would've appreciated this explanation from you earlier," I mutter.

"It is not usually the king's job to give."

"Nothing about this is usual!" I throw out my arms and gesture to the room around us. The motion sets me off balance and I sway. Doing anything more than standing is doing too much. I take a step backwards. My knees buckle and I try to figure out how I'm going to ease myself to the ground while preserving *any* remaining scraps of my dignity.

Eldas is at my side in a breath. One arm wraps around my back. He leans forward and tucks the other underneath my knees. My stomach sinks into my pelvis as I'm hoisted up.

He's stronger than he looks.

I stare up at the man. He turns his gaze to mine and neither of us say anything. My cheeks turn red and I can't blame it entirely on the fever...not when the strong muscles of his shoulders and neck are underneath my hands. I wonder if he feels the same tingling sensation when we touch? We both fall silent; I am captured by his hands and he seems captured by my stare.

"Eldas," I say softly. "I need *someone's* help here. I don't have many options. Regardless if it's your job or not...please, teach me?"

His eyes darken at the mere idea of helping me. "I have duties that can't be ignored."

I try and shift uncomfortably. It only presses me closer to him. The tingling sensation overtakes me and I'm dizzy, but not uncomfortably so. I try and keep my focus.

"I know about duty."

He regards me skeptically.

"I do," I insist. "It might not have been the same as all your duties as a king. But I had my own duties back home."

He doesn't believe me. I can see that much. I'm getting nowhere trying to reason with him.

Let's try another approach, Luella. "If we're talking about duty... Wouldn't one of your duties as king be helping the Human Queen transition into her role?"

He sighs heavily and shifts his grip on me. His strong muscles ripple underneath me. I've never been held like this before. The few times I was in Luke's arms they held me more like a cage. I didn't feel it then, but I can see it now. Eldas's hold is surprisingly sturdy, safe—as if I could wriggle out of his grasp any time I wanted, but while he has me I have nothing to fear. I'm here only as long as we both want me to be.

"Please." I can't meet his eyes as I beg. I hate that I'm so helpless here. But it's not the first time I've had to rely on the kindness of others to find an education and it certainly won't be the last. "I need something to do here, some kind of purpose."

"Very well." He says it so gently I wonder if I imagined it.

"Really?" I ask skeptically. I didn't expect to get my way. I think I should be excited, but apprehension strangles the emotion.

"For now, let's put you back to bed. You're not learning anything in the state you're in," he says almost tenderly. I feel his voice as much as I hear it. The sound rumbles across his chest and reverberates through my side. Heat spreads from my head down, pooling in my lower stomach.

Get a hold of yourself, Luella. He may be the most attractive man I've ever laid eyes on. He may also *technically* be my husband...but he resents this marriage as much as I do.

All he wants is my existence. The sooner I grasp that, the better.

I purse my lips and allow the flush to cool as Eldas carries me back to my rooms. Poppy is there waiting for us. She tuts about as Eldas speaks for me, giving the summary of what happened.

"Your brother is worse by the day," Poppy says grimly. "I fear for whatever lands he's given lordship over."

"He will find his discipline once he has real responsibility," Eldas says coolly. He lays me down on the bed, his hands lingering on me for just a second longer than I think is necessary, and then hastily steps away. The tender touches were all my imagination. He's clearly all too glad to be free of the burden that is me. A fact further proved when he turns to Poppy. "Heal her. No one is to come in or out of this room but you and Willow, including her." Eldas looks to me. "We'll begin work again in two days. You must learn to control your magic if you're going to survive here, and if I must be your teacher then so be it. Make sure you're strong enough to keep up with my tutelage."

He stalks toward the door. I prop myself up. Poppy is already working on the gashes on my legs.

"What happens if I don't manage to control my magic?" I'm a bit afraid to ask, but I have to know.

Eldas looks between me and the sleeve of his jacket, inspecting where I bled on him. He scowls. I can barely watch him lamenting the stains in his rich blue satin more than he did my injuries.

"You will," he says, finally. I expect him to backtrack, or make some other cutting remark, but he doesn't. I watch as the king leaves in silence and am left wondering if that is the best encouragement he can muster. And, if it is…then maybe there's some hope for me after all.

eleven

A FIRM KNOCK ON THE DOOR HERALDS RINNI. "How are you today, Your Majesty?"

"I'm fine." *I'm not.* I stare at the window, dressed in an emerald-green, silken gown. Its long sleeves taper to points over the backs of my hands. Unlike the last dress I wore, this one isn't boned and the skirt is simple, offering me more mobility.

"Very well, let's go, then," Rinni says thoughtfully. I wonder what she sees in me and what she heard about yesterday's incident. But I don't ask. I follow silently, guarding my last shreds of hope that today will be productive. Today Eldas will help me begin to learn my magic, and with that knowledge I might start to find my place here.

We go down the same path to the throne room. Just like before, Rinni listens at the door, presumably for anyone Eldas might be speaking with.

"Who does Eldas meet with?" I ask, quietly, before she can open it.

"Kings and queens of the other folk of Midscape, the elf lords and ladies of Lafaire who oversee his vassals, and the citizenry who live in the valley here in Quinnar."

"Quinnar is the city we're in now? And Lafaire is the kingdom of the elves?"

"Yes, on both counts." She answers my question without making me feel bad for not already knowing the information.

In fact, she does me one better by continuing. I hope it's a good sign for the day to come. "The Elf Kingdom—Lafaire—is situated at the point of the Fade at the southernmost reach of Midscape. To the north-northwest of us there are the fae clans littering the fields and forests. It used to be the fae kingdom of Aviness, before infighting tore them apart two thousand years ago. They still fight over territory between themselves, rarely with us these days. The vampir live in the eastern mountains and the lykin to the north of them in the verdant forests. Mer are in the waters to the far north, beyond the swamplands, right along the edge of the Veil."

I swallow thickly, still coming to terms with the idea that there is so, *so* much more than just the elves on the other side of the Fade.

Rinni continues, "Remember, all those people bent the knee to the elves when the Veil was made—to the bloodline that Eldas is the heir to. That means, by extension, they bend the knee to you."

"I'll try and remind myself of that whenever I'm face-to-face with a long-fanged vampir," I murmur.

"Unlikely to happen… They haven't emerged from their mountain strongholds in centuries. Not one peep from them." Rinni moves to the door. I stop her again by grabbing her other hand.

"One more question."

"What?" Now she looks annoyed.

"The vampir, do they really…do they really *feed* off of humans to live?" *Like the old stories said.*

"If they really fed off of humans then how are they still alive? Since humans are on the *other side* of the Fade." Rinni gives me a withering look.

"Well, you said they hadn't been seen in centuries."

"That doesn't mean they're all dead. We do hear rumors from time to time of their activity."

"Okay, you have a point." Though I kind of wish they were extinct. "But other creatures, animals, even—what I'm asking is, do they need to eat blood to live?"

"Don't be silly." She shakes her head and I breathe a sigh of relief. "Vampir don't need blood to live. They eat normal food like the rest of us. They need blood for *magic*. Be careful to never give it to them or they may steal your face clean off." My stomach clenches with dread. Rinni opens the door before I can ask anything further. "Your Majesty, I've brought the queen."

"You're late." Eldas stands from his throne the moment I enter; his eyes dart from me to Rinni.

"It's my fault; I had some questions for Rinni and held us up," I say quickly. Rinni gives me an appreciative glance. I return it with a small nod. I'm not going to have her kindness be punished.

"Is this true?" He looks to Rinni. She nods. Eldas purses his lips. "Don't let it happen again. Now, leave." Rinni departs and his curt demeanor returns to me. "Well?"

"Well, what?"

"You were late. Don't you have an apology for me?"

I blink several times. Gone is the protective and mildly attentive Eldas I saw yesterday. But rather than fighting him, I force out, "I'm sorry."

"If we're working on your magic, we should also work on your manners. There's little time before your coronation and you must be the vision of a queen by then. Your subjects have waited an extra, long, bitter year to meet you. Honor them by being what they expect of you and more." The way he says it makes me think that *he* is the bitter one. "So, I'm sorry, *Your Majesty*, would be more correct."

"But you're my husband." Even if he hasn't really acted like it and this is a sham of a marriage, I'm going to at least try and use the fact to my advantage. "Is that really necessary between us?"

"I am your king first." Eldas's lips pull into a disapproving frown. "Thus it is very necessary."

"All right, *Your Majesty*," I force myself to say. I have lived to people's expectations before. I can do so now. I just wish those expectations were something more than pretty dresses and fancy manners. Something more…useful. "I permit you, however, to call me Luella."

"I will call you however it pleases me to do."

"Fine. Shall we focus on the matter at hand, *Your Majesty*?" Every time I say those two words I draw them out just a little more.

Eldas clearly picks up on the slightly snide tone. His eyes narrow, but he doesn't address it. A small victory for me, I think. If he wants to be difficult then that's what he's getting thrown back at him.

If he wants to be kind and thoughtful, like the glimpses I saw yesterday…then maybe he'll get that back too. But I'm not holding my breath.

"There is no better teacher of control than the throne. We'll have you sit again."

The suggestion makes me physically recoil. Every part of me revolts. I try desperately to keep my composure when I say, "I actually have another idea."

"Oh? Do tell. I cannot wait to hear it," he drawls.

"For the time being, wouldn't it be possible for me to wear some black obsidian, I believe you called it? It suppressed my magic for years." I can already tell he's going to say that won't work.

"Black obsidian suppresses your magic, yes, for *your use*. It doesn't get rid of or change the depth of your power. If anything, wearing black obsidian would only make you more vulnerable to attack because you won't be able to effectively defend yourself."

"But—"

"Moreover," he interrupts and approaches me. The man can't even walk without being terribly handsome and intimidating at the same time with the way the light plays on the sharp edges of his face. It's unnerving. "At some point, you will be required to perform magic. What happens if you lack control of your powers?"

"I get—"

"And, the real question is…why would you *want* to get rid of your power?" Now he stops. Judgment alights in his eyes. "You are the Human Queen. You are the embodiment of life and nature itself. And you would throw it all away. You spit in the face of all the powerful women who came before you. You shame their names and memories."

"That's too far," I snap. So much for hoping today might go peacefully.

"Is it?" He shakes his head and the judgment hardens unfairly into disgust. "There are people who need your magic. And you would turn your back to them. Why? Because it is *too hard* for you? You would rather go back to the pathetic existence in that gods-forsaken town. You speak of duty, but I doubt you've ever cared about anyone other than yourself."

I strike his cheek and the slap echoes through the room. I swore an oath to help others, rather than hurt. But the royals of Midscape are making that oath impossible to keep. I'm surprised by how much my hand stings. Perhaps he really is made of sculpted marble. His cheekbones are so sharp they could've drawn blood.

Eldas's face hardly moves. Even though I whacked him, he continues to stare down at me. But his expression is now a blank slate.

His pale cheek isn't even red.

I had come here with the best of intentions. I had come here willing to learn. And yet he throws it back at me.

"*Don't* insult me again," I say firmly. "You know nothing about me. You don't know what I've done, what I've fought for, what I *earned*. I spent years studying, learning, and practicing at the expense of wanting anything for myself. I earned the respect of my community and patients enough that they gave me their hard-earned money to get an education so I might better serve them.

"My life might not have looked like much to someone who came from a grand castle. But you know what, *Your Majesty*?" I sneer. "I worked for what I had and worked every day to keep it—to keep the esteem, respect, and trust of my community. I worked for it because it was what I chose for myself.

"You know nothing about me and yet you insult me at every turn. Fine, two can play that game, *Your Majesty.* What did you do to earn this castle? *Be born?* What have you done for your community? Breathe? Forgive me for not being impressed with your grand sacrifices."

Strangling silence settles around us. He continues to look at me with that guarded expression of his. But I can see angry sharks swimming in the cool pools of his eyes. I'd take a step away from him if my body would move. His radiant anger has me pinned to the spot.

"Strike me again, and it will be the last thing you freely do," he whispers, deathly quiet.

"You can't control me."

"Are you certain?"

"Try me!"

His eyes flash blue. The word—the name—*Saraphina* echoes in my mind. My blood turns cold. Gooseflesh prickles my skin as my arms go rigid at my side.

Eldas flicks a finger, pointing toward the redwood throne. With jerky, forced movements I march toward it.

No! I want to scream, but my mouth is sewn shut with invisible thread. The name *Saraphina* must be my true name, and he wields it against me crueler than any blade.

I try and walk backwards, to no avail. I fight against the unseen hands that push and pull me along. It's no use. I am helpless.

If only I could steal my name from his mind. If only I could take it back. I was Luke's metaphorical puppet for years and now I am Eldas's literal puppet.

Be different. The words resonate within me. *Something else, anything else!*

All at once, I'm freed. I collapse to the floor gasping for air. I look up to Eldas's stunned eyes. There's the shimmer of something I would dare say is impressed.

"You…you changed your true name. You've already managed the Being." A smile slithers across his lips. "So there's hope for you yet, when pushed. Maybe you're even stronger than I first thought," he adds hopefully.

The Being? I know the Knowing is when an elf finds a true name by magic sight. What does that make the "Being"? I don't even bother asking for clarity when I know there is none to find with him. I don't even *want* to find it from him. That was the final straw.

I stagger to my feet. "We're done."

"Come back," he demands. "We are done when I say we are."

I begin walking toward the door. His footsteps clop across the hall. *Now who is the horse?*

"Touch me to perform the Knowing again"—like he did at the town square in Capton to bypass the labradorite's protection—"and I will never even *attempt* to forgive you for this!" I spin and shout in his face. Unlike with Harrow, I might actually be strong enough to make good on my threats. "I came here willing to learn, willing to make an effort, and what you just did has *burned to the ground* any hope of a productive relationship between us."

He staggers, startled, as if no one has ever spoken to him this way before. I wonder if this is the first time he's suffered consequences for his actions. "First you strike me, now you..." He can't seem to form coherent words and I'm deeply satisfied by the fact. "I have a right to know your true name."

"You have a right to nothing of mine that isn't freely given."

"I am your king." Eldas takes a step forward and I lean back. But he's still too close. His long form is oppressive. He looms over me.

I plant my feet and refuse to let him make me feel small. I will be the bud that sprouts from the gray rock of this place. I will be the flower that blooms even despite his shadow.

"You are a moody prince glorified with a thorny-looking, iron crown," I snap back. "You're selfish and self-centered. You have no idea how to speak to people or relate to them. Any compassion and effort you exert to know someone is nothing more than a ruse to get what you want out of those around you."

"I am above compassion and relationships," he seethes. "I do not have a reason to lower myself to the emotions of the rabble. I walk above them."

"If you're always walking above people you risk walking *on* them, Eldas. And that's how you make enemies."

"I won't be lectured by a human who entered my world days ago. And certainly not by one who has never ruled a day in her life."

"Good," I say. "Because I have no interest in lecturing a man who won't listen." I spin on my heel and start for the door again. Blessedly, he doesn't follow.

"You will respect me!" Eldas shouts.

"Be someone worthy of respecting first!" I slam the door behind me.

twelve

I HAVE GONE THE WRONG WAY, I REALIZE INSTANTLY. There are six doors in the throne room, three on each side. I usually enter from the far-left door, farthest from the thrones. But he made me so angry I turned myself around.

Did I go through the middle or far right door? I'm not sure.

I'm face-to-face with a long, quiet hallway. Doors are on the left, windows on the right. Every door at my left has a heavy padlock. At the end of the hall is a stairwell.

Up the stairs? Or back? That's not really a question. I'm certainly *not* going back and risking running into *him*. Up it is.

On the next floor there's a landing that has a single sofa and small table at the far end in front of a lavish tapestry—likely a waiting room for those anticipating an audience with the king. I'm about to move on when a glint catches my eye.

I pause, shifting my weight back and forth. Something is shining in the bottom fringe of the tapestry. I cross over quickly, crouch down, and reach forward to investigate. The tapestry gives way to my hand. I pull the heavy fabric aside to reveal an opening and crawl through.

The glint I saw was sunlight from a skinny window at the end of this impossibly narrow hall. I have to side step as the walls try and crush me. But as I do, I notice there are small perforations in the stone. It is as if the builder didn't completely fill in every gap with mortar.

Through these holes, I get glimpses of the throne room below. Voices echo up to me. Eldas paces the floor before the thrones, hands gripped so tightly at the small of his back I'm surprised his bones aren't shattering. Rinni is there too. She's relaxed before the raging king. This is clearly nothing new to her.

"How can I do this, Rinni?"

"If anyone can, it's you, Eldas."

"She will not listen. I cannot work with her. I waited for the queen I was promised and did not get her." Eldas stops, slipping his long hair over his shoulder. "Her power is only a fraction of Queen Alice's. It's further indication that the line of queens is diminishing. If the power of the Human Queen dries up entirely, then our world is doomed."

"That is a concern for the future. Focus on the here and now," Rinni advises calmly.

"The here and now is that she might be the last Human Queen."

"You're being dramatic," Rinni says. It's accurate, yet there's the ghost of doubt drifting around her words. "You've only just begun working with her. Give her a chance."

"How can I 'give her a chance' when she delights in disrespecting me?" Eldas stops, turning to face his knight with a palm on his cheek. "She actually struck me."

The full spectrum of emotions runs across Rinni's face. I see her brow furrow with worry. Then her lips part in shock. I see her close them quickly to hold back what looks like laughter.

"Rinni—"

"About time, Eldas."

"She's won you over already? She's even stealing my allies." Eldas scowls and resumes his pacing.

"You've become unbearable these last few months." Rinni doesn't mince words and folds her hands together smugly. "Someone needed to put you in your place, and I certainly wasn't getting through to you."

Eldas pinches the bridge of his nose and hangs his head, raven hair slipping over his shoulders and shielding his face. "I suppose I have been somewhat curt."

Rinni snorts. "Somewhat?"

My words exactly. I'm not sure if I'm relieved that Eldas is admitting it or all the more angry. If he *knew* he was being an ass then why allow himself to act that way?

Eldas comes to a halt, staring at the door I left from. There's a murky expression clouding his gaze. I can't make out the depths of it all...but dare I say it? Is that remorse?

No, it can't be. He was cruel and he knew it. Those facts trump everything else. Yet, the longer I stare at him, the cloudier my own feelings become. *Your heart is too soft, Luella*, I scold myself.

"I wonder if..." Eldas murmurs.

"If what?" Rinni presses.

"If she's all right," Eldas finishes. I was right, there is worry in his eyes. "I should check—"

"Don't." Rinni rushes over and catches his elbow. "I don't know exactly what you did, but I suspect it might be best to give her some space. You're likely the last person Luella wants to see right now."

"I doubt—"

"Eldas, am I wrong?" Rinni cuts him off with the deadpan question and a harsh stare.

She's not, I think. I don't know what I'd do if Eldas tried to run to me and apologize right now. I'd like to think I'd accept it. But part of me wants him to stew a bit more over what he just did, make sure he's really sorry before accepting an apology.

"Fine," he mumbles. "I'll apologize tomorrow."

I doubt he will. I doubt it strongly.

"I think that's wise," Rinni says.

Eldas drags himself over to his throne, sinking onto it heavily. "First the fae, now her. The Fae King has made it clear that he thinks I am softer, weaker than my father. He wants land returned to them and wants recognition at the Council of Kings."

I lean closer to the openings. I watch as Eldas angles himself, slumping onto an elbow. He props his head up with his hand, as though his crown is suddenly too heavy to bear. He looks weary... vulnerable.

He looks nothing like a king right now. He looks like a man. A tired and weary man.

Then I remember how he used my true name against me to treat me like a puppet and any sympathy evaporates.

"Waiting for her this last year was a mistake. I stayed too long secluded in the castle, keeping everyone away, waiting for the coronation," Eldas murmurs, so softly I almost don't hear it. "My people think I abandoned them. The other kings of this land think I'm weak."

"You stayed secluded in the castle because you were waiting for your queen and her coronation—to introduce yourself to Midscape as one with the Human Queen. It wasn't a mistake; you were honoring our customs," Rinni says gently and reassuringly. "The people will understand as everything returns to normal."

Eldas was secluded? Waiting for me? He mentioned something about that yesterday, but it was lost amid all the excitement. My nails scratch lightly against the stone. I've only thought of him as a powerful Elf King—cold and unfeeling. I've thought of him as lording over this castle in delight.

But…what if he's as much of a prisoner to this terrible system as I am? The thought betrays me, sparking sympathy that I don't want to harbor for this man.

"The seasons have returned and the people are rejoicing. Preparations are already beginning for springtime rites," Rinni continues. "At the coronation, the other rulers will see her power and they won't question you."

The bud of sympathy promptly withers at the reminder of my role to him. I am a tool. I gave his world spring and now I'll reinforce his reign. My purpose here will never have anything to do with what *I* want.

Eldas sighs. "I hope it's true."

"I'm certain it will be."

Eldas stares off into a far corner of the room. Rinni continues to stand, expectant. She sees something I don't. I would have taken this as the end of the conversation. But she lingers.

"Rinni," he says, finally, his voice thin. "You are the only member of the fairer sex who's ever dined at my private table. You have been at my side longer than any of my counselors or magistrates. You—" Eldas chokes slightly on more emotion than I thought him capable of. "—You're the only friend I've ever had.

"Tell me what I should do? Spring is here, yet winter's gusts blow from the Veil. If she doesn't learn to manage her power, I fear the worst. I fear I will fail her. I fear she will only know this place as I have—as suffering. And through it all the coronation grows near. I would like her to find her place before then."

I push onto my toes, leaning against the wall for a better view. I wish I could see his expression. I want to know if the worry and sincerity I hear in his voice is genuine.

Rinni slowly approaches the throne. I watch as she reaches forward and rests her hand on the king's cheek. My stomach knots for a reason I can't quite explain.

Eldas raises his gaze. He looks up at her with yearning eyes. Rinni doesn't remove her palm from his face and Eldas makes no motion to move her away. I doubt he would do the same if I were the one touching him. Then again, the first time I did touch him, my husband, was to strike him.

I shouldn't be seeing this. Yet I can't take my eyes away.

"At your core, you're a good man, Eldas. But you're *very* rough at your edges. You know that." Her thumb strokes his cheek. Something about them looks good together—looks *right*. It makes my stomach even more upset. "She doesn't understand *why* because you won't let her. And you aren't making an effort to understand her, either.

"I admit I had the same shortcomings. I was bitter toward her for hiding and for what her absence caused you to endure this last year. For her to have forced you to expend so much power maintaining the Fade and still see it weakening as Midscape dies.

"But none of it was her fault. I believe that, and I know you do too. You can't blame her for Midscape's or your circumstances. I'm trying to know her now, and you need to also."

"If she only—"

"Don't make excuses," Rinni says firmly, dropping her hand. "Get to know her. Alice wasn't what you expected once you opened up to her. Maybe Luella will be the same."

Eldas considers it and for a moment his face is soft and thoughtful. A mask of marble has given way to a man. But he retreats behind the walls he's built the moment he must realize he's exposed. Eldas shakes his head and pushes himself off his throne. He catches Rinni's hand in both of his, giving it a squeeze.

"I respect your council, Rinni. You know I do... But Alice was a rare thing. I am not meant for love—"

"Those are your mother's words," Rinni says cuttingly.

Eldas ignores her remark. "I was born for one thing: my duty to Midscape."

"And those are your father's words." She sighs.

"Anything else is a distraction," Eldas finishes, completely ignoring Rinni's objections. "I cannot give her what she had in Capton. I cannot give her family and community. I can't give her what I've never known. But perhaps I can teach her to manage her magic and navigate this brutal world; I'll do my best to give her that much."

thirteen

I watch as Eldas departs and then I ease away from the perforations in the wall. My calves have cramped from standing on my toes and I shift my weight from foot to foot. It serves to work out some of the nervous energy in me.

Part of me wishes I hadn't been privy to that conversation. I don't know what to think of Eldas now. I find a corner of my heart is already aching to be sympathetic toward him. That is tempered swiftly by the other part of my heart that bleeds for Capton and everyone I miss more by the hour— bleeds from his cruelty.

He was right. Midscape is brutal and it is a world I wish I could have none of.

Your duty, I remind myself on instinct. Whenever times were tough, I would focus on my duty to the people of Capton as their healer. But now…that duty is gone and without it I am little more than Eldas's puppet wandering the halls of the castle.

I don't want my purpose to be fortifying his rule with my mere existence. Everything in me yearns to do more. But what can be done? My place here feels shallow and empty.

Slowly, I trudge up the stairs. I don't know where I'm going, but I follow along the hallway the top step leads me to. I wander from room to room until the scent of peat and earth tickles my nose, stealing me from my thoughts.

The smell is like a lightning strike on a clear day—

seemingly out of nowhere. This cold, gray castle is void of life, so any signs of it spark my curiosity. I follow the aroma down a stretch of connected rooms that open up into a space I would best describe as a laboratory.

Shelves packed with jars line the walls above counters filled with colored beakers, bubbling cauldrons, and herb-drying racks. Tall tables flank me on either side, stools around them, tools scattered atop. The far wall is made of glass that steams with humidity. Greenery is blurred by the fog.

Sweat instantly dots my skin as I enter the attached conservatory. The greenhouse takes up the whole width of the castle. There's stone below, stone above, and glass on either side facing north and south. Plants grow along trellises, arcing up to the ceiling. There are shelves of pots and aboveground planting beds.

Here I smell lavender and dandelion mixing with rose—which nearly makes me gag after the incident in the lunch nook—and the earthy aromatics of sage and rosemary. I spy elder shrubs, valerian, primrose, mint, and lemon balm. There are plants I've never even laid eyes on before and some I've only ever seen in books.

"*Oh.*" I startle, stopping in my tracks. The man I've spotted jumps to his feet. I've nearly scared him out of his skin. "Hello, Willow." I smile.

"Luella." He breathes a sigh of relief. "What're you doing up here?"

I shrug, not ready to open up about what happened with Eldas. "I was wandering."

"A good place to wander to; welcome to the royal greenhouse." He pulls off his gardening gloves and puts them in the basket at his side. Pruning shears and bushels of peppermint accompany them. He smiles brightly. "Would you like a tour?"

"Very much," I say without hesitation. Anything to distract me.

He shows me their intricate watering system and their compost bin in the far back corner. Willow is especially proud of the organization of the gardening shed and drying rooms. But my attention remains where the plants are growing.

Alive.

I am aware of them as I walk by in a way I've never experienced.

Their aura is like a subtle greeting, a nod that they're aware of my presence. The sunflowers turn to face me instead of the sun as we pass. I'm as eager to meet them as they are me.

"What's this one?" I stop at a plant with a black, bulbous base and red, waxy, heart-shaped leaves.

"Heartroot." Willow steps beside me. As he speaks he checks the plant, looking for bugs.

"What does it do? I don't think we have it in the Natural World."

"Odd." Willow hums. "I thought all plants in Midscape were also in the Natural World. Perhaps you're just not familiar with it?"

"Perhaps," I say. But I doubt it. I've spent years learning every herb known to man. If I don't know about it, I'm confident in saying *no one* knows about it.

"In any case, the leaves are used in a lot of antidotes to increase potency and how quickly they're absorbed into the blood. But the bark, that's the really interesting bit. You can use it to slow a person's heart to almost nothing—the bare minimum for life."

"Also used in poisonings, I'd bet." He nods in affirmation of my suspicion. I can see how it would be useful to slow the spread of poison.

"It's said the bark can also be used for memories…but that's something not explored by many."

"Why not?"

"It's more of a rumor than anything solid. 'The heartroot remembers,' is how the old adage goes. Though no one knows where that saying comes from." Willow shrugs. "I've experimented, but I've never been able to find a way to bring out any kind of mental properties with it."

"I see." I reach out and lightly touch the smooth leaves of the heartroot. A vague sense of nostalgia overwhelms me.

I can feel earth, wet and damp all around me. I can almost see the outline of a woman wearing a crown of leaves. Her hands envelop me—safe. Then, darkness. I am buried. Deeper and deeper I grow as the earth shifts above me, thickening, hardening.

Memories, not my own but held somewhere beyond its ruddy base, swim in my mind.

Then, the sensation shifts. It becomes more of a tug. Two buds sprout and I quickly pull my hand away, holding it to my chest.

"I'm sorry."

Willow stares in awe. "Don't be sorry; this is magnificent."

"What?"

"Usually the plant takes three hundred years to mature. What you're waiting for are the flowers. *Those* are what can cure any poison. Heartroot only produces them at a certain age."

"Oh."

"This is magnificent." He beams at me. Willow saw something wondrous just now. I saw yet another sign of my magic out of control.

"Does... Do other properties come out at a certain age?" I ask. "Perhaps the memory ones?"

"I doubt it. But we can test it."

"No... I should go." I push the phantom sensations from my mind and look at the plants sadly. If I had just been Luella the herbologist I would've spent hours in this place. But I'm now Luella the Human Queen who can accidentally make plants grow. Will they be good plants like the heartroot? Or nasty plants like the vines I made in the lunch nook?

I shouldn't stay and find out.

"Wait." Willow grabs my shoulder, stopping me from leaving. "There's something else."

"Willow, I'm sorry—"

"Journals kept by the past queens." He beams, knowing that I'm certainly not going to say no to that. "Poppy told me about them when we were talking about your situation. I thought they could help make you feel more at home here...maybe even help with your magic?" He starts heading back to the laboratory as he speaks and I follow. Willow goes over to a bookshelf in the corner and retrieves a stool from between it and the wall. "Top shelf. Help yourself."

I inspect the top shelf. There are twenty-five journals of all shapes and sizes with names written on each spine. Some names are duplicated with ordered numbers beneath them. The last one in the line has "Alice" scribbled in ink on it.

"Did you always know these were here?"

"Truth be told, I never look at that shelf." He laughs. "But I was talking with Grandmother Poppy about you and she mentioned she was thinking of asking you to help us here. I wondered if Eldas would allow that…but she said there was precedent."

"Precedent for the Human Queen to help?" I don't dare get my hopes up. I've had them dashed too many times here already.

"It's actually been rather common. Which makes sense, when you think about what the queen's magic does." Willow grins and it's a bit lopsided. Just the sight of it tugs a smile onto my own lips.

"What would I be doing?"

"You could help tend the plants. Or mix things for us as you'd like and if we need."

It's a start. "Would I go into the city?"

"Maybe after your coronation." His expression is now worryingly uncertain.

"Could I have patients?"

"I…doubt it." He frowns and my expression mirrors his. I look back to the journals longingly. How were they happy here? *Were* they happy here? I guess there's only one way to find out. But I can already tell that if my journal lines this shelf, it will not be filled with joy as long as my days are spent merely watering plants.

"Anyway, the other queens kept those records," Willow continues. "You may find something useful somewhere in these journals that would help you get acclimated. Poppy gives her permission as well."

"There are some queens missing." Namely the first five.

"I guess the earlier ones didn't keep journals? Or maybe they've been lost or destroyed. That was three thousand years ago. We're lucky to have the journals we do." He shrugs and starts for the exit. "It's almost lunch time. I think I'll go grab us food. Do you have any preferences?"

"Nothing spicy," I say quickly. "Other than that, anything sounds good." I hook my finger on Alice's journal.

"Be back with food shortly," he calls over his shoulder and strolls off.

As I slip the book from the shelf, the thought of taking it to Mr. Abbot crosses my mind. He would no doubt love to merely *hold* something his sister touched. I wonder if I could somehow get the book to him. The thought seeds an idea as I flip through the pages.

If I could go back... I'd do a lot more good in Capton. Spring is here in Midscape, the folk will be fine, and I'm sure Eldas can make himself look tough without me.

My fingertips tingle as though the book is giving me permission.

Alice arranged her notes neatly within. There's the name of an herb at the top of every page with a gorgeous and meticulously detailed sketch of the specimen in question. To the right of the sketch are properties and preparation instructions.

Under all of the above, there are notes on magic—the *queen's magic*—and how to use it. I set the book down on the table and begin eagerly flipping the pages, scanning the magical notes.

Focus on balance. Nature gives back what it receives.

This one stores magic well—can load with magic to be used for greater equilibrium exchanges.

Best to let grow naturally for greatest potency.

Easy to manipulate and sacrifice for larger exchanges of life to power.

Chew and spit out before making adjustments to weather patterns.

One after the other; it's a treasure trove of information. I turn back to the bookshelf and grab another journal at random. This queen has set up her pages slightly different. The sketch of the herb is less skillfully done and it takes up the whole page. Each segment of the plant is noted directly over the sketch. Then, a page of additional information and some life anecdotes are recorded to the right.

I go back for a third journal. Yet more information awaits me. Personal notes line the corners of this queen's pages as she waxes poetic about her situation.

Red rose. Properties: love. The king gave one to me on our fifth anniversary and I shall work to keep it alive so I might treasure the token of his affection forever.

I snort. At least some queen, sometime, seemed like she was in love with the king. Eldas clearly never heard this story. He has no interest in even being my friend, much less loving me.

"You find something amusing?" Willow has returned with a platter of food that he sets on the table between us.

"I did." I set the journal down and move to get another. When I return to the table I tear off a hunk of rosemary bread and dip it into oil and herbs. "I have an idea."

"Oh?"

"These journals are a good start"—and much better than Eldas's sorry attempt at training—"but I want to learn more about my magic, and the elves' magic. I need a safe space to practice."

"All right," Willow says with an appropriate note of caution.

"I want to make this my training room. And I want you to teach me."

"What?"

"Tell me about elf magic and guide me as I work on learning my own." I can't count on Eldas.

"But—"

"Please, Willow." I grab both of his hands. "You're the only friend I have here."

He purses his lips, looking between our hands and my eyes. Finally, he says, "All right."

While we eat, he tells me about the elves' onomancy—the wild magic of names. Every group of folk in Midscape has its own unique wild magic. The fae have ritumancy—magic charged by rituals based on actions performed in set ways. The vampir have sanguinmancy—magic from blood. On and on...

I focus mostly on the elves' magic, since that's what I'm dealing with. Willow reiterates what Eldas told me about the Knowing and how elves use it to find a subject's true name.

As long as the elf knows the true name of someone or something, they can manipulate that thing however they please. It's as Eldas said: their limitations only come from their own imagination and the strength of their magic. Willow explains how some elves are uniquely adept at suggesting emotions, others can manipulate hair into beautiful weaves; they can levitate objects, summon memories, communicate telepathically, and more.

I am surrounded by people of immense power. I wasn't born with magic, and I might never learn enough to stand a chance. The best and safest thing I can do is leave.

Willow knows nothing about the "Being" that Eldas mentioned. After lunch, I spend the afternoon scouring the journals for any notes on it. I can't find anything.

But what I do find is enough instruction on how to use my magic that I have renewed hope and a plan for later tonight.

The day drags on until the chime of a clock startles me from my work. Willow is finishing cleaning up his workbench. "Just leave all your things where they are. We can resume again tomorrow, if you'd like."

"Sure." I force a smile and refrain from saying that I won't be here tomorrow if everything goes right tonight.

fourteen

I WAS EIGHT THE FIRST TIME I SNEAKED OUT OF MY HOUSE.

The tiny window at the back of the attic was *just* large enough for my child body to wriggle through. The ledges that framed the windows were *just* wide enough for my nimble feet. And I was *just* stupid enough to think that climbing tall trees meant I was perfectly capable of scaling down from the third story of a brownstone so I could go and collect rare flowers that only bloomed at night.

I was young and reckless.

Now I'm older…and apparently still reckless.

Moonlight streams in through the windows of the lunch nook. Somehow, the room I destroyed has already been put back together. A shiver wriggles up my spine and I wonder if it's the phantom sensation of the elf magic that I know had to have been used to repair the damage, or if there's truly a chill left behind by the power.

My satchel is slung across my body and I'm in the clothes I arrived here in. Sturdy garments that can hold up to climbing the tallest redwoods in the forest or skidding down a hillside. The sort of clothes I'd wear in the shop I long for now.

I take a deep breath, debating with myself over this course of action. What will happen if I actually leave? The Elf King needed a Human Queen. Well, he got one. Even if I'm far away, we're still married, technically. Midscape needed a recharge through that queen from the Natural World. They got that too.

And, based off the conversation I overheard with Rinni, I've caused more harm than good in Eldas's life. Great, that feeling is mutual. If I leave we can both go back to living how we want now that we've fulfilled our duties.

"I have to go," I say to steel my resolve.

Maybe the other queens had nothing better to do than exist, but I have work. I've made the trees bloom and Midscape flourish. My job here is done as far as I can tell. Now, it's time to see if there's another option that no queen has dared attempt to explore—going home.

I open the window. Even though the trees in the city below are now in spring's embrace, their boughs heavy with fresh growths, my breath frosts the air. I wonder if this city is perpetually chilled by the magic of all the elves living in it.

Whatever it is, I'm looking forward to the much warmer weather of the coast. I imagine the sun on my skin as I collect flowers and herbs growing wild on the hills. I imagine the crash of the waves being muted by the trees as I gather clippings to fill the jars of my shop.

The memories embolden me. The thought of staying another moment here with Eldas and Harrow is too much. I will slowly wither if I'm forced to live out the rest of my days here.

I hold a rose in my right hand; I've cut off the thorns this time to prevent the magic in my blood from getting involved in my magical equation. Several more thorn-less flowers are in my left hand. My bag has damp spots from all the other flowers I've stolen from the now-empty vases around the lunch nook.

Based on what the journals said, and what I saw during my practice with Willow today, I need fodder to use my magic. Wild magic is powerful because it defies the laws of nature. But I am the embodiment of the natural and nature thrives on balance. So everything I do must be kept in equilibrium.

"Let's try this again," I negotiate with the flower. "This time, you have to listen to me, okay?"

It seems to wiggle under my fingers. Surely my imagination. But, if not, I hope that bodes well.

I steel my nerves and remind myself that I can do this before placing the flower on the windowsill. I press my right fingers into it to keep it from blowing away. I inhale, as if I'm sucking in the life and energy from the flowers in my left hand.

Balance and equilibrium, I think. I take the life from the flowers in my left hand and transfer it to the rose underneath my palm. I am not destroying, nor creating, just shifting and rearranging raw essence. Power surges through me, tingling, rushing underneath my skin. It emboldens me in a way nothing ever has before.

Peering out the window, I look down the sheer seven stories to the city street far below. The rose shudders to life. Tendrils grip the rock. The stem lengthens. I watch as it becomes a trellis all the way down the mountainside.

Maybe Eldas was right and controlling magic isn't so hard after all, once you have the basics.

"You better hold." I sit on the sill and place my heels into the weave of vines. I'm putting a lot of trust into some old journals and a few preliminary tests. But I don't have a lot of options at present. Eldas doesn't think I have any control over my powers, so now is the time for me to run if I'm going to. Once I start showing mastery, he might lock me up tighter.

Carefully I shift my weight, turning while I can still grip the sill. I close the window behind me, and begin to slowly descend.

There're a few other windows I pass, but they're dark or have heavy curtains pulled in front of them. By the time my feet are on the ground, my hands and shoulders ache, but the climb wasn't nearly as hard as I expected. The vines seemed to cradle my feet and make convenient holds for my grip.

The plants were looking out for me, I realize. They've always been. Tree branches straining to support me, or bending so I could reach them… it wasn't solely my imagination even when I was told it was as a girl. All this time there were little signs and hints about who I really was and I ignored them.

My thoughts wander to Luke. I hope they haven't had a trial for him yet, because the first thing I want to do when I'm back is really let him know how I feel. Then, I want to explain just what he was risking for all of Midscape, too, by hiding me. No one in Capton seems to really understand what's happening behind the Fade.

The city is quiet. Lampposts shimmer with blue fire, giving everything a sapphire-crusted sheen. The houses are just as tall as my brownstone in Capton, if not taller. I can see the dark shops of milliners, cabinetmakers, smiths, and cobblers—all the trades one would expect to find in a city, but the wares in their windows have me slowing my steps despite myself.

Elf goods are rare in Capton, and extremely precious. Here, my elf-made kettle is just a kettle. I see another one just like it in a silversmith's shop window as I pass.

Everything I once saw as exotic, precious, and magical is common in Midscape. From blue flames to cool magic and all-too-perfect architecture that spires into wicked points on many of the buildings, it's a land that somehow feels like both home and anything but.

A few nighttime revelers are milling about, but they keep their distance. I mostly avoid the taverns where they seem to be congregating. I rake my hair over my ears, trying to hide the fact they aren't pointed like everyone else's here.

I see the occasional city guard patrolling in pairs of two—their outfits just like those who arrived in Capton with Eldas. But it's a peaceful night. Everyone keeps mostly to themselves and no one casts suspicion my way.

Laughter and shouting echoes across the lake, catching my attention. I look to see Harrow and his friends emerging from a dimly lit alleyway. Harrow is suspended between the two men. Aria twirls around them, laughing and prodding at his limp form.

I walk faster.

When I arrive at the end of the stairway that leads into the mountain tunnel Eldas and I emerged from, I pause. There's no stealthy way to ascend. It's a strip of pale moonlight leading all the way up.

Looking back, I can barely make out the vines on the side of the castle, like a green ribbon unfurled from the window. They'll know by dawn that I've sneaked out. But shrinking the vines back down to a rose was a risk I didn't want to take. I need my strength for whatever is about to come next.

Yes, they'll know I ran. So the best thing I can do is get a far enough head start. If I can make it to Capton tonight, then I can explain that I've held up my part of the bargain here and the council will hopefully shelter me. Maybe Luke—for all I loathe the idea of working with him—still knows a way to conceal me. Or maybe there can be an exception made for the fact that a sleepy little coastal town needs a healer desperately.

I take a deep breath and begin running.

Elves don't cross the Fade for anything other than the rare trade of goods, wives, or war. There's no reason a lone elf would be leaving the city at this time of night. I have no doubt Eldas personally picks who can cross the Fade and when. I run as fast as I can and pray no one sees.

I don't stop running as I plunge into the earthy darkness of the tunnel. I sprint into the obsidian mist that blots out the light. I nearly run headlong into a tree, stopping at the last second as it emerges from seemingly out of nowhere.

With two hands I prevent myself from smashing my nose on the trunk. I lean back and look around. The light from the city of the elves has vanished. Sentient darkness surrounds me.

I don't remember taking any turns when Eldas escorted me through the Fade. But perhaps we did. I step around the tree and move forward more slowly and deliberately this time.

It's only possible to see a few feet in front of me at a time. All visibility has vanished and now it is as if I am the light. I am the only entity that is real here. Everything beyond me is shadow and nightmares.

The damp moss sags beneath my feet. I look for stones and signs of the temple pathways. I've been walking for a while now, haven't I? Though perhaps it seems longer because I'm alone. I am very, *very* alone.

"*Meet me in the copse of trees,*
Where the grape vines don't grow."

I sing to myself. It's one of the songs I remember singing as a child but can't place where, or who, I learned it from. It's a macabre song about a human who falls for a creature of the deep wood, and my singing is terrible, but it's better than silence.

"Meet me underneath the silver boughs,
No one else has to know.

Meet me under the veil of secrets,
Before the day expires.
There, my love, I'll steal your face,
Before anyone inquires."

A twig cracks behind me. I spin in place. The haunting melody lingers in the air as I can barely make out movement in the darkness.

I hear the snarl first, a low growl that activates my primal prey-drive to flee. Then, a glint of light breaks the mist. Two, luminous, glowing yellow eyes peer at me.

Step by step, the hulking beast approaches. It's the largest wolf I've ever seen, with paws nearly the size of my booted feet. Its fur is a dark slate color, as if it were born from the mist itself. Its lips are peeled back from its razor sharp teeth.

I match its steps by inching backward.

"Don't," I whisper. The word quivers. "Please, don't."

Why did I have to sing? I might as well have basically shouted, *Here I am, terrible beasts of the Fade! Come and eat me!* Now I'm going to die alone in the dark because of a song I don't even like that much.

My back presses into a wide tree trunk and I glance around, looking for somewhere to climb. Damn. Of course there're no branches.

I look back to the snarling beast, meeting its eyes as I reach in my satchel and retrieve the other roses. If I can make a branch grow, I might be able to climb high enough. Though, judging by its powerful legs, I'm already in lunging distance.

"I'm not a good meal," I say. "Why don't you go back where you came from?"

If it were possible, the wolf only snarls more.

My hand closes around the rose stems. I press my other palm into the tree behind me. What do I want to do? Grow a branch? Will I be able to swing up in time?

I could try and make a cage of roots, like Eldas did to Luke. But the complexity of making something large and strong enough makes me nervous. Meanwhile, the wolf continues to approach.

Choose, Luella, before you're food.

Branch it is.

The roses wither and crumble under my fingers. But nothing happens. Magic flares in me and fizzles out harmlessly in the air.

The wolf lets out a roar and goes to lunge. I try and scramble up the tree, uselessly. In the process, I slip on the damp moss and fall backward.

The world moves slowly.

This is it. This is how I die. Mother always said I went too deep in the forests. She always told me that if anything did me in, it would be that I wandered too far from home.

You were right, Mother.

My back slams into the earth and my bones rattle. I nearly bite my tongue clean off. My teeth sting and ears ring. I imagine the sensation of the throne clawing under my skin. It's the wolf claws on me now. Then there will be the teeth, and blood, and—

Hot breath is by my ear. Sniffing.

I pry open my eyes and am met with the wolf's luminous gaze. It sniffs the side of my face. The boy—as I can now affirm—circles me. He sniffs my hands and buries his nose into my bag.

When he's done with his inspection, he sits, curls his bushy tail around his paws, and stares expectantly.

"What?" I slowly sit upright. "You're not going to eat me?" The wolf continues to watch me. "Then what was all that growling for?" I rub the back of my head. It's still aching. "And what made you stop? Not that I'm complaining."

He tilts his head at me. His ears twitch. It's then that I notice a deep gouge in his right ear.

"Wait…are you…no, you couldn't be…" I shift onto my knees, finally getting a good look at the wolf. He continues to stare expectantly. His tail lifts and then drops heavily. "Are you the same wolf as that day in the woods with Luke?"

It has to be. He has the same bright, knowing eyes as the wolf we saw then...now that he's not snarling at me.

"Is this the second time you've startled me out of my skin?" I laugh airily. A sane person would likely begrudge the animal, but I'm actually slightly amused. "How long have you been watching me? You're cheeky, aren't you? Did you know long before I did who I was?"

He tilts his head in the other direction. Maybe it's a yes.

"Do you know the way out of here?" I've lost my mind. I'm talking to a wolf. "You can get to the edge of the deep wood, right? Where it meets the temple grounds? That's where we met last time; I want to go back there."

The wolf continues to stare at me for several more seconds. With a sigh, I pull myself onto my feet. Wolf guide? A little too much to hope for.

"Well, anyway, thanks for not eating me, again." I hold out my hand in a low wave goodbye.

The wolf moves. His legs are just as powerful as I imagined because before I can blink he's crossed the gap between us and pressed his head into my palm. I stare in wonder as my fingers sink into the rough, dense fur. Even though he looks like he's born of the Fade's mist, he's solid. Then, he backs away slowly, holding my gaze.

He turns, and disappears into the darkness.

"That was..." I start to say, but am cut off by a flash of gold. I can barely make out the wolf's body from the curling mist. But I can see its glowing eyes. He looks almost expectant. "Do you want me to follow?"

The wolf begins to trudge ahead. I dash over to keep up. I'm likely following it to its favorite tree to pee on. I don't even know if this animal does pee. Is it an animal at all? Or a beast made of shadow, like the horse Eldas rode to Capton on?

Doesn't matter. He's the best chance I have of getting out of this place. We walk through the dark woods for what must be another hour before I let out a groan of frustration.

"Thanks for nothing," I mutter. "I'm going to go this way now. It seems just as good as any other direction we've gone in."

A bark and a growl stop me mid-step.

"*What?*"

Another low growl.

"Fine, I'll follow a little longer." I throw my hands in the air, resigned.

We walk until the trees give way to a mossy clearing. A circle of stones rings a larger tablet in the center of a small rise. It almost looks like a tombstone and I shudder.

"This isn't the temple grounds," I scold. The wolf huffs and walks over to the large, vertical memorial. He lies down next to it. "Is this your favorite place, though?"

He tilts his head and raises his eyebrows at me, as if to say, *Isn't this where you wanted to go?*

"No, it's not where I wanted to go," I mutter as I approach the large rock.

There's writing on it, faded with time. It hides behind a cloak of the same green moss that grows out from its base. There's something distinctly temple-like about this place. It reminds me of the old shrines that dot the pathways that wander forgotten in the deep woods.

"What does it say?" I whisper, reaching forward to wipe the moss from the etchings.

"Nothing you can read." Eldas's voice breaks the still silence, and I don't even bother suppressing a groan.

fifteen

"ARE YOU SURPRISED TO SEE ME?" he asks with gravel weighing down his voice.

I turn to face him and can't decide if he's more like a wraith, or an agent of the Forgotten Gods. The darkness of his hair is teased by the mist of the Fade. The gray pallor of his skin is like cut stone, unnatural and ethereal in this world of living night. If it were possible, he looks even more powerful than he did in the throne room. And several times more severe. I fold my arms to protect myself from his judgment.

"I suppose I shouldn't be."

"No, you shouldn't be." Eldas scowls. "What were you thinking?"

"I sat on your throne; I brought about spring. You clearly don't want or need me here anymore and I am little more than a burden to you. I was going home."

He blinks slowly and shakes his head. "You…you think you were a burden?"

"Given how you've treated me, what else was I supposed to think?"

"I have made an effort to be civil to you."

"You have not," I snap without thinking. He takes a step back, as if he's taken aback someone would speak to him in such a manner. Given our experience in the throne room, I'm the one who's surprised I can still make him shocked.

"Well, I…I've given you apartments. I've given you the royal purse to furnish them with. I've not locked you away or barred you access to anywhere in my castle—a decision you've made me very much regret."

"You treated me like a puppet! You *controlled me* with my own true name!" I continue without remorse. I'm in too deep by now, might as well keep digging. "I don't want to be some pawn for you. I'm not going to spend the rest of my life training my magic just so you can scare some other kings of Midscape."

He takes another step back. I see anger rise on his cheeks, furrowing his brow. Until his whole face softens.

"I'm sorry. I was wrong."

"I don't…" *I don't want your apology*, is what I want to say. But I gather my composure and rephrase. "I don't want words, I want action. It's easy to apologize, Eldas. It's harder to mean it."

"I will try harder then."

"Or you can let me leave." A wet muzzle presses into my palm, as if the wolf is trying to remind me he's still here, beside me. I scratch him between the ears, grateful I have someone on my side. Eldas's eyes drop to the beast and narrow slightly, but he returns his attention to me. "You don't want this marriage; I don't want it. I did what you needed and brought about spring. So why are we trying to navigate living and working together?"

"Because we must."

"Why though?" I take a step toward him and the wolf matches my pace. The idea of advancing on the king with a beast of the Fade emboldens me some. "Stop…stop shutting me out, *please*. If you're really sorry for how you've acted, here is your time to change it. If you want me to help you then help me sincerely. Teach me like I asked, don't berate and put me down."

His eyes widen slightly and, for the first time, his walls don't immediately come up. He studies me and I keep myself open, bare before him. This is the last chance I'm giving him, though I don't say so outright.

"The Human Queen is our link to the Natural World and the redwood throne is her link to the foundations of Midscape. The magic flows through her, and from her, to nurture the earth and give it life. This connection is something that must be nurtured. You don't sit once and that's all."

"Wait, are you saying that I'm to be magically leeched by the throne *regularly*?" I say in horror.

"Yes, you charged the earth of Midscape, but the magic you put in will fade over time. So you must continue to sit on the throne to keep fortifying the land."

"That's too much..." I wrap my arms around myself, fighting off the phantom sensation of the throne grabbing for me.

"Yes, eventually you will be depleted. As your strength wanes over the year, Midscape will cool, and the earth will wither."

"Then you cast me aside because I am no longer useful?"

"No," Eldas says sharply. "You truly think so little of me?"

"You haven't given me a lot of reasons to think positively of you," I admit.

He grimaces. "Your magic will grow thin, but you will return to the Natural World when it is most strong—midsummer—to recharge and reaffirm your bonds."

When I arrived, it was a deep winter here in Midscape. After I sat on the throne, spring bloomed into existence. Summer will come next. As my power fades, so too will the earth.

"Seasons," I realize. "You're talking about the seasons."

Eldas nods.

"When I leave for midsummer in Capton, it will be winter again in Midscape because my power will have grown too weak to keep charging the earth."

"It will be Yule, specifically. Midscape will swing closer to the Veil than the Fade—closer to death than life. But this is part of a necessary cycle to sustain our world that mirrors yours, but in reverse. We are in the process of resetting the balance now, but it will find its equilibrium soon and everything should be better then."

Nature requires balance, I think. I feel more powerful than I ever imagined. It is because of me that the seasons will turn in Midscape—there can be life itself.

"Our time apart will also be when I reaffirm my power," Eldas says.

"How so?"

"You are my antithesis, Luella. You are the queen of life."

"And you are the king of death," I whisper, staring up into his frozen eyes. Not for the first time, a twinge of fear blooms in me at the power this man holds. Of course, like the completely sane person I am, I decide to turn it into a joke. "Good to know that we were never meant to get along."

A flicker of amusement alights his eyes. It's the first real emotion I think I've seen in him and it brings a smile to my lips. At least until he steps forward; then my expression falls.

But Eldas brushes past me to stand before the large stone tablet. A pulse of magic thrums through the air like a winter's wind as his fingers lightly sweep across the etched words. Liquid silver magic, mixed with the deep blue of twilight, spills across the carvings and pushes back the moss. The air around us grows thicker.

"So you understand, now," he says. It takes me a moment to realize he doesn't mean whatever magic he just performed. "You cannot be free of this any more than I can. We are held in tandem, you and I. That is why we must learn to live and work together, as you so aptly put it."

"No, I don't understand," I say.

He looks at me incredulously, as if he can't believe I could be that dense.

"Well, I do. Sort of. As much as I think I can understand the high-level explanation of an ancient power forged thousands of years ago. What I don't understand is why everyone has just gone along with it this whole time?"

"Maybe because none of our predecessors wanted to condemn an entire world to be consumed by the death of the Veil?"

"Of course I don't want to condemn anyone to die. But what if there's another way?" I say.

"Another way?"

I'm heartened by the flicker of interest in his eyes. I think of my father's discussions around the dinner table, talk of the council lamenting how there was no alternative to the treaty—wondering if there is another way to be free. The memory of his impassioned voice emboldens me. "Why don't we try to both be free of this?"

"There is no way to be free of this."

"Have you ever tried?" I ask. He's silent. "Has anyone?" More silence. "Why don't we work toward a solution that doesn't involve Midscape dying and the worlds being thrown out of balance *and* one that doesn't involve war breaking out between wild magic and natural magic? A solution without Human Queens?"

"You speak of things you don't understand." He looks back to the stone grimly. "Our only hope is to preserve this arrangement as long as possible." He mumbles under his breath, "Which may not be possible for much longer…"

His hesitation gives me hope. "And you know this because you've looked for an alternative?"

He sighs dramatically. "Luella, I know you look at me and see a regular man—"

"*Nothing* about you is regular," I say quickly. His lips part briefly and the severe expression vanishes from his face, making him all the more handsome. I purse my lips together and fight a stirring I don't want to have when looking at Eldas.

"You see me as a mortal," he rephrases. "But my power stretches beyond your imagination." He motions to the stone he was examining. "*This* is a keystone of the Fade. Do you even know what that means?"

I shake my head.

"It's the cornerstone of Midscape, a foundation for the Fade. Can you see its power?"

I shake my head again.

"Can you comprehend the intricate magic woven all around you, tethered to this rock? Magic that splits worlds?"

"No." He opens his mouth to speak again, but I'm faster. "Can you comprehend what it sounds like to have a thousand, a hundred thousand, *millions* of living things screaming for you? Can you imagine what it's like to have the earth clawing under your skin, scraping your bones for life and power? Will your mind recreate the torture of knowing they would gladly eat you alive if given the chance?"

He blinks. There's that slightly startled expression once more. I'm finding I like the softer, unguarded side of him much more than the severe edge. If I can just keep him off balance maybe we could get somewhere...

"You're right," I continue. "I can't comprehend your magic because, as you put it, I am your antithesis. But that means you can't understand mine, either. And maybe none of the other kings ever gave their queens a chance to really explore their power. Perhaps there's something I can make, or do, like your keystone, that would tether Midscape's seasons to the Natural World's without a Human Queen. *Hmm?*"

He says nothing as his expression hardens once more into something passive and unreadable.

"All I'm saying is...give me a chance—a real chance," I beg. "What do we have to lose?"

"Everything, if we're not careful." There's not a hint of levity in his voice.

"Then *help me*. My power, your knowledge, we can do this together if you let us."

Eldas's lips press firmly into a line. I search the deep waters of his eyes—search for something human. I have no reason to think he'd help me. But I have to at least make an attempt. I owe Capton that much.

"Why is this so important to you?" he asks, finally. There's a trace of hurt. It's the shadow of something lurking in the deeper currents of his personality. I think about what Rinni said—about him secluding himself. "Help me understand."

Here's hoping he listens.

"I had a life. You're right, I'm not like all the other queens. I wasn't groomed for you, for any of this. I had my own dreams and plans. I had people who *depended on me* and I swore to protect and serve them as best I could. They gave their precious little coin for my education and I gave my skills, my years. Capton needs me just as much as Midscape does; I'm the only herbalist they have.

"So maybe that's why none of those other queens dared to question if there was a way out. They didn't have any expectations to be anything other than what they were because they were identified as queens young enough that being the queen *was their dream*. But

I'm not them. I *am* questioning for myself and every other young woman who comes after me."

The king looks between me and the stone, as if he's choosing either me or the world he's always known. I don't even bother holding my breath. I know what he'll pick and it's not my wild idea.

And then...

"All right," he says.

"What?" I gasp.

"I agree to let you pursue this."

"Truly?" I round over to his side. "You mean it genuinely? No more agreeing to teach me and then acting like a right ass?"

He cringes but nods. There's an urge to take his hand and squeeze it, almost like I would do to a friend. But I quench the notion before my body can act on it.

"There are terms to this deal." He regards me warily.

"Of course there are." Still, this is progress. "What are they?"

"The first is that you must keep me appraised of your work. You might not care about Midscape's fate, but I am its sworn warden."

"I never said I didn't care—"

"I will not have you accidentally unraveling the fabric of my world," he finishes, completely ignoring my objection.

"Fine, that's fair." Not like I wanted to do any unraveling.

"Furthermore—"

"Oh, there's more, shocking." I fold my arms. Is that the ghost of a smirk I see on his lips? I'm rewarded once more with a twinge of amusement, bolder than the last. If he keeps giving me sly smiles and shimmering eyes I'm going to think he's beginning to like a determined and slightly bold Luella.

"Furthermore," he continues. "You will not tell anyone else of this plot. I cannot and will not deal with the rumors of the woman who is supposed to rule at my side trying to escape me like I am too weak to win her over. I've already had my rule cast in enough shame by how long it took to find you."

The wolf seems restless with Eldas's agitation. He paces between us and I hold my hand out. He quickly trots over and I scratch between his ears until he settles.

"Eldas, I never meant for you to endure hardship because of me."

"Spare me your fake pity." Anger flashes in his eyes, though it's not directed at me. I can tell that much.

"It isn't fake," I fire back. "I'm sorry. Truly."

My sympathy stuns him. He staggers, taking so long to compose himself that I worry I've broken him.

"I..."

"You?" I encourage.

"I'm sorry as well, for what you've endured."

A smile splits my lips. "Was that so hard?"

Eldas grimaces. "You really can be annoyingly insistent, you know that?"

"I've been told, usually by my patients." I can't help but laugh. "Though I prefer calling myself tenacious." He snorts and, for a brief second, something I'd dare call peace flows between us. I'm hesitant to break it. But I must... "Is there anything else for the terms?"

"Yes. You will not attempt escape again for much the same reasons. The Human Queen isn't meant to be seen before her coronation. It's tradition, but also for your own safety so that no one might perform the Knowing on you or any other magic—especially before you have control of your powers and can defend yourself."

"I can agree to that." Though I think less sequestering would be better for everyone.

"Finally, you have until the coronation in three months to break the cycle."

"Three months? What can I do in three months?"

"I look forward to finding that out," he says, somewhat coyly.

Three months, I'll have three months to find a way to free myself. "If I don't succeed in three months?" I dare to ask.

"Even if I wanted to give you more time, I can't. At the coronation you will be fully accepted by the world of Midscape—you will be part of Midscape more than the Natural World. Only our food will nourish you. Only these lands will be your home. While you will still return to strengthen your magic, it will be limited. Too much time beyond Midscape will kill you."

"You're saying after this coronation there is no going back," I whisper.

"Save for a few days at Midsummer for the sake of your magic, yes."

A shiver rips through me. I succeed, and am free. I can return to Capton. I can help the people I've sworn my life to.

I fail, and I'm trapped for the rest of my life. At least this way, there's a chance. There's hope.

Eldas's eyes bore a hole into my skull, as if trying to gain direct access into my brain and see what my thoughts are. I'm torn between the urge to look away, and being stuck entranced by whatever magic his gaze has. "Tell me, do you accept my terms?" he asks, voice deep and ominous.

"All right, Eldas, you have a deal." I hold out my hand. His long, chilly fingers clamp around mine. I barely resist a shiver at the jolt of magic that dances under my skin at his contact. Too late I think about the fact that I gave him the opportunity to perform another Knowing. But, in shocking respect to my wishes, his eyes don't flair. "But I should warn you; I'm a very hard worker. Three months is going to be plenty of time. I will be free of this."

"I dare say I am looking forward to what you can accomplish." There's an implication of respect there that steals my breath. "Let's return you before anyone has a chance to notice you're gone."

Before I can react, a sudden jolt of power freezes me in place. I panic, thinking he performed the Knowing after all. Dark mist steams off Eldas, mingling with the Fade. It pools at our feet, encasing us. I want to scream, but I can't. I can't move at all. The only light in the darkness is the glow of his eyes.

The world shifts around us.

The stale air of my castle room fills my lungs as I exhale the Fade in plumes of black smoke. Tremors wrack my body, causing black ice to fall off my shoulders. The condensed magic evaporates to steam, dissipating.

"W-what?" I say through chattering teeth. I grip my knees, trying to catch my breath before righting myself. Eldas is unfazed. "What was that?"

"Fadewalking. It's a skill very few are capable of."

I wonder what other incredible feats he can perform. Before I can ask, the air at Eldas's side writhes like heat off a brick street.

From between the shadows and light, a wolf bounds forth. The now-familiar beast happily trots over to me, rounds my feet, and sits at my side.

"What the—" Oh, good, Eldas is as confused as I. The king scowls at the creature. "Yet another sign the Fade is weakening. It's becoming unruly," he mumbles. Then, louder, "Go, beast."

The wolf tilts his head to the side.

"By the order of the Elf King, you are a creature of the Fade, and there you shall remain."

The wolf wags his tail and I don't bother suppressing a giggle. "I guess he does what he wants." I bury my hand in the wolf's fur.

"Like someone else I know." Eldas gives me a side eye and somehow I laugh. For the first time, it feels as if we're working together—as though we're equals.

"If it's any consolation, he didn't listen to me either."

Eldas looks up to the heavens as if silently beseeching the gods for assistance and then heaves a monumental sigh. "He'll go back soon enough. He was likely just following our scent through the Fade."

"Fadewalking seems a lot less impressive when an animal can do it too." I can't help a grin. Eldas narrows his eyes at me, but his scowl has lost some of its bite.

"He can Fadewalk because he is of the Fade—a creature caught in the rift when worlds were severed."

"He's a good boy, that's what he is," I coo to the wolf.

"Fine. It is now my choice to allow this beast to stay as long as it pleases."

I don't know if he's saying that to me, the wolf, or himself. "Of course it is *your choice*."

"If you destroy anything in my castle, I'm sending you back by force," he says sternly to the beast.

"I'll look after him."

"Don't get too attached. He'll be gone before morning," Eldas grumbles, and starts for the door. "And you, Luella, we will practice your magic again tomorrow."

"You've given me even more incentive to learn," I say earnestly. He seems somewhat startled by my shifted tone and gives a small nod. I bite back the urge to tell him that if he gives kindness, he'll likely get it back.

Eldas yawns. "Now, I will make an effort to get some sleep, if the Human Queen will stay put long enough to let me."

"I'll allow it, I suppose."

He clearly wasn't expecting me to answer. A smirk pulls on the corners of his lips. Eldas puts his back to me before I can enjoy the expression.

"Eldas," I say right as his hand falls on the door handle.

"What is it now?"

"Thank you for our agreement... It's a good start in proving that you're not so terrible, after all."

As soon as I say it, I dip my head and focus on petting the wolf to hide my smile. I don't want to make him even more uncomfortable. The sight of his icy facade crumbling at someone else's gratitude is satisfaction enough.

He says nothing and slips out of my room, leaving me and my unexpected new companion alone.

sixteen

RINNI CRACKS THE DOOR. "Your Majesty? Are you ready?"

"Yes." I'm perched at the edge of my bed. Alice's journal is balanced on my knees and I'm scouring through for any information that could give me a starting point for how to approach my predicament.

I've already managed to figure out that the "Being" is the mirror of the "Knowing" in that it is the essence of existing rather than just *understanding* existence. It's a tricky concept, but the important bit is that I now know my powers can change the true name of something.

A useful discovery to dedicate my morning to.

Rinni says nothing. The silence drags long enough that I glance over to her. Her eyes are focused on the wolf that's taking up nearly the entire foot of my bed. She has a confused, bewildered, and slightly afraid expression.

"Rinni, meet Hook." I named the wolf after the hook shape of his one, damaged ear.

"Hook… You have a wolf?"

"Yes, and his name is Hook." I close up the journal. "Before you ask, yes, Eldas knows Hook is here. And yes, he's all right with it."

"Eldas… I'm missing something."

"Maybe." I smile sweetly and saunter over to the closet. I feel better than I have in days. "Hold on just a moment while I get dressed."

Rinni studies me when I emerge.

"What? Did I pick poor clothes for a queen?" I ask.

"It's not that. I like that you went with green again. It complements your hair. Perhaps you do have a bit of fashion sense to you."

I gasp. "Rinni, did you just say something nice about me?"

She rolls her eyes. "You say it as if it's a shock."

"Well, I didn't think you liked me much."

"I like you fine." Rinni's eyes fall to Hook at my side. "You're not bringing that beast into the throne room."

"You want to try and tell him he can't come?"

Hook tilts his head at Rinni. His eyes say, "pet me." But his long muzzle full of razor sharp teeth says, "try me." It's only been a day, but I think finding Hook was one of the best things I could've done. It's like we were meant to be together all along.

"Fine, but if Eldas asks, I said he should stay in your room."

I shrug. After last night, I'm already more confident around Eldas. As long as he keeps up his end of the deal, maybe there's hope.

Maybe, somehow, we got through to each other. A little?

We walk through the main room of my apartments. It's still barren, and getting furniture slots higher onto my to-do list. It's solidly underneath "figure out my magic" and "stop the cycle of the Human Queen." But it may be more attainable than either of those goals and, moreover, having a furnished apartment might make me more comfortable during my—hopefully short—three months here. At the very least, it'd be nice to have an actual desk to read journals and take notes at.

We go down the same path to the throne room. Just like before, Rinni listens at the door before opening it. "Your Grace, Her Majesty and…Her Majesty's wolf."

Eldas stands before the great window behind the two thrones— one crafted by nature, the other by mortal hands. His hands are folded behind his back and his long silhouette is cut sharply against the morning light. I think I hear the echo of a sigh.

"Thank you. You may leave, Rinni."

Rinni bows and departs through the side door we entered through. Eldas turns to face me, looking down his blade-like nose. His face is so severe that I wonder strangely if it would be painful to kiss it. I already know his words are sharper than glass. Would his tongue match? I push the thoughts from my mind. I'm here to *work*.

His gaze shifts to Hook.

"The beast is still here."

"His name is Hook."

"Very well." He shakes his head, resigned. "We have work to do, wolf or no."

I summon my courage and say, "Yes, we do."

"Come here." He senses my hesitation and adds, "I'm not going to force you to sit on the throne."

"Really?" This is already going much better than the last time.

"Truly. It's obvious we need to start with the bare minimum. We'll begin with you exploring your powers and becoming familiar with them. We need to learn just how much of the past queens' strength you inherited," he instructs as I cross over. "Close your eyes."

I oblige him. With my eyes closed I'm somehow *more* aware of his presence. I hear his footsteps. I'm keenly aware of the exact moment he crosses the line of my personal space. He's achingly close and the air shifts as he moves around me.

A low growl breaks the trance. "Hook, *shh*," I hiss. Maybe Rinni was right about leaving him behind.

Is that a soft chuckle I hear? Eldas smothers the pleasant noise quickly. I peek through my lashes, but he's not in front of me any longer.

"Reach within you." The resonance of his voice behind me, nearly close enough to move the tiny hairs on the back of my neck, makes me shiver.

Get yourself together, Luella.

"Feel the power that's there."

"I feel nothing."

"You're not going to master anything with sixty seconds of effort," he says dryly. I can't help but smirk. "Try harder." His hands rest on my shoulders, feather light. I shiver again as he trails his fingers over the velvet that covers my arms. "Feel the magic being drawn in through the air, the power that gathers in your hands. Feel it as your feet root to the earth." His hand slips around my hip. I let out a gasp as his fingers spread across the flat plane of my stomach. It's as if with every caress my magic activates, eager to respond to him, as if my power could arc from me to him. "Do you feel it? Gathering within you? A wellspring of life waiting to be unleashed?"

"I…" *I feel something, all right.*

"*Shh,*" he says, a little too gently. "Keep your focus, Luella."

Why does my name sound so much better when he says it in that deep voice of his? I press my eyes tighter and try to shift my focus. The only things I'm feeling well up in me are dark desires I certainly am not about to admit to anyone—myself included—anytime soon.

"Breathe," he whispers. I do as he commands. "Exhale."

I'm putty under his hands. Breathe in, breathe out, focus. Eldas stands behind me, one hand on my stomach and the other resting lightly on the backs of my fingers. He breathes in time with me. And, slowly, the carnal urges he woke with his touch fade away.

We breathe together as one and, in the darkness, something new is blooming.

Power flows between us. My magic is more like a wide, shallow lake than a deep well; he stands on the far edge. We look toward different skies, broken by the other's silhouette.

Our power is connected, but we see that power differently. And because we understand it differently, the power functions uniquely for each of us.

I see life. He sees death. Two sides of the same coin. Two halves that require the other to exist.

I imagine myself kneeling at the lake's edge. Yet my eyes never leave him. Not even as I dip my hands into the water.

It's not wet, as I would've thought. The water is warm and swirls around my fingers with a faint glow. When I take my hands from the lake, they have the same green shimmer on them.

"Little by little," Eldas murmurs.

Does he see the same thing I do? Is this vision beyond my own mind? Is it actual, or just how I'm comprehending the shifting power that pulls between us like helpless tides trapped between two moons?

"The magic responds to you, Luella. You are its master. It is not the master of you. It exists to serve you and you are its sole commander; never think otherwise." His hands leave my body and I bite back an inappropriate groan of frustration. My skin is flushed, hot under where he touched. "Open your eyes."

I pry my eyes open as he walks around me. The light of the throne room is too bright. I blink several times, returning my mind to the here and now—the physical world.

"Was that real?" I ask.

"That was how your mind is attempting to comprehend your magic."

"Did you see it too?"

He seems startled I'd probe for his experience. "I saw... something." Eldas turns away from me, hiding the expression that accompanied those words. I take a step forward, drawn toward him as he moves away. He speaks before I can probe further. "Come to the throne."

The gentle heat that filled my body vanishes. The redwood throne stands before me, tall and imposing. Threatening.

It's softened only slightly by Hook's presence. The wolf has curled up at its foot. His chin is on his paws and he looks up at me with golden eyes. Somehow, even the animal seems to expect something from me when it comes to this throne.

"You said I wouldn't have to," I whisper.

"This is your power," Eldas says delicately. "You must commit to learning it. Especially if you want any hope of breaking the queen's tie to the throne."

"But..."

It takes only two of his wide strides for him to be before me again. Eldas slowly moves for my hand and I allow him to take it in his. Somehow, this touch is sturdy and reassuring.

"You can do this. You must."

I shiver and force my body to move. It's just a throne. A throne that nearly killed me the last time. Nothing to be worried about. *Right*. Maybe if I tell myself that enough I'll believe it.

Eldas guides my palm to the throne, holding it just above the corner of the armrest.

"Just this, for now. Greet the throne and its might without giving yourself to it."

I am frozen in fear.

"Are you ready?" he asks softly.

"Just one more minute." My voice quivers slightly. He gives me the time and then some, standing patiently, holding my hand in his. When my composure is gathered, I nod and he presses my hand against the wood.

There's a spark sizzling under my skin. Popping crackles my ears. But I stay grounded in my body. This time, I'm not pulled deep into the magical clutches of the redwood throne. I blink and breathe slowly. Hook lets out a low whine.

Eldas has unhanded me. I continue pressing my palm to the throne of my own accord. My connection with it is stable and calm this time. I can once more sense those deep roots fanning beneath me in the foundation of worlds.

"What do you feel?" he whispers. His hands are behind his back again and yet the ghost of them is still on my body.

"I feel it...stretching, reaching. I feel the earth, mighty and solid, coiled in the roots' grasp. I feel..." Rock. A hard layer of rock that the roots can't penetrate. Instead, they cluster just before it, around something, like a cage. I can't tell what that "something" is. It's a black spot in my awareness—a place where my limited senses go to die. I don't remember it from the first time...but that whole experience is just a jumble of pain in my mind now.

"When you're ready, close your eyes."

I take a deep breath and do as he instructs yet again.

"Feel the Fade you crossed, just south of the city; we're right at the edge of Quinnar. Traverse the plains and hills to the eastern mountains. Feel their white-capped and snowy ridges. Enter the deep forests of the fae. Find, at the water's horizon, far, far to the north, where the Veil separates our world from the Beyond. See, but never touch."

As he speaks, I go on a journey behind my eyelids. I'm jerked around from place to place. It's as if I race between one location and the next to keep up with his words. As my thoughts change, so too does my awareness.

I shiver as the bitter cold of the mountains brushes against me. I hear the chirping of the birds awakening to spring in the forests. I smell the salt air as I look out to a vast, dark horizon at the world's edge.

One place, and then to the next. Each location tries to tie vine tendrils of magic to me. The earth leeches from me on instinct. And a small piece of myself is left behind at every turn.

Opening my eyes, I pull my hand away and try to catch my breath. The world spins and I sway. Eldas moves in the corner of my vision. Hook is faster.

"I'm fine." I bury a palm in the wolf's fur. He comes up to my thigh and leans against me for support that I hate I need. Just that little bit of magic left me drained. "I just... I need to catch my breath."

"This is a significant improvement over last time."

"Careful, Eldas, that sounds like approval."

"Well, I am a king, I must be discerning with my approval." He adjusts his coat, smoothing out invisible wrinkles. A movement I'm beginning to associate with uncertainty. I almost find it endearing.

A tired grin pulls at my lips. "Even with your wife?"

"Especially with my wife." His eyes meet mine. "Because none have greater responsibility, or power, than her. I am the most discerning with those that are the most capable."

"And *that* almost sounded like a compliment."

"Take it as you will." He looks to the throne as if my sly grin made him—the mighty Elf King—uncomfortable. "What did you feel?"

"The world, again. But this time with more control. I didn't feel like vultures were picking me down to the bone." I straighten, no longer leaning on Hook. The room has stopped spinning.

"Yet it still took magic from you," Eldas observes. I nod. He frowns. "Tomorrow, we'll work on shielding your magic from forces that would try and leech it away."

"Are there more forces that would leech from me than the earth itself?" I ask.

"The earth may be the greatest force, but sheltering yourself from it may be the easiest task. Guarding yourself from an attack by a sentient being is much harder." It sounds like he's speaking from experience.

"Who would do that?"

"You are a queen now. Moreover, you are my wife. Both titles bring enemies."

"This isn't the first time you've brought up enemies... Who are they?"

"That's not your concern."

"Clearly it is." I blink several times at him, waiting for his agreement. Eldas purses his lips.

"You will be safe in the castle. Stay here until your coronation," is all he says as he strides away toward one of the doors on the opposite side of the room. It's like he's retreating from allowing himself to get too close to me. As though the very notion makes him afraid. "Come again tomorrow morning."

"Where are you going?"

"I have business to attend to."

"Maybe I could help with it?"

He pauses. "Don't you have your own work to do on ending the cycle of queens?"

"I thought you were going to help me accomplish that task?"

"I do things my own way." Eldas smiles thinly.

"But—"

He closes the door tightly behind him. I whirl away and am face to face with the thrones.

"Fine, be that way," I mutter, and head to the greenhouse.

Willow is there waiting for me. Hook quickly becomes his new obsession and our magic practice today is slow going as a result. But that's fine; I'm tired and I could use a bit of a break. We work up until lunch, when he excuses himself much like he did yesterday to go and get us food.

I have my nose in one of the past queens' journals, absorbing as much information as I can, when Hook perks up. I see him move from the corner of my eye. He lets out a low growl.

Footsteps stop at the entrance to the laboratory.

"Hook, what is—" I freeze.

Harrow leans against the door frame, gripping it for support.

seventeen

"WELL, DON'T YOU LOOK JUST LIKE THE PROPER QUEEN?" Harrow slurs his words. The prince's hair is stringy and clings to his cheeks, which have a sickly pallor. "Already up here, spending your days with plants rather than people."

"I find plants rarely attack me, unlike people." I slowly close the book, resisting the urge to run over and inspect him to determine what ailment he has.

"I beg to differ." He pants.

"You need medical attention."

"I need Poppy. Where is she?"

"Willow mentioned she's off on some kind of a special assignment." I think that's what he said earlier? I was too focused on studying to get the details and Willow was too focused on scratching behind Hook's ears to elaborate on what Poppy was doing.

Harrow curses.

"Willow will be back soon—"

"I don't want the understudy," Harrow seethes. Pain is pinching his face, making it even uglier than normal.

"Then how about a queen?"

"Like I would ever let you touch me," he says, but he makes no effort to leave.

"*Mmhmm.*" I roll my eyes at the child he's being and point to one of the stools. "Sit."

"How dare you—"

"How dare I try and heal you even after you were an ass to me?" I snap. "Now, sit, you arrogant prince, before your stubbornness has you toppling over or throwing up." Either looks equally possible.

Harrow stares at me blankly. His eyes are glassy and dull—because of fever, likely, given all the sweating he's doing. His shirt clings to the doorway and then suctions back to his skin as he moves to sit. I quickly thumb through the journals. I know how to cure sicknesses, but there may be even more effective ways locked in these dusty pages.

Do I dare try using my magic now of all times?

"Did you wake up not feeling well?"

He chuckles and shakes his head. I glance over at him. The stool creaks as he leans against the table.

"So this came on later in the day?"

"A lot of things came on later…last night, this morning, sometime…time, slipping between my hands, fingers…life…ah, damn it all." He's not making any sense.

"Harrow, tell me what doesn't feel good."

"Everything." He snorts and slumps. I see his head go limp and Harrow catches it quickly as he relies even more on the table for support. I race over to him, my hand on his shoulder.

"Unhand me, human."

"Stop," I say, softer, trying with all my might to take the venom from my voice. An ugly corner of me wants to let him suffer. But my training—everything I have dedicated my life to until this moment—won't let me. "I can heal you. But I need to know what must be done. Your wounds are on the inside right now, I can't see them. So I need you to tell me what's wrong."

"Too much partying is all."

I saw him last night, I remember. He looked in bad shape then. But he was with his friends, surely they were looking out for him? Though Aria seemed fairly gleeful, given his state…

"You don't look like you came from a party," I murmur. "You look like you came from a fight and lost."

He glowers. "Are you done mocking me?"

"I'm not sure. Can I mock you into being a model patient?"

Harrow snarls at me. It's echoed by Hook's growl, low and fierce.

Harrow blinks, startled, focusing on the wolf for the first time. He points and lets out a blurt of laughter.

"Wait… Is there actually a wolf there? Or am I hallucinating again?"

"There's actually a wolf there." I pull away carefully, situating him and making sure he won't keel over before I get back. "I'm going to get something that'll make you better. Please don't pass out in the next five minutes."

I move deliberately through the greenhouse. I pluck aloe, dandelion, red clover, milk thistle, nettle, and a large bunch of basil. Back in the laboratory, I mix them all with turmeric, honey, dried ginger, and willow. As I inspect my concoction, one other idea crosses my mind.

Hallucinating again, he said. Harrow continues to sag. If I don't get this in him soon, he'll be a puddle on the floor. Possibly a dead puddle.

I don't know what he ingested, but I run back out and carefully take a single leaf from the heartroot plant. Willow said that it enhances antidote properties. If there is anything suspect in his system, it'll hopefully help.

Holding the bunch of basil in my left fist, I place my hand on the pot. I take a deep breath and brace myself. *I give life to gain a more potent mixture*, I think loudly to myself.

The basil withers as I draw out the life from it. Power surges through me, mingling with my own magic. The magic swells in me and I push it through my palm on the cauldron into the mixture I've created.

Strengthen the herbs, I command as magic changes my mixture from a murky color to bright green. I take a tentative sniff. It smells right. Everything about it seems right.

But can I trust my instinct when it comes to magic?

I glance back at Harrow. He's fading fast. He doesn't even look like he'd make it until Willow is back.

I have to try.

Slowly, I ladle out a thick glob of the mixture into a cup. I've only added just enough water to make it drinkable. Harrow looks up at me skeptically as I present it to him.

"Are you going to kill me now?" he whispers. "Strike when I'm weak to get back at me for what I did to you?"

"Please. I have better things to do with my time than kill you." I bring the mug to his lips. "Drink. And don't you dare complain about the taste. You're lucky I threw in honey."

Honey is actually great at preventing inflammation and stinting infection. But I doubt Harrow knows that, and I'd rather he think I did him a favor.

Harrow drinks slowly. His throat bobs and color begins to return to his cheeks. I can almost see his fever breaking. He sits straighter and wipes his brow.

I move back to the pot to scoop out the second cup. I just performed magic without issue. Last night, this morning…the fizzle when I tried to make a branch in the Fade aside, I'm getting better. Perhaps there's hope for me yet. When I'm not overthinking things or panicked, my hands seem to know what to do.

Though I know I'd be a fool to think the redwood throne will be conquered so easily. Still, it's nice to have something go right for once.

Harrow is far more skeptical of this mug than the first. I hate the fact that I must take it as a good sign that he's back to his ornery self.

"What's in it?" He sniffs the mug.

"You saw everything I put in it. I doubt you'd understand the why. But you don't need to; just drink. The more you get in you the better."

"It's foul." Harrow scrunches his nose as he takes a sip of my infusion.

"But it's clearly helping." I fold my arms.

He resigns himself to sipping the concoction in silence. I turn my back to him and return to the journals. I pretend to flip through them, but I'm too on edge with Harrow's presence to focus. And I keep glancing at him to make sure my magic isn't going to unexpectedly kill him.

"Why did you heal me?" His question interrupts my thoughts and I meet his eyes. He looks much younger when he doesn't have that wicked smile he's been wearing since the first time we met.

"Because it was the right thing to do," I say finally. "Because that's my job."

"I think my eldest brother would disagree on it being your 'job.'"

"*Eldest* brother?" I arch my eyebrows, focusing on that instead of lingering on Eldas and his control over my circumstances. I'm not going to let Harrow, of all people, shake the level foundations Eldas and I are currently standing on. "There are more of you?"

"At least pretend to hide your disappointment at the fact." He rolls his eyes. "Eldas is the oldest, then Drestin, and then me."

"Do you all have the same mother and father?"

"What kind of a question—*yes* we all have the same mother and father."

"I know your mother wasn't the last Human Queen." I rest my hand lightly on Alice's journal. She seemed to have a...*strange* relationship with the former Elf King.

"*Aww*, are you looking into our parentage because you want to know if you'll have to birth Eldas's little screaming spawn? Don't worry, the Elf King takes lovers for his heirs."

I ignore the remarks. I'm not going to be here long enough to broach the topic of who's dealing with siring heirs. Fortunately, the subject of consummating our marriage hasn't come up either in conversation or in the journals I've read. I'm pleased to see that the people's investment in the nighttime couplings of their rulers was also greatly exaggerated in the stories I read as a girl. "Where's Drestin?"

"He's out in Westwatch." Harrow takes another sip of his drink. "Oh, that's right, you know *nothing* about us. Let me explain."

"I can find out on my own," I say curtly.

"Westwatch is the fortress along the great wall that borders the fae forests," he explains anyway. "It was built a few hundred years ago and helps keep their infighting out from our lands. Such an honorable appointment for the *noble* Drestin." Harrow looks at the corner of the room, angry at something I can't see.

I laugh softly and shake my head.

"What's so funny?"

"You remind me of a friend, is all. She has two sisters and the fights they got into are legendary." I wonder how Emma is. I hope her heart is holding up enough that Ruth isn't flying off the handle at every turn. She should have enough potion in stock to last a few days...but she'll have to take the ferry to Lanton for more when she runs out. Now it's my heart that's aching on her behalf.

"Don't compare me to you humans and your pathetic plebeian problems."

I laugh, loudly. "Forgive me, mighty elf prince. Because you sound *so* far above us lowly folk when you're clearly just jealous of your brothers."

"You don't know anything about me." Harrow throws the mug across the room. What little liquid was left in it splatters across the floor before it lands with a loud *crash*, shattering.

I jump, but immediately work to keep my composure.

"Clean that up, human." He points at the mess he made and storms toward the door.

Harrow freezes when Hook's growl turns into an angry bark. He turns, and the moment his eyes meet the wolf's, Hook lunges.

"Hook, no!" I shout. Magic thrums within me. I see the potion I made for Harrow steam off the floor and disappear. Balance heeds my demands on instinct—potion in exchange for a barrier.

Fresh growth springs up impossibly from the wooden floorboards. Hook stops suddenly, barking at the wall of saplings I've erected between him and Harrow. He looks back at me with his golden eyes as Harrow glances between us.

"Hook, *no*," I repeat, somehow managing to keep my voice steady despite the magic I just performed. *How did I do that?* Luckily Hook backs down.

"You..." Harrow's eyes take up almost as much space on his head as his massive ears.

"That was the second time I saved your life today. A thank you would be appropriate," I say with narrowed eyes.

All I get is a glare, and Harrow's swift departure, leaving me with the thrill and awe of the magic still tingling in my fingers.

eighteen

I NEVER TELL WILLOW WHAT HAPPENED WITH HARROW. I'm not quite sure why. I know Willow would take my side and I know, if anything, he'd be proud of me for how deftly I used my magic.

But something about the exchange felt private. I have a wriggling notion that Harrow wouldn't want people to know about his vulnerable state. As much as I want to ignore that sense, I can't. The privacy of my patients is sacred to me, in the Natural World and in Midscape.

So Willow and I part ways with him none the wiser, some excuse made about a potion attempt gone wrong to explain away the floorboards Willow fixed with his wild magic.

That night I burn the midnight oil and I'm up with the dawn. I scour the journals I've taken from the laboratory, searching for any clues as to how equilibrium is created between the queen, the redwood throne, and the seasons. I start with Alice's journal, but the quality of her entries diminishes with age.

Her pen lines are shaky. The once masterful drawings are rough sketches, wobbly and hard to decipher. Without warning, they stop altogether.

It fills my chest with a deep pain unlike any other I've felt. I can see her in that laboratory, working the last energy from her fingers while they will cooperate. I imagine her hands trembling without her permission until she can no longer hold a pen. I imagine her alone, longing for her brother—the comfort of family—and to smell the salt air of Capton just once more.

I imagine myself, ninety years from now, withering in this cold place with nothing but the agony of the redwood throne filling my days. It's a cold and bleak thought, one I try and put away with Alice's journal.

After that, I read the writings of the queens before Alice. It's easier to thumb through the pages that lead up to their ultimate demises when I don't have any kind of personal connection with them. I succeed in hardening my emotions after the third journal—the journal with the loving notes about the roses.

She had been heartbroken by the thought of leaving her king's side, even in death.

A knock on my door jolts my eyes from the page. I rub them. Hook has curled up at the foot of my bed yet again. He's long since given up on trying to place his muzzle over my book pages or nudge me for attention.

"Are you awake?" Rinni asks through the door.

"Yes." I stretch my arms overhead and my spine pops in several places.

Rinni enters. "I came to let you know that an urgent matter has arisen."

"Oh?"

"It seems a delegation from the Fae King arrived last night," she reports.

"I thought there wasn't a Fae King, just a bunch of infighting between clans?"

"Every now and then they scrape together enough unity to declare someone king and swear to the rest of the world they're presentable. This one has lasted the longest, but we'll see if he can keep it up. No king has ever kept his power long enough to make it to the Council of Kings." Rinni shrugs. "Regardless, Eldas has sent me to inform you that he will not be able to meet with you this morning as planned."

"Oh well." I hop off my bed. "What're you up to today?"

"What am I...up to?"

"Are you busy?" I rephrase.

Hook stretches with a low whine and shakes out his fur.

"Usually, I would be assisting Eldas with the delegation…but he has appointed me to your care."

"I can't tell if you're upset about that or not." I grin.

Rinni bristles. "I—" she clears her throat "—Your Majesty, guarding you is an honor."

"Is it?" I arch my eyebrows and walk to my closet. I leave the door open while I change so I can talk to her. "I still can't tell if you like me or not."

"It's not my job to like you, it's my job to serve you."

"Yes, but—" I pop my head out and Rinni promptly glances askance at my bare shoulders. "I would much prefer if you *liked* me. If not, I'm sure we can find another guard who does."

She huffs and purses her lips. "I think I've told you already; I like you fine."

"Oh, good. And you're sure I'm not keeping you? You seem like you're someone pretty important."

"I *am* the king's right hand." The mention gives me pause, bringing back the memory of Rinni cupping his cheek. I can't help but wonder if there's more there. Harrow had mentioned something about the Elf King taking lovers… "But that's precisely why he has me guarding you. There's no one else he trusts to keep you safe."

I barely refrain from asking if there's anything she can do about Harrow.

"Well then, I'd like to furnish my room today. You said it was something the queens got to do." I emerge from the closet. Rinni tilts her head in an uncanny mirror of Hook. I barely resist laughing at them both.

"Yes, but usually they do it *after* their coronation, when they can go into the city."

"So I'm stuck without furniture for three months?"

Rinni purses her lips. "I have an idea—I believe the furniture of the past queens is stored somewhere in the castle. You could start with that for the time being?"

"All right, lead the way."

We wander through the lifeless castle to a back room. It's clearly being used as a storeroom, but it's the size of a small ballroom. The only dancers are tarp ghosts propped up by furniture underneath.

"All this…belonged to past queens?"

"By my understanding."

It's like a graveyard. With morbid curiosity, I peel up the first sheet and reveal a chaise covered in supple brown leather. *It's just a piece of furniture*, I try and insist to myself. But I can see the outline of where the queen sat.

I shiver and lower the sheet. The room is suddenly ten times colder.

"I think I want to pick out my own."

"But—"

I turn back. "Isn't there a way we could sneak out? I can cover my head, tuck my hair, and—"

"Your eyes," Rinni interrupts.

"What?"

"Your eyes give you away. Elves have blue eyes."

I curse under my breath. "I can't use any of this…" I shake my head. "It's a good effort, thank you, but I can't… It'd be strange. As though I'm living with ghosts." Rinni gives a sympathetic sigh. At least she seems to understand why her suggestion won't work. "Are you certain there's no way I can go into the city to get furniture of my own?"

She pauses, curling and uncurling her fingers around her sword.

"Rinni?"

"Perhaps there *could* be a way, if we're very careful." Rinni's eyes are shifty, as if she's doubting herself for saying anything.

"Oh?" I encourage eagerly.

"I'll tell you as we walk." Rinni motions for me to follow her and I quickly fall into step.

The plan is fairly simple.

Rinni takes me back to her room and there I change out of the gown and into some of her clothes. She has a modest apartment— the racks of weapons I expect. The painting supplies I do not. Rinni says nothing about her hobby, so I follow her lead. I don't know if it's supposed to be secret that the right hand of the king is also an artist. Either way, I don't want to risk the peace we've found.

I carefully tuck my hair underneath a cap. Even though no one knows me yet, Rinni says the red is too distinct a shade to have flowing freely. Though a few red-orange sparks float stubbornly around my ears.

The final bit of my ensemble is a pair of green-tinted glasses. Apparently, elves all having the same eye color has given rise to some thinking it fashionable to wear spectacles of varying tints. It's like I'm wearing one of the stained glass windows from the Keepers' temple on my face, but I'll accept it if this is the way I get out of the castle without issue.

"I think this'll work." Rinni appraises me one final time. She's changed out of her usual military garb into plain clothes.

"It'll be great." I appraise myself in her tall, skinny mirror. "Shall we?"

"One last thing." Rinni looks to Hook. "He has to stay here."

I purse my lips. "Hook is—"

"Hook is going to quickly become identifiable as the queen's wolf." Rinni folds her arms over her chest. "If your hair can't be shown, then neither can Hook."

Sighing, I turn to Hook. "You're going to have to stay here." He whines. "No, I insist. Rinni is right, there's no other way." A bark. "Do not take that tone with me. You are headed back to my quarters, now."

He gives a defiant yowl and hops about the room. Before I can stop him, the air shimmers, the shadows lengthen, and the wolf slips between them into the void. Rinni is as startled as I am.

"What did you do?" she whispers.

"I… I don't know." Panic claws its way up my throat and is let out as a soft, "Hook?" Nothing. "Hook, come back." I raise my hands to my lips and let out a shrill whistle. The wolf comes bounding back on command and I bury my fingers in his fur. "Good boy. Did you hear my whistle? You really are the best of boys!"

"Now *that's* useful," Rinni says in awe. "A Fadewalking wolf… I've seen everything."

"Okay, Hook, go back and play in the Fade. I'll call you later."

He heeds my command and Rinni and I set off through the back halls of the castle. All paths lead back to the main atrium, and the two doors that Rinni unlocks with magic.

I take a deep breath the moment we enter the city. As if I'm welcoming spring with a big hug, I reach my arms out, over my head, and rise to my toes. The days are becoming undeniably warmer, even if they're still a little too cold for my taste and frigid at night.

"You seem happy," Rinni finally comments as we walk around the great lake in the center of the city.

The frost has vanished off the statues and their details are clearer. The queen wasn't merely kneeling…it looks as though she's burying something. Perhaps? I see a large mound under her hands and maybe a small sapling that almost looks…familiar? I've seen those leaves before, haven't I? But the significance of her burying something, or what she might be burying, is lost on me—something to search for in the journals.

It's likely just the queen planting a commemorative tree, or something similar. I quickly shift my focus back to Rinni.

"It's nice to get out of the castle." I keep an eye on her face, looking for any sign that she knows about my escape two nights ago. I see no indication.

She thinks about her response for several steps. "I can see how it might seem that you're some kind of hostage, especially before the coronation. But once you're introduced properly to Midscape, you can explore Quinnar at your leisure. Past queens would even make trips out to the various strongholds and lands throughout the Elf Kingdom…or to the royal cottage. And, of course, you'll cross the Fade every year to commune with the Natural World."

I purse my lips. I can see where she's coming from—how her logic is set up. I look up toward the long stairway leading into the mountain tunnel that crosses back to the Natural World.

"Rinni, why did you want to become a knight?" I ask.

"I… Because my father was a knight and I was his only child," she says, tension raising her shoulders slightly.

"So it was always assumed of you?" I reason. She nods. "If you could be anything you want…what would it be?" Based on what I saw in her room, I suspect I already know the answer.

"A knight, like my father, and his father before him. I come from a long line of knights who have served the Elf Kings for centuries."

"*No.*" I stop walking and Rinni does as well. "What do *you* want? Forget your family. You're an orphan for one minute and have no idea who your parents were or what they did. What would you be?"

Rinni purses her lips. I can tell the question is uncomfortable for her. But she seems to be making an effort nonetheless.

"A painter," she says, finally. "But—"

"No buts," I interrupt. "*You* want to be a painter. You're a knight because it's what's expected of you. And that's fine." I try not to judge her for it. Willow comes to mind as well, following in the steps of Poppy and Poppy's grandparents before. Elves seem to enjoy doing things for tradition's sake. "But you didn't make that choice for yourself, not really. You made it because it was assumed you would and because, I'd guess, it would create tensions in your family if you hadn't become a knight."

She sighs and starts walking again, as if she can leave this conversation behind. I'm not ready to quit yet. But I do shift the focus.

"I'm not trying to attack or upset you," I say.

"I wouldn't let you upset me," she mumbles.

"Good!" I laugh and smile at her. I see the tiniest smile in return. "I'm just trying to say…we're not so different. And, maybe, because of that, you can understand how I feel. I had my own dreams, too, Rinni. I had a shop. I wanted to help people with my talents when it came to herbs and potions. The whole town depended on me and invested in me so I could do it. That profession—herbalist—was *my* painting. But the world wanted me to be something different.

"So, no, I'm not held hostage in the literal sense. But it can feel that way, especially because the life I planned for myself is out of reach."

Rinni sighs and runs a hand through her blue-streaked hair. "I suppose, phrased like that, I can understand."

"Thank you." I nudge her and Rinni looks at me in surprise. I flash her a bright smile. "I appreciate the effort."

A faint blush crosses her cheeks. Is she shocked by someone paying her a compliment?

"In any case," Rinni says hastily. "We're here."

"Here?"

"The best cabinetmaker in Quinnar."

The cabinetmaker's shop is filled with showpieces and books with diagrams of intricate furniture. Sawdust floats in from the woodworking room in the back, resulting in the cabinetmaker fastidiously dusting his counters. I decide on a few pieces that he already has pre-fabricated, rather than going for anything too custom.

"I suspect he knows who I am," I say to Rinni as we leave the shop.

"Maybe, likely, especially after seeing me with you, but he's from a long line of cabinetmakers," she says. Why am I not surprised? "They've been working with the castle for generations, so I trust his discretion. I wouldn't have brought you there if I didn't."

We're halfway back to the castle when she pauses. "Oh, here, there's something I want you to try."

We navigate through the flow of people out on the street. In the daylight, Quinnar is a completely different city. Elves bustle about, carts line up in front of shops: people selling everything from food, to jewels, to suspect potions that have me curling my nose.

Rinni leads me to a cart where a woman is grilling dough on a flat griddle. Rinni orders two and the woman takes the small cake, slices it in half, and fills it with cheese. After another minute on the grill, the melted concoction is handed over to Rinni.

"Here. They're one of my favorites to grab whenever I'm out patrolling the city in spring," Rinni explains as we head over to the lakeside, sitting on a bench. "They start making them leading up to springtime rites."

"What are springtime rites?" Harrow mentioned them before.

"A large festival of the arts to welcome back spring to the world. Usually the borders of the kingdom are opened...likely why the delegation from the fae is here. There will be music, and dancing, performances, singing and poetry." Rinni sighs wistfully. "You'll love it. And then, on fire night, the sky itself is the canvas and the Elf King paints blazing colors across it."

"Literally?" I can't help but ask.

"Of course." Rinni laughs. "Eldas is the closest to the Veil and the strongest among us. There's almost nothing he can't do."

I try and imagine Eldas painting with fire in the sky, his nimble hands commanding magic with the skill of a weaver on their loom. Rinni looks up, as if she can already see the glowing strokes. There's admiration in her eyes. It makes my stomach twist, a sensation I promptly ignore.

"When does it happen?"

"Usually a week or two after the coronation."

"Oh." I stare at the food in my hands and suppress any glumness. I don't need to see Eldas make fire sky paintings. I need to go home. I need to tend my patients. In fact, I don't *want* to see the springtime rites. Because, if I do, I've stayed in Midscape too long and I can never really return to my world again.

"Is something wrong with it?" Rinni asks, pointing to the fried dough and misreading my expression. "I promise it's good."

"Oh, I'm sure." I quickly take a bite. The cake is crisp on the outside but soft and fluffy on the inside. The charring on it adds a nice bite to what tastes like the corn base of the dough. The cheese strings between my mouth and the cake as I try and tear off a bite, prompting laughter from both Rinni and I.

For a moment, I forget who and where I am.

By the time I realize I've forgotten, the cheesy griddle cake is gone and the carefree moment with it. But, briefly, things weren't so bad. They weren't bad at all. I was eating delicious food and laughing with a friend. We were enjoying the weather and the quiet bustle of the city around us.

It was accidental happiness. A brief glimpse of what my life could've been like...maybe should have been like, if I had been prepared for this all along. If I had come here ready to be the queen, I wouldn't be spending my time looking for a way to break the cycle. Instead I would be finding ways to explore and enjoy my new circumstances.

I sigh as my gaze drifts back to the opening in the mountain that leads through the Fade.

"We should get back to the castle," I say.

"Yes, before someone sees you."

We start heading back in earnest. Until something catches my eye, stopping me in my tracks.

There, in the back of an alley between two buildings, is Aria. She talks with shifting gazes and nervous glances to a lithe creature that has two deer antlers sprouting from the top of his head and dragonfly wings. I see the horned man hand over a small pouch to Aria.

Then, her eyes meet mine. She freezes and I quickly turn away to take several quick steps and catch up with Rinni.

"Are you all right?"

"Yes, fine." I lightly pat the brim of my hat, feeling for any stray strands of hair. There's no way she noticed me in this getup, right? "I thought I saw something strange. But there are many strange things here, for me." I force a smile and Rinni grins.

"We'll be back in the castle soon." She nods at the looming castle ahead of us and takes two eager steps ahead. "That's at least a little familiar—"

A blur in the corner of my eye solidifies into the weight of a shape behind me. A hand clamps a wet cloth over my mouth before I can say anything. The scent of something sharp and tangy fills my nose and I quickly hold my breath on instinct.

But it's too late.

I don't know what concoction the rag has been soaked in but it's not good. My muscles begin to go limp and my vision blurs. My lungs are already burning from holding my breath. But I can't take another gulp of air. If I inhale any more, I'll slip out of consciousness.

I lose sight of Rinni as I'm dragged between two buildings.

I'm not even able to scream.

nineteen

FARTHER AND FARTHER, I'M DRAGGED OFF THE CITY STREETS. The bright sunlight of the day is dimmed. A silhouette appears before me—horns and sharp angles, gossamer wings that stretch unnaturally out from his back.

That creature I saw with Aria.

"Keep holding, she's still awake," a man snarls.

I blink slowly and fight every instinct to inhale gulps of air. My lungs are revolting. I'll *have* to breathe soon. Hopefully, if they think I've passed out, they'll remove the rag.

As naturally as I can manage, I finally shut my eyes and allow my body to go heavy. Eldas had said there were enemies. Why didn't I listen? Why didn't I take it more seriously?

The movement stops as I hear shouting in the distance. It's garbled, frantic words. The darkness behind my eyelids is quickly becoming more than pretend. I will pass out soon.

Yet, right when I think I'm about to lose my battle for consciousness, the rag is removed. I fight every urge to gasp in fresh air, instead inhaling slowly so I don't alert my assailants.

"Go and throw them off the trail." My eyes are still closed, but I can recognize the horned man by voice alone. "I'll hide her."

"You don't have any ritumancy prepared," another voice

hisses, so low that I can barely hear the words. Ritumancy was the wild magic of the…fae?

Is it Aria? I think the speaker is a woman…but I can't be sure. There's more movement. Are there three, or four people here now?

My heart thunders in my chest. I want to call for help—for Eldas. He walked through the Fade itself and found me when I had tried to run away. I don't know how the Fade works, but he'll come if I call, right? I doubt it…there's no way he'd hear me. He thinks I'm still safely tucked away in his castle.

Yet the thought sparks an idea.

Rinni has to have looked back and noticed I'm gone. The commotion I hear rising in the distance must be her leading knights to me. I just have to hold on and put up enough of a fight that they can't take me too far away.

I can do that much, can't I?

Two hands grab me, hoisting me up. I hear the buzzing of mighty wings. My stomach sinks as I'm suddenly weightless.

Are we flying?

I crack open my eyes and see the blurred flapping of the horned man's dragonfly wings. *He's going to fly away with me*, I realize. I take a deep breath and think of the square in Capton. I used my magic to turn what human hands made back into the natural world. I turned iron into trees. I turned stone into moss. I can do *something* to save myself.

It's now or never. I open my eyes wide and look up at the face of the horned man. He has yet to notice I'm not as incapacitated as he thought. I'm surprised at how human his face looks, despite his wings and horns. But I don't allow myself to get distracted.

I reach for the beaded necklace around his neck and curl my fist in it. He looks down, nearly dropping me. A hiss and a curse escape him.

Transform, I command, *change into vines, tree branches, anything*! The beads shudder, nearly coming alive. He jostles me in his arms, straining his neck away. I try and focus on my magic, but I slip from his grasp.

The necklace breaks and I fall back to the ground, landing with a hard *thud*. Luckily, I wasn't too high up yet. But I was high enough that the impact steals the wind from me.

He lands next to me, stalking over with a snarl. "How dare you, human."

I don't even waste my breath on engaging. My magic might still be too ineloquent for me to command at whim. But I know something else that will heed me.

Bringing my fingers to my lips, I let out a shrill whistle. "Hook, come!" I shout. The horned man lunges for me as I see the air beside him shimmer. Hook bounds from between the shadows. "Hook!"

My wolf lets out what sounds almost like a roar rather than a growl and charges toward the horned man. My attacker barely has a chance to react before Hook is upon him. Hook sinks his teeth into the man's wings and he lets out a scream of agony.

I scoot away until my back hits one of the dingy walls of the buildings. "Hook," I call weakly. The beast has become nothing but rage and teeth. Hook rips one of the man's wings clean off. "Hook, stop!" I push myself onto my feet.

He attacked me. He tried to kidnap me. And yet, just like with Luke, I can't bring myself to see him maimed by Hook's vicious attacks.

"Hook—"

"There!" Rinni's voice echoes over mine. She's at the entrance of the alley. Soldiers pour in around her, rushing toward us. The man has been brought to the ground. Hook's jaw is clamped over his knee and the wolf refuses to let go.

Still, he raises his hands, laces his fingers, and brings them down on Hook's head.

"Stop it!" I shout. The knights can't reach us fast enough. He continues beating Hook until the wolf releases him, and even then, the horned man doesn't relent. "I said stop!"

He reaches for me as I rush to catch his arms. The man draws a blade from his sleeve and yanks me close. The cool silver is underneath my jaw; the wicked, sharp edge bites into my chin.

"Don't come any closer! Come closer and I'll kill her."

"Kill her and you doom us all, you fool." Eldas's voice comes from behind us and it is malice incarnate. It slithers across the ground, rising to fill the air. The shadows seem to lengthen. The air drops in temperature.

The horned man goes stiff. He goes to turn but he can't. His arms unravel around me and I watch as his body slams limply against the wall opposite. Shivering, I look at his bloodied form, contorting and popping.

A hand hooks around my elbow. Eldas pulls me to him. His arm slips around my waist and my side is flush with his.

Protected. Safe. The Elf King looks out at the world with rage and writhing power. Yet I am the antithesis to it all. He clutches me firmly but gently.

"Eldas…" I whisper. "Don't." My eyes dart from the man to Hook. The wolf whines softly. Just the sight of my attacker beating him over the head nearly makes me want to take back my words.

"Luella, this is not your world," he reminds me. I hear between his words, *this man is not Luke.* "This fae scum sought to harm you, and he will die for it."

"If you—if you had given us our land…this wouldn't have happened," my would-be kidnapper wheezes. "Midscape is dying under elf rule. We won't stop until we get what is ours and are free to control our own destiny."

"He should be brought to justice—taken captive for trial." I look up at Eldas, pleading with the statue of a man that has rage simmering behind his eyes—hotter than any emotion I've ever seen from him.

"This is justice. *My* justice."

I avert my eyes, pressing my face into Eldas's chest as a horrible ripping and tearing sound fills my ears. I may have let out a shout. Eldas's arm tightens further around me and the world goes dark as he pulls me through the Fade with him.

twenty

ELDAS DELIVERS ME TO MY ROOM. Wordlessly, he summons a fire from nothing to crackle over the andirons in the hearth. I sit before it on the bare floor. A blanket is placed gently over my trembling shoulders. He murmurs that I will be safe.

He disappears and returns once more, this time with Hook cradled in his arms. Eldas lays the wolf at my feet. Hook whimpers and his usually bright eyes are distant and glassy. But he responds with a soft huff as I reach for his head.

I look back to thank Eldas for bringing me Hook, for ensuring my wolf's safety, but he is gone. And I am alone with the wretched sound of a body twisting too far echoing in my ears.

Eldas. Civil, brutal, cold, hot, capable of kindness, but all too easily can reach for cruelty. He had called Midscape a harsh place when I overheard him with Rinni. I didn't fully grasp it then.

This…*this isn't my world*, I remind myself time and again. The rules I've always known don't apply here. I was foolish to think those rules were just related to magic and the people who wielded it.

But it's not just magic. *Everything* is different.

How could I possibly ever fit in here?

The sun has tracked farther across the sky when the Elf King returns. He doesn't Fadewalk into my room. This time, he uses the door.

Eldas hovers just inside, waiting for something. I can't even look at him. I don't know what I'll see. Will it be a killer? Will it be the man whose caress lights my flesh?

My hands are buried in Hook's fur for strength. I press my eyes closed and take a shuddering breath. All I see is the face of a man—a fae—who was killed...*killed by Eldas*...

I stare at the fire, trying to burn the memories away. I don't want to face this truth. I can't handle things becoming any more complicated. The weight of Eldas suddenly appearing next to me jostles me from my trance. It isn't until his arm timidly wraps around me that I even realize I'm still shivering. I lean into him despite myself. Part of me thinks I should fear him. The other part needs him and every bit of stability he can offer.

As if sensing this need, Hook warily raises his head, resting it heavily on my knee.

"I wanted to protect you," he says quietly, finally. I jump at the sudden break in the silence I've been smothered in all afternoon. "That was why I told you to stay in the castle." I can hear his voice wavering, as if he's fighting with his own temper. But, for the first time since I've known him, he fights and wins. "Regardless of why it happened, I am sorry you had to endure that."

"You're right," I whisper, continuing to stare at the fire. "I should have listened. I should have stayed in the castle. I just wanted to have a moment of freedom, something that was my own. But if I had done what you asked, then that man would still be alive. Because of me—"

"No," Eldas says firmly, not allowing me to finish the thought. His touch is gentle in contrast to the word as his free hand rests on my chin—his soft caress replacing the memory of the blade held to my throat as he guides my face to look at him. "This was *not* your fault. I understand, Luella. Even if I wish you had heeded my warnings and not left. I understand wanting to escape this place." I see desire and longing shining in the waters of a deep sorrow in his eyes. "That man died because he tried to attack the Human Queen."

"Why, though? Why would he attack me?" I grab Eldas's shirt gently, as if clinging to an answer that's likely not there. "I don't want to hurt people. I brought spring!"

"Not everyone loves the Human Queen," Eldas says solemnly. "But—"

"Some see her—you—as an out-of-date notion. Some wish to be rejoined with the Natural World and conquer humanity." I shiver and Eldas pulls me closer. I allow him to. Killer and protector, the two words circle in my head as my side is pressed flush against his. The motion seems to have been subconscious, because, for a moment, he's as startled as I am by it. Clearing his throat, Eldas regains his focus. "Others have already sensed the line of Human Queens is fading. Each queen is weaker than the last."

"My power really is weaker?" It always felt quite strong to me. Despite myself, Luke's words about the Keepers even knowing the power of the queen was fading returns to me.

"You might find it hard to believe," he admits, as if reading my mind, "but it is. Think of how the throne ravaged you the first time you sat on it. Moreover, nature in Midscape is not as stable as it once was and that is creating hardships as food becomes scarcer, and viable land is more prized than ever."

I duck my head. "And they blame the Human Queen for the land's plight."

"They don't understand the queen does all she can."

I shake my head. "We must find a way to break the cycle."

"I know." Eldas shifts. He now wears a hardened but not closed off expression. He's resolute, everything I would expect of a king. His eyes are heavy as he stares into the flames. I wonder what he sees in the dancing light. "We must for our world, and for future kings and queens. I fear you might be the last queen. But even if none of that were true, no one should have to endure what you have...what you will continue to endure. And no other king should—" He stops himself short.

"Should what?"

"Should have to see their queen with a knife to her throat." His gaze turns to me. It's filled with an emotion I don't dare name—an expression trapped hopelessly between desperation and desire.

My breath catches in my throat. "Were you...worried about me?"

He laughs airily. Our faces are close enough that his amused huffs wash over my cheeks and tease my hair.

"Of course I was worried about you. It's my duty to protect you." Eldas reaches up and tucks a wayward strand of hair behind my ear. The tender movement is in contrast with his utilitarian words.

A weight sinks in me. "Am I nothing more than your duty?" I don't know what I want him to say. I regret asking instantly.

"You are…" His eyes narrow slightly, as if trying to see me better.

The pause is terrible. My brain can fill in a thousand words trapped behind his enigmatic eyes. I imagine him saying yes. I can hear him saying no. I straighten, trying to distance myself from him and the question.

"It's all right," I say hastily. "You don't have to answer. I understand the weight of duty." And my duty has me searching for a way to end this cycle. Ending it would be the ultimate help to Capton, wouldn't it? And then I could go back and escape this land of wild magic.

Eldas eases the tension by changing the topic. "Hook seems all right." He reaches to scratch behind the wolf's ears. Hook allows it, though doesn't move from his spot.

"Thank the Forgotten Gods."

"You really care for the creature."

"I care for all my friends." I glance his way. I hope he hears what I'm implying—*be my friend and I'll care for you too.* Eldas holds my eyes intently, as if he's expecting me to say more. But my throat is too gummy. I look for an alternative, instead. "May I ask you something else?"

"You may ask me anything." His sincerity startles me.

I quickly move past it. Talk of politics will cool the heat rising in my cheeks. "The creature was a fae, right?"

He nods.

"Do they all look like that? Deer horns and dragonfly wings?"

"Many do, yes. Though their features will vary. However, oftentimes they'll glamour themselves to look like something else."

I shudder at the thought that those creatures might be lurking anywhere. For the first time, I'm grateful the castle is so empty. I press forward. Talking is helping to erase the sight and sound of that man's death.

"So they could be anyone?" I whisper.

"Fresh water washes away fae glamour," Eldas says reassuringly. "The border with the fae is blocked by a wall and water. The only bridges are heavily guarded. Fae don't get into our lands without us knowing."

"But the fae delegation—"

"I sent them away," he says curtly. "I could not bear to look one second longer at them. And if they had anything to do with this plot I would not want them in my territory. No one else will come in or out until your coronation or until...until you're back in the Natural World. Rinni will see to their removal personally."

I barely resist asking him not to be too harsh. But then that horrible sound fills my ears and I'm fighting trembles. This is not my world, or my justice.

"How did they steal you away from Rinni?" Eldas asks.

"I lagged behind her, for a moment...it all happened so fast," I murmur. As much as I don't want to think about it, something else surfaces from those crimson-stained memories. "Aria was there," I whisper.

"What?" Eldas scowls. "With the kidnappers?" he asks quickly.

"No, no... I saw her speaking with the horned man just before."

"Are you certain it was the same man? Are you certain it was her?" Eldas shifts to look me straight in the eyes. "You must be absolutely certain."

I try and sort through my memories, but after spending the day pushing them away and blacking them out... I shake my head. "I think so? No. It must've been her. Maybe that was how they identified me, since Harrow allowed Aria, Jalic, and Sirro to see me before the coronation."

Eldas is silent, staring into the fire. He sees something I cannot.

"Do you think she was involved?" I dare to ask. I don't like the thought of someone who could possibly have been involved in a kidnapping attempt being allowed in and out of the castle. After a minute of more silence, I press, "Eldas?"

"No," he says, finally. "I doubt she is..."

"But how do you—"

"Aria is the niece of the current Fae King."

"She's fae?" I blink, startled.

"Only half. And her elf side is far more dominant. The current Fae King's brother was her father, though he died when she was young. Aria was raised in Quinnar with her mother." Eldas shook his head. "The benefits to diplomacy for not a great deal of risk on our part are part of why I permit Harrow's friendship with her. We vetted her thoroughly when they first became friends years ago. She's trouble, yes..." He sighs. "But the sort of trouble Aria can be is beneath kidnapping the Human Queen. Her trouble manifests in misguiding my somewhat impressionable brother to stay out too late or drink too much."

"Can you be certain?" I can't help but ask.

"If she was involved in a plot to kidnap you, she would be acting against her family and her own self-interest. If the Fae King was involved, then any standing he hopes to have with the elves is lost. And, Aria looks after herself. Trying to hurt you would *severely* limit her prospects," Eldas explains. I consider this. It makes sense, I suppose. And what do I know of Midscape's politics? Precious little. I've been so focused on learning my magic and looking for a way to break the cycle that I haven't had the chance to dive too deeply into everything.

"If you're sure," I murmur.

"If she was involved, I will see to her myself," Eldas swears to me.

I quickly change the topic, not wanting to think of Aria being torn limb from limb. "The man said something about wanting his land—giving it back. What did he mean?"

Eldas runs a hand through his hair. I watch as the silky curtain falls effortlessly back into place. "When the fae began their infighting, it was years of bloody squabble that spilled over into the surrounding area. There were attacks made on elf settlements when the borders of our land were blurrier than they are now. Most were unprovoked—the fae looting for resources or simply catching our people in the crossfire. That prompted swift retaliation."

"Retaliation by your father?" I wonder where Eldas inherited his brutal streak from.

"No, well before him." Eldas stares into the fire. "Eventually, the elves erected a wall—the one lined with fresh water for its entire length." I remember what Harrow had said about their brother, Drestin, receiving some honorable position on a wall somewhere. "The wall was an effort to keep the fighting out. But when the dust began to settle and the clans grew weary of their wars, it was discovered that the wall had encroached upon a large swath of formerly fae territory."

"And now they want it back?"

"They have for centuries. But by the time they made their claim clear, our people had long since settled on the land. Even if we gave it back to them, it's uncertain who would take it and who would rule. The fae delegation that was here arrived to discuss absolving the tithing to enter elf territory for the fae—they feel that if their ancestral land couldn't be returned, they should at least be able to enter it freely. But after today, I doubt I'm going to ever—"

"Don't let today change things," I say quickly. "That man paid for his crimes. Unless he was acting on behalf of the Fae King... don't let all of the fae people suffer because of his choices."

Eldas studies me so intently that I shift and pull the blanket tighter around me, as though I might guard myself from his probing stare. "You would have me not turn them away?"

"I would have you rule fairly, with strength, and with honor."

A tired smile curls the corners of his lips. "You remind me of her, sometimes."

"Who?" I imagine some lover he gave up before I entered the castle.

"Alice." Certainly not who I was expecting.

I clutch the blanket tighter. "You must've known her well, didn't you?"

A shadow crosses his face and Eldas shakes his head, as though he regrets saying anything. I can feel him retreating mentally well before he retreats physically. I watch as he stands, fighting the strange urge to pull him back before the fire with me.

"You should get some rest," he says softly but firmly.

"Eldas—"

"I'll see you in the morning to practice your magic."

"But—" I don't get to finish. He's out the door, retreating with a haste I've never seen from him before. I look to Hook, who gives a low whine and tilts his head at me in response. "I don't understand him either."

The wolf stands, stretches, and then comes to sit where Eldas just was. I lean against him for support and the beast gives a soft huff. But he doesn't move. Hook stays even as I fall asleep on his furry shoulder.

twenty-one

THE NEXT MORNING, RINNI ARRIVES AS USUAL. She says nothing of finding me sleeping on the floor. In fact, she's eerily quiet.

Hook still seems drowsy from yesterday and I tell him to stay in my rooms. He doesn't put up a fight and I'm already thinking of what I can make him later in the laboratory with Willow that might make my companion feel better.

"Rinni, about yesterday…" I start as we walk to the throne room. She doesn't so much as turn my way. "I want to apologize to you."

Silence.

"You were right," I continue with every bit of sincerity I have. "I was wrong. We should have stayed in the castle."

More silence.

"Rinni—"

"I will be waiting for you when you have finished with the king to take you to Willow," Rinni says, her words void of emotion. Anger would've been easier to handle.

"I can just go and meet Willow on my own."

"His Majesty has instructed me that you are not to be without escort, even in the castle. I'd like to make haste with this jaunt, however, as I have matters to discuss with the other head knights regarding city patrols and security."

"Eldas seemed to think the castle would be safe now that the delegation is gone."

"It is the will of our king." Rinni stops before the door to the throne room. "And it is *not* our place to go against his wishes."

Rinni doesn't give me the chance to say anything else before I'm ushered into the throne room for another morning of magic practice.

Eldas is distant once more. It's as though any time he even remotely gets close to me he overcompensates for it the next time we meet. He stays several steps away from me at all times. Which only makes me think all the more about his earlier caresses when we first started working together.

I would've thought the space would make me feel better. This is a man who tore someone else apart. But the gap between us only makes me cold. It's somehow *more* of a reminder of what he's capable of. I want the tender man who came to me last night. Yet I don't know where or how to find him.

My magic matches my emotions. At times, it heeds my will and his instruction. I continue to explore the redwood throne, trying to figure out what that dark place is. All I can uncover before my magic fails me is that the throne seems to have grown *out* from that spot.

As soon as Eldas deems us finished, he departs without a word. I'm not even given the chance to discuss yesterday. Wrapping my arms around myself, I head to the laboratory, Rinni escorting me silently.

Thankfully, at least Willow is normal.

He hears me out as I talk about the incident in the city, allowing me to air all the confusing feelings I've had knotting me up since yesterday afternoon.

"The fae are a mess," he sighs when I finish. "Which is sad, because they have such fascinating magic and traditions. I hear that some of the rituals they perform to charge their ritumancy can take days at a time. Sometimes they hunt for years to get all the items in place for their rituals. And the rituals themselves are filled with dancing, meditation, or sometimes even blood sport."

I don't want to think about blood. "I know how the elves love tradition," I say, trying to force the thought away.

Willow chuckles as he reaches across the laboratory table and squeezes my hand. "I'm glad you're all right though."

"Me too. But I'm afraid I might have landed Rinni in a heap of trouble."

"If anyone will be all right, it's Rinni. There is no chance from here to the Veil that Eldas will ever punish Rinni."

I'm taken back to that secret room overlooking the throne room, Rinni's hand on Eldas's cheek. Thanks to the journals, I've confirmed what Harrow said—the Elf Kings take lovers. The thought gives birth to a question, one I already know I need to put to rest.

"What is Eldas's and Rinni's relationship?" I gather my bravery to ask.

"Rinni is his right hand and the general of the army of Lafaire."

"And here she is, wasting time protecting me."

Willow flicks my nose and grins. I can't help but smile. "Stop that. You're the Human Queen. Protecting you is anything but a waste of time. More like the highest honor."

I sigh and rephrase my earlier question. "Are Eldas and Rinni... intimate?"

Willow blinks several times over. I can tell he's instantly uncomfortable. "Luella, that's not something you ask about the Elf King."

"Think of me as a woman asking about the man she's married to, then."

"I *really* don't know anything. I don't pry into royal affairs. You'd have to ask one of them. It's not my place."

I drum my fingers against the table in thought. "You know, that's an excellent idea, Willow. I think I'll go to Rinni when we're done here."

"You can't be serious."

"I am."

Willow scratches his scalp nervously. "Fine, but if you're going, we're making citrus tarts first."

"Citrus tarts?"

"They're Rinni's favorite."

"And how do you know that?"

"I've been in the castle practically since I was born. I was up here with Poppy, studying how to be the next castle healer. But...I suppose I heard some things about the few others I was in the castle with." He shrugs.

I barely resist pointing out that if he heard "some things" he likely heard the truth about Rinni and Eldas. But I resist. Willow is right, it's not his place to say. And some things are best asked at the source.

At the end of the day Willow takes me and a small box of lemon and orange tarts that we spent the afternoon making down to Rinni's room. There's also a small pouch of treats for Hook that Willow insisted on putting together. We'll see if Hook likes them later. I hope they set my wolf right as rain.

We come to a stop at Rinni's door, I take a breath, and knock.

"Yes?" Rinni opens the door. She has a smock tied around her waist. Her usual armor and regalia have been traded for loose-fitting, paint-stained clothing. The look suits her, I think. Her eyes dart between Willow and me. "What're you doing here?"

"She insisted," Willow says quickly.

"We need to talk." I barge in without her permission.

"All right…" Rinni exchanges one last glance with Willow before shutting the door. "What do you need of me, Your Majesty?"

"I want to talk about—" Words fail me as I land on the portrait she's working on. A familiar pair of warm eyes look back at me with a small, enigmatic smile. The detail is incredible. Though the portrait quickly becomes unfinished as the paint bleeds out from the subject's face—*my face*. "You're painting…me?"

"Yes." Rinni wipes her hands on a rag. "It was commissioned."

"By who?

"Who do you think?" Rinni clears her throat and coaxes the colloquial tone back to formal. "I meant to say, Your Majesty, that the Elf King himself commissioned this piece."

Eldas wants a portrait of me? For what purpose? I look between Rinni and the painting. *One thing at a time*. I hold out the box of tarts.

"Here, a peace offering and an apology."

"What is it?" Rinni takes the box skeptically. As soon as she opens it she growls, "That Willow."

"He said you liked citrus tarts," I say hastily.

"Yes. I love them." Yet she looks so grumpy as she says it. Rinni pushes some paints aside on her table and sets the box down, shoving a tart in her mouth. "I just hate that he shared with you my one weakness."

I laugh. "Well, now that I have you in a vulnerable state. Rinni, I really am sorry."

She sighs over her second tart. "Fine, I accept your apology."

"Thank you." I glance back at the painting, thinking of the other reason why I came. If there was anything between Eldas and Rinni, then surely he wouldn't ask her to paint a portrait of me. That'd just be cruel. "Are we friends again?"

"Oh, very well," she says dramatically. I crack a smile. "I guess we're friends."

"Good, because there's something I want to ask you."

"Go on, you have five tarts left before my guard is up again."

"I wanted to talk about Eldas."

Rinni's hands freeze. So much for five more tarts. "What about him?"

"Are you and he romantically involved?" I ask directly. Rinni doesn't look at me and my nerves go wild. "Because, if you are, I understand. Or if you're not but you have feelings toward him, I would like to know. I'm not going to get in your way."

"You're his wife," she says delicately, still not looking at me.

"Yes, and we're anything but a normal couple." I sigh. There's the ghost of pain in my stomach. It's trying to stamp out a hope I didn't know had begun to sprout. "I know the Elf King takes lovers. It only makes sense, really. Our circumstances aren't conducive to companionship."

"Luella, I'm not going to get in the way of anything growing between you two." Rinni looks up with a small smile. "We're *not* lovers. And I have *no* interest in ever being Eldas's lover."

"You're not?" I ask slowly. "But you two seem... There's..." I fumble over my words as I discover I might have been hoping they were. I might have been looking for a reason to stamp out this frustration that's begun budding up every time I'm around Eldas. "There's clearly a connection between you two."

"There is." I appreciate Rinni's lack of denial. "We've grown up together. We're about the same age. And I'm not sure if you know... but the crown prince isn't allowed to leave the castle while his father is alive. So he never left this castle as a child. Then, he made the choice to continue his seclusion to be coronated alongside you. He just didn't expect it to take a year..."

I know about Eldas's choice to stay secluded. "Why can the crown prince not leave while his father is alive?"

"Because there is only ever one Elf King. And it keeps the transition of power—one reign to the next—tidy."

I'm not sure if I agree with all that. "So he was kept in the castle, alone?"

"Yes..." Rinni briefly frowns. Not even the next tart can shake the expression from her. Even she, as someone who knows the traditions, clearly thinks that holding a young boy captive is a bit extreme. "As you can imagine, he didn't have a lot of friends."

"It shows." The words slip through my lips and I feel a twinge of regret for them.

"Perhaps." Rinni smiles thinly. "He didn't have a lot of options for companionship and I was here all the time as my father was his father's right hand. We became close." Rinni folds her arms and leans against the back wall. She meets my eyes. "I suppose I should also just tell you that yes, at one point, we did explore a romantic relationship."

"How long ago?"

Rinni thinks about this a moment. "Three, or four years ago? Looking back, I think he was panicked seeing the last Human Queen nearing the end of her life. More than just being grief-ridden...I believe he felt confined to his role and was rebelling in his own way against the idea of being married off. He was old enough to understand his fate and was losing Alice at the same time."

I wonder if Eldas sees himself in me. If my rebellion against my fate is stirring up negative thoughts for him, or feelings of hopelessness. Perhaps the mere suggestion that there could be a way out is almost more painful than the acceptance he's fallen into.

"He looked for comfort where he could find it and I was receptive. I'd be lying if I said that I hadn't spared more than one girlish thought about him and me up to that point. So, we made a clumsy attempt at it for a few months, only two or three, really. And before you ask, we didn't do much more than kissing. Also, I'm not giving you any more details on our relationship. It's over and done and he and I do not work together romantically. The colors are dry on that landscape of my life and I have no desire to go back to the canvas."

"Fair," I say. "Thank you for your honesty."

"Of course, I'm in support of you both. Eldas and I are better off as friends and allies. But, if anything, the attempt at being lovers did make us closer. So you're right in that there is a bond. There's no other man I'd rather serve in brush or sword, or any other way… *except* for the bedroom."

I let out a laugh. But the levity is cut with the lingering thoughts of Eldas struggling against his fate. I'm imagining him young, and awkward. My smile fades with a sigh.

"Rinni, I know I've asked a lot of you today. But may I ask your help with something?"

"It'll take more tarts."

"Done." I chuckle and continue, "I want to get to know Eldas better." I think of what Rinni said in the throne room about Eldas not making an attempt to get to know me. But, in fairness, that goes both ways. "I'd like to have dinner with him."

I'd like to sit at his private table.

Rinni arches her eyebrows as a somewhat delighted smile creeps across her lips. "All right, I'm sure that can be arranged."

"I don't want it to be anything formal." I think of one of the massive banquet halls in the castle and the illustrations I saw in books as a child. "I don't want to be the king and queen sitting at far ends of a table that's so long we may as well be in separate rooms."

Rinni laughs. "I know what you're saying."

"Good. Will you ask him? I'm worried if I do it Eldas will say no." Given how he seems to retreat after every time we get close, he just might. "And I'm also worried that the throne room has become either a classroom or a battle ground for us. If we meet there then we'll—"

"Be unable to relax," she finishes for me. "Say no more. I can make this happen."

"Thank you." I cross over and pull Rinni in for a quick hug. She's stiff and just as awkward as the first time I hugged Willow. But she seems to warm up to the idea a little faster than my healer friend.

"Of course, Your Majesty," she says, somewhat awkward as I pull away.

"We're well past formalities." I start for the door. "Call me Luella."

That night as Hook curls up at the foot of my bed, I stare up at the ceiling. In a week I've secured two friends and a wolf. If I'm being honest, none of this is going as badly as I expected.

But the largest hurdles remain—genuinely befriending Eldas and, with his help, figuring out a way to break the cycle.

I yawn. "One step at a time," I murmur before rolling over and falling asleep.

Eldas and I don't meet the next day, or the day after, so I occupy myself with the journals and with Willow in the laboratory. Even if Eldas won't help me, I will continue to search for a way out of this cycle—for myself, for him, and our worlds.

I worry that Rinni has asked him about dinner and it just went more horribly than I could've expected. On the third day, Rinni informs me that he's taken up some new negotiations with the fae and that's what's distracting him.

I think of our conversation and I wonder if these new negotiations were, in part, inspired by me. I dare to think they might have been. Which fills me with an effervescent sensation, like I am some bubbly beverage, held under pressure.

Luckily, I'm distracted on the fourth day when my furniture arrives. The cabinetmaker makes the delivery personally and sees to helping Rinni and me set up the furniture in the space. He's a sweet old man and I can't help but notice him massaging his creaking fingers by the time we're done.

After everything is settled to both our standards, I take him up with me to the laboratory and give him a poultice similar to what I made for Mr. Abbot. Blessedly, neither Willow nor Rinni tells me that helping a "commoner" is "beneath me."

The cabinetmaker is bashful, but at Willow's encouragement accepts the gift. The rest of the day I spend working with Willow, experimenting with my magic and learning from the books left behind by past queens.

I take my dinners in my room, alone save for Hook. My wolf curls up under my new desk that overlooks the windows in the main room—rather than the doors. I delicately skim the fragile pages of the women who came before me in search of clues. The oldest journal is just over two thousand years old. There are no records left behind by the original queen or her immediate successors. So I'm learning from women who were just as much in the dark as I was.

On the evening of the fifth day, I finally find something that may be useful. It's about midway through Queen Elanor's journal—four queens before me. Apparently, I wasn't the first person to think of breaking this cycle.

With every new queen, the redwood throne takes a greater toll. Our power seems to be dwindling generation over generation. It's possible that soon enough, there will not be a Human Queen.

I suspect that the throne itself is seeking balance with the other side of the Fade—with the Natural World. The Human Queen is not balance enough on her own. The laws of nature are stretched too thin.

If there was some way we could bring the two worlds in balance, then maybe Midscape would no longer need a Human Queen. But I have no way to prove this theory...

The next morning I'm getting ready to head to the laboratory when I hear Rinni's distinct knock.

"May I come in?"

"I'm decent," I call back.

"What are those clothes?" Rinni asks the moment she lays eyes on me.

"They're something Willow helped me find." I run my hands over heavy canvas trousers. "Don't tell me, the day I finally dare to not wear a dress, Eldas wants to meet with me?"

Rinni smirks.

I groan. "It's true, isn't it?"

"It is, but you have until this evening to change."

"He accepted my invitation to dinner?" I can't tell if the flapping in my stomach is the wings of butterflies or hornets. Am I excited or nervous? Both. There's a whole war of the winged bugs going on in there.

"He did, *finally*," Rinni mutters. She raises a hand to her mouth and coughs, as if trying to hide the fact that the last word escaped. I do her a favor and don't comment. "Yes, he has. You'll dine in the East Wing tonight."

"*Ooh*, the mysterious East Wing." I wiggle my fingers in the air. "How exciting and illustrious."

"It is; only the royal family is usually allowed there."

It's not lost on me that I'm not considered part of the "royal family." I may keep Midscape alive, but I clearly don't deserve the honor of being seen as one of them. My thoughts wander to Harrow. I still haven't seen him since healing him. Which I should be grateful for, but I'm oddly worried.

While Eldas didn't seem too worried about Aria, I can't help but think she might be up to something... No, that's just my fear surrounding the horned man coloring my opinions of her.

I push the thoughts away. Harrow is just another reason why I'm glad to not be a part of that family. I'm leaving in two months and counting.

"Thank you for letting me know. What time should I be ready by?"

"Eldas expects you at eight."

"Oh good, I can get a full day in the laboratory then, and still have time to change."

"Would you like me to help you get ready this evening?"

I think about taking her up on the offer. There are definitely dresses that I can't reach all the clasps of by myself. "No, thank you," I ultimately decide. If Eldas is going to get to know me, he should get to know the real me—not whatever hairstyle or dress Rinni thinks is appropriate.

"Then I will return at seven forty-five." Rinni gives a bow and leaves.

The day is an odd mix of too long and too short. The hours seem to drag on while I'm in the laboratory. Every time I look at the grandfather clock, I'm certain half the day has passed and it's been five minutes.

I can hardly concentrate.

But all too soon, I'm back in my room and Rinni is knocking once more.

"Enter," I call.

She appears at my bathroom door. "You chose that to wear?"

"It's non-negotiable," I declare. "He meets with me in this or he doesn't meet me at all."

"Very well." Rinni has the ghost of a grin as she leads me away. Luckily she doesn't comment on Hook following. He's become my shadow in the castle since I'm much more at ease with him around. At this point, getting to know me involves getting to know Hook.

We cross through the throne room to get to the East Wing. I assume it was a more direct path than going down to the main atrium. Rinni leads me through the door Eldas usually disappears into. She traverses silent halls, cramped with intricate suits of armor, pointed stones on pedestals, tapestries, and portraits. There's less open space here than in the West Wing. Less ballrooms, dining rooms, rooms for the sake of having rooms. They're replaced by spiraling staircases and an infinite amount of doors that block my prying eyes.

Finally, we reach our destination, a door that looks much like any other. Rinni gives a soft knock.

"Your Majesty," she says. "Your queen is here to join you."

twenty-two

I FREEZE SLIGHTLY AT THE WORDS, "YOUR QUEEN." I worry the labradorite ring around my finger, suddenly aware of its presence once more. I don't want to be anyone's. I don't want to be owned. I nearly break out running, but manage to keep myself in place.

A sense of ownership is not what those words were intended to imply. I came here of my own volition. I wanted this to see if the kind man I've caught glimpses of is truly there. If he can trust me. If maybe our partnership can shore up its footing so that we might actually manage to get Midscape out of the bind it's in. I'm not here out of obligation, or fear, or because he commanded me to be.

"Send her in." The bass of Eldas's voice resonates right through me.

The door swings out into the hall and Rinni steps to the side. I enter and try to walk tall, one hand buried in Hook's fur for strength. As the door clicks behind me, the hornets win over the butterflies in my stomach and I press my lips together, trying not to let nervous words buzz out.

Eldas stands before a great hearth. There's a table between us that looks like it could comfortably seat four but is set for two. Food glistens in the low light—roasted meat, trays of vegetables, and some kind of round, iced cake with what I hope aren't actual butterfly wings decorating the top.

I can only inspect the food so much before my eyes

wander to the man I'm actually here to see. Eldas is wearing a tufted tunic the color of midnight. Tiny pearl buttons are sewn at the center of Xs across his breast and give the appearance of scattered stars. His complexion is in contrast with his dark clothes, making him look like a king of starlight, rather than death.

"Is the crown really necessary?" I blurt, completely disarmed by his mere appearance. It almost looks like he made an effort for me.

"Excuse me?" Surprise disrupts his schooled expression and his hand flies to the dark line of iron on his head. Eldas drops his hand suddenly, as if embarrassed by the motion. "I am a king, why would I not wear my crown?"

"Because it's just me you're meeting with."

"All the more reason. I am your king. Why would I not look the part?"

Your king. The words rumble in contrast to "your queen." If I am his queen, does that mean he is my king? Is it, rather than him owning me, that we own each other? We share each other?

For the first time, I wish I spent a little more time on all this relationship and romance business at the academy, rather than being singularly focused on herbology. Maybe I would be less awkward and less inclined to over-think everything.

"I…" Words fail me. Instead, I walk over to him and feel his eyes trail over me with every step. Hook waits behind, as if he somehow knows I need to do this on my own. "I came here as myself, as Luella." I hold out my hands and let him look at the high-waisted skirt and billowing top I chose—simple fabrics, simple designs, what I would wear back in Capton. "I was hoping that I might—"

I reach up and he flinches away. I hold out my hands and wait. Eldas settles and allows my fingers to curl around his crown. It's heavier than I expected, so heavy I wonder how he holds his head up at all.

"—meet with Eldas, and not the Elf King." I set the crown down on the mantle, grateful I didn't drop it.

"The Elf King is who and what I am. There is nothing else."

Those words mirror things I've said many times before. He didn't intend for them to wound, and yet they do. Internal tremors try to knock my bones together. Nerves are attempting to get the better of me because I have never felt more vulnerable.

For the first time, I realize the clothes, the crown, that horrible, echoing throne room...they're all different forms of armor for him. They shield him from anyone seeing whoever the man is without them. And, now, I'm all the more curious about who that man actually is.

"I understand," I whisper.

"You don't." He looks back to the fire as if he can't handle my scrutiny. As if he knows the realization I've made.

"I do," I insist. "Because I had my own armor. I had my shop, my job, my duty. I had it keep me from everything because if I put myself out there for a moment then maybe I could be hurt—maybe I could lose control."

His eyes flicker back to me. The fire cracks and a log falls.

"Little good that did me," I murmur. Even trying to protect myself, Luke dealt a near mortal blow to my heart. His gaze softens further. "So I'm not going to retreat. Well, I'm *trying* not to. I want to get to know you, Eldas."

"Why?" He seems shocked someone would.

"What kind of a question is that?" I laugh breezily. Yet his tense shoulders indicate it was genuine. "I'm technically your wife."

"Only a formality... And I forced you to take those oaths." He brings a crystal cut glass to his lips. It barely hides a grimace. "I am sorry for my actions in the temple at Capton. I should have apologized earlier."

A sincere and unprompted apology? I barely refrain from letting out a shocked gasp. Progress, this is real progress.

"Thank you for your apology." I purse my lips. Part of me doesn't want to forgive him. Yet... "Honestly, without your help, I probably would have puked on your shoes."

Now he doesn't hide the grimace. "Maybe I am less sorry."

I laugh lightly. It's a fragile sound to pair with our delicate explorations. "What're you having?"

"This?" He swirls the glass. Ice clanks. "It's faerie mead. It was sent with their king's apologies for the incident in Quinnar."

"May I try some?" There's a narrow bar with an additional glass set out and a bottle of liquid the same color as what's in Eldas's glass.

"I didn't think you would want to since it's of fae make. I only opened it because it's strong and because tonight...I needed some strength."

"You needed strength around me?" I lift my eyebrows.

"You are perhaps the one thing in Midscape I find terrifying."

I chuckle as I help myself to some liquor. As I pour, Hook takes my spot at the fireside. Wolf and man regard each other warily as I return and hold my glass out to Eldas, distracting him from Hook.

"To strength, tonight."

He stares at my gesture long enough that I'm uncomfortable.

"Do you toast here?"

"We do." For the first time, his chilly gaze seems inviting. His eyes are cool, but like a brisk winter morning that you're ready to greet. Eldas lifts his glass. "To this world. To the next. To the people we meet between and the bonds we share." He lightly clanks his glass against mine and drinks. I do the same.

"Is that an elvish toast?" I ask.

"It is."

"It's lovely."

He doesn't seem to know how to respond to the compliment so he deflects instead. "I see the beast is still insistent on roaming my castle."

"Hook," I correct gently. "Yes, he still stays with me."

"You must return to the Fade eventually," Eldas scolds lightly. Yet, despite his tone, he leans forward and reaches for Hook. The wolf tenses but permits Eldas to gently scratch him between the ears.

"He goes back and forth as he needs. Sometimes he runs off of his own accord, but he always comes back. And he's a good companion whenever he's here." I don't want to think about Hook leaving me for good, as Eldas's tone implies.

"Good. This castle can be lonely." Eldas purses his lips slightly, as if that were something he hadn't intended to say.

"You would know, wouldn't you?"

"As much as you would." Eldas turns the sentiment back on me and I'm silenced. We take long sips of mead.

"Did you really stay locked away here while you were waiting for me?" The question comes out weakly. I'm afraid of the answer.

"Rinni told you, didn't she?" He doesn't look at me when he says it. I doubt he likes feeling vulnerable. But I'm not going to apologize for taking an interest in his wellbeing.

"She did. Don't be cross with her."

"You continue to tell me who I can and cannot be cross with." Eldas glances at me from the corner of his eye. I can almost see him fighting a smirk and that brings a smile to my lips.

"Consider my advice like any other counsel: recommendations." I take another sip as the conversation lulls. I wait. Nothing. "You didn't answer my question."

"I did continue to sequester myself. I wanted to present myself to the world at the same time as my queen but…" He runs a hand over his hair and shakes his head. "Nothing is going according to plan. Then there was you…and your nature shredded the last notion of my carefully concocted designs. You really are nothing like I expected." Before I can remark on the almost tender sentiment, he turns to the table. "Shall we eat?"

"Very well." I am quick to abandon what Eldas expected of me. I'm almost afraid of what I might find is the answer. No…not that… I'm afraid of discovering what I *hope* is the answer—I'm nothing like he expected in a way he might be enjoying. A feeling that's dangerously mutual. "Did you cook all this?"

He scrunches his nose in disgust. "Of course not. I have someone who does that."

"Yet the castle seems so empty." I take my seat, and he takes his. "I've wondered who does all the cooking."

"There are inner passages. Think of them like a castle within a castle. The servants operate there. Very few can be seen on this side." He pauses, eyes flicking to mine. "Magic helps as well."

"Magic helps," I repeat with a laugh. "I suppose it would."

"Well, I know you cannot summon a rack of lamb with a thought in your world."

"Can you—"

Before I can finish, Eldas lifts his hand, motioning to the corner of the room. A blue mist collects on his fingers, mirroring a small cloud in the corner. With a blustery burst, it condenses into—sure enough—a rack of lamb.

"Enjoy, Hook." Eldas leans back in his chair, swirls his glass, and takes a swig. When he catches my stare he bursts out in laughter. "You didn't think I could."

"*How?*"

"I learned the true name of that rack of lamb, and I can create duplicates of it."

As he speaks, Hook gnaws on the offering.

I have a thousand questions, but all I can muster saying is, "You must *really* like lamb."

Eldas blurts out laughter and quickly covers his mouth with a hand. His embarrassed expression leads to my own outburst. Suddenly, we're laughing together.

"How have there ever been any food issues in Midscape if that can be done?"

"Only elves can do it, and very few among us possess the skill. And that food is not nearly as nourishing as something natural— something real." He stares at me over the top of his glass as he takes a swig. Something about the muscles in his throat contracting is oddly entrancing.

I quickly return to my food, changing the topic to learn more about the upcoming springtime rites. Eldas is eager to tell me, especially about his part in them. He lingers on his duties as the Elf King—how he opens and closes the ceremonies, how he is seen as presenting the queen as the bringer of spring. I can't help but smile as he goes on and on.

He's genuinely excited to be king, to finally rule. And yet... we're working on ending the cycle. I will not be here to see these springtime rites. I will not be presented.

As we talk, we help ourselves to the spread. Eldas is a proper gentleman, almost to the point that I'm uncomfortable. He makes it a point to see my drink is refilled whenever it's low—which is often, since the mead is sweet and effervescent. He serves me when I express interest in trying something.

As we tuck in, I'm not surprised to find everything is delicious. The food in Midscape is its own sort of magic. All the flavors seem brighter, more unique and rich. Had I truly tasted anything before coming here?

"I hear you're helping in the greenhouse." Eldas makes an attempt at small talk.

"Willow has been good to me." I instantly rise to his defense, even though there was nothing in Eldas's tone that would suggest I couldn't be assisting. "Not only has he let me help with the plants, but he's given me access to the past queens' journals and taught me more about elf magic."

He tilts his head slightly when I bring up the journals. "Yes, I've heard you've made the place your own. Even to the point that rumor of the queen's ability to heal ailments has spread through town."

"I'm sure I'm not the first queen to do so." I think back to the small poultice I crafted for the cabinetmaker.

"Queens do not have an interest in meeting with the common folk of Quinnar, or common folk in general."

I snort at the remark.

Eldas sets down his fork and arches his eyebrows. "Did I say something amusing?"

"It's not that queens don't have an interest, but they haven't been *allowed* to have an interest."

"That is untrue."

"Oh?" I grin. The expression slips across my flushed cheeks a little too easily. What number glass of mead is this? "Perhaps you should read some of the past queens' journals. You may find their lives enlightening. If you're making an effort to get to know me, then you could do the same with them."

"I made an effort with Alice."

"Did you really?" I grin, but abandon the expression when his tone becomes unexpectedly thoughtful.

He hesitates, voice suddenly heavy and sad. "She... She was a kind woman."

"I have her journal, if you'd like to read it," I say gently.

He stills and an almost child-like excitement flashes in his eyes. "I'd like that very much."

"I'll lend it to you; I'm finished with it."

"That'd be very kind of you."

"I want to be kind to you."

Eldas busies his mouth with a long sip of his liquor and then focuses on the food still on his plate. Perhaps it's just the firelight. But I think I see the faintest of flushes on his cheeks. I yield, turning back to my own food.

"You're right," he says without looking up from his plate. It's good because he won't see my surprise. *I'm right?* "I have never taken the time to properly enlighten myself on the past queens beyond Alice, and that is something that I should remedy if I am to be an effective king both to you, and to my future heir."

He's still operating under the assumption that I will be here longer than two more months. I barely refrain from pointing out the fact. Tonight has been cordial and there's something that makes me sad about the thought of leaving right now.

No sadness that a bit more mead can't fix.

"I'll recommend passages to you beyond Alice, then," I say, finally. "Some on the life of the queens. And some about interesting tidbits surrounding their magic that I've discovered that may help us end this cycle."

"You still think you can remove the need for a Human Queen?"

"My plan hasn't changed."

Eldas stands and moves over to the fireplace again. He leans against the mantle, his towering form striking a dark line against the firelight. I scratch Hook behind the ears, watching—no, *admiring* him.

The light hits his cheekbones in just the right way that it makes them sit even higher. His eyes are highlighted, hauntingly beautiful. And the hidden rainbows of his raven hair have never been more noticeable.

"It's for both of us, you know," I say gingerly, standing, glass in hand as well. The room sways and nearly draws a giggle from my lips. But now is not the time for giggling. I still have enough of my wits to know that. "As well as for the benefit of everyone to follow. Think of what we could change, Eldas. Dream of how your heir's life could be different—how your life might be."

"I've long since grown past the age of dreaming." His haunted, cold eyes speak only truth around the statement.

"Maybe you should try starting again. It's easy: just dream, Eldas, and then follow those dreams." I touch his elbow lightly and it summons his eyes to mine.

"I am not made for dreams. I am made to rule."

"I think you're made for whatever you want to be."

"You don't know me in the slightest." Worry drifts in and out of his words.

"I think I'm starting to. I know I want to." My fingers trail down his arm to his hand. They dance across his smooth skin, playing with the cuff around his wrist, asking for more. "What did you want as a child? Tell me your hopes?"

Eldas looks from my touch to my eyes. He inhales slowly. His pupils are blown wide.

"My whole life has been training to be the king. To serve my people, to protect the Human Queen and the cycle. My father never warned me…"

"She would be the one trying to destroy that cycle?" My chest tightens.

"She would be the one I needed to protect myself from."

"I only struck you once." A light giggle escapes and I bring the glass up to my lips, grateful he seems amused as well. "Sorry again for that."

"I'm sorry for insulting you. Shall we call things even between us?"

"Even is a start."

"The start of what, exactly?" When did he get so close? We lean like trees in a windstorm, back and forth, both of us edging on each other's personal space until there's hardly any gap at all.

Hook nudges my lower back. Wasn't he curled up in the corner a moment ago? I was already too off balance. I stumble forward. My drink spills down Eldas's luxe tunic only for me to land against the damp spot now covering his chest. His hands catch me. But he doesn't push me away as I would've expected. He stares down at me, red faced in a way that makes me dizzy.

The hard line of his lips is suddenly softer, glistening with faerie mead. The light on his face washes him in gold, not marble. I wonder what he would taste like if I were to kiss him right now.

Is this what I've been running from my whole life? Is this what it's like to care for someone else? The rogue thought wanders across my mind as I stare up at him. *How could I have wanted to hide from this?*

"Sorry," I murmur. "I didn't mean to. It was Hook's fault."

A lazy smirk crosses his lips. He knows something he's not telling. That's what that expression says. But I don't get to probe. He distracts me with a hand on my face, his thumb dragging across my lips.

"Apologize to the drink. Because rather than being on your tongue it's now merely on my clothes—a sorry demotion."

"Eldas," I whisper thickly. My head tilts slightly into his palm. I have an ache in me, a deep need I've never yielded to, and everything in me tells me that giving in is the worst idea possible. But I can't think straight. Between the mead and his touch, I don't want to.

"Luella?" My name is a question. What is he asking?

"Yes." *Whatever it is, yes.*

His grip on me tightens; he pulls my face upward. My mouth meets his. His arm tightens around me, yanking me even closer. We smell of honey and taste of forgotten dreams. We move like desperation.

The glass I was holding falls, shattering, nearly breaking this trance with it. But Eldas runs his tongue along my lips and I let out a whine I didn't know I could make. I allow him entry into my mouth and his tongue slips against mine gently—so gently.

Yet his movements are somewhat rough and needy. He's a man of contrasts. Soft and hard. Cold yet he sets me aflame.

My back is against the mantle by the fireplace. My shoulders arch and I press against him. He holds my face to his until we both are lightheaded and gasping, coming up for air.

Eldas stares at me, lips shining and parted. I meet his gaze with as much shock and awe. The fire burns as blue as his eyes. The shards from my shattered glass are now rose petals.

"We... I..." He breathes heavily. Then, without warning, Eldas steps away. There's panic in his eyes and fear in his movements. "You're leaving."

"I'm right here." I reach for him; all better judgment has left me.

"No, you're leaving Midscape. Leaving me. We... I can't." The truth sobers us both. "I must go."

"Eldas—"

He's gone before I can say more than his name. The fire burns orange once more and the only traces of the king are wisps of the Fade he just fled through.

twenty-three

THE WALK TO THE THRONE ROOM IS VERY, *VERY* LONG THE NEXT MORNING.

"Are you all right?" Rinni asks, pausing right before we enter.

"What? I—yes, of course I am. Why do you ask? I'm perfectly fine."

"*Uh huh.*" Rinni abandons the door and folds her arms over her chest. "What's going on?"

"Nothing. Now if you'll excuse me, I'll be late and Eldas will—" I try and move for the door but Rinni blocks me. Hook growls up at her but I stop him with a hand. Rinni knows Hook well enough by now that she's not intimidated in the slightest.

"Yes, you don't want to be late. So out with it; how did last night go?"

"It was fine," I say a little too quickly.

"Fine?" She arches her eyebrows and repeats, "*Fine?* You've wrung your hands at least fifty times on the way here. Something happened."

"No, nothing."

"You're lying."

I groan and bury my face in my hands. The anticipation of seeing Eldas again has been prickling me all morning to the point that I couldn't sit still. I had to read my journals while pacing before the sun was even up or the restless energy in me might spark lightning.

All night, the sight of his silhouette outlined in raw blue magic illuminated my mind. All night, I heard the whispers of the softer tones of his voice; his more delicate expressions haunted me. The phantom sensations of his lips on mine had me sighing and gasping in ways that embarrassed me come dawn.

"Really, it went fine. We'll just have to see how the rest goes from here."

Rinni studies me for another long minute. But then finally eases away from the door. "All right. But if you want to talk about anything, I'm here."

"Thank you." Though Rinni would likely be the last person I talk to about wanting her king to press me against a wall and do obscene things with his fingers somewhere between my—*stop with those thoughts right now, Luella.*

"If it's any consolation, Eldas seemed out of sorts this morning."

I bet he was, I bite back and enter the throne room.

Eldas is seated on his iron throne. His right ankle rests atop the opposite knee. Balanced on his thigh is a familiar journal. His chin rests lightly on his fist as his eyes dart across the page.

I walk silently over and stand right in front of him. But he doesn't look up. His strong cheekbones frame his thin lips, pursed slightly in thought to match the slight furrow in his brow. I know what those lips feel like now—not cold, not cutting, but velvet.

I wonder if he doesn't know I'm here. It would seem impossible, but with such a look of intense focus...

"I believe I need to thank you," he says, finally. I nearly jump out of my skin as the words echo through the throne room.

"For what?" My mind is still on last night.

Eldas holds up Alice's journal. "Telling me this existed. I went to retrieve it from the laboratory last night." He stands and stretches out his arm. "Here. If you don't mind returning it to the laboratory for me?"

"Did you...finish it?" I ask, crossing over and taking the journal from him. He's acting normal. But also not. There's a kindness here, a warmth that wasn't there before.

Does he want to kiss me again? I can't tell and I hate that. I want to know him so well that I know every time he wants to kiss me and every time he'd let me kiss him. *Do I want to kiss him again?* I can't seem to get my thoughts in order.

"I did."

"That must've taken you—"

"All night." Yet he doesn't look any different than normal. His skin is the same shade and no dark circles line his eyes. If looking refreshed after spending all night reading is some elf ability, I am going to feel extremely shortchanged as a human. "It completely enraptured me."

"Really? I mean, I'm glad." I try not to let my surprise give him the wrong impression and force a smile. Everything is awkward.

Eldas regards me with a guarded expression. "I would care for the next one you recommend."

"Pardon?"

"You had others, correct?"

"Yes, but—" Eldas is already crossing the room. "Wait, where are you going?"

"To your apartments," he says, as if the fact is obvious.

"Excuse me?"

"The other journals are there, yes? I would like to start the next one you recommend. I admit I glossed over some of the more detailed notes on plants, however. So please give me one with more margin notes and personal anecdotes alongside the herbology."

"All right," I say, as if this conversation is totally normal. "Actually, come this way." I start for the door in the back of the throne room.

"But—"

"There are two specific ones I want to recommend to you. Well, three, but I'm not finished with the third yet. The last one I have in my apartments, but the others I've already returned to the laboratory."

"Very well, lead on."

If he's trying to be normal then I will also. If he doesn't want to address last night, then I don't need to either. Ignoring it is the best, healthiest, most mature response, right? Right.

Hook pushes past me as I open the door. The wolf scampers

halfway up the stairs, stopping to look back at me, as if frustrated I'm not going fast enough. He clearly already knows where we're headed.

"Go on ahead," I encourage. "We'll be right behind."

Hook lets out a small bark and bounds away.

"I started doing some other research last night," Eldas says.

"Other research?" I laugh. "You had time to research something else and finish that whole journal?"

"I already told you I skipped the sections of herbology," he says somewhat remorsefully, as if the very idea of not reading every word in a book is embarrassing for him.

"Fair. What is it that you researched?" I assume he wants me to ask. Otherwise, why bring it up?

"If there have been any other instances of Fade beasts wandering into Midscape."

"And?"

"It's not entirely unprecedented. But, usually, they do not linger this long. Fade beasts are the animals that were caught between when the worlds pulled apart. They might look and feel mortal...but they are part of the Fade itself."

"Part of the Fade itself," I repeat. "So every animal, tree, creature, was trapped in place when Midscape split from the natural world?"

Eldas nods.

"The Fade is almost like a creature unto itself, then. Isn't it?"

I pause on the stairs, noticing Eldas has fallen behind. He stares up at me with his shining blue eyes. He stares at me in a way I haven't had him look at me before. Yearning, if I had to describe it.

"That is correct," he says gently. "The Fade is very much like something living, breathing, thinking."

"And trapped in stasis." Somehow, I pity that dark, primordial mist.

"No one has ever recognized that before," he says with a note of surprise.

"I'm sure someone has."

"No, they haven't," he insists and takes another step toward me. I wonder if he'll kiss me again. I wonder how it'll feel with both of us sober and sensible. I'm doing a very poor job of ignoring these thoughts. "It gives me hope that you're so fond of something from the Fade."

"Why?"

"Because it speaks to your capacity for compassion if you could care for something of the Fade. It is a cold place."

Cold like me, I realize is what he wants to say. If the Fade comes from the Elf King, and I care for something of the Fade, does that mean I care for him? Is that what he sees? Is that the truth?

"The Fade..." That seemingly sentient wall is a part of Eldas. "I thought the first Human Queen helped make it?"

"Yes, the Human Queen's magic, her gift from the earth, and the Elf King's powers bestowed by the Veil. It took both of them."

"See, we're stronger when we work together," I murmur. I'm against the wall again and he looms over me.

"Perhaps you're right." Eldas wears a small smile and continues up the stairs. I breathe a sigh of relief. I don't know what I would've done if his attention was on me like that for a moment longer.

When we arrive at the laboratory, Willow is on his knees, knuckle deep in the most rigorous belly scratches I have ever seen. Hook is clearly loving the attention with tail-wagging, body-wriggling delight. "Who's the best Hookie? *You're* the best Hookie! Best boy gets his tummy scratched. Yes he does. *Yes he does*."

"Oh, Hook, my fierce defender, what am I going to do with you?" I laugh and cross back to the bookshelf. Willow hardly acknowledges me. "You spoil him, you know."

"He's the best boy and deserves to be spoiled," Willow says defensively. "Oh, I've been working on the biscuit recipe. Let's see if we can't find something you'll finally eat." Hook has had no interest in food, much to Willow's dismay. Whatever Fade beasts eat, it's not anything Willow has concocted. At best, Hook has politely indulged him for the sake of more scratches. "They're right over—oh. Oh! Your Majesty!"

I glance over my shoulder to see Willow bowed at the waist before Eldas. Hook continues to lie on his back, as if satisfied by embarrassing the poor man. I roll my eyes.

"I see this is how my resources are being spent," Eldas says, suddenly brisk again. "To make biscuits for creatures of the Fade."

"I… Well, that's… You see…" Willow still has yet to straighten. I can see him almost trembling.

"Leave him alone, Eldas," I scold and step down from the stool, journal in hand. Crossing, I hand it to the Elf King. "He's the best healer this castle will ever have and you know you're not going to get rid of him just because he wants to spoil my wolf. Especially not when Poppy is away."

Eldas narrows his eyes at me but says nothing. I dare to grin up at him. I can almost see him fighting a smile.

Movement behind Eldas catches my eye. Any retort I had in mind fades into a soft, "Oh no."

Harrow is slumped against a man with long lashes and wavy brown hair. He was the quiet one with his nose in the book when I first met Harrow and his motley crew. *Sirro*, that was his name.

Sirro has a panicked expression as he struggles to get Harrow to the laboratory. Harrow, for his part, can barely stand. His head is slumped and every other step seems to give out with his feet dragging limply.

"What is—" Eldas turns and stops short. I see his whole body tense. The room is noticeably colder. "What is the meaning of this?" he says, his voice deathly soft.

"Harrow, he…" Sirro looks between me and the king. I'm surprised when his eyes land on me. "He told me to come here and find you."

"Find *me*?"

"He said you could heal him again."

I curse several times under my breath. I hadn't told anyone about that day. This certainly wasn't how I expected Eldas and Willow to find out.

"Put him here." I point to the stool I healed him in last time. "Tell me what happened."

"We… Well, we…" Sirro glances between me and Eldas as he continues to bring Harrow forward.

"Whatever happened, I need to know." I can only imagine the debauchery they've been up to. "I can assure you the king will be much more cross if you *don't* tell me what's going on and something terrible happens to his brother."

"You do not speak for me," Eldas says, perhaps mostly on instinct. I stick out my chin and glare at him. "But the queen is correct," Eldas relents. I press my mouth closed to keep it from falling open in shock. He admitted I'm correct without prodding. "And I am most interested in why my brother is in this state. Willow, you may leave."

"Luella, do you need—" Willow tries to ask but Eldas won't let him get a word in.

"Luella clearly does not need help if she is healing him *again*." The way Eldas says the last word tries to knot my stomach, but I suppress it defiantly. I'm not going to regret helping a man in need. "Go, Willow," he barks.

Willow glances at me and hastily departs. Hook growls at Eldas's tone, and likely because his belly scratcher was just sent running. I'm too focused on Harrow to worry about Hook or Willow right now.

"Tell me, Sirro," I say and look the man right in the eye. *There's only you and me right now*, I want to say. *Ignore the mighty Elf King standing right next to you.* "What's wrong with him? What did he do?"

"We were out at Harpy's Cranny," Sirro starts, still glancing at Eldas.

"Harpy's Cranny? That no-good—"

"Eldas, enough," I interrupt the king sharply. "Sirro, look at me; what happened?"

He takes a deep breath. "Last night we went to Harpy's Cranny, the four of us. Aria was celebrating because she just got a part in the Troupe of Masks and found out she'll begin touring with them before springtime rites, starting in Carron in a few weeks. There was faerie mead and I remember dancers..." Sirro shakes his head. "I don't..."

"You're doing great," I encourage. "Did he just have mead?"

"That's all I saw. But he did go off with Jalic at one point? Maybe Aria? I'm not sure. I think that happened. Jalic was interested in some sweetchime I had. I gave him some earlier in the day. Perhaps they did that?"

"Sweetchime?" I've never heard of it.

Eldas grimaces. "It's a pathetic substance that some say enhances the effects of alcohol. They hear chimes and laughter and dance with the spirits under the full moon on it."

"It's harmless. Or, I thought it was. You don't think there maybe was something more, do you?" Sirro says worriedly.

The sight of Aria in the alleyway with the horned fae returns to me. I can't let the fae's attack on me prejudice me against Aria. If Eldas still hasn't uncovered anything there—and I'm somehow certain he would tell me if he had—then I won't worry. "I'm sure it's just too much," I lie and start for the conservatory.

"You may leave," Eldas commands Sirro.

"But Harrow—"

"Out!" One word sends Sirro scampering. I can almost see frost crackling along the glass of the conservatory as Eldas's rage increases. I ignore it for the time being.

Once more, I go through the steps of making a remedy for the ailing prince. Once more, I add a leaf from the heartroot and other herbs to detoxify. I don't know what sweetchime does, but if there was anything else that Harrow took then he can use all the help he can get cleansing his system. I also add in a few other herbs that come to mind based on my readings of the past queens' journals. Eldas hardly watches me. Instead his arm is around his brother, supporting him as he teeters on the stool.

"What happened before?" Eldas asks as I bring over the concoction. "The last time you healed him."

"He looked much the same. Of course, I couldn't get any solid information from him."

"Of course," Eldas mutters. Worry is plastered across the king's face, a frantic and pained expression I've seen once before—when he thought I was in trouble.

Harrow is barely responsive as I lift the mug to his lips. "Come on, drink."

Eldas's eyes flash blue. A chill whips through me like a winter's gale. Harrow shudders and I see his throat tense as he swallows.

"What did you—"

"Focus, Luella. I assume he needs to finish that." Eldas has yet to take his eyes off his brother.

Thanks to Eldas's magic control over Harrow, we get the entire mug of potion down.

"Harrow!" Eldas says as his brother goes limp in his arms.

"He's just asleep." I rest my hand encouragingly on Eldas's shoulder. It's turned to rock with tension. "The potion will help his system clear everything up…but the best medicine is often rest and allowing the body to work on its own. I put in some herbs to help him sleep; with any luck he'll stay asleep and wake up right as rain."

"All right." Eldas sighs. "Come on then, brother." He shifts and lifts Harrow up with ease into his strong arms. I can see the outline of corded muscle bulging from under his tunic. The worry on his face is easing into relief. A relief I helped create. The thought brings a rush of joy I haven't felt in some time.

This is what I was meant to do—help people. I miss my shop and Capton more than I have in weeks but I force the thoughts away. They're sharper than they've ever been and I need to stay focused.

"Here, when he wakes he'll need another dose. More rest…and then he should—"

"I cannot carry him and half the laboratory. Please bring what he will need and follow me to his room."

twenty-four

HARROW'S ROOM IS THE LAST PLACE I WANT TO BE. But I can't outright say so. And I can't abandon a patient.

"I...sure." I quickly load all the essentials I can think of, and then some, into a basket and follow behind Eldas. "Hook, go," I command the beast. I don't want to bring him to Harrow's room. I wouldn't be surprised if the young prince found out after the fact and tried to get Hook taken from me somehow as a result. Hook looks at me with his yellow eyes and tilts his head. "It's all right, Hook, go back to the Fade. I'll whistle for you later."

Hook skulks between the shadows of the world as Eldas and I depart. We walk through the quiet castle and into the East Wing. I recognize the cramped hallways filled with relics and tapestries from dinner the night before. We arrive at a landing not unlike my own and enter into a wreck of an apartment.

Signs of debauchery litter the floor. Clothes are strewn about. There are remnants of a party long gone, waiting long enough to be cleaned that a stale smell hangs in the air.

Eldas pauses with a heavy sigh. He glances over his shoulder at me. "Sorry for this... The bedroom is right through here."

We carefully step over suspect objects as we navigate through an archway paneled with sheer curtains. Behind is a large, circular bed that's just as much of a mess as the rest of the room. Eldas sets Harrow down and I take the liberty of cleaning off a side table to arrange my clerical items.

"Tell me what he will need." Eldas gently situates the blankets around his youngest brother.

"When he wakes, he'll need to drink the rest of this. Then, after that, this powder should be mixed with water and he should get all of that down at once. But I can come back and see to his care."

Eldas looks up at me from the edge of the bed. His knee almost touches my thigh as he shifts to face me more. I continue to focus on my herbs and salves.

"You would do that for my wretch of a brother?"

"Even wretches need care." I pause and my eyes drift to Harrow. He no longer looks like the antagonistic terror I first met. Asleep, he looks younger and softer—vulnerable, almost. "No…he's not a wretch, just a bit misguided, I'd bet." The people who act the worst are often hurting the worst. "He especially needs care." More than I can give. I suspect Harrow's problems are deeper than physiological.

"He does," Eldas agrees faintly. "It's my fault that he is this way." I stay silent as Eldas speaks. "Managing the spares to the Elf King has been tricky throughout history. The Elf King has always been able to ascend to the throne, thanks in part to the protections that surround the heir from birth. So spares have never been needed… Our brother, Drestin, was simple. He had drive and gladly accepted his post at Westwatch.

"But Harrow… Our mother has always been soft on him. He was the one son who she could cling to the longest. She dotes on him; Father did too. And I…"

"You resented him for it," I finish.

"Yes." Eldas presses his eyes closed and buries his face in his hand. "I was the heir to all of Midscape, and I envied my little brother."

"You didn't have it easy." Sorrow wells in me. It's as though I've finally penetrated through the overwhelming wall of permafrost that surrounds this man and caught something real, something warm—pain. "You couldn't go out. You were the heir from the moment you were born and groomed as such. Your father was in a complicated situation between your mother and his queen. Being between him and her and Alice couldn't have been easy—"

"Alice was my savior," he interrupts. "Without her, I would've gone mad."

"Oh." All his past mentions of Alice take on new meaning.

"She was good to me. My mother knew that I was destined to be king and that destiny would take me from her. From the moment I was born she handed me off to the wet nurses and washed her hands of me."

Family dinners flash before my eyes. I can still hear the echoes of my parents tucking me into bed, assuring me that there were no monsters lurking in the corners of our attic. I remember the first time my mother took me out into the fields to show me what she knew of herbs and plants. Her wails as I left fill my ears and the sight of my father's red eyes flash before my eyes.

Did Eldas hate me then? Did he hate me for the family I had that he was denied? Did he rip me from them so callously because of spite?

The questions sting my tongue as tears sting my eyes. It's likely true. I should likely hate him all the more now.

But...I don't. I can't. Something in me is shifting now that I've seen him like this and know what I know. It's shifting more than it did from kisses against a wall. I may never be able to look at him the same way again.

Maybe I don't want to. I feel for him deeper than I ever expected and I don't dislike it.

"Alice took pity on me when no one else would," he continues, oblivious to my turmoil. "She was the best thing I had. And I mourned her death daily for far too long."

Just like I mourn your departure when it hasn't even come to pass—I can almost hear the unspoken words and I wonder if I've fabricated them entirely.

"Eldas, I—"

"Where is he?" A curt voice cuts through the air as the door to the main room snaps open. *Speaking of mothers...* "Where is my darling boy?" A woman with sharp features and eyes just as cold as Eldas's storms in, curtains fluttering behind her. I wonder if part of the reason why she couldn't tolerate Eldas was because of how much he looks like her. "What have you done to him?"

I blink, realizing her attention rests solely on myself. "What? *Me?*"

"You come into this castle and have caused my sons nothing but torment," she scolds and rounds the other side of the bed. "You're not even supposed to be in the East Wing. Keep to your side, *queen.*" She says queen like an insult.

"I—"

"Mother, Luella has been helping Harrow," Eldas says curtly, standing from the edge of the bed. "Without her—"

"Without her my baby boy would not be in this turmoil; just look at him." She smooths away Harrow's dark hair from his sweat-slicked face.

I want to pity this woman. I want to find sympathy for her as I have for Eldas. I try and imagine myself in her position. She's in effect the mistress of the former king with no real title. From the first moment she pursued a relationship with Eldas's father, she must have known her firstborn son would be taken from her. I try and reach deep for compassion, but her murderous glares in my direction make it very hard.

"You know what Harrow will need next," I say to Eldas. "If you need me or have questions, you know how to find me."

"Yes, thank you, Luella." The way he says it leaves no doubt that he means it.

"He will not have anything that girl has made." The woman glares at my nightstand of supplies.

"Mother—"

"She is, what? Eighteen?"

"Nineteen," I correct calmly.

"A child. Get Poppy."

"I am unable to do that," Eldas says coolly. "I have sent Poppy away on an important mission that will take at least two months still; and I will not call her back. So if you wish for Harrow to receive care you will allow Luella to—"

"Poppy's grandson. Even that mouse of a man would be better than *her*."

I see Eldas's hands tighten behind his back to the point that his knuckles are paper white. The muscles in his jaw tense. But his eyes are full of sorrow and longing, even as he speaks with all the bitter ice I've ever heard the man muster.

"I am the king, and what happens in my castle is my sole discretion."

"'Your castle.' You do not lord over me. I am your mother."

"A shame you have failed to ever act like it."

"Eldas." I touch his elbow lightly, trying to snap him out of this.

"How dare you speak to me that way."

"How dare you speak to my wife that way!" Eldas's words reverberate through me. They ward against the ever-rising chill and generate a warm heat that flushes up my arms and settles in my cheeks.

He's not defending you, Luella, not really. I'm just an easy opportunity for him to jab at his mother. I look away from them, hiding my face as I try and lie to myself.

"Harrow needs his rest," I say quietly.

"Yes, we're leaving." Eldas turns and his large palm rests on the small of my back as he ushers me out of the room. He's silent as he leads me all the way back to my apartments.

The entire time, his hand remains on my person. It's warm, for such a cold man. I make no effort to step out of his reach.

Hook is already back and he lets out a soft whine the moment he sees us, lifting his head from his paws.

"Sorry about sending you away," I apologize to Hook and finally step away from Eldas to crouch down and scratch the wolf behind both ears. "I didn't want to risk Harrow waking up and being mean to you."

"No one in this castle will harm Hook. If they did, they would have to face my wrath."

I look up at Eldas. He seems to sway slightly. Exhaustion is creeping in at his edges and I resist the urge to run to the laboratory and make something to help him relax and sleep deeply.

"Because he is part of you?"

"No, it has nothing to do with me—because you care about him. You, and anything that is yours, are my responsibility to protect."

"Responsibility," I whisper, chasing it with a sad laugh.

"Are my *honor* to protect," he clarifies without hesitation.

"Thank you," is all I say. What else can I say to that firm declaration? It brought the heat right back to my cheeks.

"Thank you, Luella." His eyes linger on me, almost expectantly. "For..." He shakes his head, as if he can't come up with the words.

"For last night?"

Panic flickers in him. Eldas seems to lean forward, as if drawn to me by the memory of our kiss. I wouldn't mind if he kissed me again, I finally admit to myself. The thought stirs my own panic and I swallow hard. Seeing it, he instantly pulls away.

"Last night is better left at the bottom of the bottle of mead," he says finally.

"Is that your way of saying you were drunk?" I ask. Disappointment floods me. I try and erect dams before it can overtake me.

"We both had too much."

And that's his way of saying he regrets it. Eldas studies me from the corner of his eye, clearly waiting for my response.

"Right, we did," I force myself, albeit painfully, to agree. If he wants to back away then I'll let him. I'm trying to leave anyway.

He has his duties. I have mine. Ignoring last night and anything that might be simmering between us is for the best. We're only destined for heartache if we continue.

Yet, Eldas seems to deflate some. But he quickly corrects the hunch in his shoulders, no doubt arriving at the same conclusion as me.

Without another word, he departs. I watch him go before taking Hook into our apartments.

For the first time since finding Hook, it feels lonely in the vast landscape of my chambers. For the first time, and despite every last bit of sense telling me not to, I wonder what it would be like to have Eldas stay.

twenty-five

"You're up early," Willow says as he enters the laboratory.

"Yes, well, I wanted to get a few things sorted before I go and check on Harrow."

"How did all that go?" Willow hops up onto one of the counters. He's more interested in me than starting his duties for the day—more interested in me than scratching Hook's belly, and that's saying something.

Hook is not amused by this change in events.

"I…" My hands hover over the basket I was loading. "It was strange. Harrow is fine, or he should be. We'll know soon." I quickly recap the events of yesterday, leaving out some key details of intimate family tensions and the odd push and pull going on between Eldas and me. The former I doubt he or Harrow would want me to talk about. The latter I'm not ready to talk about.

"So you met her, Heir Mother Sevenna."

"Sevenna. Just the name sounds severe." It suits the brisk woman I met yesterday.

"They call her the castle wraith in town," Willow confides in me.

"The castle wraith and the ice king. Quinnar certainly has strong opinions of their royal family."

"Other people's words, not mine," Willow adds hastily.

"I've never interacted with the royal family much, despite being here."

"You've said as much. And even if those were your words, I wouldn't report you to Eldas." I give a wink at Willow and watch him relax once more. He flashes one of his earnest smiles. No, I wouldn't do anything that could harm Willow, not after all he's done for me.

"She doesn't leave the castle much. Well, ever. They say she died with the last king and it's now her ghost that wanders the halls."

Sevenna must've loved the king. Surely she did. Once more I try and find sympathy for her, as hard as it may be.

"I can assure you she's very real. Oh, speaking of her, she did mention something. Or rather, Eldas did."

"What?"

"Eldas mentioned that he sent Poppy away and she won't be back for at least two more months." I finish gathering the supplies I think I'll need and proceed to check them twice. "I remember you saying she was on some kind of a trip a while ago... Is it the same one? Is everything all right?"

"He sent her to the Natural World."

"What?" I gasp softly.

"I thought you knew..." A frown briefly crosses his face. "I'm sorry, I would've mentioned it sooner."

"No, it's fine. What did he send her for?"

"He was worried about the city across the Fade not having its healer after you left, or that's what Grandmother told me. It seems a bit odd, if you ask me. I've never heard of a king sending aid to your side."

I pretend to focus on my basket as my insides knot. I remember the conversation we had in the Fade and the fears I confided in him. Here I was going about my days, oblivious to this kindness... I merely figured Poppy was busy elsewhere in Midscape. *Why didn't Eldas say anything?*

"Are you all right?"

"Yes, I'm fine." I sling my arm through the basket. "Do you mind watching Hook while I run this errand? If he gets troublesome you can send him off."

He gasps. "I would never send my Hookie off!" Willow hops from his perch to grab Hook's face with both hands. "Are you ready? We're going to figure out those biscuits today. Yes we are. Yes we are." His puppy talk brings a grin to my face and I depart knowing Hook is in good hands for the time being.

I recall the way back to Harrow's chambers from memory. It's slow going and I second-guess every step. But the leisurely pace gives me time to think about Eldas's gesture in sending Poppy back, as well as Sevenna, Harrow, Eldas, and the unconventional family I've found myself not quite a part of.

I knock on Harrow's door and pray Sevenna isn't there. There's no response, which I take as a good sign. It's possible he's still sleeping.

"Hello?" I say as I crack open the door.

"Is that my brother's queen?" Harrow rasps.

"And your personal healer," I respond and shut the door behind me. Someone has cleaned up the room. There's much less for me to dance around as I make my way to his bed.

"Lucky me," he says dryly.

"We both have the best luck, it seems," I retort, just as dry.

"Fair. You had to end up married to my bastard of a brother."

"He's not half as much of a bastard as you."

Harrow snorts and gives me a tired grin as I check on the status of the medicines I left behind. Both the powder and second dose of the potion are gone. And judging from the color that's returned to Harrow's cheeks, my concoctions worked.

"Careful, Luella, if you keep talking to me like that I may end up liking you."

"The horror."

He snorts. "I do find I prefer the company of people who treat me like shit."

"And why is that?" I ask offhandedly, though I'm genuinely curious of the answer.

"Who knows? Maybe because I know I'm not worth anything better?" Harrow speaks as I finish the potion I started in the laboratory. A bundle of thyme turns to dust in my fingers as the liquid in the mug I'm holding shifts in color to a murky brown.

Magic tingles on my palm. I have more control of my powers, I think, more confidence at the very least.

"That's not true," I say as I hand the mug to him. I sit on the edge of the bed. He eyes the movement, but doesn't tell me to get out... which is progress I didn't know I was after.

"What do you know?" he says, half hidden behind the mug.

"Everyone is worthy of decency. It's why I'm helping you, after all."

"And I bet you think you're so much better than I am because of it." He sneers. But the expression lacks the same kind of venom it once held. Or perhaps I've become immune to his particular brand of poison.

"I'm not better than anyone." I sigh. "Though I wish I was better for myself." If I was, I might have known I was the queen earlier. I might have been able to figure out a way to stop the cycle and fix the seasons of Midscape by now. I might have seen Eldas's kindness. I might not be ignoring the stirrings in me toward him.

"Don't we all?"

"So, what happened?" I divert the topic and my thoughts. "Tell me what actually happened to you this time."

"So you can report to my brother?"

"It'll stay between us. I swear it to you." I look Harrow dead in the eyes.

"You swear it?" He arches his eyebrows.

"I take the relationship I have with my patients seriously, Harrow. You have my word I won't tell Eldas—or anyone else—anything."

"I guess I can believe that. You didn't last time." He sighs. "I...I may have involved myself with something I shouldn't."

"What?" I ask as he passes his mug between his palms.

"I can't believe I'm telling a human this," he mutters.

"I'm your healer; think of me that way and nothing more."

"Right. Well...I don't know how it happened. It wasn't supposed to."

"*What happened?*"

"A few weeks ago, I think I took glimmer for the first time. You have to believe me, it was completely by accident. I would've never sought out the stuff," he says defensively.

"I don't know what glimmer is."

"Oh, right, *human*." He rolls his eyes and I roll mine right back. "Glimmer is a...substance made by the fae. It heightens the connection with the Veil and, because of that, can improve elf magic. The sensation of power flowing through you is like none other. As if you're halfway into the Beyond—halfway to the immortality we once had. Some people take it to perform incredible acts. Others... for pleasure."

"Like you?"

"I told you, I didn't intend to. Not originally..."

I frown. At the academy there were students who experimented with various substances, natural and created. Some I even heard of selling such things on the streets of Lanton. But I never gave the matter much attention, choosing instead to distance myself from the shadier acts as much as possible. My studies kept me from everything I couldn't grow in dirt.

"We were at a party. People were having a good time. I think something was slipped into my drink. That must've been it. But after...I...I craved it. Just a little at a time. But the allure of the Veil is overwhelming."

I resist frowning. I don't want him to interpret my worry as judgment. Instead, I keep my face passive and listen.

"Plus, when I take it, I don't think about anything. The world slips away into that hazy blue void." Suddenly, anger flashes in his eyes. "Do you know what it's like to hunt for your whole life for a place you can just exist?"

"Yes," I answer honestly. He's startled. "It's something I've always pursued—a place of my own, built by my own hands—a corner of the world I can make my duty to look after. Not for the same reasons as you, Harrow...but I know that feeling."

"Look at me, relating to a human. They'd never believe it in the salons and lounges if they heard," Harrow muttered.

"These are strange times indeed." I grin slightly. But my expression quickly becomes serious. "Harrow, you can't—"

"Before you say it, I know. I know I can't keep doing this. And I don't want to. But that siren call..." He stares off at nothing, as though he can hear it even now—the pull of this substance known as glimmer. "They call it glimmer because elves get a 'glimmer' of their immortality back. Now that I've tasted it, I want more. I don't know how to stop the cravings."

"I'll help you," I declare. I don't like the way he's talking about being closer to the Veil. Then, I add, "That is, if you want me to."

"What can you do?"

I wish I had access to the library at the academy and its wealth of knowledge on all topics. Or that I could write to one of my past teachers who dealt with students who became trapped by the substances they created. But I may have something just as good here.

"Plants are magnificent things. They can create something as powerful as glimmer and they can also create ways to stave off such cravings." I look him in the eyes. "Would you like me to try and make something like that for you?"

Harrow finishes his mug and passes it to me. He looks away like an obstinate child. Yet, despite all his body language to the contrary, he says, "Fine, I suppose. It's not like I can stop you. I'm drinking whatever you put in front of me, anyway."

"All right." I take the mug and set it down. "I'll see what I can do. In the meantime, don't leave the castle."

"But—"

"No, Harrow. If you must, bring Jalic, Sirro, and Aria here." I cringe inwardly at the suggestion. They're the last people I want here, but if it helps Harrow then it's what must be done. The wellbeing of my patients comes first, always.

I remember Aria in the alleyway and something passing between the fae and her. I bite my lip. Even if she wasn't involved with the horned fae who tried to kidnap me, she still might be up to something. But if I bring up any suspicions now, Harrow will likely become defensive. I can't risk him shutting off to me. Instead, I simply say, "Make sure they bring nothing harder than alcohol."

"I'll try."

"Good." I know that's all he can do. Hopefully, he's still toward the top of the slippery slope he's sliding on. But the sooner I act, the better. "I should be going."

"Yes, get out of my room, human." Even the word "human" lacks all bite.

"Gladly, *prince*." I say the word with offense, but Harrow grins at me. An expression I mirror—like we now share a secret.

I suppose we do.

The door to his room closes behind me and I'm flipping through my mental catalog of herbs as I start down the hall. I'm so focused on finding a good starting point for Harrow that I don't notice someone in my way and I nearly walk face-first into Eldas. He stops me with a strong hand on my shoulder, which jerks me out of my trance.

"*Oh!* I-I'm sorry."

"It's all right." He smiles—*smiles!* It's like the sun rose on his face. But the clouds quickly roll back in and the expression vanishes as he releases me, as if catching himself. "I was actually coming to look for you."

"You found me."

"I did." He glances over my shoulder. "Where's Hook?"

Even if the beast is a part of him, I can't help but be warmed by the fact that he's asking after my wolf. "He's with Willow. I thought he'd enjoy it much more there than attending Harrow with me."

"*Ah*, how is my brother?"

"Well enough to be trenchant." A shadow crosses Eldas's expression. His jaw is set instantly. I hold up my hands. "No, no, it was fine. I know his quips mean he's getting better." I laugh. "Plus, I'm getting used to him."

"You're...getting used to my brother?"

"People can drink poison if they take it in small enough doses for long enough," I retort.

Eldas snorts, another flicker of amusement crossing his face. I do like amusing him. I like his small smiles and mischievous looks.

"How is he doing?"

"He'll be fine. He just needs to enjoy the nightlife less. I told him he should stay in the castle for a while and rest—no going out."

"Hopefully he'll listen to you. He certainly doesn't listen to me," Eldas mutters.

"We'll see... But I'm not confident I'll have much success." I glance over my shoulder and back toward Harrow's door. Really, I'm keeping an eye out for Sevenna. I can only acclimate to so much poison at a time and I have no energy for her withering stare today. "In any case, I should get back to work."

"As should I," Eldas says. Yet, we both linger. "Oh, I almost forgot, I wanted to return this." He holds out a familiar journal. "It took me a little longer than the last one to get through."

"You still got through it in record time." I take the journal with both hands and stretch my fingers in search of the jolt that happens when our skin touches. But the tome is too large, and our hands don't meet.

"Yes, I'll need another," he says thoughtfully, his voice low. "Would I..." He clears his throat and it dislodges some of the gravel in his voice. I rather *liked* the gravel. "Would it be all right if I were to come and retrieve another from your apartments later?" Eldas asks with all the primness and propriety expected of a king.

I bite in a laugh and smile. "Of course, Eldas. You're welcome anytime."

"Good." He nods and breezes past as if things haven't just fundamentally changed once more between us. "I'll see you later, Luella."

There's something about the way my name rolls off his tongue, or the husk of his voice as he passes, that has me standing in place, toes curling into my boots, long after he's disappeared into Harrow's room.

twenty-six

I TAKE DINNER FROM MY DESK, MORE DETERMINED THAN EVER TO SCOUR THROUGH THE QUEENS' BOOKS. Specifically, I look for information on the heartroot. Harrow's recovery has, in both instances, exceeded my expectations. Since all the other herbs are ones I'm familiar with and have used many times over before, I can only assume that the variable is in the heartroot.

To my delight, Willow joins me for dinner and we spend late into the evening discussing heartroot and its magical properties. He helps me skim through journals in search of the first queen to work with the rare herb. The only thing we find is a single mention in the journal of the queen who brought that heartroot from the northern marshes—the same queen who spoke of ending the cycle. I search to see if the two are connected in some way, but when the hunt yields nothing I know I'm just seeing what I want to see.

Willow sits in a chair across from me, occupying one half of my desk. I sit at the other end, food forgotten as we scour. Hook is curled up between our feet, gladly accepting scratches with our toes.

The clock I ordered chimes nine and I'm broken from a trance. I look up for the first time in hours and rub my bleary eyes. Hazy, pale shadows dance outside the windows of my room.

"Oh…"

Willow looks up as well, turning from me to the windows behind him. He pauses, lips pursed, studying the falling snow with as much intensity as he was the journal moments ago.

"*Snow in spring, warn the king. Snow in summer, the queen yet slumbers.*"

"What?"

Willow repeats himself at my question.

"No, I heard you…what's that?"

"Oh, it's an old rhyme." He turns away from the window. "Snow in spring, warn the king—I think it implies that there may be something wrong with the queen. Because we shouldn't have snow once spring comes. Snow in summer—"

"The queen yet slumbers," I finish. "Meaning, she hasn't come back yet. The last queen is dead and it's winter when it should be summer." Willow nods. I stare at the fat, falling snow, apprehension filling my gut. It mocks the bright spring weather here mere hours ago. "I think you should go."

"Are you sure?"

"I need to see Eldas." The words hurt to say and the pain of them will only be the beginning of tonight's agony.

Willow sighs and closes the journal he was thumbing through. The notes he was taking are tucked inside. He stands and Hook stands with him. Willow gives the wolf a scratch between the ears.

"I'll see you tomorrow, Hook. And you too, Luella."

I wish he didn't sound slightly worried and doubtful saying that. "I'll see you tomorrow." *I hope.*

"If you need me, summon me no matter the time." Willow departs and I pace my room several times in front of the large windows.

I'm not surprised when there's a knock on my door.

"Come in, Eldas."

The door opens and I don't even bother looking. But, sure enough, his voice cuts through my rampant thoughts. "How did you know it was me?"

"Lucky guess." I glance over my shoulder with a shrug.

"I haven't made it a habit to come to your room in the evenings."

"Well, given that it's snowing…"

His gaze shifts, as though he saw only me from the first moment he opened the door. A frown pulls on his lips. His eyes are hard and severe. "So it is."

"You weren't coming here because of that?"

"I was coming for a new journal. But you are correct in that this is a more pressing matter."

"I will have to sit on the throne again, won't I?" I worry the labradorite ring on my right hand nervously.

"You will." He sounds apologetic, the words rife with worry.

"Let's go, then."

"Now?" He seems startled by the idea.

"When else? It must be done, and I'd rather get it over with when I have all night to try and recover." More like, while I have my courage together. Before the fear really sets in.

"Luella, you'll be fine." Even he doesn't sound convinced.

I shrug. I know what I've read. The throne doesn't get easier. Queens just get used to it. I have no choice but to endure the world trying to drain every drop of life from me.

"Luella." The soft note in Eldas's voice brings my eyes up to him. "You have had more time to allow your magic to settle and to acclimate to Midscape. You know what's coming."

"I just want to get it over with," I say faintly. "Please, take me there."

"Very well." He obliges.

In what seems like no time at all, we're in the throne room. It's almost so cold that my breath clouds and I fight a shiver. I'm in a simple shift dress—long sleeved, luckily—but the cotton isn't nearly thick enough for this.

"At least when I sit on the throne again, it'll get warmer." I make an attempt to grin, but Eldas doesn't mirror the emotion so it quickly falls from my face. He exudes worry with every step.

"I'll be here the entire time," he says as we pause before the throne. "I'll pull you out like last time, if need be."

Last time. The thought has my body aching. I square off against the throne. If I can leave home, go to Lanton, become an herbalist, become the Human Queen, and manipulate the earth, then I can do this. I refuse to let a throne control me.

"Let's get this over with," I say, sounding more stable than I feel.

Turning, I tip backwards and allow myself to fall into the seat. If I try to ease myself down, I may pull away at the last second. Fear could get the better of me and turn the inevitable into something more unbearable than it already is.

Right before my body hits the throne, I look up and all I see is Eldas.

I'm here, his eyes seem to say. *I'll be here*.

I don't get a chance to thank him. The air is sucked from my lungs and I'm plunged into darkness. *Keep your wits about you, Luella,* I command myself. I know what's coming and I'm not going to let the shock steal my senses.

Deeper and deeper, I sink into the core of the earth. The sensation is somewhere between the first and second time I interacted with the throne. I am as immersed as the first. But it's less violent, like the second.

Eldas's phantom fingers splay across where I imagine my stomach would be, if I had a stomach in this form. *Focus*, I can hear him command. *The magic responds to you. You are its master. It is not the master of you.*

Slowly, awareness comes into focus. It's not quite like seeing, but more like my awareness sharpening the world around me. I am within a cocoon nestled deep in the roots of the redwood throne. I am in the dark spot I previously could not see within, trapped in a cage of gnarled roots.

Everything stretches out from here. Everything originates from this spot.

The seed, I remember reading another queen call it in a journal. From this seed, the life of Midscape is sustained. This is the seed of the tree that nourishes the world of wild magic. The Fade creates the borders, but without the seed it would be an empty vessel.

The first Human Queen and Elf King worked together to make the Fade. The rogue thought wanders through my head as if someone whispers it to me.

Hello? I try and ask.

Silence.

I try and reach out to the world around me, but am met with

nothing. Yet my hands seem to touch everything. In this murky place of primordial beginnings, I see a hazy image.

A woman with a crown, reaching forward. *Planting…*

Planting? Planting what? Have I seen this before?

The heartroot remembers.

Remembers what?

But the fleeting images are gone, and with them exhaustion follows in their wake. I must stay focused on my task. The echoes of a thousand queens exist in this dark void and I cannot allow myself to get lost among them.

Magically, I tap into the great roots that prop up Midscape. I feel the same cries from across the land. But they are less hungry and demanding this time.

They know I've returned, I realize. The plants, animals—life itself on Midscape knows the queen has returned to attend them. They are not screaming into the void of a seemingly endless winter, but making their needs known so that summer can break over a world still waking.

Fine, I relent. *Take what you need.*

As soon as permission is given, I feel the tendrils worm underneath my flesh. They dig into me with an inevitable violence. I grit my teeth against the pain. It's numbed as the world begins to drain the magic within me from my marrow.

Enough, I try and demand. *That's enough.*

But Midscape does not listen. This unnatural world is needy, and hungry. *More, more, more*, it seems to say. Everything is out of balance and it doesn't know when to stop.

Enough!

The vines tighten around me. I can't get a word out. They writhe within me. They will tear me apart in this dark and lonely place.

All at once, the invisible tendrils release themselves. My lungs are my own. My mind is free and exists only within my own head.

I'm pressed against something solid and warm. Two roots still cling to me but—*no, they're not roots*. They're arms. I blink up in the dim light of the throne room.

Eldas is all I see.

He cradles my shaking form against him; his embrace is the only thing keeping my bones from rattling apart. I want to thank him, but I'm too exhausted. Talking is hard. Thinking is hard.

"You did well," he murmurs. My head rests against his shoulder by the crook of his neck.

"Was it enough?" I rasp.

"It was enough. You are more than enough."

I hope so. My eyes flutter closed. It feels like enough. This once-cold world is now warm. In the back of my mind, I realize I know this sensation. I've felt it once before.

He held me like this when he hardly knew me after the first time I sat on the throne. The vague thoughts slip between my fingers, as much of a victim to the overwhelming darkness as I am.

I wake in my bed several hours later.

Dawn has broken, painting the room with a watercolor brush of periwinkle and honeysuckle hues. I feel as though I've run a marathon. Not that I've ever done such a thing in my life before. But I watched my classmates do it in Lanton and it looked *exhausting*.

As I push myself off the bed, a chorus of popping and snapping in my bones wakes Hook. He whines and eagerly jumps up to my face. Wet nose, hot tongue, and warm breath is my greeting party back to reality.

"It's good to see you too," I say softly, running my fingers through his dark fur. "Sorry for worrying you."

Once Hook has been reassured that I'm not dead—despite how my body tries to claim otherwise—I swing my legs off the bed and make an attempt at standing. I ache, and just walking to the bathroom has me winded. It's not as bad as the first time but I still can't imagine doing this regularly. I already have to suffer each month because of my womanly body. I wouldn't like to suffer each month, or more, because of my magic.

A soft sigh disrupts the quiet and I pause, looking toward my bedroom door. There's shifting in the main room. Hook's ears twitch, but he's already settled back at the foot of the bed, only raising his head when he realizes I'm not coming back. I bat away the idea of some thief or fae assassin rummaging through my things. If Hook doesn't deem the sound a threat, or even worth investigating, then I won't be worried.

Soundlessly, I slip into the main room. There, on my richly upholstered settee, is a cramped-looking Eldas. His long legs are tucked against one end, knees hanging over the edge. A thin blanket I found in the back of my closet and had out as a complement to the lush velvet of the furniture is draped over him. It's comically small, almost like the lanky man is using a napkin to keep warm.

Padding on light feet, I sneak back into the bedroom.

"Move, Hook," I whisper and yank at the duvet folded at the foot of the bed. I haven't needed it for warmth since Hook took up residence with me. "*Move*."

He whines and relents.

I drag the blanket back to the main room. The fabric whispers over the carpet and Eldas stirs, muttering in his sleep. Gravity threatens to pull the duvet from my tired fingers, but I hold fast, waiting for him to settle once more. Carefully, I situate the blanket over him.

Eldas shifts slightly, but doesn't wake. His eyes don't open until a good hour later. I'm leaning back in my desk chair, journal in my lap, feet propped up against the desk as I stare intently, deep in thought. There's something on the edge of my mind. Something I remember reading that connects with…

I hear him stir and glance over my shoulder. "Good morning," I say.

"Good…" He blinks sleep from his eyes, rubbing them.

"Good?" I repeat with a small grin. Tired and slightly vulnerable is not a terrible sight to see first thing in the morning. The tangerine glow of the late dawn kisses his skin, making him look more man than ethereal creature of wild magic and death.

"Goodness…your hair."

"What's wrong with my hair?" I raise a hand to my yet-to-be-combed tresses, the grin slipping into a frown. The last time I even thought of my hair was when Luke commented on how he wanted it to be long again.

"It's like fire in this light," he murmurs.

"Fire head. Yes, I've heard it before." I close the journal and sigh, dropping it on the desk harder than I intended. "All throughout grade school. Don't make the fire head angry, smoke might come out of her ears. The fire head—"

"You look like a goddess," Eldas amends. "I would not change a single thing about you, Luella." My traitorous heart skips at his words. Then, as if remembering himself, he clears his throat and sits upright, the blanket pooling around his waist. "Where did this…"

"My bed. You looked cold this morning," I answer the unfinished question. It seems Eldas has a hard time forming complete thoughts first thing in the morning, and there's something surprisingly endearing about the fact.

"I'm used to the cold." He chuckles darkly. "Ice king, they've called me."

"Good thing you have a fire queen, then." The words leave me before I can think through what exactly I'm saying. A flush rises to my cheeks.

"Oh, and why is that a good thing?" He stands, lips quirking slightly. I don't answer, tongue heavy and gummy in my mouth as Eldas approaches. "Will you keep me warm?"

A single eyebrow arches and somehow that is what sets me aflame. I purse my lips together, trying to think of something witty to say. Trying to prevent my nerves from making me say something stupid. Trying not to remember the feeling of those smirking lips on mine.

I thought we had agreed, more or less, to not go down this route after some drunken missteps?

"I think I already did." I point at the blanket that's now on the floor.

"Oh, right." He chuckles. "Of course." Do I hear a note of disappointment in his voice? Surely I'm imagining it. Eldas studies my face as I will the blush to cool. "You're flushed; do you have a fever again?"

"No, I'm fine." I stand quickly, a little too quickly as the world sways. Eldas catches me with a steady hand.

"You're not."

"I am." I touch the back of his hand lightly. I want to tell myself it's just to reassure him. But, in truth, I want the shock that shoots from my fingertips straight into my chest whenever I touch him.

I want the feeling of him there with me, in me. *In me?* My mind sputters.

"Let me take you back to bed."

You're not helping, Eldas! I want to shout. "Thank you, but I'll be all right. I don't need your help." I fumble over my words, trying not to think of every implication he certainly doesn't mean.

The trance is broken. As if realizing his hand was still on my person, he quickly jerks away. Eldas speaks as he hastily folds the duvet. A king folding a duvet is a sight worth leaning against my desk and watching. Especially as the broad muscles of his back strain against the thin tunic he's wearing.

"Well, you should continue to get what sleep you can to gather your strength. Tomorrow you'll be meeting with the finest seamstress in the city."

"I have plenty of clothes."

He pauses and gently sets the duvet on the settee. When he speaks again, he doesn't look at me. "She will be measuring you for your coronation gown. It is the honor of the top seamstress to clothe the queen for the event."

"I see..." I murmur.

"Of course, she doesn't know you intend to be gone by then." Eldas turns and the broad back I was just admiring now has become like an icy wall that I will never be able to scale.

"Eldas, I—"

I don't get to finish before he closes the door behind him. The sound rings in my ears louder than the silence that crashes down on me in his wake.

twenty-seven

THE SEAMSTRESS SETS UP A MAKESHIFT SALON IN THE CASTLE. She is now one of the "elite few" who's able to see me and has, by my understanding, been intensely vetted by Eldas. It's hard to believe it's now been over a week since the attack. In some ways, it still seems like yesterday. I'm still jumping at every sound and movement in the corner of my eye when I round corners. In other ways, it's like an eternity.

Rinni escorts me to a room with large windows that overlook Quinnar on three sides—almost like a closed-in balcony. Here, the seamstress has set up three tables under each window, yards of fabric, lace, and jewels glittering in the sunlight. I'm directed to stand on a pedestal in the center of the room as Rinni and Hook stand guard outside the door.

The seamstress steps around me. She flicks her fingers and invisible ice is dragged over my skin as measuring ribbons unfurl down my arms and legs. I do as she instructs, holding out one arm and then the other. The measurements are endless and it gives my mind time to wander beyond the window panes.

Quinnar is getting dressed up like a spring maiden. Heavy garlands of wildflowers plucked from the fields that my room overlooks have been magically woven across awnings, balconies, and porches. Minstrels have begun walking the streets, standing on benches surrounding the central lake and belting their songs.

It's a joyous veneer on a dying world. The throne was less aggressive but somehow more exhausting than the last time. Its toll is less physical and felt more in the recesses of my magic—a hollowing out of the powers I have.

My power—the last power of a long line of Human Queens—is diminishing, and I fear for this world if Eldas and I don't end the cycle.

I frown at the thought.

"Apologies, Majesty, did I prick you?" the seamstress asks, looking up from the muslin she's draping over my body.

"Oh, no, I'm fine." I force a smile. I had been frowning at the realization that I've begun to care for this world—not just in the way that I care for anything living. No…I care for it deeper than that. Perhaps it's the throne, or perhaps it's Eldas, but I'm beginning to care for Midscape as though it could be a home to me.

I stare out at the statue of the first Human Queen, kneeling before the first Elf King, and can't help but wonder if they will someday make a statue of me—the last queen. There's no way to be certain that I am the last… But a nagging inkling whispers with certainty that I am. One way or another, the Human Queens will end with me.

What would you do? I wonder with an aching heart, wishing the first queen could hear me. *If only you could guide me…*

"Your Majesty!" the seamstress squeaks as I step off of the pedestal, interrupting her work. Muslin falls from my hips.

"I'm sorry, just a moment, I need a better look at something." I quickly cross to the windows, staring down at the statue.

From this vantage, I can see details that are hidden by the queen's hands when standing at ground level. Nestled in her cupped hands is a sprout. I was right—she's not kneeling before him, she is burying something. And that something is a plant.

"When was that statue built?" I ask.

"Excuse me?"

"The one in the center of the lake, when was it created?"

The seamstress hums in thought. "I'm not rightly sure. It's always been in Quinnar. Perhaps by the second or third Human Queen."

One of the first five queens—someone whose journal I'm missing. "If it's that old, how are the details still preserved?"

"I believe the Elf King tends to it." She motions back to the center of the room. "May we resume, Your Majesty?"

I go back to the pedestal, mind whirring. The sculpture was an early creation, when the throne was young and the memory of the first queen was fresh. Is there a meaning hidden in it? Or is it truly just to honor that early queen? Those questions lead me to wonder what it might actually be depicting… Is it the creation of the Fade, or redwood throne, perhaps?

My thoughts continue to spiral around what I've read in journals, searching for a link to this revelation of the statue's true nature. I might be reading into it too much. But I must find a way to break the cycle. That's the only solution. If I don't, Midscape will be in danger.

Then, I return to Capton and everything I've ever wanted.

But what do I want?

"What do you want?" the cheery seamstress echoes my thoughts.

"I'm sorry, what?" I blink back to reality. She motions to the table of fabrics.

"For your dress, Your Majesty. What do you want? Silk, or velvet? Or perhaps chiffon? I think jewel tones for your complexion but I want to make sure I incorporate your opinion. After all, a woman's natural beauty is enhanced best by her own confidence."

She would lay an egg if she knew that what would enhance my confidence best would be a sturdy pair of canvas trousers and some kind of breathable shirt or tunic that I didn't mind getting absolutely filthy.

"I trust your judgment," I say, finally.

Her face falls slightly. "Are you…are you sure? Is nothing I brought to your liking? Because if it's not I can—"

"No, they're wonderful," I interject. I hadn't meant to offend her. "Let's see…" I step down to run my hands over the fabrics, settling on one as light as air. "This one, whatever color you think is best, but this one."

"Oh, fae-spun silk." She practically purrs as she runs her fingers over it. "You have good taste, Your Majesty."

"I'm glad to hear it." I laugh. But a thought crosses my mind at the mention of something being fae made. "I hear the fae are good craftsmen."

"The fae are skilled at their looms, yes. But the elves are the best craftsmen in the land." She preens.

"Oh, of course. On my side of the Fade there is nothing more valuable than elf-made goods." I smile and she continues to relish in my praise. I'm hoping I have her enough off guard to seize another opportunity. "I've heard a good deal about the things fae can make... especially things for celebrations."

"Like faerie mead?"

"And more, I've heard." I'm not sure how to approach this casually and can already tell I'm overplaying my hand.

A shadow crosses her face, but she brightens it with a forced smile almost immediately. "You honor us all that you're taking an active interest in all the inhabitants of Midscape."

"It is my role as Human Queen." Just when I'm about to give up on learning anything more about glimmer, she surprises me.

"I'm not sure what you heard, Your Majesty..." The seamstress keeps her head down, writing notes in a ledger she brought. "But I..."

"You?"

"It's not my place." Her pen pauses.

"Please, tell me," I encourage. "This is still a new land to me. I have much to learn." Not a lie in the slightest.

"I would suspect you might have heard something of the like from the young prince Harrow." I don't need to confirm the fact; my silence is enough to prompt her to continue. "Please be careful, Your Majesty. Those of us in the cities have seen the prince's recent... dalliances. Especially since the arrival of the fae delegation."

"Such as?"

She shakes her head. "I shouldn't have said anything. Forgive me, Majesty. Please, if you might... if in your immense kindness you spare mentioning I said anything to the king?"

"I assure you I won't," I say hastily, trying to put her at ease. "But I do need to know as I am living in the same castle as Harrow. Please, tell me if there's anything I should be aware of?"

"I don't know anything more." She shakes her head and I leave the matter be. If she does know something, she's too nervous to say.

We finish up shortly after and I excuse myself from her salon. The moment I step out I'm face to face with Harrow, Jalic, Sirro, and Aria.

"Your Majesty." Jalic is the first to notice me and he bows his head. The others follow suit. Even the begrudging etiquette is a significant improvement over the first time and I wonder if my interactions with Harrow have had anything to do with their change in tone.

Hook bounds past me. He circles Aria twice, growling low. Aria steps closer to Harrow, grabbing his arms.

"This beast is getting snot on my skirts." Aria swats lightly at Hook's nose as he buries it into the layers of fabric. "Shoo, shoo!"

"Hook, come," I command. Hook looks between me and Aria and lets out a frustrated huff, but obliges. However, his focus remains intently on the woman. It's amusing to watch Aria fight an open scowl. "Good afternoon, you four. Where are you headed?" I ask.

"Why? Would you like to come? Have a bit more fun with us?" Jalic shoves his hands into his pockets and gives me a casual grin.

"Not particularly."

"Is that any way to speak to a queen?" Rinni asks and Jalic glances askance.

"I'm going to see the seamstress," Aria announces, puffing her chest slightly. "It's such an honor to be dressed by the same woman who dresses the queen." She pets Harrow's arm lightly. There's no question as to who brought this "honor" about.

"Good, the seamstress seems very talented," I say mildly, and find a small delight in watching Aria's expression tilt toward disappointment at my lack of ire toward her being dressed by the same person as me. "In fact, I think you should *all* get your clothes for the coronation made by her."

"I'm not getting something for the coronation." The way Aria stretches her neck, as if she's trying to compete against my height, is evocative of how I imagine a territorial swan to look. "I'm getting something for the Troupe of Masks."

"Oh, right, you mentioned Aria was performing somewhere. Carron, was it?" I glance at Harrow.

"You told her? That was my surprise," Aria hisses. Then, quickly collects herself. "It's a high honor."

"Congratulations."

"Thank you, Your Majesty." She acts as though I just awarded a medal to her, bowing with a dramatic flourish of her hands. "I will be going on tour soon with them. But don't you worry, we will be back for the coronation night. I'm sure it'll be a performance worth remembering."

"I can't wait to see it," I lie. Even if I wasn't trying to leave before the coronation, I have no interest in anything to do with Aria.

"Good." She smiles thinly. "Let's be off; we don't want to keep the queen from...whatever it is she does."

Rinni takes a step forward but I don't move, still blocking the entrance to the salon. "I do a lot of reading, actually." I meet Aria's eyes.

"Good for you." Her smile is quickly becoming a sneer.

"Carron is not far from Westwatch, isn't it? Right along the wall that borders the fae wilds?"

"Your grasp of Midscape geography is astounding," Aria drawls.

"Will you be seeing any family there?"

Aria narrows her eyes as her whole body goes tense. It's a subtle shift that she quickly corrects with the poise of an actress. But that was a glimpse of something real.

I've gotten too good at catching when people's guards are down, in large part thanks to Eldas.

"All the family I associate regularly with is here in Quinnar, Your Majesty. If you'll excuse me, I'd like to be respectful of the seamstress's time." She seems too eager to dismiss the whole topic of conversation. "The hour is late already and we have a soiree tonight."

"A soiree?" I glance to Harrow.

"Here, in the castle," he says, giving me a knowing nod. Then, his voice reverts to the more careless and somewhat cruel tones I first heard from him. "I doubt you'd be interested."

"Yes, nothing you have to worry yourself with. We already know that you humans don't find the same sorts of things amusing as us elves," Aria says somewhat snidely. I can't help but wonder if she means glimmer.

"I have other, more important matters to attend to, in any case." I grit out a smile and step aside. "Enjoy yourselves."

The four go into the salon, closing the door behind them. I promptly reach out a hand and Hook is at my side. I scratch behind his ears, staring at the door.

"Rinni, take me to Eldas."

"But he—"

"Now," I say firmly. Then add, softer, "Please. There's something I need to urgently discuss with him."

"Very well." Rinni nods and starts down the hall. She doesn't seem cross with me, and yet a brief sensation of discomfort passes over me.

For the first time, I gave someone in Midscape an order, like a queen would.

And they listened.

twenty-eight

RINNI TAKES ME TO THE SECRET PASSAGE OVERLOOKING THE THRONE ROOM. I act surprised for her benefit. She places a finger over her lips and we move silently, staring down.

A screen of iron has been erected in the center of the room, bisecting the space. Eldas is on one side, sitting on his iron throne. On the other is a man dressed in lush velvet and mother of pearl. The screen is intricately woven, mostly obscuring Eldas's appearance. He continues to seclude himself, as much as possible, even as he is forced to rule due to the delay in coronation.

"This is how he's governed for the past year," Rinni whispers in my ear. "While he waited for you."

All I see is a cage. A physical barrier separating Eldas from any kind of real connection with anyone beyond Rinni, Harrow, Sevenna, Poppy, or Willow. I wonder what it must've been like to finally escape the castle when he marched to Capton. Was that the day he broke? The day he could take the all-consuming loneliness of his hall no longer?

He is chained by the traditions of his station, and suddenly I want to free him of the cycle just as much as myself and all of Midscape. What would he be like without the shackles of duty? He said he's never allowed himself to dream…what would he find he wanted, if he allowed it? *Would he want me?* a treacherous voice whispers.

The two men discuss matters of the fields surrounding Quinnar.

"The plants do not grow. The soil is like ash," the lord says.

"The queen has only just recharged the throne," Eldas replies calmly. "Give things time."

"Queen Alice did not need time."

"Queen Alice had one hundred years to perfect her abilities."

"We might not have one hundred years before Quinnar starves if the fields don't become viable."

"I know these are tense times. But you must be patient." Eldas's voice remains calm, but I hear a protective edge.

"Tell that to the people who have hunger gnawing at their stomachs. Who have been foraging in the barren landscape for nuts and edible roots for months!" The man throws out his hands. Then he pauses, and bows low. "Forgive me, Your Majesty, for speaking out of turn."

"Do not let it happen again," Eldas says with dangerous softness. I lean toward the wall as I catch a glimpse of the type of ruler he is—of the harsh man I first met. "I will open the granary stores of the castle. You'll have an allotment of three wagons. Divide as you think best."

The man steps backwards, bowing and mumbling thank yous the entire way to the back exit. Rinni squeezes my hand and we slip out and down the stairs. She doesn't hesitate before opening the side door to the throne room.

"Your Majesty?" she says.

"Rinni? You know I—" Eldas's eyes shift and the initial scowl he wore drops the moment he sees me. Hook bounds past, rushing over to the throne. Eldas frowns slightly, but his hands bury into the fur on either side of Hook's face. "What's happening? What's wrong?"

"I need to talk with you about something." I approach him. Eldas's eyes flick to the back doors that are obscured by the iron screen. "I know you have other people you're meeting with, but—"

"You are my priority," he says, almost like it's a decree. I fight a blush. "What is it?"

"Two things. Foremost, Aria."

"What has she done now?"

"Nothing, explicitly… But I don't trust her," I start.

"I looked into Aria personally following the incident in the city," Rinni says.

"I know. But it's something other than that. I think she's—" I stop myself short. I promised Harrow I wouldn't betray his trust. Eldas arches his eyes. "I think she's perhaps involved in something."

"I don't think she's capable of attacking the crown." Rinni frowns.

"Maybe nothing that serious, but still serious?" I dance around the topic. "I don't know what. But she seems suspicious."

"Luella," Eldas says thoughtfully, descending from the throne. His hands are folded behind his back. He's the model of a king but the voice of a friend—of... I dare not think of what else my name on his tongue sounds like. "You are still tired from the throne. I know it's a toll."

"That's the second thing...but I'll finish the first by saying, look into Aria, *please*. She's going to Carron. She has connections with the fae. And ever since the fae delegation was here, bad things have happened to the royal family—Harrow's suspicious illness, my kidnapping."

"Your kidnapping was performed by a rogue fae group—Acolytes of the Wild Wood—that's trying to claim the fae throne. They'll do anything to show their power...except exposing where their leaders hide," Rinni says.

"And Harrow has always been trouble. His illness is hardly more than a night of too much indulgences." Eldas sighs with a note of finality. I want to scream. I don't know how else I can spell it out for them.

"I don't think Harrow's—" I don't get to finish before Eldas keeps speaking.

"Now what is the second thing related to the throne?"

I hadn't come here for this. But after what I heard, I can't ignore it. "I need to sit on it again."

"Luella—"

"Now." I lock eyes with Eldas and see apprehension tempered with what I'd dare say is admiration. "I overheard the discussion. Your people need fertile fields and forests filled with game."

"You're still too weak."

"I'm strong enough."

He takes a step forward and his hands release from his back to scoop up mine. I'm shocked he's touching me in front of Rinni. The tender expression on his face is one I never thought I'd see in the daylight, and certainly not around others.

"I can't risk something happening to you."

"For the sake of Midscape?" I smile weakly.

"For…" He hesitates. I wait expectantly, but whatever it is he intended to say, he's not going to be forthright with it. So I retreat to where the topics are safe—our responsibilities.

"This is my duty," I say softly. His eyes widen slightly. "As much as looking after Capton, it is my duty to look after Midscape."

"Very well, but sit for only a little," he relents.

I give a nod and he releases my hands. I brush past him and I think I see him twitch, as though he's resisting the urge to reach for me. Something in me aches for him, to allow Eldas to envelop me in his arms so that I can leech whatever strength I'm able.

But I don't stop.

I head right for the throne and brace myself for the pain that's about to follow.

For two weeks, I dance with the throne.

I wake and take breakfast in my room as I try and read through the journals. But by the second week, I'm too tired for reading. Eldas begins to eat breakfast with me as well, reading nonstop. I wonder if he's compensating for my fatigue. He never says much—as though he knows I am too tired for pleasant conversation—so I hope he somehow knows I am grateful for his silent, reassuring presence.

On the days that I am strong enough, I return to the laboratory. Willow expresses worry for my sunken cheeks and the slowly lengthening shadows underneath my eyes. But I make no complaints.

I don't want anyone to know just how empty the throne is leaving me. I can hardly trust Eldas with that truth. Every time I am honest with him, his expression darkens, and I can almost see more worry blooming in the grim gardens of his mind.

No matter what, I make sure I am strong enough to keep good on my promise to Harrow, crafting jars of teas and powders to help with his constitution. As I suspected, he was in worse shape after the night with Aria. But he's defensive the moment I try and even make a pass at the topic.

I never find out if he gave in to glimmer again.

At the end of the second week, I lie in bed awake, staring up at the ceiling. My skin is too heavy. My joints ache. My hair has lost its luster.

The throne is killing me. It is making up for what I don't have in magic with my life itself.

"There has to be a way to stop it," I whisper into the air. "I *have to* stop it."

Repeating that mantra, I free myself from the warm covers of my bed and shuffle out to my desk. The journals are spread across every flat surface in the main room of my apartments. Notes in both my and Eldas's script scribbled between them. But there's nothing useful there. We've been through them countless times now and have found nothing.

I think of the statue, of the first queen who made the redwood throne and helped make the Fade. If only I had her journal—or the journals of those who came after. Perhaps I'd be able to piece together the final part of this grand picture I'm missing.

Then, an idea strikes me.

A knight is posted at my door. I vaguely recognize him from the legion that came to collect me from Capton. Rinni has been pulling people from her core squadron to guard me whenever she cannot due to duty or necessity—like sleep.

The man startles at my presence, but dips his head.

"I'm going for a walk," I declare. "Hook, stay here and guard the room." The wolf obliges and the guard follows behind me as I lead us to a large hall occupied by ghosts.

I stare at the tarps placed over every piece of furniture purchased by the past queens. Someday, my desk, my chair, the small table, and the settee Eldas slept on will be neatly stacked in here and covered like forgotten tombstones. Moonlight streams through the high windows of the ballroom. Where the light lands is washed bone white. Where it doesn't is shrouded in an eerie gray.

The knight stands at the entrance as I wander into the maze of furniture. Around halfway through, I grab a fistful of fabric, yanking it off. Dust rises in a plume and I cough.

The glittering motes settle back on the couch, shimmering in the moonlight, almost like the frost of elf magic.

I discard the tarp on the floor and keep moving back. It's as if I'm revealing these forgotten queens once more to the world. They sacrificed too much to be pushed into a corner of the castle and a lone shelf in the laboratory. I find desks, dining tables, sofas of all shapes and sizes. The fashions change from the utilitarian style the cabinetmaker crafted for me to more ornate, gilded swirls. I walk back through time as told by the changing design sense of Quinnar.

Dusty confetti rains around me as I yank at the tarps. I finally make it to the back of the room, where a final piece is pushed against the far wall. If there's any lingering old journals of the first five queens, this is the last place I could think to look for them. A line of fabric litters the floor behind me, furniture exposed. Taking tarp in both fists, I pull and expose a long writing desk.

A loud creaking fills the air. The desk groans as if the tarp was the only thing holding the time-worn and worm-eaten wood together. With a snap, the wood comes apart and the whole piece comes crashing down.

Jumping back and coughing, I try and avoid the bugs that scuttle out, dashing across the floor. As the sawdust settles, I look at the pile of broken wood and splinters.

"Sorry." I'm not sure if I'm apologizing to the once desk, or the memory of the queen. A wave of sorrow passes through me, as if this desk was the last thing holding her presence to this world. "I wonder whom you belonged to," I murmur.

This far back, it must've been a very early queen, pushed away and forgotten by time. I don't know what I was hoping for. Anything that survived her would be little more than sawdust by now.

Crouching down, I pick through the wood, trying to find some signifier of which queen it may have belonged to. Though I know the mission is futile. Or, at least, I think it is, until the moonlight glints off a small metal box in the framework of what once was a drawer.

"What're you?"

Lifting the box from the wreckage, I open it with delicate fingers. There's a small journal inside next to a necklace. I inspect the necklace first.

Wrapped in silver filigree is a shining black stone. Or I think it's a stone at first because of how brightly polished it is. When my fingers smooth over the pendant, I find it warm to the touch. *Wood.* A dense, black wood, polished and carefully set as a pendant on a silver chain.

Magic lives in it. Memories make my mind tingle and the back of my head itch as the power dances underneath my fingertips—*a glimpse of woman and then I'm buried.* I've seen these memories before, haven't I? There's a hazy, uncomfortable quality to the thoughts evoked by the pendant. I quickly put it down and pick up the journal.

The pages inside are at the point of crumbling under my fingers, and I abandon the idea of inspecting it here. I need to get it back to my room. I'll copy whatever notes are still legible into a fresh journal.

I carry the box with both hands and walk lightly back to my room, careful not to jostle it. The knight is silent all the way back. At least until we return to find my door slightly ajar. The man puts a hand on his sword, inching forward toward the door.

"You're dismissed." Eldas's voice breaks the cool silence. The guard bows his head and departs.

I push through the door and find Eldas on my settee, his nose in a book and one hand lazily scratching Hook's stomach. The wolf is splayed out on the floor alongside him, tongue lolling. "Some guard dog you are."

"Hook knows he has nothing to fear from me," Eldas says without looking up from the journal. I can tell he's about to finish yet another. Between us, we've almost read everything there is twice, which makes the contents of the box all the more exciting. "And hello to you too."

"To what do I owe the honor of your presence, Your Majesty?"

I use the title with a bit of jest and Eldas doesn't bother hiding his amusement. It quickly wavers when he looks up at me. I imagine I'm a bit harrowing to look at right now.

"I came to check on you," he says smoothly.

"Check on me?"

"I've done it once or twice, I admit. Usually when I have something keeping me awake that I wish to discuss. Or when I'm plagued with nightmares of fae kidnappers stealing you from your bed." I shudder and banish the thought by admiring him. There's something about Eldas tonight. Something... *Oh*, his hair is pulled back. He's corded it loosely at the nape of his neck. Fine strands slip the tie and frame his face, resting lightly against his collarbone and chest. "Fortunately, I heard you coming up the hall and let myself in."

"Do you make a habit of letting yourself in when you come to check on me?" I arch my eyebrows.

"You did say I would be welcome anytime."

"I did, but I didn't think you would be stepping into my room when I'm sleeping." I give him a pointed look that earns me a chuckle.

"I assure you, most of the time I come to talk in the off chance you're awake, or just to reassure myself no one has spirited you away. I don't linger and I've never touched you while you slumbered." He considers this, then adds, "Well, once, the blanket had slipped off your shoulders and you looked cold."

"I see." I wish I had a better response. I suspect I should be more disconcerted by the notion of him checking in on me, but I find it reassuring. The idea of a fae spiriting me away in the night is now in my mind, too. I cross to the desk. I hear him move behind me as I gently set the box down.

"What did you sneak off to steal from my castle?"

"I didn't steal anything," I insist quickly.

He laughs and the sound makes my toes curl. It's a rough and unused sound. But not unpleasant in the slightest. "Everything in this castle is yours, Luella. You can't steal from yourself."

My nails dig lightly against the metal. *Everything here is mine.* There's too much in those four words to unpack right now.

"In any case, I found it in the ballroom of old queens' furniture."

"Ballroom of old queens' furniture?" He tilts his head to the side.

"Don't tell me...first the journals and now I know something *else* about this castle that you don't?"

"It's a very large castle." He gives a nod to the box. "Are you going to open it?"

"Perhaps. Say please?"

"Kings don't say *please*." He looks at me through his long lashes with a lazy smirk, arms folded across his chest. I lament all the previous opportunities I've missed to appreciate the way his muscled arms strain against the tight tailoring of his sleeves up close.

"Technically, you just did. So close enough, I guess." He rolls his eyes at me and I tear away my gaze, trying to focus as I open the box.

"A necklace and a journal... May I?" His hand hovers over the necklace.

"Go ahead. The journal is very fragile, though. I brought it back so I could transcribe whatever I can before the pages disintegrate."

"You won't need to worry about that." Eldas turns the necklace over in his hands and sets it aside. I can't tell for certain, but I suspect he doesn't feel the same sensations I did when my fingers came in contact with the polished wood. The only explanation that I can think for why is that the necklace holds some of the queen's magic—intrinsically different from Eldas's.

"And why is that?"

Rather than answering, Eldas stares intently at the journal. His eyes flash a pale blue and the temperature in the room plummets. As he lifts his hand, a blue shimmer traces the outlines of his fingers. It condenses in a blink. One second, his hand is empty, the next his fingers have closed around an identical journal.

"True name duplication," I say, taking the journal from him and remembering the rack of lamb he created during our dinner.

"You may need a couple to get through all the pages. But this way you won't destroy the original."

"Thank you." It's a thoughtful gesture, one I deeply appreciate.

"It's the least I can do." A frown tugs at the corners of his lips. He shakes his head. More strands of hair slip out of the loose knot at the nape of his neck and I barely resist the urge to tuck them behind his ear. "I've tried to read all these journals to understand your magic, but I still have yet to grasp even the beginning of it. Which means I have no idea how to help you."

"You—"

"You're such an enigma to me, Luella," he whispers longingly.

There are volumes there in that simple statement. We hold each other by gaze alone as my heart threatens to rip itself from my chest and fall at his feet like a humble offering. I take a slow, tense breath.

"Eldas, you do more than enough," I whisper.

Eldas, his lean frame washed in moonlight, a shadow given form and outlined by the soft glow of my room's lamplight... As I look at him, I'm reminded once more that he really is the most handsome man I have ever laid eyes on. And I have wasted half my time with him frittering away my hours on projects and missions that will keep me from him.

Would it be so bad if you stayed? a tentative voice in the back of my mind poses. *You could stay here, with him, forever.*

But then I see the redwood throne picking at my bones, scraping me raw until I wither and there is nothing left to be with him. I see a life hollowed out until I don't even have the energy to want him any longer.

I see my mother and her tear-streaked face as I left. I see my parents alone at their table. I see Emma on the ground, dying from an attack that won't abate. I imagine kindly Mr. Abbot coming to my shop on instinct, only to remember I'm gone. All of Capton, my home, my patients—my duty to them and, by extension, Midscape— pull on one side of my heart.

Eldas pulls on the other.

No matter what, I won't survive becoming the Human Queen intact.

"I had an idea of something I'd like to do for you—something that might help you."

"What is it?" I shift to face him. It places me a half step closer. My attention drifts toward his lips. I can think of several things I'd like for him to do to "help" me.

His every touch these past few weeks has been agony. Agony

because my skin is ablaze from the redwood throne. Agony because I can feel him holding back coupled with the stinging memory of his kiss. I can feel him shying from whatever it is growing between us.

"My brother, Drestin, his wife is with child," he says awkwardly.

"Oh, congratulations." I try not to let my surprise at this sudden revelation, and shift in tone, diminish my sincerity. This wasn't where I was hoping things were headed.

"Yes, he's very excited." The ghost of a smile crosses Eldas's mouth. Longing taints any sweetness there is to it. I wonder if he's imagining himself as a father-to-be. "In any event, his wife will come to term right around the coronation. Naturally, they won't be coming."

"Understandable."

"Yes, and as the brother of the king, he has leeway in such matters that other lords may not be given." I resist the urge to say that any lord should be allowed to be home for the birth of his child. Luckily, Eldas continues before I risk insulting his people and their ways. "But he has offered to host us at Westwatch before the coronation. It's his way of an apology, and trying to endear himself to the new queen." Eldas glances at me. "I haven't told him that you will be gone soon."

Don't look at me with such longing, I want to beg. I can already hear the stress fractures forming in my heart. They crackle like ice too thin. They crackle like the feelings he wove in me without me realizing.

"You think I'll actually manage to do it?" I run my finger along the spine of the journal.

"If anyone can, it's you," Eldas says softly, his voice deep with emotion. "And you're right in that it must be done. The queen's power is diminishing... I cannot take another day of you dying before my eyes. The cycle must end and you have to leave."

My breath catches in my throat. He worries for me. He's doubled down on his support of my mission to end the cycle. Yet the way he says those words, almost expectant, almost waiting to see if I contradict him—like there's some way out of this that will allow me to stay...

A voice whispers in the back of my mind, *This is what you wanted, isn't it?*

Well, Luella, is it?

"In any case, I don't have a good reason to reject my brother," Eldas continues in the wake of my silence.

"Will the throne be all right if I leave?"

"We'll charge it once more before we depart," he answers solemnly. "But regardless of Midscape's situation, you need a break from it. You won't be effective if you keep pushing like this."

I can't argue. Just like I still can't bring my eyes to his. "I'll pack my things. When do we leave?"

"In a week." One week more to work, then we travel for who knows how long. Another week, maybe? That will only leave me about two more weeks before the coronation and my deal with Eldas running out. "Unless…"

"Unless?" I look to him and he seems startled by my sudden eagerness.

"Unless you and I leave a little early," he says gingerly, eyes searching.

"Where would we go?"

"There's something I think you would enjoy and that should rejuvenate you."

"Is that all you'll tell me?"

"Yes, I think so." The corners of his lips are pulled into a smile. "I was denied showing you my castle. Willow beat me to sharing the conservatory with you." I resist informing him that he *could've* shown me the castle at any point in those early days. But things between us were different then. It's astounding how much they changed in a handful of weeks. "I would like to share this with you."

His fingertips trail lightly from my shoulder to my elbow, resting there as he waits for my response. I shiver, but not from the cold. Suddenly I'm burning. I realize I want that lazy touch of his *everywhere*. I want his icy fingers on my arms, my legs, my stomach…

"Yes." The word is almost a croak. My tongue has gone heavy and useless. "I would like to see this surprise."

His face lights up brighter than the dawn rising on his cheeks the morning he stayed on my settee. "Then we will leave in the morning."

"In the morning? That soon?"

"It'll take about a day to get there. And then another day out to Westwatch." Eldas steps away, starting for the door with almost giddy strides. My chest bubbles at the sight of him like this— knowing that I had a part in making him so happy. "And I think you'll want to spend more than a night there."

"All right." I can't help but laugh. "I'll pack my things tonight."

"And I will see you at first light."

twenty-nine

A GILDED CARRIAGE AWAITS US IN THE LONG TUNNEL THAT STRETCHES UNDERNEATH THE CASTLE AND THROUGH THE MOUNTAIN RANGE SURROUNDING QUINNAR. Eldas informed me when he came to collect me that we would be riding by carriage. "I want you to know how you could get there without me," he explained when I questioned why we wouldn't just Fadewalk.

It only made me more curious as to where "there" is.

I've brought only one bag with me—a piece of luggage I found in my closet. My single bag is loaded by the footmen onto the back of the carriage on top of several others.

I cast a look Eldas's way but hold comment until we're in the carriage. "Do you think you packed enough?"

"I suspected you would pack too little. So I was certain to have the servants pack extra for you, just in case. You can thank me when you're appropriately dressed in Westwatch." Eldas settles into his seat and I stifle a laugh at his playful smugness. The carriage looked large enough on the outside. But, somehow, our thighs are still touching on the bench within. There's another seat opposite, but he chose to sit next to me.

I try and ignore the solid presence of him at my side. The effort becomes easier as the carriage jostles forward, plodding down the long tunnel and emerging into the sunlight at the far end. I push aside the heavy velvet curtains, pressing my nose to the glass as we emerge along the winding road between the fields I've seen for weeks from the windows of my room.

"Here," Eldas says. He leans over me and what was once the touch of his thigh is now half his body. I press against the far wall and windows, pretending to focus on the scenery more than his dexterous hands tying back the curtains. Eldas shifts back in his seat and retrieves a worn journal from the small satchel he brought into the carriage.

"What's that?" I ask.

He chuckles. "I thought you were more interested in the scenery?"

"I'm most interested in you." As soon as I say those words, I contrast them with a sudden jerk of my head back to the windows to hide the deep scarlet blush rising up my neck, rounding my ears, and painting across my cheeks. I wait for him to make a smart remark back. But he spares me. Though I do hear the soft huff of a chuckle that turns my midsection to jelly.

"Would you believe me if I said that the queens aren't the only ones to keep journals?"

"I'd believe it." My face is starting to cool as I'm distracted by the meandering landscape. Fields line up against pastures with farmhouses wedged between them. In the distance, I can see the land rising up into hills. There's the faint silhouette of a keep on the crest of one in the distance.

"My father impressed on me the importance of cataloging my thoughts and keeping journals," Eldas continues. "I've actually been comparing the journals of the kings against the queens to see if I can glean anything important for our research."

Our research. Not mine alone. Not anymore. He really has committed to this mission. I bite at the insides of my cheeks and wait before speaking for my stomach to untwist itself.

"So, what I hear is that you've been holding out on me?"

He laughs again. I have never heard Eldas laugh so much before. As the gray and hollow castle shrinks behind us, it seems the empty void in his chest—the cold and bitter pit that I couldn't traverse when we first met—is vanishing to nothing.

"Yes, Luella. I have been holding out on you. After all I have given you I thought it would be good sport to deny you something now."

"I knew it." I shift in my seat, trying to find a comfortable position after bumps in the road jostle the carriage and nearly place me in Eldas's lap. "Why have you given me so much?" I ask softly.

"*Hmm?*" Eldas's pen has stilled. I'm amazed he could write anything at all with the swaying.

"I never expected you to be the doting husband."

"And that is the true crime in all of this, isn't it?"

I'd meant to make him feel better with the remark. But his sour and tired response has me looking for his eyes, his face. What expression was he wearing when he said that? Whatever it was, I missed it. I was too focused on my skirts and now Eldas is looking out the windows of the door at his left.

"Well, this isn't exactly a normal situation."

"Not for you," he admits. He's been training for this his whole life. Though, little good that seemed to do in actually preparing him for a Human Queen.

"No, not for me..." I bite back a sigh and look out my own windows. If only the throne hadn't been trying to kill me. If only I hadn't been at the end of a three-thousand-year line of queens. If only I had been stronger, or more prepared, or was still able to wish to be queen like someone trained for this from a young age might. "I wish everything was different," I whisper aloud.

I hadn't meant for him to hear. But, with those long ears, I should have known better.

"I don't," Eldas says, just as soft. I have to strain to hear him over the creaking carriage.

"You don't?" I look over to him, but he's still turned toward the window.

"If things were different, you wouldn't have been you." He finally looks back to me. His once icy eyes are now tepid pools as inviting and warm as the creeks I would strip bare and swim in underneath the redwood trees deep in the forests around the temple. "And I've found I'm very fond of exactly the woman you are. I wouldn't change a single thing."

I don't know how to respond to that, so I don't. I peel my eyes away from his and look to the window. Eldas returns to his journal. And I silently thank the carriage for being noisy enough that I think it'll hide my racing heart.

"Luella," Eldas whispers. "Luella, we're here."

At some point I dozed off. With how exhausted the throne has made me, I can't seem to sleep enough these days. I blink slowly and near darkness greets me. Eldas must've pulled the curtains because they are now shut tight. What light sneaks through is honey colored and dimming. The copy of the journal Eldas made me is in my lap, mostly unread still.

And my head…

I straighten quickly. "Sorry," I mumble. At some point I slouched in my sleep and my temple ended up on his shoulder.

Eldas gives me a wry smile. "It's all right." That's all he says and yet I find myself trying to read between every word.

Get yourself under control, my mind commands. But I've already discovered my heart is a poor listener.

The king knocks on the door and it swings open. He steps out first and then turns to assist me. I take his cool hand, noticing that his touch is no longer bitter and icy. Perhaps something has changed in him. Maybe I've become accustomed to his magic. Or maybe it's just the fact that I've come to want those cool fingers against my skin.

"Where are we?" Gravel crunches under my feet as I step down.

The carriage is parked at the apex of a wide arc of a lane. Tall hedges round all sides and continue along the edges of what I assume is all a single piece of property. They stretch down one side of a tree-lined road.

In front of us is a quaint cottage. The thatched roof is in good condition and the wide porch in front has been freshly sanded and repainted. There's the same tang in the air that the temple has every midsummer when the Keepers spruce it up before celebrations.

"This is yours," Eldas says, guiding me forward. As we walk away, the footman gets back in the driver's sseat and spurs forward the horses attached to the carriage. "There's a town only about an hour's drive away," Eldas answers my unspoken question. "The footman will stay there since there's not room for him here."

"I see…" No servants. No attendants. Alone with Eldas in the middle of rolling hills and creeping forests nestled against the shade of a mountain that almost reminds me of home.

"Go ahead," he encourages, motioning to the door as we walk up onto the porch. "It's yours, after all."

"You keep saying that." My hand hovers on the doorknob. "But what do you mean?"

"This is the queen's cottage." Eldas smiles proudly. "It was gifted three queens before you as a private escape for Her Majesty. Close enough to Quinnar that you can make the trip within a day. Far enough that it feels like an escape. And, as I mentioned earlier, no need to depend on a king's Fadewalking to get you here. However, myself and past kings have put up strong wards around this place, so even though it is away from the castle, it is just as safe."

I open the door and behold the most adorable cottage I have ever laid eyes on.

It's like the oil paintings I would see sometimes in the Lanton markets of idyllic countrysides, promising a world most people never know. Wide beams stretch across the ceiling. I see hooks for drying herbs lining each of them, begging for greenery. The downstairs is split by a center staircase. To the left is a kitchen of large brass pots and ruddy tile; the right is a living area with seating framing a large hearth.

The wood of the banister glides smoothly under my fingers as I head upstairs. The second floor is smaller than the first and I see immediately why Eldas said there was no room for the footman. This is another single room…with a single bed.

"What do you think?" Eldas asks as I appraise the quilted blanket covering the bed.

"There's only one bed."

My remark is met with roaring laughter. "Don't worry, I'll be sleeping downstairs." He smiles, oblivious to the twinge of disappointment that stabs my side. I try to ignore the sensation too.

"But, shouldn't you—"

"I slept on the couch as a boy when I would visit Alice here." He starts downstairs again. As I follow, I notice that my bag and an extra trunk were carried up here and his things are situated in the corner of the living room.

"But you're not a boy anymore."

"And yet, I've still slept on a couch for you before."

I think back to the settee. "I didn't ask you to."

"You were weak after the throne and I was worried. What if you needed something? What if the throne sapped more power than we thought?"

I don't have a response, especially after how I was the first time I sat on the throne.

"You didn't need to ask me to look after you. I should have been doing a better job of it all along."

"I never thanked you for that."

"You never needed to thank me."

"Thank you," I insist on saying anyway.

"You're welcome." The smile that graces his lips is brief but warm. He looks out to the doors that line the back of the cottage. "Unfortunately, I think the grounds will be more impressive in the daytime. Shall we turn in for the night?"

"I'm still a little tired," I admit. Gone are the days when a long nap could keep me up all night.

"That is why we're here, so you can rest. Past queens have said they find this place rejuvenating."

"I'm sure it will be. But I don't think I'll be able to quiet my mind enough for bed yet." My thoughts are still pinned on Eldas and me here, in a scenic spot, together, alone...with one bed.

"Then perhaps a nightcap of some sweet wine will help dull any racing thoughts?" Eldas heads into the kitchen.

"Wine, not mead?" I cross over, resting my elbows on the worn butcher's block countertop. I'm momentarily entranced by Eldas rolling up his sleeves to his elbows, exposing muscular forearms beneath.

"Faeries make mead. Elves make wine. And it's a crime you've yet to try the latter." Eldas gives a wink. A *wink*. I have to sit on one of the stools so I don't fall over with shock. Is this the same Elf King

I met weeks ago? Gone is the marble and here is the man and all his glory. I hope he stays.

"Well, whose fault is that?" I ask playfully.

"Yet more blame you can lay at my feet. I will need a lifetime to make up for my previous transgressions against you." *But I only have a few more weeks,* I hear unsaid.

Eldas retrieves a dusty bottle from a lower wine rack. He moves nimbly through the kitchen. He knows exactly where the corkscrew and glasses are. His movements opening the wine are fluid, as though he's performed this task a hundred times.

"I wouldn't have expected a king to seem so...*natural* in the kitchen," I appraise.

"Even kings have hobbies." Eldas pours generously. "Alice was an incredible chef. I learned from her." I remember the plethora of cooking-related notes in her journal.

"Yet you looked so offended when I asked if you cooked our dinner a few weeks ago." That was the dinner when he kissed me. I can almost see the moment Eldas has the same thought as his movements slow to a brief pause he quickly recovers from.

"Things were different then."

"Things change quickly with us, it'd seem."

"Maybe it's because we don't have very much time." He meets my eyes as he sets down the bottle next to the glasses. There's desperation there. I know the look of a man who wants something. But I've never felt my body react in such a way to that look. I'm aflame, heat pouring into my lower stomach faster than wine from the bottle. Every part of me is so sensitive that just the shifting of my clothes is almost too much.

"You—" I clear my throat. "—you came here with Alice?" I try and guide the topic back off us as I accept my glass from him.

The wine within is a deep plum color that seems to swirl with twilight as I tilt my glass. I wonder if a normal human would find it ominous. I wonder if I should. Instead, I'm entranced.

What grapes went into this? What other fruits? What process gave it that magical color? I have a twinge of regret when I realize I likely won't be in Midscape long enough to even scratch the surface of this magical world.

"I did, as often as I was allowed. It was one of my few retreats as much as it was hers."

"I still don't understand… Why do the elves insist on keeping a young man locked up just because he's an heir?" It seems so unfair.

"There are logical reasons, such as protection or ensuring he doesn't shame himself by getting into trouble. Most likely because that's just how it's always been done and whatever reasons might have been there originally have been lost to time." Eldas shrugs easily enough, but I've seen the ghostly scars on his spirit left behind by those years in solitude—his mannerisms, his looks, his hesitation and awkwardness in how to handle someone new coming into his world.

"Just like elves follow in the footsteps of their parents?" I reference Willow and Rinni.

"Humans have odd enough customs themselves. I hear you are actually allowed to have your own dreams and study for what it is you want to do, regardless of your parents and their wishes or wisdoms. Seems a bit selfish, doesn't it?" He gives a coy smirk.

I burst out laughing. "Fair. One can be just as odd as the other. Though I think the humans win on this one." Eldas chuckles and holds out his glass of wine for a toast, and I raise mine to hover next to his. "What're we toasting to, this time?" I ask.

He thinks a moment. "To tomorrow."

"What's tomorrow?"

"Everything. May tomorrow hold every possibility. And may we be bold and hungry enough to take them for our own."

The toast is sincere and unscripted, unlike the last time, and I gladly clink my glass against his. The wine is warm on my lips and complements the warmth in my stomach from his sentiments. Eldas gives me a sly smile from behind his glass, one I return.

For the very first time since coming to Midscape, I realize, in this moment, I don't want to be anywhere but here.

thirty

DAWN BREAKS CLEAR AND CRISP. It winks at me through the small second-floor window opposite the foot of the bed. I roll over, yanking the covers around me.

My head throbs a bit. Likely a little too much elf wine last night. I thought I was drunk on conversation. But I know now that I was just a bit drunk. Unfortunately, unlike last time, there was no drunken kissing to be had.

I crack open my eyes, remembering where I am. This room evokes memories of my attic back home. From the exposed wood of the floors and walls, to the dust that hangs in the air like what I once imagined faeries to look like.

Five more minutes, I would've begged back then. Sleeping in for five minutes was a pleasure. I had work to do those days. There would be fishermen who would come and pick things up for themselves or their families before heading out to sea for the morning. I knew when every customer would show up and always had to be preparing for the surprise walk-ins throughout the day.

Now… I'm not sure where I'm meant to be.

Is it the throne? Is it Capton? Is it with Eldas? The uncertainty fills me with shame. I should know unequivocally where I belong; I always have. The duty I've always trusted guides me. So many have sacrificed for me—my friends, parents, all of Capton. Any hesitance feels like a betrayal.

"Don't do this," I quietly beg my heart. I press the heels

of my palms into my eyes until I see stars. I didn't ask for this, for any of it. And now…now there's a part of me who doesn't entirely want to give it all up. Half of my heart is growing roots here, as deep as the redwood throne's. There's so much of this world I have yet to see and explore. So much magic that I could delight in if I dared.

I hear the sizzle of something hitting a hot pan and drop my hands. The second the smell of bacon hits my nose, my stomach growls loudly and I'm out of bed. If I must berate myself, I can do so on a full belly.

Wrapping a silken robe around my nightgown, I tiptoe down the stairs. I knew the house was too small for any kind of attendants. I also knew that Eldas said he enjoyed cooking. But there's something entrancing about actually *seeing* the man working in the kitchen.

He's in a simple cotton tunic, thin and humbly made. It has a wide neck and exposes his strong collarbones. Of course, it's long sleeved, but he's once more rolled the sleeves up. A canvas apron has been tied around his narrow waist, colored by stains old and new alike. It hides the tight-fitting black trousers underneath. Inky strands of hair have freed themselves from the knot he's placed half his tresses in to frame his jaw and neck. The other half of his hair moves in sheets of midnight.

I rest my chin in my palm and watch him move. He's graceful, unhesitant, and easy. *Comfortable*, I realize at once. This is the look of a man in his element. His brow isn't weighted by the iron crown, but rather furrowed slightly with focus. Eldas's eyes are intent and intense. But he wears a small smile on his lips as though every turn of the spoon and flip of the spatula delights him.

It's almost impossible to imagine that this is the same severe man I first met in the temple all those weeks ago. *And he's your husband*, I remind myself. That prompts me to take yet another look at him in yet another way.

He's as agonizingly handsome as I've always known him to be…as I've rarely allowed myself to appreciate. His attractiveness has disarmed me on many an occasion. But permitting myself to appreciate it *as a wife would* has my thighs tensing.

Some women would kill to be you. To have all this, I scold myself. *And you want to run away.*

It's as if he senses my turmoil. Because he looks at me with those stunning blue eyes, startled to find me. I try and plaster on a smile and nonchalantly continue down the stairs, as though I weren't just shamelessly admiring him.

"Good morning."

"Good morning," he repeats. "How did you sleep?"

"Very well. The past queens were right; this place is surprisingly refreshing after the redwood throne." I neglect to mention the dull throb in my head. The last thing I want is for him to suggest we skip the wine tonight, given how delicious it was. "And you?"

"Excellently." He smiles.

I glance at the couch. I have my doubts about that. Sure, it would be fine for a boy. But there's no way he can spread out there. "You can have the bed tonight. We can swap."

"Luella—"

"It's only fair."

Eldas has a mischievous glint to his eyes. "I am the king; I think I decide what's fair."

"I think you're wrong. The queen should have a say as well."

"If she insists, I'd be a fool to fight her."

"Glad you've finally realized." I assume the same seat as last night, admiring the spread he's prepared. "You weren't joking about enjoying cooking."

"It's not much."

"Humility doesn't suit you." I flash him a teasing grin and begin to dig in. There are rashers of bacon, fried eggs, hunks of sourdough grilled on the skillet, and every thing tastes better than the last.

"Slow down, no one is going to take it from you," he says.

"I can't help but notice you piling your plate just as heavy."

Eldas merely grins.

When we're finished, Eldas loads the dishes into a deep sink and sends me upstairs to dress. I try and move as quickly as possible. My mother always insisted that whoever cooked in the house didn't clean. But I'm too late. By the time I'm back downstairs in my own shirt and trousers he's drying his hands on his apron, a slightly smug satisfaction alight in his eyes.

"Cooking and now cleaning?" I arch my brows. "Are you really the same Eldas as in the castle?"

"Here I am free of the castle and free of its burdens. This place is an escape for me as well." He stands a little straighter, as if no longer crushed by the weight of his position or trauma those walls haunt him with. I narrowly resist saying that he should just live here, for good. "I think it's time to show you the grounds."

We leave through the double doors at the back of the kitchen. Creeping vines cover the entirety of a pergola, offering a shaded area over a patio. The pavers spill over a ledge, down a staircase, and wrap around a pool of sparkling blue. I walk over to the low stone wall next to the stairs.

"This place is..." The words escape as a whisper.

To the left of the pool is a copse of trees surrounded by gardens. They terrace upward and into the mountain until they're entirely claimed by the forest at the mountain's foot. To the right of the pool is a field of wildflowers have taken over. There are more gardens at the far edge and I can see the sheen of water between the rows of plants that I suspect will only grow in swampier environments.

"It's yours," Eldas reminds me again. His breath moves the edges of my hair at the nape of my neck. My whole body aches at the sound of his voice so close.

Before me is a garden I couldn't have dreamed about if I tried. Behind me is a house, simple and comfortable. A house that I would've longed for if I'd ever thought of moving to the countryside.

"It's wonderful."

"I'm glad you like it. The Human Queens have tended it alongside the Elf King. These plants were transplanted from the Natural World. Alice said they always helped restore her power when she couldn't return to the Natural World."

"You can transplant things between worlds?" I arch my eyebrows.

"It takes significant magic and tending, but yes. The Natural World to Midscape, and the reverse." Eldas nods. "Hidden away in the Natural World is a mirror of this garden. Alice told me it keeps the plants alive here and can help rejuvenate the Queen—why I thought coming here might help you. She always said a bit of the magic from her world flowed through, enough to make her strong."

Mirror—*balance*, is what he means. It's natural magic—the queen's magic—suspended between the worlds. Could this somehow be used for the seasons? That's a lot more magic than just keeping some plants alive. But it could be a start…couldn't it?

The palm of his hand lands on the small of my back, distracting me. I stand a little straighter.

"Go on, explore."

We spend the entire day wandering the grounds. It takes all of my energy not to tear apart the cottage for a clean journal so I can begin cataloging all the various plants and noting their needs. *This is a dream*, I begin to tell myself. It's a beautiful dream that I will, eventually, wake from. But for now, I will enjoy it. I will delight in the lush gardens, the wild overgrown brush, and the magic that seems to hang as happily in the air as the eager pollinators buzzing from flower to flower.

"What's up there?" The gravel pathway that snakes between raised beds winds between the trees, slipping into the dense forest and shadow of the mountain in the late twilight.

"The last thing I would like to show you."

"What is it?" I demand, somewhat firmly. The path reminds me of the temple and that long walk that took me across the Fade.

"It leads to the Fade." He affirms my suspicion without realizing.

"But I thought that Capton was the only entrance of the Fade?"

Eldas sighs. It's the only indication I have that he's shouldering a burden of worry I don't understand. "Capton is where the Human Queen is chosen from. The act of doing so honors the ancient pact made between the elves and humans, as the first queen's home was on that isle and the first keystone was placed there—where the Fade itself unfurled from. However…that is not the *only* point where the Fade can be crossed."

"Really?" I'd heard whispers in Lanton from time to time… traders spreading rumors about vampir attacks to the south or ships going down in the north due to beasts with wild magic terrorizing the seas. But I thought those stories were like all the other stories of magic from my childhood—grossly exaggerated and grounded in more fiction than fact.

"May I show you?" He holds out his hand. "I will Fadewalk us there, if you'll allow? Otherwise, it's a long trek."

"You may." I take his hand and the dark mist that is his power envelops us both.

We step through twilight and into a realm of swirling darkness. Every time I walk with Eldas across the Fade it becomes a little easier than the last. Still, this place between worlds—not quite one or the other—makes invisible bugs scuttle across my skin.

I do not belong here, and the entity that is the Fade makes the fact known.

"I recognize this place." It's the same mossy clearing I stumbled on with Hook. A circle of smaller stones rings a large tablet at the center of a small rise.

"You think you do," Eldas corrects. "You've never stepped foot here before."

I look at the stone and its faded writing. "Another keystone of the Fade?"

"Indeed." The shadows swirl around Eldas as he moves toward the stone. They reach for him hungrily. Tendrils curl around him with eager embraces.

No, I realize. The Fade does not reach for him. It resonates *from* him. I was blind to the fact the last time we were here. But now that I understand his magic, I can see the corona of midnight darkness that radiates off of him in waves with his every movement.

Eldas reaches a hand to the stone and a pulse of magic thrums out from him. His power no longer rattles me with fear. It echoes in a hollow, needy portion of me that cries out to be filled.

A starry twilight illuminates the engraved words. Writing I don't understand shines in tandem with Eldas's eyes. The power sinks into the earth and the Fade around us thickens.

He pulls his hand away and his shoulders sag slightly.

"It is the Elf King's obligation to tend all the keystones across the Fade. We charge them with our power to ensure that the Fade remains strong. The keystones weaken with time, and when they are weak...the Fade can be crossed by lesser creatures."

"One man can't keep up with all the keystones." I surmise that's how the rumors of magical creatures wandering my world from time to time were started.

Eldas shakes his head grimly. "Midscape is a fragile balance, pulled taut with time. Generation after generation, we hold our breath wondering if these will be the final years of peace. Most kings focus on the Veil. Keeping the order of life and death is far more important than keeping humans in the Natural World and those of wild magic here."

"Let me help," I offer before I can think better of it.

He chuckles and his tired eyes sweep from the stone to mine. "Certainly, right after you somehow manage to break the cycle of queens by creating naturally occurring seasons in this unnatural world. And then fundamentally change your magic to become something that can manipulate the Fade."

I purse my lips, not wanting my gut to get the better of my brain. Eldas stands before me, his eyes fading to their natural shade of blue as the spike of magic dissipates. He lifts up a hand and slowly traces his fingers down my jawline.

His hair is a cascade of night, blending in with his clothes, becoming eclipsed by the living darkness around us. The dusty pallor of his skin has grayed, as if the shroud of death has covered him. He has one foot in the Beyond. I have one foot in the world of life.

The only thing that is linking us together is that trailing touch igniting me.

"Besides, you will leave me the moment you are successful. You wouldn't be able to stay and help."

You could stay, the voice in my mind is now screaming. *Stay with him!*

Is this what I really want? Or am I swept up in the moment? Perhaps he has truly transported me to yet another new world with a mere carriage ride; he's taken me to a place where my guard is down and I can pretend this will all work out. Somewhere I can ignore that I am allowing my heart to be set up to be broken.

Or do I actually feel nothing for him? Is all of this yearning and gnawing desire somehow the magic of the Human Queen trying to ensure its own preservation by driving me to stay with him?

I press my eyes closed and take a quivering breath. I don't know the answers. But I want to. I *need* to. If I stay in Midscape, it must be *my* choice. I must finally make a choice, of my own volition, free of the influences of any man, with where I stand. I have to take my own advice and choose what I want for myself, not what others want for me. And it can never be my choice if I don't succeed in breaking the cycle. What I really want might not even matter if I fail.

"I'm here now," I whisper, finally opening my eyes to look up at the face of my antithesis. "Kill the thoughts of tomorrow. Let's live for today."

I don't entirely know what I'm saying. But I know what I want in this moment—*him*. Eldas's eyes widen a fraction and that's how I know he hears.

I tilt my head up slightly. His hand still hovers on my skin. His knuckles hook my chin.

"Kiss me again," I demand breathlessly. "Kiss me like you did that night in the castle. Let's give in to this waking dream, Eldas."

"No," he murmurs. Everything in me shudders at his denial. But then he pulls me toward him, snaring me with the lightest touch imaginable. "I will not kiss you like I did then." My breath hitches. Through the fan of my lashes I watch him lean forward. "I will kiss you better."

His other arm fabricates from the darkness, suddenly around my midsection. Eldas envelops me as he pulls my body to his for the first time. His lean form is long and firm against me. My hands, awkward and inexperienced, land on his hips, quivering like skittish birds about to take flight.

Everything aches in that moment. The second his breath is on my face is the longest second of my life. I was right when I realized all those months ago that wanting to kiss someone makes all the difference.

And I have never wanted to kiss someone more than Eldas. This is not drunken desire. This is not loneliness or unattended needs.

I want *him* to kiss me. Now. Here. Forever.

He holds my eyes until the last moment. His lips meet mine and I burn.

I let out a whimper. He pulls me closer, heeding my unspoken command, trying to smother the blazing agony in me with his cool body. His tongue runs along my lips, seeking entry, and I grant it. Eldas deepens the kiss with cruel laziness.

More, my body demands with a need that makes me blush. I want his hands to move. I want those long fingers to brush down the curve of my neck, my breast, my hip. I want to feel things I've only known in concept. I want him to teach and guide me down all these carnal paths I've yet to walk.

But, to my supreme displeasure, he pulls away. His lips have a wet shine in the darkness and they curl into an unreadable smile. Color has flooded his face, giving it a natural hue once more.

"Luella," he whispers, husky and deep. "You're glowing."

I realize it's true. A barely perceptible glow covers my skin and dances with the darkness. Our powers radiate together, mingling, wrapping around each other in a dance of opposites.

"Then," I reply with a sultry tone I wasn't aware I could make, "I think you should keep kissing me. So that we may properly investigate this strange phenomena."

His smile turns into a smug smirk and Eldas leans forward once more with hooded eyes. "My queen, ever the researcher."

My queen. The words make me weak in the knees. They no longer fill me with fear. *My queen*. Those two words are almost as sweet as losing myself in the taste of his mouth.

"My king," I murmur in reply. "Eldas, *my* king." I am his, and he is mine.

Eldas holds me to him with a crushing grip the moment I say his name. He presses forward and I expect us to fall to the mossy ground below. But the shadows rise around us, and we slip between worlds.

thirty-one

MY BACK SETTLES INTO THE QUILTED BLANKET THAT I LOOSELY THREW OVER MY BED THIS MORNING. The mattress sighs around me, accepting my weight and Eldas's. My arms wrap around his back, pulling him closer. I bend a knee and press my hips upward against his.

I'm clumsy, and no doubt awkward, but Eldas moves with me fluidly. He responds to my every movement with eager attention. He shifts just as I need him to and my breath hitches as he grinds against me for the first time.

Supporting himself with one hand frees the other to rove my body. I am outlined by his fingers. I am his to be molded and sculpted—his to cut from the night itself. With his index finger alone, he draws constellations into my clothing. Every point connected by a different aching need that I never knew I could feel so keenly.

His lips pull away and my eyes snap open as his teeth sink lightly into the flesh of my neck. Eldas kisses me like the creature of darkness that he is, determined to consume every last flicker of my light. Another groan slips past my lips and it fades into a pleasant sigh.

"Luella." He growls my name, as hot and needy as the exhale it's said on. I never knew my name could be such an erotic combination of sounds and caresses.

"Eldas," I respond in equal measure. He grinds against me hard. A gasp escapes me at the feeling of him.

"I can leave." Yet, as he speaks, his body contradicts him. He continues to kiss me. His hand hitches up my shirt, sliding over the plane of my stomach. How I've longed for him to touch me there again…

"Leave, and I will find you," I whisper breathlessly in reply. "Leave me here, unsatisfied and yearning, and I will hunt you down, Eldas."

His lips meet the shell of my ear and his fingers finally make their way up to my chest. The moan that his touch unleashes almost drowns out the husk of his whisper. "Oh, Luella, I would never even dream of leaving you unsatisfied or yearning."

Then, as if to make good on that promise, his lips crush against mine. His weight pushes me farther into the bed and my hands come alive with permission I didn't know they were waiting for. My nails dig into the lean muscles of his back as his hand closes around my breast.

For years, my body has been asleep. Now, like a dead limb returning to life, shocks and prickles dance across my entire being. I've never truly felt anything before now. I arch off the bed, pressing into him, begging him without words to touch me more—to give me all of these delicious desires that I have been denied.

Consume me, I want to say. But all that escapes are moans between increasingly eager kisses. The shadows darken, closing around us as he peels off my shirt. I take the opportunity to do the same and eagerly explore him with eyes, and hands, and mouth the second his broad chest is exposed.

He's initially tense at my touch. His eyes follow my hands, explore my face, waiting for some kind of reaction. The only reaction I can offer him is a mixture of awe, admiration, and desire. The ridges of his muscles are illuminated by the faint glow of our magic. The sounds he releases as my nails lightly brush over his nipples drives me wild.

I want to go slow. I want to go fast. I want everything all at once and yet want the clock to stop so I may savor every second.

I'm too distracted by the taste of his mouth to be embarrassed by my own increasing nudity. The yearning is too strong to question my hands as they tug clumsily at his belt and trousers. Eldas's fingers leave me to assist and I let out a moan that would make me blush under any other circumstances.

But I doubt nothing in this moment. My world has shrunk to pinhole focus on this man alone. This man? No. *My husband.*

Husband. The word smooths across my mind, as erotic as his caresses. It feels as right as his weight above me and his mouth upon me. This incredible, powerful being of a man is my husband. Through a twist of fate I never expected, our lives were forever entwined. I hook a leg around his hips, begging him closer with the movement.

Eldas hovers above me, his hair a waterfall of midnight that pools on the pillow around my head. His eyes study mine. I can see him probing for hesitation, waiting for me to back down.

I snake my fingers through his raven hair and pull his mouth to mine once more. There is nothing but magic and *him*. I invite both in me with a hiss and a sigh.

Eldas remains still and for a moment we simply exist, together as one. His hands caress my face as he continues to watch, waiting for yet more permission. Once I'm acclimated to him, I give a small nod and he pulls away only to quickly return again.

Our bodies move together, unrelenting. We are a chorus of gasps and moans. I never knew there were so many shades of shadow until I knew this man. He moves with all of them—through all of them—as ethereal, eternal, and incomprehensible as the Fade itself.

In that moment, we exist beyond time. We exist for every king and queen who came before us as the treaty is fulfilled in more than name. The redwood and iron thrones are finally united once more.

Somewhere distant, a clock chimes. For the second time, I wake hazy and exhausted. The events of the night before are as fresh as a hot summer's rain on my mind. They're as real as the heavy weight of Eldas's arm around my middle.

Whatever glow covered my skin faded with the night that cloaked us. I wonder if it was my magic responding to his. Or perhaps it was my magic coming forward in a misguided instinct to protect me against my eternal opposite as he took me with fierce passion.

With a sigh that almost sounds content, I let my eyes flutter closed once more and I lace my fingers with his. He returns my grip but his breathing remains level. Even in his sleep, he reaches for me. His arm tightens, as if affirming the rogue thought.

I could spend forever like this. There's no point in denying it. This prickly, awkward, and somewhat emotionally stinted man has become mine. And whether I intended to or not, I have allowed myself to become his.

But errant thoughts of what must be done—of my duty to this world and my own—finally pull me from the bed and that warm embrace. I slip out unnoticed into a gray dawn. Eldas murmurs as I grab my robe and tiptoe out of the room.

He finds me a few hours later on the terrace, overlooking the pools and the gardens. The journal he made a copy of for me is written in the old tongue. I can read it, but the words are stilted and grammar awkward, which makes for slow going. I'm searching for some kind of notion of balancing the two worlds. I can't get that thought out of my head, even now.

But when I hear the door behind me open, I know that any hope I have of focusing on this lost queen's journal has evaporated like the dew. A delightfully shirtless Eldas crosses over to where I'm sitting underneath the vine-covered arbor and sets down a steaming mug of tea.

Eldas sits in the chair opposite me and looks out over the gardens. I glance at him from the corner of my eye, but he doesn't seem to notice. His focus rests solely on the mountain's ridge. I can imagine him tracing the pathway that leads into the Fade. I wonder if he's thinking of all the other keystones that need attending to.

"Thank you," he says, finally. The words are soft and somewhat bashful. They bring a gentle heat to my cheeks.

"For last night?" I arch my eyebrows. "I should be thanking you for that as well."

He looks away, eyes distant but expression relaxed, open, tender—all the emotions I never thought him capable of. "For allowing me to feel not so alone. For showing me every magnificent side of you. For giving me something I did not deserve but will cherish forever—not just last night, but our entire time together until this moment."

When he brings his eyes back to me I don't know how to react. My heart has swollen to the point that it pushes painfully against my ribs. I bite my lip, trying to stop myself from saying something foolish.

The world hasn't changed. It's still the same. My fears, my duties still stand in complement and contrast to his own. Yet, somehow, the world seems like it's shifted, if only slightly. Like something finally clicked into place.

"I should thank you as well. Last night was exceptional." I finally reach for the steaming mug and bring it to my lips. I know half of the herbs in the infusion by scent alone, and confirm them and identify the rest by taste. "This is good," I interrupt whatever Eldas was about to say next. "Did you make this blend?"

"I wish I could take credit for it." He smiles as well and any initial awkwardness following our first night together evaporates like dew. "But, alas, I cannot, and you would likely call me out for lying the moment I tried."

I grin. "Maybe you've been keeping a secret green thumb and affinity for plants from me this whole time. You kept cooking from me, after all."

"If I had such an affinity, you think I would keep it a secret when it might endear you to me?" He chuckles. "No, this is the last of some of Alice's blend."

"Ah." I stare at the tan liquid in the mug. Mint, lime rind, dried strawberry, and camellia sinensis withered under a hot sun, all dance across my tongue. "It tastes like summer."

"Her favorite time to drink it," he affirms. "You two would've gotten along."

"It would've been nice to meet her." I take another sip. The flavor has become somewhat sad and full of yearning. "I would've had so many questions."

"Perhaps you could ask me?" Eldas runs one of his very dexterous fingers across the rim of his mug. I shift, my seat suddenly much less comfortable as the motion elicits memories of our night together.

"At this point, they would mostly be questions about my magic."

"I see." He pauses. "At *this point?*"

I take another long sip so I don't have to answer right away. I have to choose my next words carefully. "At first, I may have asked how any queen put up with this situation. How no one else was as adamant about finding a…solution."

"A way out, you mean." The words are easy enough, but there's a cool edge to his tone. One that I now easily interpret as hurt. He sees me as yet another person running away from him, condemning him to seclusion. His eyes fall to the journal on the table, almost accusing it for trying to take me away.

"A way to strengthen Midscape," I insist. That's what my mission is about now. Ensuring the safety of Midscape. Doing so is the best way to help everyone here and, moreover, it'll be the only way to know if what I'm feeling for Eldas is real. Or if all of these deep and complex emotions are just born of proximity and the appearance of necessity.

Love is choice, I told Luke, what seems like forever ago, and I have never found it to be truer. I cannot be certain of what I feel for Eldas if I don't choose him freely.

"But you don't have those questions any longer?" He glances over at me through long, dark lashes.

"No, I don't." I wave an arm toward the grounds. "This alone is paradise. And the conservatory back at the castle is a welcome balm that would suffice between trips out here."

"I see." Do I hear disappointment in his tone?

"Moreover…" The second I speak, Eldas looks at me with intent. I shouldn't have said anything. Hope has brightened his face more than the sun—more than the magic flush that coated my skin last night as we made love. "I can understand how some queens found companionship in their kings."

I make the attempt at giving him a coquettish smile and emphasize the word "companionship." Not *love*. I can't say it just yet. What would happen if I'm successful and then return home to find I can't leave again once I'm surrounded by my shop and patients? What if the Fade strips away these feelings from me the moment I emerge back in the Natural World? What if I do truly care for him but I can't leave my shop again?

He would be crushed. And that is a fall I will not even risk setting him up for. Let him think this is casual enjoyment. I'm past the point of being able to guard my heart. I'm helpless for the fallout. But him? Maybe I can still spare him.

Of course, all this assumes that he feels anything for me in return. Just because he wasn't with Rinni doesn't mean he's never been with a woman. His skill in bed makes it difficult for me to imagine that last night was his first time. Though…having never been with a man before, I don't exactly have a large list of comparisons for skill.

I banish the thoughts from my mind. I refuse to imagine him being with another woman and I can't imagine that these feelings that threatened to burn me alive last night are one-sided. For now, we'll dangerously ignore all of those unknowns like we ignore our time together here dwindling. That's safer for both our hearts.

Eldas chuckles, ignorant to my countless worries about what the future holds for us. "And tell me, my queen, was I a sufficient *companion*"—the way he says the word is a bit chilly, but with a joking edge—"to you last night? Because if you found me lacking in any way, that will be something I must immediately remedy." He licks his wicked smile and it stirs me at my core.

"Well, you know me. I am fastidious in my collection of information on a topic. More data is necessary."

He lets out a low growl before grabbing my face and crushing his lips against mine. I happily comply as he tugs me onto his lap. My stiff body tries to protest, but I move anyway. My legs straddle either side of him and he grinds against me.

I bite on his lower lip, which elicits a delicious sound. He rises, holding me with both hands, my legs wrapped around his waist. With a sweep of his hand and a burst of his icy magic, the cups vanish from existence. I barely notice as my back hits the small table.

He tugs at the bindings of my robe as my fingers grope at his pants in equal fervor. *Why did we even bother dressing?* As if we didn't know this was what we'd end up doing.

As bare as we were last night, Eldas wastes no time. His hips crash into mine again and I let out a cry of delight. I'm filled with a deep ache and satiation at the same time. My body is exhausted, yet eager to move with him—eager for his touch.

Our moans and gasps fill the valley as all shame and hesitation is forgotten and we collectively continue to dream that insatiable dream of all we could be.

thirty-two

THREE DAYS TOO SOON, THE COACH RETURNS.

We packed our bags the night before and, at my insistence, stacked them by the door. Eldas refused to let me help the footman load up. So getting them ready to go was the least I could do.

As the footman begins loading the bags I wander back out through the kitchen, already like the ghost of another forgotten queen—one of many to float through this world, enjoy its pleasures, and then be swept away. I grab my elbows, looking out over the pool, remembering Eldas floating in it the afternoon prior. The sun glistening off his perfect, wet, and deliciously naked body. So delicious looking that I had to take a bite…

"Are you all right?" he asks softly. I didn't even hear him join me outside this time.

"I wish I didn't have to leave," I admit.

His hands settle lightly on my hips. Eldas takes a small step closer and plants a sweet kiss in the crook of my neck.

"Duty calls, for now. But we could come back after seeing my brother." He pauses, grips me tighter, then adds solemnly, "And after you recharge the throne once more."

The air is already cooling around us. I am stronger than I have been in weeks, thanks to the natural magic living in this place. Strong enough that I can resist the temptation of coming back here. It was a lovely dream, and like all dreams, I have to wake up. There's still work to be done and three-thousand-year-old cycles to end. I shake my head.

"By then it'll be too close to the coronation." Too close to when I will be cemented into this world and all possibility of choice along with the pursuit of truth will vanish. After the coronation, there can be no return and I will never freely explore the feelings I have for him. "We should go back to Quinnar and continue searching for the way to end the cycle."

"Time is relentless," he mutters. I'm forced to agree. I had told myself that my time here was a dream and I enjoyed it like one. Now, the dawn is cruel and I wonder if I will ever find another morning kind.

"Thank you for taking me here, for showing me this, for giving me rest—"

"I did not give you that much rest." He smirks and I can't stop myself from kissing off the expression between chuckles.

"Thank you for everything," I whisper over his lips.

"You seem to have enjoyed yourself." His voice has a delighted and sultry tone. He knows full well I enjoyed myself all over this place. He was the source of the majority of that enjoyment.

"It was all right." I grin.

He releases me, aghast. "Just *all right*?"

"Perhaps you should work harder." I glance over my shoulder and it's his turn to claim my coy grin with his mouth. Our kisses are still the hungry sort that has him almost pushing me up against the wall and hiking my skirts. Even when they linger, they're filled with desire deeper than any emotion I've ever known.

"Don't challenge me," Eldas growls, biting my lower lip and drawing forth a moan. "Or I may exceed your expectations."

"Maybe I want that."

"Oh, I know you *want* it. But can you handle it?"

Even as I look at him, determined, I shiver with delight. He's a sensual dream of a man. The footman saves us before we give into baser instincts.

"Your Majesties." He bows and keeps his eyes on the ground. Eldas takes a half step away from me, but his palm still rests on the small of my back. He's not afraid to touch me in front of others anymore, a fact that I think I might like. "The coach is ready whenever you are."

"Let's not delay," Eldas declares.

A pang of longing constricts the muscles around my heart as I step over the threshold of the cottage. I can imagine the curlicues of the vines wriggling for me, reaching like the hands of children. The land itself begs for me with a whisper I feel more than hear. It resonates through my feet.

With one last look at the queen's oasis in a desert of wild magic and gray castles, I step into the coach.

We're silent for most of the way to Westwatch. The silence is a comfortable third companion, someone we met one night while sweaty, tired, and satisfied, and now know well. Eldas's journal is back on his lap and we spend most of the journey writing and reading. I finally have a few hours uninterrupted reading time when I'm not too distracted by his presence to focus.

"*Oh,*" I exhale. My eyes are stuck to a page. *I know whose journal this is.* My heart races. Perhaps this journal was waiting in that desk, holding itself together for this moment. My searching that night was rewarded.

I'm holding the journal of the first queen.

"We're here," Eldas says with a note of affirmation. He misinterpreted the sound I made. I jerk my head upward, about to correct him, but am distracted as the coach rolls slowly across a wide drawbridge. Eldas points over my shoulder at a wall that stretches upward into the sky and sprints toward the horizon east and west. "That's the elf border," he says. "My great, great grandfather was the one to build the wall to keep out the fae fighting and other agitators from elf lands. There's the river I told you about as the added protection."

"The fae lose their glamour whenever they come in contact with fresh water, right?"

He nods.

Talk of the fae brings back that day in the city. I suppress a shudder and focus on the other thoughts fae mentions give me—thoughts of Harrow and glimmer. I've only been away a few days, but it seems like too long.

"Harrow will be here too, right?"

"Yes, and our mother as well, since it's a family trip," Eldas says with a note of apology.

"If she's civil then I will be too." I've long since learned that it's impossible to make or expect everyone to like you. Of course, I would've preferred if Eldas's mother, of all people, at least tolerated me. But if my suspicions are correct, her hatred lies with Alice, not me, and whatever dynamic Eldas's father and Alice had. The best I can hope for is that in the future, if I stay—if I return—then she can learn to accept me. But, for the time being, I put Sevenna aside.

"We shall see." Eldas doesn't sound too hopeful.

Across the expanse of water is the arc of a city. When the city could no longer build out, it built up. I see the familiar architecture of Quinnar here in the towering buildings and gray stone. At the heart of the city is a large keep nestled within the wall. Much like at the castle of Quinnar, a many-gated tunnel snakes through the base of the keep—the only entrance and exit, I presume, to the fae lands.

We step out of the carriage and a wave of servants bows to greet us. I walk at Eldas's side, adjusting my skirts. I wish he had helped me by suggesting I wear something slightly more formal. Wasn't that why he packed so much for me? Perhaps my mission to get him accustomed to the clothes I usually wear was a little too successful.

Eldas's brother, Drestin, is the odd man out of his siblings. He didn't inherit his mother's black hair. His is, instead, a dark shade of brown that I presume belonged to their father. It's cut even shorter than Harrow's and gives him the distinct air of a military man.

Drestin's wife, Carcina, is ready to pop at any moment. The entire way to our room she ambles alongside us with one hand on her very pregnant stomach, apologetic for being unable to curtsy or bow properly. I assure her not to worry, but that only seems to fluster her more.

"What do you think of them?" Eldas asks the first moment we're alone.

"They're pleasant," I answer honestly.

"They are a delight."

"Might I ask something about them?" I take off my traveling cloak, draping it over a settee situated near a hearth.

"Anything."

"Carcina is Drestin's wife."

"Yes?"

"And she's the mother of his child?" I ask somewhat timidly.

"Why wouldn't she be?"

"Well..." I'm not sure why I'm dancing around this topic. I clear my throat and collect myself. "I know the Human Queen wasn't your mother. I know Elf Kings usually take lovers. I know the elves value tradition, but I'm afraid I still haven't sorted out what 'tradition' is when it comes to elf lords siring their heirs."

"Ah, that's right. Talk of heirs has never really come up."

A fact I was all too ready to leave to the side when I'd first arrived, as even the thought of being intimate with Eldas was unfathomable. But now... "I don't mean to imply you and I, that I was going to—" I start to add hastily, thinking of our past few days. He cuts me off with a laugh.

"It's a fair question; I didn't think you meant to imply anything." Eldas unbuttons his coat, distracting me for a moment with the elegant movements of his fingers. "The Elf King is permitted to take lovers and the Human Queen is as well. It has been tradition for the Elf King to sire his heir with a lover—like my mother—because it ensures the Elf King will be wholly elf, and his deep connection to the Veil wouldn't be at risk."

"I see." I mull this over. "So there's never been a child of an Elf King and a Human Queen?"

"No. It's not—"

"Traditional?" I finish with a slight grin. I meander into the bedroom, coming to a stop as I take note that there's only one bed.

"I figured it wouldn't be a problem." Eldas's voice is deep with a hint of mischief. He leans against the doorframe, his silvery tunic like liquid metal over his lean shoulders. "My brother offered separate rooms, however..."

"Of course not." I gasp with a mask of mock offense. "How dare you suggest we inconvenience them further!"

"No, we wouldn't want that, now would we?" He smirks, hands sliding around my waist, tugging me to his hard body.

"Though I must insist that I have time to get some work done in the evenings." I retrieve the small journal from my coat pocket, trying to show it to him.

Eldas has none of it. He pushes the journal away and hooks my chin. "Very well, but it's not evening yet," he growls over my lips. "Which means I have every right to distract you now."

I shiver, body responding to him, journal forgotten. I'm helpless, putty as his hands slide up my sides, grabbing my breasts through my clothes. I inhale sharply and he crushes his mouth against mine.

I've so much I need to tell him. There's so much work to be done and things to worry about. This journal is the key we've been waiting for. But his caresses as he leads me to the bed we'll share smooth away all thoughts of leaving.

The colors of the world around me blur and smear under his gentle palms until he is the only thing in focus. We tumble back onto the duvet and spend the afternoon focused solely on each other.

"Harrow and Mother should have been here by now." Drestin looks to the tall grandfather clock wedged between full bookcases in the lounge we've collected in for drinks before dinner.

"The rain might have held them up." Eldas stands by a blazing hearth, the orange light casting his form in shadow. Outside, rain pounds the glass.

"This is not the rain. Harrow is still up to his antics. I hear the rumors of the youngest prince even out in Westwatch. I've no doubt he's the cause of this delay." Drestin takes a long swig of his drink. Mine is mostly unfinished. "We need to be done with it, marry him off and give him land. The sooner he gets real responsibility on his shoulders, the better."

"He's not ready," Eldas protests.

"I wasn't ready when you gave me Westwatch and was only a year older than Harrow is now. It was the best thing that could've been done for me." Drestin's bright blue eyes flick over to Carcina. She's seated next to me on the couch and looks significantly more comfortable than she did at our earlier meeting. "Best thing, aside from meeting you, of course."

"You don't have to flatter me. I know I was merely a requirement with the title," Carcina says with a playful grin.

"Ah, yes, forgive me. That's all you are, mother of my child, light of my world, goddess among women—merely another box that I had to check." Drestin jests back and I'm pleased to see genuine fondness in his eyes. Those eyes flick over to me and then back to Eldas just as fast. It was only a glance, but I know what he's thinking.

A marriage made of necessity but sustained by genuine love that grew against all odds. I take a sip of my drink to avoid saying anything on the topic. If Eldas is even aware of the undercurrents, he says nothing.

"We should have dinner," Eldas suggests, looking to the clock once more. "Carcina, you shouldn't go this late without eating."

"I'm fine." Carcina pats her stomach. "Perhaps if this babe is hungry enough, it'll come crawling out at the table and demand food." She laughs. "I'm ready for it to be over with."

"Most women are at this stage," I say. She looks to me with an inquisitive stare. "Back in Capton—in my world—" I clarify, not knowing how much they know of the other side of the Fade, "I studied at the academy to be a herbalist. I didn't specialize in midwifery, but I worked closely with those who did. There are many balms and draughts that you can have to help with various ailments at this stage…such as swollen feet or aching back." I took note of both when she was hobbling with us to our rooms.

"Perhaps you could tell my healers of this knowledge from the Natural World. I need any assistance I can get."

"I'd be happy to make it for you myself, if the supplies are here."

"Your Majesty—"

"Just Luella, please," I remind her, not for the first time.

"Luella," she says sheepishly. "I wouldn't want to trouble you."

"It wouldn't trouble, it would delight me." I beam.

"It's best not to fight her when she's made up her mind," Eldas adds with a small smile. I remember not too long ago helping others was "beneath me" as the queen. Now, it's unquestioned.

"Then perhaps after dinner I will show you the healer's laboratory." Carcina rests her hand on mine. "Thank you, Luella."

"You're very welcome."

Dinner is an intimate affair. Since Harrow and Sevenna have yet to arrive, we adjourn to a smaller, more informal dining room that I first caught a glimpse of on our way to the lounge. It reminds me of the first dinner Eldas and I shared.

Usually, the thought of that dinner would have me fighting lingering fantasies of him pushing me up against a hearth. But not tonight. Worry for Harrow and what could've held him up nags the back of my mind.

However, selfishly, I am grateful for the absence of Sevenna. It gives me an opportunity to get to know Carcina and Drestin. And for them to get to know me without Sevenna's opinions poisoning the air.

After dinner, the men decide on a nightcap while Carcina and I make our escape to the Westwatch laboratory and gardens. It gives the brothers an opportunity to catch up, and me the chance to find my way to the stash of healing supplies in Westwatch. Paranoia has now taken residence in the back of my mind as there's *still* no word from Harrow.

Something is wrong and the air is thick with whatever it is.

"Here we are." Carcina lights the lamps of the room with a sweep of her hand and flash of her eyes. Little things about wild magic make me envious of its blatant disregard for logic.

The laboratory is similar to the one in Quinnar. Instead of a conservatory attached, it opens through arched doorways to a terraced garden facing the city of Westwatch. The layout is somewhat different, but a quick sweep of the room yields where the healers here are keeping similar supplies.

"Everything we should need is here," I say as I poke my nose in cabinets. "I could bring it to you in the morning?"

"I wouldn't want to leave you alone here."

"Is it unsafe?" I can't help but ask.

"We have added extra security for your visit." She smiles proudly.

"Then it's fine. I'm used to working alone. It's how I would work in my shop. My favorite hours were first thing in the morning before anyone could disturb me."

"Your shop?"

"I had a shop I opened up after I finished academy." It seems like years ago now. Time twisted as I passed through the Fade. It must pass faster in Midscape because the memories of my worn counters and rough-hewn bowls are leaving my fingers. It seems as though I've been in Midscape all along.

The fading of those connections terrifies me. I have to go back. I can't know who I really am or what I'm feeling until I do.

"I see." She's clearly confused, but accepts the remark in stride and doesn't probe further.

"In any case... If it doesn't bother you to have me working alone in your healers' laboratory, I don't mind doing so. You look tired and need rest."

"This child hasn't even come into the world and he's already sapping my energy and patience." Her body emphasizes the point with a yawn.

"Go and rest; I'll have it ready by breakfast."

"Thank you again, Luella." She goes to leave but pauses just before. "I didn't know what to expect of the Human Queen. I admit...I was a bit nervous. But I'm glad that it is you."

I can think of no response before Carcina excuses herself for the night.

As I work, I try and place the wrenching, restless feeling that's propelling my hands with frantic purpose. Guilt, I finally realize. I feel guilty. But for what?

For leaving.

I frown at the liquid bubbling in a small cauldron. I have nothing to be guilty over. I'm doing the right thing for both our worlds *and* for us. I could never stay with Eldas and be happy, not truly, unless I know I'm staying of my own volition.

"Is it more effective when you make that face at it?" Eldas's voice cuts through my thoughts. My body jerks, startled, and I face him. He's lounging against a table, arms folded, looking delightfully smug.

"How long have you been there?"

"Long enough to see you work."

I must've been truly lost in my thoughts to not notice Eldas come in.

"And what a sight it is."

"What?" I say the word on an exhale, already trying to fish out all the complex emotions he's somehow fit into the small pools of blue that are his eyes. There's admiration, a note of sorrow, longing, resignation? More I can't name.

"You were born to do this," he says.

"You've seen me work before." I run my finger along the top of a jar before putting it away.

"I have, but I never truly watched. I never paid attention." The sorrow I saw in him is given sound. "Luella…if we are unable to break the cycle before the coronation…I would do whatever I could, even then, to help you manage the throne. Whatever you needed, I would give you. Perhaps we could even find a way for you to work as a healer in Quinnar too. Maybe, even though you would be a part of Midscape, we could even explore options for you to visit Capton more than just midsummer."

My stomach twists and when I speak I can't look at him. I know he's trying to help. But this conversation dredges up the tangled mass of emotions that I can't completely pick through when it comes to thinking of my life before, my life now, and whatever awaits me in the future.

"Wouldn't that be unconventional for a queen?"

"Yes, but convention is always new at one point. I've read the journals too. Others have longed for something similar—for a purpose beyond the redwood throne. Helping the healers wasn't enough. It's too late for them, but for you, for future queens…" He runs a hand through his hair and looks away. I watch him from the corner of my eye. "If there are future queens, that is."

"Speaking of all that." I turn and lean against the counter. "There's something I need to tell you."

"Yes?" Eldas is clearly startled by my sudden shift in mood.

"The journal I've been reading…I figured out today whose it was."

"Whose?"

"Queen Lilian."

"Lilian," he whispers. He's no doubt heard the name from stories he was told all his life. "The first queen. Then—"

I nod, knowing what he'll say next. "I think I know how the seasons, the redwood throne, and the queen's magic are tied together. I think I understand what the first queen and king did and how it all works." I've figured out a great mystery. I should be happier. And yet I watch with dread as Eldas rises to his feet. We're standing on an edge from which there's no going back. "I need to read more, and research, of course. And just because I understand how the Fade was made and the seasons turn doesn't guarantee I'll be able to do anything with the information, but—"

His hands clasp around my shoulders. Eldas wears a bright smile. But his eyes are heartbreakingly sad.

"This is excellent. If anyone can figure it out, it's you. I've said it all along and now you have what you needed."

"I know, but…"

"But?" He falters.

Don't be happy about this, I want to say. I don't want him to even pretend to be happy about me leaving. The fact that he would be swells my heart to the point of pain. The smile on his face mocks me and I find myself doubting the traces of hurt in his eyes; are they real, or am I just imagining them to be because I *want* them to be?

"Eldas, what do you feel for me?" I dare to ask, small and afraid.

"What?" His hands fall from my shoulders. Perhaps that's answer enough.

"What do you feel for me?" I ask again, louder and more certain.

"When you say—"

"Do you love me?"

He looks as if my words materialized and struck him between the ribs. Eldas's mouth opens and closes several times. Perhaps he had run the numbers in our equation and arrived at the same result as I—that it was better not to think about what these feelings truly were. It was better not to ask or know, for both of us.

As he stares at me now, deathly silent, I want the thick night air to envelop me. I want it to take me away and carry me through the Fade here and now. I can't handle waiting for his answer.

If he says he doesn't love me, then my heart will be crushed. If he says he does, then my heart will still be crushed if—*when*—I inevitably leave. And, if I don't leave…I will wonder if his feelings, like mine, could've been somehow manipulated by magic or circumstance. If they were ever real at all, or a twisted survival of the heart. I will question everything forever and that alone would be our undoing.

"Don't answer that." I shake my head. "It's better if you—"

"Luella, I—"

Neither of us get to finish. Drestin comes sprinting in. He's panting as if he's been running for some time. His eyes sweep over me and land on Eldas.

"It's Harrow," he pants out. "There's been an attack."

thirty-three

"AN ATTACK?" Eldas repeats, looking somewhat dazed. I have whiplash as well from the sudden shift in conversation.

"Before we sat to eat, I sent out riders. I was worried. They met with mother in her coach just outside of Westwatch. But Harrow wasn't with her. She said he'd wanted to stop in Carron before coming here and she couldn't say no—of course not, not to her darling Harrow. So she let him go. His horse and guard were found gutted just outside of Carron. There's no sign of Harrow."

"Carron, why was he—"

"Aria," I stop Eldas. "He went to see Aria perform. She mentioned to me that she was performing in Carron with the Troupe of Masks as the start of performances leading up to the Coronation." I look between the two men. "How far is Carron?"

"It's up the wall, an hour from Westwatch," Drestin answers.

"Let's go."

"You should stay here," Eldas says firmly.

"I'm coming," I insist with such force that I can almost hear it echoing in their thick skulls. "You two will need me."

Drestin glances between Eldas and me, eyebrows arched with a somewhat surprised look. Rinni might be familiar with Eldas's and my comfortable rapport. But it seems Drestin is not yet. "Your Majesty—"

I ignore his surprise and wave off his objection. "Is there a gate to the fae lands in Carron?"

"No," Eldas answers.

"No way to cross the wall?" I press.

"No," Eldas repeats.

"Well..." his brother starts, earning an arched brow from Eldas. "There were reports of places where the wall has been weakened. Farmers talking, spreading rumors of fae getting through. But I've yet to confirm..."

My mind is moving as fast as my frantic hands. While the men speak, I finish off the potion I was making and jar it, placing it in a leather satchel I steal off of a peg by the doors out to the gardens. I leave them for a moment to search the gardens for anything fresh I might need for magic or emergency healing.

Unfortunately, I can't find any heartroot. It seems Willow's early mention of the plant being incredibly rare holds true.

"Luella, stay—" Eldas tries to say as I reenter the laboratory.

"I already told you both, I'm coming." I stare both elves in their cerulean eyes, trying to communicate with my wide, planted stance alone that this isn't a negotiation. "I have information you may need."

"What could that possibly be?" Drestin asks.

"We're wasting time, just trust me." I look to Eldas. "Please."

He gives a small nod and holds out his hand. "To Carron."

My fingers close around Eldas's. Together, we step into the dark mist that rises from underneath Eldas's feet. We Fadewalk to a muddy road a short walk away from a town about the size of Capton. Drestin emerges from a plume of mist at our side. Dark swirls whorl in the air for just a moment before dissipating on the wind and leaving a man where they once were.

Carron is snug against the wall, just as Drestin said. Much like Westwatch, there's a bridge that crosses this thinner span of river. If I were a fae looking to sneak something into the elves' territory, this would certainly be the place I'd try and do it.

In the fields to the far right of town, tents have been erected. They glow from within, their colors shining like candy in the glittering darkness that follows in the night after rain. Flags made small by distance flutter in the nighttime breeze. We can hear cheers faintly across the fields.

"Go and investigate the Troupe of Masks," Eldas commands his brother. "Look for any signs of foul play there."

"And you?"

"I'm going to the scene of the crime." Eldas doesn't wait for Drestin to respond; we're already moving through the Fade again.

We emerge a little bit down the road at a scene of butchery. One horse has been flayed open, its entrails spilled out. Its rider—a guard whose face I don't recognize, but wears the city armor of Quinnar—has been ripped nearly in half.

"Wolves?" I ask, noting the claw marks.

"This is no wolf," Eldas says darkly. "Those are fae claws."

I shudder and think back to the antlered creature in the alleyway. So fae can have wings, and horns, *and* claws. They're the creatures that haunted my nightmares, not elves.

Eldas crouches down, looking for any hints as to who might have done this or what happened to Harrow. I keep staring at the dead elf: eyes wide, blood pooled in the mud. I pull my gaze away and sweep it across the plains that surround the road. In my mind, I try and recreate the scene that transpired.

There is no place to hide, which means Harrow and his guard would've had to see their attackers coming. Fae glamour? I look down at the road. *No.*

"Eldas, something isn't right here."

"Yes," he growls. "My brother might be dead!" Eldas rises with his voice. "Something is *very* wrong. We need to search the area. They can't have made it far."

I remain calm in the face of his rage and panic. I've had families take out their grief over sick relatives on me. Worry twists the hearts of men into something unrecognizable. But better sense ultimately prevails, sooner or later.

"Look." I point to the road. "It rained during dinner, which means any fae glamour wouldn't have worked. You said fresh water washes it away, right?" He pauses, slowly nodding. I continue, "Additionally, any footprints should have also been washed away. Here's ours. Then, there's these..." Deep divots of pooled water collect in two sets of footprints. One set are boots, the other are paws larger than any I've ever seen. Larger than Hook's.

Speaking of... I raise my fingers to my lips and give out a shrill whistle.

"Hook, come," I command. The wolf bounds from between the shadows of the night. It's good to see him again after a few days— good to know he'll still come when I call. But this is not the cuddly Hook I know. He lets out a low growl at the carnage. His eyes are alert and his ears press flat to his head. "Hook." I draw his attention to me. "Can you find Harrow for us?"

Per usual, Hook seems to understand my command. He walks over to the horses, sniffing around them. As I presume—hope— Hook is picking up Harrow's scent, Eldas asks, "What're you getting at?" I can see him trying to shake the worry from his mind so he can think clearly once more.

"I think the bodies were put here."

"Why?"

"To throw us off and have us waste time searching along the fields and roads." I look back to Carron. "Harrow was off to see Aria perform. Aria, presumably, knew he would come. She could've tipped off a fae party he was on his way."

"Aria wouldn't act against her family. Harming Harrow hurts her father's chances."

My suspicions persist strongly despite this reminder. But airing them now won't help. "She might have done it unintentionally, said the wrong thing to the wrong person?"

Eldas grumbles at the idea of his brother being betrayed, but finally doesn't object.

"We need to search the city." I grip the bag at my side tightly and the jars of herbs I brought with me clank softly around loose plants. When do I tell Eldas that I'm worried about what state we might find Harrow in? How much longer can I keep Harrow's secret before it's a detriment to him? "Take us there."

Eldas says nothing and grasps my hand. I bury my free fingers into Hook's fur and we three step through the Fade onto the muddy streets of Carron. Immediately, Hook's nose is to the ground.

He sniffs along the road, tracking back and forth until he seems to have a scent.

"I can go with Hook, you can search—"

"I'm not leaving you," Eldas says firmly and strides off after Hook.

The small town is eerily silent. Every resident has locked up and gone to see the Troupe of Masks perform. The liquid shine from lamplights catches on dark windowpanes and hangs on corners, casting alleyways in darker, more ominous shadows than I have ever seen.

It would be a perfect time to attack a prince. Harrow was lured in by Aria and, if my suspicion is correct, the appeal of glimmer she might have been providing him. I can imagine him walking these silent streets, telling his guard to hang back while the deal was done to preserve his secret. I imagine his shadow lingering in the alleyway Hook leads us down. I imagine money exchanging hands for glimmer while his guard was gutted. Aria smiling sweetly, knowing she'd joined the Troupe of Masks for the sole purpose of this first performance venue—to get Harrow so close to the fae lands.

By the time Harrow knew anything, it was too late.

"I don't understand." Eldas keeps his voice hushed. He moves with almost cat-like grace and quiet. "Harrow should have been able to overpower a few fae. He has as much of a connection with the Veil as Drestin does and, while he might be dense, he's smart enough not to fall for their half-truths."

"Unless it was more than a few fae?" And unless he'd ingested so much glimmer that it put him out of his right mind.

"With his guard—"

"Unless he told his guard to wait elsewhere."

"Why would he do that?" Eldas stops to face me. My expression must betray something, because his eyes narrow. "What do you know?"

I've said too much, and I know it. "I don't know anything other than we have to find Harrow."

"You're lying to me," he hisses. His brow is furrowed with anger, but his eyes are wounded. "I know you well enough that I know how the air shifts around you when you try to deceive."

I swallow hard. "There's no time now—"

"Tell me the essentials, then."

"I'm trying to respect my patient," I say weakly.

"This is a command."

"But—"

"Luella!" he presses, worry contrasting with the frustration in his voice.

"Harrow was using glimmer," I blurt.

"*What?*" The white fights to consume Eldas's eyes as his lids hold themselves painfully open. "How would you—"

"He told me," I say quickly. Then nerves and fear prompt me to speak even faster. I rush to tell Eldas of what I saw in the alleyway— what I suspect was glimmer changing hands to Aria from a fae accomplice. Of what Harrow told me on his bed and his confusion of how he'd become addicted to the substance he'd never meant to take in the first place. My theory of Aria using it to lure Harrow here, alone.

"They were planning this… Going after you that day was nothing more than an unexpected opportunity. That was why their kidnapping attempt seemed so haphazard. It was a crime of convenience. But the real plot was Harrow all along because the fae instigators knew they had a woman who had his ear," Eldas seethes. I hope the rage in his eyes is directed at the fae and not at me, but I'm not certain. "You and I will discuss your choices to keep all this from me in more detail when my brother is safe."

"Fine." I want to object that I tried to tell him while respecting my patient's wishes, but I know this isn't the time or place. He's right. Harrow's safety is priority one right now.

Hook lets out a low whine and we begin following him again. The wolf leads us to a back, forgotten corner of the town. Refuse piles line the wall and fill the air with their stench. Eldas plugs his nose, rearing away. I've smelled worse from some rare plants, but the aroma still staggers me.

Somehow, Hook manages to keep the trail through it all and he leads us to a series of boards leaning against the wall—out of sight with the trash piled in front of them. Hook scratches and then lets out a low growl. As Eldas and I near, we hear the faint echo of people talking, words indiscernible. Through cracks in the boards, the dark line of a tunnel in the wall is visible.

"Stay here," he hisses.

"But you need—"

"I do *not* need you. You are a liability because I can't allow something to happen to you. And if you had been forthright with me from the beginning, all of this might not have happened," he snarls at me with rage I didn't think Eldas could harbor toward me. I stagger back as if he struck me. Yet, even through his anger, his worry and compassion for me shines through. It reminds me that the Eldas I've come to know and care for is still the man standing before me. "Stay here, hide, and *stay safe* with Hook. If something happens to you I'll be forced to rip apart every fae with my bare hands."

Before I can say anything else, Eldas pushes the boards aside, steps off into the darkness, and leaves me alone. I grit my teeth. Hook lets out another low whine and scratches.

Images of Eldas ambushed, injured and bleeding, fill my mind. Surely Aria knew he'd come after Harrow? Unless they thought they could get Harrow long away before anyone realized? These thoughts swirl around the image of Harrow, drugged to the point of incoherency.

I meet Hook's luminescent golden eyes.

"What would you do?" I whisper. The wolf looks back to the hole in the wall. "If you insist, I can't argue with that."

I fish in my bag for a sprig of briar. I picked the plants I took from the gardens at Westwatch carefully. Every one for a different reason, based on the insights of a past queen. For weeks I've been reading and practicing their written methods.

The memory of my last attack lingers. I wasn't confident with my magic then. I *needed* Hook and Eldas to stand a chance. But I'm not the same woman as I was. I know how to use my powers and I trust the land beneath my feet to keep me safe.

"Let's go." I nod toward the opening and Hook strides into the darkness, unafraid. I try to emulate him, following close behind. As

we walk, I push magic from my hand into the briar, charging it with
energy to use in a large burst.

The silence is broken in the distance by a sharp cry being cut
short with a sickening crunch.

"Go!" I urge Hook and he bounds ahead. I stumble through the
darkness, running my hand along the rough-hewn wall. It bites into
the flesh of my palm but I keep pressing firm.

Soon, a sliver of light guides me. I can make out Hook's shadow,
racing onward. He crosses into the moonlight before me. The noises
of fighting rise in my ears. I keep pumping my feet forward.

I've never been in a real fight before. I studied how to heal,
not hurt. But I'd never been married before, crossed the Fade, had
magic, slept with a man, or loved like this before. I've been able to
take all those firsts in stride.

I can do this.

I emerge into a forest. Instantly, I notice how the fae lands are
different from the Elf Kingdom. Motes of magic drift through the air
between the trees, casting everything in shades of blue and green.
Vining flowers I don't recognize hang like curtains from the trees'
leafy boughs. Even the earth seems different under my feet; it's more
untamed, magical, and much more like what I think I originally
expected of Midscape.

Hook's growl followed by a shout brings me back to reality. I
sprint forward, dashing around the trees to a low-lying clearing.
Two fae lie dead, their throats slit with a violent dark line. Eldas
faces off against a beast with paws that match the prints we saw
in the road. The animal is the size of a bear, covered in fur around
its face and paws, but the rest of its body is coated in wet-looking
scales, like a serpent's.

Hook's whimper draws my attention across the clearing to where
the wolf has been beaten back by another fae with ram's horns. The
man's eyes gleam a bright violet and his hands move through the
air, vaporous magic tracing his motions. Both beast and man wear
necklaces weighted by labradorite around their necks.

I hold out the briar and sink my feet into the ground.

An arm closes around me and the blade of a dagger is at my
throat.

"King Eldas!" Aria shouts over my shoulder. My ears ring. I was right; it was her all along. I've never been so angry about being correct. "If you won't parlay with us for your dear brother, then perhaps your queen?"

Eldas's bright eyes leave the beast to face us. A rage unlike any I've ever seen twists his handsome features into pure malice. Waves of shadow radiate off of him and the presence of the Fade thickens with his magic.

"Let her go," he growls.

"Let us go and agree to give us the land that's rightfully ours!" She pushes the dagger closer to my throat.

"Aria, don't do this," the man with the ram's horns says, voice weak with emotion. "You were supposed to get away." I see something I recognize—an emotion I've seen in Eldas numerous times now. Admiration, *compassion*. I'm beginning to piece together the simple plot this seems to have been…Aria fell in love with one of the rebel fae. Love was the one thing that could make someone act against their own best interests.

"You insult your people's—your family's—attempt at diplomacy and hurt your cause with this." Eldas holds out his arms and an array of silver blades pop into existence. He summons each one with nothing more than a thought—a true name of a weapon he learned and saved in his memory throughout the course of his life. "Kill her and you kill us all."

"Our lands are cold and cruel," Aria shouts. "She only makes the Elf Kingdom viable for food and game."

"That's not—" I can't get out a word. Aria yanks me tighter and the dagger bites into my throat as I dare to speak. Blood slips down the blade, dropping to the earth.

"Silence," she snarls at me. "We have a way that you're no longer needed. A ritual that will restore this land."

Ritumancy… Willow explained it as the act of performing rituals to gain magic. I never expected Aria to be the one to give me the missing piece that finally put together the puzzle of how to end the cycle. But she did.

I just have to survive long enough to test my theory.

"Don't take another step closer," Aria shouts as Eldas begins to move; his eyes are still stuck on me with panic. "I know you, you won't dare risk the life of the Human Queen."

Droplets have been dripping from the hand I cut on the wall for a good minute now, mingling with my blood streaming off her blade. I smirk; I learned very early on how dangerous my blood can be when mixed with nature.

"He won't," I whisper. "But I will."

Magic explodes out from around me with a force I haven't felt since the afternoon with Harrow in the lunch nook. I release my control and it flows into the earth unfettered.

I am like a blight on the land. Death spreads out from around me as the power is consumed and leeched from the earth itself. Balance, it all requires balance.

The briar falls from my fingers and writhes outward. The thorny vines wrap around Aria and she lets out a shout. I can feel their tiny daggers digging into her flesh as if the vines were a part of my own body.

Yet, none of the thorns face me. Aria is cocooned in a wicked prison—trapped, but not dead—and I am free to step away as the vines wrench her hand holding the dagger away from my throat like violent puppet strings. The earth cracks under my feet as I walk. Thorny, angry briar follows me and races toward the beast as I point in its direction.

The clawed and scaled creature makes an attempt to get away. But it can't outpace my magic. The air shifts as Eldas turns his attention onto the remaining fae. The weapons he summoned rain like a hail of steel on the remaining man. Aria lets out a scream of pure anguish—cold and lingering.

I lower my hand the moment the last fae is wrapped in briar. All at once, energy leaves my body and I sink to my knees. They slam into the rocky ground, now cracked and dry—void of any life but my snaring vines.

thirty-four

HOOK RACES OVER TO ME, LICKING MY FACE AS I SUPPORT
MYSELF ON ALL FOURS. It's as if I have just sat on the
redwood throne. My body trembles and aches. Exhaustion
clouds my vision.

"You killed him!" Aria screams. "My love, my love…"
Her words devolve into sobs. I'm not sure if she stops
talking, or if my mind stops paying attention to her—
focusing instead on keeping me conscious.

I really was made to bring life, and not death. Even using
the latter as a method to achieve equilibrium demands a
high toll. Waves of magic roll within me like a choppy sea
and I sway slightly. I'm slimy all over, slick with sweat, as
if my body is trying to expunge the uncomfortable sensation
of making the earth barren.

"Luella—"

"I'm fine," I say as Eldas kneels next to me. I look up
at him and then back at Aria. She now stares numbly at the
world around her, my vines sinking into her flesh at multiple
points. No matter what, I couldn't kill her. It's just not in
me. So I'll leave it to Eldas and his justice to decide what
happens next. "You deal with her. I'll take care of Harrow."

"I'm taking both of you back to Westwatch," he declares.
"I will return and deal with them when I know you're safe."

"But…"

"They're not going anywhere for the next five minutes."

Eldas gives a nod to the thickets surrounding us. "You truly are incredible," he murmurs as he slips his arm under mine and around my shoulders. With Eldas's help we stagger over to where Harrow is. He's in some kind of daze; his eyes are glossed over and half open, unfocused. Eldas's mouth is set in a grim line.

"I'll help him," I say.

"I know you will." Eldas leans forward, resting his palm on Harrow. He adds with a slightly bitter murmur, "Helping him at all costs seems to be one of your strengths."

The shadows thicken around us before I can comment on his remark and then are promptly chased away by the lights of Westwatch's entry. Two guards startle at our sudden appearance. Eldas barks orders and disappears once more, leaving Harrow and me behind. I notice that Hook didn't join us and selfishly hope he's looking after Eldas back in the fae lands as Eldas deals with Aria and the aftermath.

At my request, Harrow is taken to a room not far from the laboratory. Every step is harder than the last, but the clanking of the concoctions in my bag keeps me moving. Harrow needs the medicine I made and so much more.

Sevenna is nowhere to be found while I'm treating Harrow—a blessing. I can move alone and unhindered for the first hour of his treatment. After that, I'm swarmed by other healers. Harrow is stable enough, and I make my escape before whatever is holding back Sevenna gives way.

My rooms are cold and vacant when I return to them shortly after dawn. I look over to the bed but the idea of sleeping alone without Hook or Eldas to keep me warm is unappealing. Instead, I bathe, washing away the night's events, and then curl up on the sofa of our parlor, drifting asleep despite myself.

Half the day has burned away when I wake. Eldas is the first thing to come into focus. Lilian's journal is on his knee, split down the middle. Even with his superhuman reading speed, he likely didn't sleep if he's that far along.

"You're awake," he says without so much as looking up.

"So it seems." I pull myself upright. Every muscle screams in protest. I could sleep two more days easily. "How's Harrow?"

"They say he's stable. The healers cleared up the...what did you refer to it as to them? Fever he got from being out in the rain? Though he has yet to wake." Eldas's eyes finally flick up to me.

"I figured you wouldn't want everyone to know about the glimmer," I say gingerly.

"So many assumptions you make." He closes the journal slowly. "You assume I wouldn't want people to know about my brother being involved with glimmer."

"Was I wrong?"

"You assume *I* shouldn't know."

"I was trying to respect his wishes," I say calmly.

"He clearly couldn't be trusted to have an opinion on what was in his best interest if he was using glimmer!"

"That's not my choice to make."

"You *assumed*"—every time he says it the word becomes more of an accusation—"you could navigate a situation you were woefully unequipped for."

"Eldas," I say softly but firmly. His eyes are haunted and tired. Now is not the time to be having this conversation. I take a deep breath and try and start from the beginning. "I didn't tell you about the glimmer because I didn't want to betray Harrow's trust. I doubt he'd told anyone about it—save for maybe Jalic or Sirro, who might be in on Aria's plot too. I don't know. If I betrayed the trust he placed in me, he likely would've retreated further and kept that secret guarded to his grave." A grave that could've come far too soon if last night had ended differently. "I genuinely feared for him, Eldas. And I was worried that if I gave him reason to push away the one person he'd begun to open up to, that would be far more detrimental than anything else. I'm sorry I couldn't imagine any of this happening."

The king purses his lips and looks to the window. He rests an elbow on the arm of the wingback chair he's sitting in and brings a hand to his lips, as if he's physically trying to force himself not to say something he'll regret. "The fae were part of a group called the Acolytes of the Wild Wood. One benefit of them not being able to lie is it can make them easy to interrogate after a point."

I remember Rinni saying the name once before and ignore his

remarks on interrogation. I don't think I want to know what he means.

"Aria was helping them infiltrate her uncle's court. That was how they could sneak in with the dignitaries but without the Fae King being aware. I can't believe I allowed her into my home." Eldas directs his frustration inward. He doesn't even seem to be speaking to me.

"What did you do with Aria?" I have to ask. I might not entirely *want* to know, but I *need* to know.

"She will be locked up and the key misplaced for a while," Eldas says, finally. "I might have wanted to kill her then and there. But she's still the Fae King's niece; he should be the one to decide her fate. Allowing him to will be a display of good will and will show me if he is serious about our kingdoms' relationship or not."

I grimace at the idea of having to pass judgment on a family member—on someone I love.

"And the rest of the group?"

"Those I could hunt down faced my justice." There's not a hint of remorse in his voice. *Dead, then.* I swallow thickly and try not to judge Eldas for what he must do as king. "Hopefully this long-planned plot of theirs being thwarted will push them back for a while. Then, when we end the cycle, that will really put an end to their claims of elf favoritism from the Human Queen and the land dying. What we're doing will help everyone...even if they don't know it yet."

"Speaking of, I think I know how to do it—break the cycle," I say. He arches his eyebrows. "I think the solution is simpler than we could've imagined. It's a matter of restoring balance between Midscape and the Natural World—like the queen's garden." I can see the solution begin to light up Eldas's eyes as I speak. "I think with something like the fae's ritumancy, we can assemble the necessary requisites to find equilibrium. Which can make sense—the Human Queen's magic is more like the fae's than the elves'... likely because the fae are closer to the dryads and all that." I believe my logic checks out, since the fae were descended from dryads and the dryads later made the humans, but it's been a while since Willow and I discussed the history of Midscape.

"Good." Yet he contradicts his word with a shake of his head as he stands.

"You don't seem happy." I watch as he faces the crackling fire in the hearth behind his chair.

"Of course I am not happy," he murmurs darkly.

My chest tightens. I expected him to be angry. But I didn't expect how painful it would be. "Eldas, I—"

"My brother could've been hurt. *You* could've been hurt." He looks over his shoulder.

"I didn't know the extent of the situation, not really. I just thought your brother was in a tough spot. I didn't think about the politics that might be involved." I slowly rise to my feet, allowing the world to spin and settle. My magic and body are both exhausted.

"It's for the best," he murmurs.

"What is?"

Eldas turns and his expression is unrecognizable. I haven't seen those frigid eyes since our wedding. "That you'll be leaving soon."

"Do you mean that?" I whisper.

"Of course I do. It's what you wanted, isn't it? You have an idea and based on what I've read of that journal, you're not far off." Eldas stares down at me. "You'll no longer be needed here and you can go—be free of me. No king will ever have to suffer with a Human Queen again."

"Stop this," I whisper. Every word is like a physical wound, cutting me deeper than I thought possible. I'm shocked the floor isn't bloody. "I know you're upset and…you have a reason to be cross with me. But Eldas, I—"

"What do you feel for me?" He turns to face me as he turns my question back on me. I lean against the chair for stability. Otherwise I may be bowled over by his stare.

"You never answered that either," I remind him weakly.

"If you asked, then you may have some kind of idea of what I might feel." Eldas gathers his height. "But I want to know about you, Luella. What do you feel for me? Do you love me?"

Every pore, every raw part of my essence screams, *yes!* But my lips don't move. They quiver silently and my eyes burn. *Yes, say yes, Luella.* But if I say yes now…I will always doubt myself.

"Tell me, Luella, do you love me?" His voice takes on an almost begging note.

I press my lips harder together, fighting every instinct. My mind is at war with my heart. My better sense of duty to Capton and Midscape against an impulsive streak these feelings have brought out in me. Silence is the best thing for us, even if he doesn't see it now.

"Tell me now or I will wash my hands of you for good."

How can I make him understand? "Eldas, I—"

"Yes or no, do you love me?" His voice raises a fraction.

I watch as he shatters under my silence and hesitation.

"No. Of course not. Who could?" He chuckles sadly and shakes his head. "I already suspected you didn't, given the secrets you chose to keep."

"Eldas, it's not that simple."

"But it is." He skewers me with a look and I can't breathe. "It's a simple question, with a simple answer. Your actions and everything you can't say have told me all I need to know."

"I wanted to—our situation is—we can't be certain—I have to go to know—" It's impossible for me to form a cohesive sentence. The world is rumbling under my feet. I hear the groans and stress fractures spiderwebbing out around me. *Make him understand*, I have to make him understand. But when I need words most, they all fail me, even the frantic kind. "Eldas—"

He shuts the door behind him. The soft click of the latch engaging strikes me like a drum. I sway and then rush to the door and yank it open. But I already know what awaits me—an empty hall.

He's gone.

thirty-five

ELDAS RETURNS TO QUINNAR ALONE. He Fadewalks without so much as a word to me. I find out through Drestin that he's gone and that's really the biggest jab of them all. The carriage back is as cold and lonely as the castle halls that await me. Not even Hook's presence can ward off the chill. I spend the hours having a long debate with myself on what I could have, or should have, done differently along the way.

When Quinnar's castle is visible in the distance, rising up in line with the mountaintops and towering over the fields, I'm not sure of what I feel. A part of me is oddly nostalgic for the place. Another part of me would rather be anywhere other than this carriage, drawing nearer and nearer.

Rinni is waiting for me as the carriage comes to a stop before the castle's tunnel entry.

"What happened?" she asks—no, *demands*.

"Harrow—"

"I know what happened with Harrow. I am Eldas's general, so of course he told me about *that*." Rinni steps over to me, hooking her elbow with mine and leading me to the doors. Hook follows closely behind. Her voice drops to a hush as she glances back, looking to make sure the soldiers that rode on the outside of my carriage aren't following. "What happened between both of you?"

"Nothing happened," I lie.

"That's what he said and it's *obviously* false."

"Rinni—"

"I'd started to see changes in him—changes for the better, Luella. I started to see a warmer, gentler side of him. It gave me faith and hope in the man that leads us." We come to a stop in the large entry hall. The grand stairway arches upward on the opposite end, splitting to the empty mezzanine. It brings back memories of when I first arrived.

Incredibly, I think everything was *simpler* then. When Eldas was nothing more than a king. And I hardly understood my role as queen.

"But ever since he's been back… He's his old self again," Rinni finishes. "And I know that must mean something happened between you two."

"I can't change him, Rinni." I shrug as if the weight of the world isn't pulling on my shoulders. If Rinni believes I don't care, maybe Eldas will too, then maybe I will. And somehow this unbearable spot I'm in might become easier.

She blinks, startled. "I'm not asking or expecting you to. He was changing himself because he believed he could be a man worthy of love—*your love*."

I can't take her words. I don't want to hear them from her. I wanted to hear them from Eldas. No, I didn't want to hear them at all. It's impossible, we can't love each other. Not under these circumstances, not so quickly.

But what do I know about love? What have I ever known about love? Nothing, and that's why I messed this up so badly.

I need to return to what I understand and what won't hurt me— my duty.

"Sorry, Rinni, I think you might be mistaken. But I don't really have time to discuss it. The days are getting cooler and I have work to do. Hook, come along."

Rinni stares listlessly at me as I start toward my room. She eventually shadows behind me, but I can tell it's only out of obligation. She doesn't say anything else as I tuck myself away to plot and work.

I hope she ends up taking Eldas's side…he needs her a lot more than I do now.

Eldas doesn't speak to me for three days. By the fourth, he breaks the silence with a letter. Four simple, emotionless lines, nothing more.

It looks like it will snow again soon.
My kingdom needs you to sit on the throne, or break the cycle.
Which will it be?
How much longer until you're done and gone?

Done and gone. He wants to wash his hands of me. Rinni was wrong; he doesn't want love any more than I do. We're not built for love. We were made to focus on our work.

So that's what I do.

On the fifth day I'm up in the laboratory, Willow is with me, stealing worried glances until I can't take it any longer.

"Go ahead and ask," I say without looking up from my journal. I almost have my plans outlined. There's just one more thing to be done. I can spare a word for Willow. He's been kind to me, and none of this is his fault.

"What really happened in Westwatch?" His eyes are tender, gently probing. "You haven't been the same since you came back."

"Nothing changed," I answer placidly. Nothing did. Eldas is still the icy Elf King. I'm still forced to be his Human Queen. Whatever we found in that cottage was a dream, a moment, as fragile as butterfly wings.

"Something did." He frowns and sits across from me. "Is it what happened with Harrow?"

"How's he doing?" I ask, continuing to allow Willow to think that my general malaise originates from the incident with the fae. Since we've returned, Willow has taken over Harrow's treatment. But the youngest prince still hasn't woken. That's another thing for Eldas to resent me for. I've no doubt he blames me for the non-responsive state of his brother since it was I who first treated him.

"He's fine, but still no changes." Willow pats my hand. "I'm sure he'll come out of it soon."

"Yeah…" I finish looking over the last of my plans. There's only two weeks left before the coronation. I bite my lip and sigh. There's something I'm missing to achieve the balance, I know it. But my thoughts are scattered like dandelion seeds on the wind.

Part of me can only think of Harrow—worried for his recovery and wondering why he has yet to wake. Part of me wonders if I'm making the right choice. I wonder if there's any other choice to be made. Then, there's Eldas…

"I need to grab a few things from the conservatory," I say, slipping out before Willow can probe again. I've become too fragile. I'm teetering on the edge of spilling all the feelings I'm carrying at once just so someone else can see them all—so I no longer have to carry them alone. Yet I can't. It's better to pretend none of this exists.

The heat clings to me from the second I step into the conservatory and doesn't let go. I inhale deeply the now-familiar scent—the unique aroma of the plants that grow here, the moss, the earth, the compost Willow fastidiously tends in the back.

"Be good when I'm gone," I say softly to all of the plants. They seem to rustle in reply.

I wander the rows of planters, looking for what I might want to take with me. I need to find something that will mirror the strength of the redwood throne. Something that can grow deep roots in the natural world and provide a counterweight to the throne in this world. I thought about taking a trimming from the throne itself, but another queen tried that once for other reasons and the throne was impervious to all knives and chisels.

The first Human Queen planted something to make the throne—I believe that's what the statue in the center of Quinnar is showing. The Fade and throne, made at the same time in a magical process, almost like a ritual. But what can I plant that could possibly mirror the throne in might? What is still outstanding in the balance?

Then a small, bulbous plant catches my eye. I stare at the heartroot, blinking several times. It's as if I see it for the first time.

"The heartroot remembers," I whisper, echoing Willow's words.

There's the seed of space that my consciousness goes to within the throne. It's the seed from which the throne was born. In that place I felt the life of past queens, the energy of the world.

Lilian wrapped a piece of dark bark—bark that mirrors the heartroot and that seed at the core of the redwood throne—on a necklace with filament. It was the necklace she hid in the box. A necklace of magic that Eldas couldn't understand.

She commissioned her statue at the center of Quinnar to have her kneeling. Not because she intended queens to be subservient, but because she was showing the way everything came to be…and how everything would end.

"That's it."

The two flowers that bloomed instantly when I first touched the plant seem to wink at me, as if overjoyed that I've pieced it all together. Carefully, I scoop up the pot cradling the unassuming plant. I can almost see the phantom memories I first witnessed when I touched it, reaching out to me.

I saw Queen Lilian taking the heartroot and planting it the first time I came in contact with it. This is what she was planting in the statue. I know it. I feel it with every part of me. This was what the redwood throne grew from, and what will help bring balance in the Natural World.

"Did you plan for this all along, Lilian?" I murmur. A human woman who negotiated peace with a warring Elf King. She was clever. She pulled the heartroot intentionally into just Midscape. She *made* the worlds out of balance. Lilian built in a way out for the Human Queens for when the time was right—when peace was stable and Human Queens were no longer needed as trophies. She left the clues behind—starting the tradition of journals, the statue, using the heartroot that would trap memories of her—hoping someone would find them.

I'm going home.

Rushing back into the laboratory, I put the plant down and sweep Willow up into a tight embrace. He goes rigid, startled, and just as he moves to return it I'm already pulling away. "Thank you, thank you," I say.

"What?" He blinks.

"It's because of you, because of the heartroot, because—oh, never mind. Listen, I need you to do something for me."

"All right." Willow nods slowly. "What?"

"Take this." I carefully snip one of the flowers. His eyes widen. "And make it into an elixir for Harrow." The heartroot has helped in my healing of Harrow to date. The flower will be just what he needs—a merger of the plant's body and mind properties.

"The flower, but it's for…" He trails off.

"Poison, I know. I can't explain why I think it'll help," I say apologetically. "Please just trust me because I need to focus on my other work."

"Oh…okay." Willow slowly begins to move, doing as I instruct. Meanwhile, I'm running through my plans. I search the laboratory for everything I might need to sacrifice to equilibrium to make the heartroot propagate faster.

My hands pause before the magic pours from them. If this works…I'll be headed home before nightfall. I'm dizzy from excitement and apprehension.

Then, another thought crosses my mind. If this works, it will be the last time I see Eldas. My fingers tremble and I swallow hard.

The cycle must end, I remind myself firmly and get back to work.

Before I know it, I'm standing before the door to the throne room. Rinni has made herself scarce this past week. Maybe it's because I've been locked away in my room. Or perhaps it's because Eldas finally told her everything and I was right in thinking she'd take his side. Perhaps, when I'm gone, she and Eldas will try again at romance. The thought makes me ill and I focus instead on the heartroot in my hands.

"You're late," Eldas says curtly as I walk in. "I summoned you to sit on the throne an hour ago."

"I know." I meet his eyes and my chest squeezes further. Those icy eyes are the same that looked to me in the darkness with such longing…with what I had dared think might be love. "But it doesn't matter. This is all about to end."

The cycle.

Us.

"You figured it out," he whispers, not even a corner of his mask slipping out of place.

"Yes, I'm leaving tonight." I wait to see a flicker of emotion on his face. There's a flash in his eyes, but one not even I can read. It could be just as easily relief as regret. And, because I don't know, that's how I'm certain I'm making the right decision. None of this will be clear to me until I'm back in a world I know, a place that makes sense, and I have some amount of freedom to sort through this mess of feelings trying to strangle me.

"Then I will grant you passage through the Fade," he says slowly, "and hope that you never return."

thirty-six

IT'S SO LATE THAT ONLY THE VERY FIRST HAZE OF DAWN HAS
BEGUN TO KISS THE SKY.

Only Willow and Rinni have come to see me off. Eldas
allowed me to depart into the night without so much as a
goodbye. He dismissed me from that vast, lonely throne
room with little more than a wish of good luck. No one
else will see me off because this mission is still our great
secret. If I succeed, Midscape will rejoice in a security it's
never known; it will no longer rely on a single person for the
wellbeing of its lands. If I fail…Eldas will come to collect
me before the coronation and no one will know his queen
"tried to escape him."

I am like a lump of coal, slowly being crushed underneath
everything that surrounds me. Though I do not know if I'll
become a diamond…or dust.

Willow stares at me with bright red eyes, sniffling. "I
thought… I had no idea you were leaving. Not like this… I
would've… I would've…"

I pull him in for a tight embrace, one he returns without
hesitation. "It's all right. I'm sorry I kept it a secret from you.
But I had to." Willow was my one insistence to Eldas and
Rinni about this departure—he would know where I went
and he would be here. He's been far too good to me for me to
just leave without so much as a word to him. And he'd notice

I was gone and raise an alarm otherwise. So keeping it a secret from him wasn't an option any longer.

"It's all right," he says with a quivering voice. "I'm not mad, I—there's so much more about Quinnar and Midscape I wanted to show you. I wanted you to be here for springtime rites, and then harvest festivals, and Yule."

My heart breaks a little for everything I won't get to see. But I still wonder if those fractures will be smoothed over the second I return to Capton. Will all of the longing and kinship I hold toward this magical world vanish when I'm no longer operating under the assumption that I *must* be here?

"I would've loved to see them with you. And, who knows, I just might. All this might fail. I could be back for the coronation in two weeks." Eldas made that much clear to me before I left—our deal was for three months. It doesn't matter if I'm in Midscape or in Capton. If the timer runs out without the cycle being broken, I will be at the coronation.

We break apart and I rub his shoulders. The man is barely holding back tears and that prompts my own eyes to sting. I never imagined when I started hunting for a way out that leaving would become so hard.

"Besides," I say, cementing my brave face. "With me in Capton, you'll have Poppy back. You won't be so overworked."

"I was managing," he mumbles. Then, in an uncharacteristic display, Willow wraps his arms around me tightly. "You stay safe, Luella."

"You too." When we step back this time, I turn to Rinni. Her face is more twisted by emotion than I expected. Just when I thought she was beginning to abandon any friendship we might have forged.

"This is a mistake," she finally says.

"No, the line of queens is getting weaker. Lilian never intended for it to go on this long. We must—"

"You leaving him is a mistake," she interjects. Willow stares at his feet, clearly wishing he wasn't here for this particular conversation. "He loves you, Luella."

Then why didn't he say it?

Why didn't I?

I force a smile through the deep sorrow that's rooting around my heart. For now, the roots are as thin and spindly as the heartroot that I'm bringing back with me. But, over time, they'll thicken with resolve or regret. I hope for the former.

"Some things just aren't meant to be."

"That's a pathetic excuse and you know it."

"Rinni," Willow says with a note of scolding.

"You're running from him because you're afraid, because you know it's real." Rinni skewers me through, staring me down. "You were brave enough to come here with your head held high. You were bold enough to try running away when you first arrived even though you had no idea what we'd do to you for it. You were strong enough to take on Acolytes of the Wild Wood for Harrow—*of all people*—'s sake."

"But…"

"*But* feeling something real is what you run from." She speaks over me. "Why?"

I shake my head. "I don't expect you to understand."

"Good, because I don't." Rinni surprises me by stepping forward and tugging me to her. The hug is rough, as if she hates herself for doing it, but would hate herself more if she didn't. "Listen," Rinni whispers. "The Fade only responds to Eldas and his magic. His blessings on you are what will allow you to get back. But once you're there, remember you have something very few ever do—a guide. When your better sense catches up to you, we'll be waiting."

"I don't—"

"Now, go and fix things." Rinni almost pushes me toward the archway. She turns and doesn't watch as I walk through. She's already heading back to town. Willow lingers. His sad eyes are the last things I see before the Fade surrounds me.

Eldas's magic is wrapped around my ankles as I walk into the darkness alone. *I grant you passage*, he said, and bestowed the magic on me like I imagine a king to bestow knighthood. But this mantle on my shoulders is cold and lonely.

A low whine breaks my thoughts.

I stop and turn to the source of the noise. Hook is perched on a boulder. The darkness merges with his fur and all I can see are his eyes. But I know it's him.

"Come here." I crouch down and Hook bounds over. He looks at me sadly, as if he knows. As if he can smell the sorrow on me. "I have to," I whisper to the first part of Eldas I ever loved, long before I even knew Hook was an extension of him in a strange yet beautiful way. "Please know, I have to do this. There's no place for me in Midscape, not really. This is for both our worlds, and for all the young women who could come after me."

Hook whines again and I hang my head. The wolf moves closer and my arms slip around his furry neck. The dam I've built against the tears breaks. I sob into Hook's fur.

I mourn for the loss of time. I mourn for all that could've been. I mourn for the sweet memories I will never have a chance to make because the love I might dare say bloomed between us was doomed by circumstance before it could ever truly begin. I mourn his skin underneath the pads of my fingers, his silky hair brushing over me, the gravel that could rumble in his voice. I even find I already miss the view of Quinnar through the castle windows, and the festivals I never got to see.

I'm not sure how long I'm hunched in the Fade, crying. But I cry until there are no tears left. With my palms, I dry my cheeks and push my face back in place. My breaths are still ragged when I stand. I've cried out everything and all that's left is my resolve.

"Let's go, you and I, one last time."

Hook walks with me through the Fade. The tendrils of mist that surround me begin to thin and a twilight forest begins to come into focus. The line between my world and his thins and the moment I cross over is like a crack to the back of my head.

The last of Eldas's magic leaves me, vanishing on the wind, as though it had never been there to begin with. I've taken ten steps when a final whine alerts me to the fact that I am now walking alone. I stop and look back to Hook. He sits on the edge of the Fade, daring to go no further. His ears and tail are low and still, brow tilted with sorrow.

"Go back," I command weakly. "And thank you, for everything."

Hook gives a bark, then another. "Take care, Hook," I force myself to say.

A lonely howl echoes through the sun-dappled redwood forest as I make my way down the path and to the temple.

I don't look back. I keep my eyes forward on the world I've been longing for. The air is as I remember—sweet with peat, the smell of redwood sap, and a tang of ocean spray. Late spring is in the woods and it fills me with a vitality that can't be replicated on Midscape. It smooths over the pains of leaving, invigorating my steps. It is *life*, not just the illusion of it that reigned in Midscape.

A Keeper sweeping the area in front of the main temple is the first to see me. He scrunches his brow and tilts his head, as if trying to figure out why someone from Capton has ended up in the deep wood by the Fade.

"You..." His broom clatters against the stone walkway as his grip goes slack. The muscles in his jaw fail him as well. *Words* have failed him. "You— You— You're—"

"I need to speak with the Head Keeper." I look up at the sanctum in the shadow of the mountain rising above Capton. The mountain looks the same on the other side of the Fade, like a mirror. And where the castle is in Quinnar, the temple sits in Capton.

The man runs off without another word. He comes back not only with the Head Keeper, but the rest of the Keepers of the Fade as well. They stand in shock and awe, looking as if they've all just been struck on the head.

"Luella?" the Head Keeper whispers. "Is it truly you?"

"It is." I nod. "I'm here on a mission for both our worlds."

"A mission?" she whispers almost reverently. They stare at me like I'm some kind of goddess incarnate, walking among them. I suppose I am the first queen who's returned outside of Midsummer. And returned without a host of elves surrounding her.

"May I walk the temple grounds freely?" I ask. I know there are some places relegated to the Keepers of the Fade only.

"Of course, Your Majesty." The Head Keeper bows and I start into the sanctum, not bothering with the discussion of titles just yet. I don't know what people in Capton will refer to me as. I don't even know if I'm staying yet.

I pause at the altar that Eldas and I stood before nearly three months ago. It seems like a lifetime. A dull ache thrums through me like a low drum with every heartbeat until I can't bear to stare at it any longer.

If my theory is correct, and balance must be restored, then the temple is a mirror for the castle of Quinnar, and what the Keepers refer to as the sanctum is merely the entry hall.

Turning, I walk as if I'm back in Midscape, just in reverse. I slowly progress, Keepers following me, until I arrive at a clearing in the center of the temple grounds. There before me is the largest redwood tree of the forest.

"The throne was the roots for this tree," I whisper. A similar energy hums within its mighty trunk. It rains down from the leafy boughs soaring above me.

"Pardon?" The Head Keeper steps to my side.

"Sorry, I'll explain soon."

I cross the threshold of stone and grass and walk over to the tree.

Everything was meant to be in balance, for it to work. Lilian based her part of the first king's and queen's magic on ritumancy— the idea that the arrangement of items and actions in time can hold inherent magic. It's not identical, as there is no equal to the queen's magic. But it was close enough that Lilian could leave a piece out of place.

I walk over to the large tree—the mirror of the throne in the Natural World. At its base, I kneel down and set the heartroot on the ground next to me. I begin to dig with my hands.

This soil…the earth that nurtured this tree and the young women who came from it for decades. It will hold the first heartroot back in the Natural World. I remove the necklace I found with Lilian's journal from around my neck and bury it first. Then, I carefully unpot the heartroot and arrange its roots around the token.

The tree represents the throne.

Lilian's necklace represents that dark place my consciousness would go to.

The heartroot encases it all. It restores the balance. The heartroot remembers where it has been, and my hands pat earth tightly around it.

A perfect mirror of Midscape in the Natural World, now complete. The missing piece that kept the worlds out of balance, restored. I sit back on my heels, staring up at the tree with a little smile. All it took was a plant, a necklace, and some understanding.

"Thanks for making it simple, Lilian," I whisper.

"What did you do?" The Head Keeper asks.

The Keepers have surrounded me, looking on in confusion. They can't feel the magic that's beginning to flow through this tree. They don't know that the essence of this world is being soaked up by the branches that scrape the clouds and pushed through the Fade—through a tangle of roots—and into Midscape.

They aren't aware of any of it. But I am. Because even though I might never return to Midscape again, I will always be the last Human Queen.

I finally say, "I ended it."

thirty-seven

FOR FIVE DAYS, I WAIT.

I've commanded the Keepers to keep my presence a secret. It's a painful demand and I spend every night staring out the window of the room they've given me, looking down at the glittering lights of Capton and second-guessing my choice. But I know it's the right choice. If I'm wrong, giving my parents and Capton hope the cycle has ended and then immediately taking it from them would be too cruel.

I don't sleep much. Everything is too...*normal*. This place, these people...they've managed to continue on with their lives like nothing has happened. It was *my* world that changed in the past three months, not theirs. A fact that has me shifting in my suddenly too-small bed like I'm lying on pins.

Because of this, I'm awake when the elf messenger arrives. A Keeper comes to my room in a rush, breathless. "Your Majesty, we need—there's a messenger here from beyond the Fade."

"What did he say?" I step away from my window.

"Nothing other than he'll only speak to you."

"Let's not keep him waiting, then." I'm not sure what to expect from this interaction, but I gather my courage to ask, "Is the Elf King with him?"

"No, thank the Forgotten Gods," the Keeper mumbles. He doesn't even bother apologizing. He assumes the sentiment is mutual. After all, who in Capton could ever think of Eldas as anything good after his last display during the Town Hall? It took me weeks to soften to him.

The messenger wears the armor of a Quinnar knight and I vaguely recognize him as one of the knights who first came to collect me. He waits in the center of the sanctum, relaxed in the face of the wary stares given to him by the Keepers. I see some of them reaching for their labradorite on instinct and I can't suppress a smile. I remember being just like them, afraid at the mere sight of an elf.

"Your Majesty." The elf bows his head at me.

"What news from Quinnar?" I ask, somewhat eager. I assume that this man's presence means there's been a sign of my success or failure. When I left, the throne was in need of charging. I brace myself to hear words of snow, to hear Eldas's demands funneled through this man, commanding me back.

But then he says, "The redwood throne has sprouted limbs and holds leaves. General Rinni asked me to tell you that the Elf King sends his congratulations. That your efforts on behalf of the Natural World and Midscape have worked."

"If that's true…" The Head Keeper steps forward, looking to me. "Then what you explained to us on your arrival has come to pass?"

The first night was a long explanation with the Head Keeper and a few of her most trusted advisers. I had filled them in on the broad strokes of my mission and what was occurring in Midscape while they told me that Luke had been sent to the prison in Lanton for what he'd done.

"I believe so." I smile for show. The world doesn't seem to glisten or glow with joy. I have done something previously thought impossible. I have helped save two worlds. And yet…I am hollow. There's a void in me that can't be filled. Nothing is quite as sharp, or bright, or colorful as I expected.

"With that," the elf messenger continues, "the king has concluded your business is finished, and wishes you well. I will retrieve Poppy and we will depart."

Nothing seems quite real as I drift from one room to the next. I speak with people, I think, but I can't be sure. There's a vague sense that I thanked Poppy for her work, telling her to squeeze Willow tightly for me before bidding her farewell. The Keepers continue to ask me questions that I do my best to answer as much as I'm able—as much as I think they'll understand.

The cycle is over. I ended it. I will never have to return to Midscape. Eldas won't come demanding me.

I should be excited. And yet—

The world comes back into focus the second I see my mother standing at the entrance to the sanctum, my father next to her. I run over to them, throwing my arms around both of them at the same time. It's an awkward, weepy embrace, but I feel more than I have felt in days.

"Luella, it's really you." Mother futilely wipes her eyes as we pull apart.

"The Keeper said you'd returned, but we couldn't believe them," Father says.

"I understand. But it's me. And I'm here to stay," I say. But the words tumble awkwardly from my mouth.

How can I be so happy and so sad at the same time? I wipe my own cheeks and embrace my mother once more.

"This is truly a cause for celebration," Father says.

"I couldn't agree more." The Head Keeper nods. "I was thinking we should honor Luella's return with a grand soiree in the town square."

"The town square? But I—"

"We've fixed it up." Mother smooths my hair from my face.

"Mostly by embracing your 'landscaping' and turning it into more of a town park than it used to be." Father chuckles. I choke out a laugh as well. He turns back to the Head Keeper. "I'll discuss it with the council."

"I don't think a celebration is entirely necessary," I object weakly.

"Of course it is!" Father claps a hand on my back. "You have done something amazing, Luella. The whole town will want to honor you."

"The town has done enough for me."

"They will want to celebrate that no more of their young women will ever have to endure the title of Human Queen and cross the Fade ever again."

"Right." I bite back a sigh.

"What is it, Luella?" Mother asks.

"Nothing." I force a smile. "I'm just eager to return to my shop is all."

"In due time," Father encourages. "For now, enjoy a well-earned rest."

Three days later, I stand once more in my old room in the attic of my family's brownstone. "It's not much, but it's mine," I whisper. That's what I used to say.

There's the hay mattress, my books lined up in a corner, my chest of clothes, and everything that I once viewed as my life—save for my shop—neatly in one place. This is the first time I've seen it all since returning from the grandiose halls of Midscape. I expected to find it comfortable and comforting. And it *is* comforting…but in a nostalgic kind of way. Like an old pair of shoes, broken in just right, yet still unusable once you outgrew them.

"Luella?" Father says, climbing up the narrow stairs that wind to the loft. He holds two mugs in his hands. The familiar scent of the mint tea blend I made for him years ago fills the air. "I thought you might want something to calm your nerves."

"Thank you." I take one mug and sip.

"Your mother and I got something new for you to wear today." He nods at the dress laid out on the bed. It's a pretty sundress of bright yellow cotton, strung together with white silk ribbon. "Of course, it's likely not much compared to the gowns you got to wear as the Human Queen, but I suspect you'll have a lot more fun in it." He chuckles.

"I'm sure I will." All I want is my canvas trousers. All I want is my shop. All I want is to be normal once more.

But I don't know what normal is anymore. I don't know how to find something I can't recognize.

"You'll love the new town park." Father sips his tea, beaming from ear to ear. He wanted to show me on the way, but the Keepers didn't want to risk my being seen before the "big reveal." So we came right home; that way I could get ready in my own room, with my own things—as my mother insisted. "The council is even talking about naming it Luella Park."

I laugh softly. "What's next, a statue of me there?"

"Funny enough, the idea was floated and it seemed well received." Father laughs as well, but I'm silent.

A statue of the first queen in Quinnar. A statue of the last queen in Capton. The balance is maintained in yet another way. It makes sense I would stay, that I would leave Eldas, when I look at it from a perspective of the natural order. The first queen stayed with her king. I left mine.

My nails dig into my cup.

"What is it?" my father asks, noticing my heavy silence.

"Nothing." I shake my head. "You were right, I'm a little nervous; that's all."

"It'll be fine. Everyone will be so happy to see you. A perfect resolution after all the ugliness Luke brought on us. It'll be closure for everyone."

"I hope so," I murmur.

"Leave her be, Oliver," Mother calls up from downstairs. "She needs to get ready. As do you!"

"Coming, Hannah!" Father gives me a kiss on the crown of my head like he would when I was a girl and goes to leave.

"Father," I say timidly, stopping him. "After today, everything will go back to normal, right?"

He stares, confused. "Why wouldn't it?"

"Nothing. Good. That's all. Thanks again for the tea." I sip as I watch him leave, hoping he's right.

When my mug is empty, I put on the dress my parents picked out. It's to the knee, loose in the skirts, with charming front laces and capped sleeves. I feel worlds better finally out of Midscape clothes and borrowed robes from the Keepers.

Wandering downstairs while I wait for my parents, I take a turn around my shop. I can see Poppy made some adjustments while I was gone. I'll need to put a few things back into place.

I can also see the ghost of Luke, standing in the doorway. But even that hateful memory isn't as bitter as it once was. For all he risked, for as foolish as he was…maybe it was because of what he did that Eldas and I could finally see eye to eye. If I wasn't so desperate for a way out, I might have just accepted Eldas as he was. Not as the man he was becoming.

The phantom sensation of his hands on my skin gives me a shiver. But the memory is immediately chased away by my mother's voice.

"Are you ready to go?" She and Father stand at the bottom of the stairs.

"Yes," I say, and we head off.

We take the long way through town and end up behind where the stage used to be. I can see signs of the new improvements made in this area. There are cuttings of the vines that grew over buildings piled up in the street, waiting to be burned or used for compost.

Father leads me around the side of the stage. I catch a glimpse of the entire town—the people I came back for. The people I love and owe. I take a deep breath.

"Let's go," he says.

I'm ushered onstage before I can collect myself. I think I was announced by the Head Council member, or Head Keeper? Maybe both? I stare out, standing where Eldas did months ago, looking out at the faces of everyone I once knew.

My heart is in my throat, trying to strangle me. *Wrong, this is wrong*, something in me screams, *the Human Queen isn't meant to be seen before her coronation.* I'm not in the right place, I realize. I'm not meant to be here, with these people. For all I love them, and even though they will always be a part of my heart, I will never fit in with this world again.

With all eyes on me, I turn and run.

thirty-eight

I RUN THROUGH TOWN, HEART RACING WELL BEFORE I'M
WINDED. I run with skirts tangling around my knees, hair
loose to the wind, tears streaming down my cheeks. But
I don't know what I'm running from—or toward. I don't
know why I'm crying.

All I know is there is this hurt deep within me, deeper than
I've ever known. It's gnawing, insatiable, and impossible to
describe. Even though I have calmed the redwood throne,
its roots are still in me, calling me back.

No, these aren't the roots of the redwood throne. These
are roots of my own making. These roots have grown from
something I never asked for and never wanted. They've
shaken the very foundation of my world—my duty—and
now I'm falling into a deep abyss from which I might never
escape.

I sprint beyond the edge of town, slowing as I reach the
rolling hills by the woods. I see the river that runs through
the forest, winding through the Fade. I think of following
it, but Eldas's magic is no longer on me. I would be just as
hopeless at navigating the Fade as I was the first time I got
lost.

I can't bring myself to go into the forest, either. I don't
belong there. Those trees grow too closely to my memories.

I look over my shoulder and back down at town. Most people are still in the square. I can imagine their confusion and hurt.

My damp face burns. They'll be angry with me. After all they invested in me, after all I did to return to them. I ran.

And I ran because…because…because I don't have a place in Capton any longer. My former position in the community is still here, but nothing seems right. This place isn't my home anymore. Am I to spend the rest of my days here, longing? Making potions with half my heart? I turn to the sea, wandering toward the cliffs, and stare out over the horizon line, looking at the vast expanse of land beyond Capton.

I could explore this world now, I suppose. If I don't belong here anymore, and didn't belong in Midscape, then maybe I'll find where I belong out there. As I think those thoughts, guilt rises up in me, drowning them.

My chest tightens and I let out a strangled hiccup. Not quite a sob, not quite a laugh. "Well, you got what you wanted, Luella," I mutter with a note of self-directed anger. "Now what?"

"And what did you want?" My mother's voice cuts through my thoughts. I turn, surprised to see her standing there. Her fiery red hair is struggling to escape its braid in the sea breeze.

"Mother…" I say weakly. "I'm so sorry."

"Don't apologize; you've been through a lot and I suspect the Keepers—while kind—didn't properly check in on you," she says gently. "May we sit?"

"Sure." I sit on the grasses where she motions.

Mother sits next to me, pulling her skirts around her as I do the same. "I told your father it was too much, too soon for you. He's been worried about you. Funny enough, I think he's more worried for you now than when you left."

"What?" I turn to face her. My mother wears a tender but otherwise unreadable smile. "But I'm back…"

"And you've not been the same." She tucks some hair behind my ear. "What was it that you wanted?" she repeats her question.

"I wanted to live up to everyone's expectations. I didn't want to let the people of Capton down after they invested so much in me," I say. "I wanted freedom. I wanted purpose. I wanted…"

"You wanted?" she encourages.

"I wanted to know if what I felt for him was real," I admit, both to her and myself at the same time. The words are small and fragile, as if saying them aloud might shatter these trembling feelings in my chest.

"*Him*," she says softly. "You mean the Elf King?"

"Yes, Eldas."

"What did you feel for him?" Her expression is unreadable. Will she be mad if I admit to finding a way to love someone she has only known as a brute of a man? Could she understand that even though he took me from her, there's a gentle and thoughtful side to him? That he sent Poppy back, and stayed with me when I was weak after the throne because he cared, and cooks bacon, and does that thing with his tongue that I—

I blush and turn back to the ocean, the heat reaching all the way to my ears. "I don't know."

"What do you *think* it was?" Mother isn't letting me get out that easily.

"Love," I admit.

"Tell me why you think that?" she says in that plain voice, void of any clues as to what she might really be thinking.

I take a deep breath, and tell her about my time in Midscape. Unlike the Keeper, who got the necessary overview of basic facts, I tell my mother everything but the moments we shared at the cottage that still make me blush. She hears of every ugly, beautiful, and improbable emotion I discovered within those gray castle walls.

My voice is as raw as my heart when I'm finished and stars are blooming in a distant sky.

"I see," she says thoughtfully.

The silence that follows is heavy in my throat and hard to swallow. I stew in agony and my mother has an enigmatic smile on her face as she looks out over the dark waters that span between us and Lanton.

"What're you smiling about?" I finally ask.

"Many things. I'm smiling because I'm still very proud of my daughter, for being strong and capable. For doing something that's so impressive I can hardly comprehend it." Mother had been a little lost when I tried to explain the Fade, redwood throne, and seasons both the first time and this time. "I'm smiling because I'm happy my daughter found somewhere she belonged and could be happy. Really, that's all a parent ever wants to hear."

"But..." Was I happy? The image of Eldas floating in the water of the pool at the cottage while I tended to the garden drifts across my mind. I think I was.

"So, what're you going to do now?" She ignores my hesitation.

"I'm not sure," I admit.

"Are you going to go back to Midscape?"

I draw my knees to my chest and wrap my arms around them. "I can't leave."

"Why?"

"I can't leave you and Father."

"Darling one..." She wraps an arm around my shoulders. "Every child must eventually leave. Sometimes, it is to a house down the street. Other times, it is to somewhere very far away. But if that child ends up where they belong, and are happy and loved...that's all a parent wants."

Her words sting in a nostalgic sort of way. It's the same feeling as when summer ends for a child, the same feeling I had when I looked at my old room. It hurts because of how happy I was here, yet know I can't be any longer.

"I can't abandon Capton's needs."

"Capton will be fine," she insists.

"You had Poppy." I look at her with a bit of an accusatory stare. "Poppy is gone and she won't be coming back. Now who will look after the elderly of Capton? The sick? The wounded?" Mother opens her mouth but I continue hastily. "And don't say that people will just be happy for me. They deserve to get back what they invested in me. Everyone sacrificed so much—you and Father too. If I left, I wouldn't be putting the academy education everyone bought me to use." *I'd let you down*, I want to say, but can't bring myself to.

She takes a deep breath. I can tell just from the way she inhales that she has a lot of thoughts she's about to share. I brace myself.

"Firstly, it sounds to me like you already put that education to use by saving all of Midscape and stopping the cycle of future queens.

That's a pretty good outcome of your studies. If anyone has earned a rest, it's you."

"But that's not…"

"Not what you went to school for?" Mother arches her eyebrows in a *don't mess with me, young lady* sort of way. "Not explicitly, but a worthy application and outcome of your studies, don't you think?"

"But, healing—"

"Yes, this matter of healing. Foremost, we *did* manage just fine and will continue to with or without you. Luella, you are talented, and an amazing help, but the town doesn't need you to survive." Her sad but strong words shake me to my core. I grow still, trying to just focus on the grass swaying around me and the ground beneath me. I have wrapped up everything I thought I was and needed to be in this town. If I'm not needed…then what do I do? "But if you are that worried, then you should know your father and the council got word this morning from Royton."

"Royton?" I echo. The Royton Academy is known for producing some of the best herbalists in all the land. It's farther down the coast, nestled in warmer, more tropical lands where all kinds of plants can be grown year round. "What about Royton?"

"There's an academy student they're sending. She'll be here within the week to assist with anything Capton needs as you settle— for however long that takes. It says she's been paid in full for at least one hundred years and we can use her services for as long or as little as we like."

"But Royton is days away…" My fingers tremble.

Eldas did this. He got the news to Royton. He saw that someone came so I didn't even have to worry as I settled in. He paid them a king's sum to serve this small town. There's no other explanation for how a graduate of Royton knew and why they would come here of all places.

What was Eldas thinking when he arranged for this new healer?

The cynic in me would say that he was trying to prove that I wasn't as necessary to this community as I once thought. He did it to take my purpose from me and force me to stay in Midscape. But, if that had been his intent…he would've no doubt told me before I left.

He was giving me choice—the choice to stay in Capton, or leave, no matter if it was for Midscape or not.

Love is choice.

Just dream, Eldas, and then follow those dreams.

I have to go to know.

Words I said to him that I didn't know got through echo back to me. He listened. Time and time again. That man is imperfect and stinted. He can be cruel and cold. But he's willing to try and hear me. Somehow, he heard things I didn't even know I was saying. He listened…and I didn't do the same.

Our interactions flash across my mind. His looks, his touches, even in front of others. The way he held me in the night. The way our magic resonated together. The promises he made me.

Eldas, what do you feel for me? My question echoes back and now I can see between the lines. *He loves you more than anything, you idiot.*

"Luella." My mother's gentle voice startles me back to the present. "The one thing that has always been most important to your father and me has been your happiness. Where will you be most happy?"

"Will everything be okay?" I don't just mean with them, or here in Capton, without me. I want her to tell me everything will be all right.

"I know you. You'll make it okay if it's not." She gives my hand a squeeze.

"If I go back…if they'll have me…I'll become more a part of that world than this one."

"But you can still visit from time to time?" she asks. I nod. "Then how is it different from what any parent endures? Children are meant to grow and live their own lives. If you want to, Luella, *go.*"

"Even if I wanted to go back…I can't." Panic is rising in me. I should have asked for a way back. Why didn't I find a reason to ask Eldas to give me his blessing to return?

"Why not?"

"Because the only one who can traverse the Fade—or give others the ability to—is Eldas himself." Even as the Human Queen, I couldn't find my way out of the Fade when I tried to run away. I was lost, turned around, hopeless until he came to rescue me. "The two times I passed through were either with the blessing of his magic, or with him as a guide."

A guide. Rinni had said I had a guide through the Fade. *Hook.* Rinni meant Hook.

"Wait," I whisper to the horizon. "I can get back."

My mother smiles as if she's known the whole time. "Then what're you waiting for?"

"But—"

"Go," she insists a final time. "Go and be happy."

My heart thrums in my ears so loudly it nearly drowns out my parents' voices downstairs as I'm packing a bag. Mother takes charge on explaining things to my father. I strain my ears, listening for his reaction. His soft voice rumbles up to me, but I can't make out what he says. By the time I walk downstairs, satchel over my shoulder, he has a weary but genuine-looking smile.

They wish me well and hold me so tightly my bones pop. I tell them that I might be back in ten minutes. But it's also possible I'm not back for a week, a month, or a year. I've no idea what changes my return may cause in Midscape. I've no idea if Eldas will even let me stay, or if the coronation will make me one with that world to the point that I *can't* return. The magic has changed, and I'm gambling with the results.

For the first time in my life, I'm acting without a plan and without a duty to guide me. All I'm listening to is that frantic beating of my heart.

I now stand at the edge of the Fade once more. I'm risking everything here. But what else is new?

I take a deep breath and step into the Fade; a finger of ice runs down my spine. Bringing my fingers to my lips, I let out a whistle that echoes in the unnatural silence.

"Hook?" I call and call again. Just when I'm about to give up, Hook's golden eyes blink at me from the darkness. "Hook!" He bounds over to me and I fall to my knees. The wolf licks my face and I waste no time. "I need to get back. I need to get to Eldas. Can you take me there?"

Much like the first time in the Fade, Hook tilts his head left and right before finally stepping away. He trudges off into the darkness and I gather my strength to follow behind, hoping he's not going to lead me back to a keystone. The moment I see soft moonlight yawning into the mouth of a cave, I begin running.

Hook bounds at my side with a happy bark. I give him a grin and he seems to almost skip around me. *Welcome back!* his movements seem to say.

I skid to a stop and overlook Quinnar. The spring air is warm now, even at night, and is almost sticky compared to the chill of the Fade. Flowers hang on the breeze, rustling on the trees. They complement the streamers and pennons that have been splashed across the city.

Music soars through the air. People are in the streets, dancing, laughing, and drinking. Sparks of magic are flung about and I see paper beasts and birds come to life and rejoice among the revelers. I smell the cakes Rinni and I tasted. I see acrobats spinning on hoops suspended impossibly midair over the lake.

I see a city in celebration—as if they somehow knew I was about to return. The world I first saw as dead and gray is now in full bloom. It's magical, and looks like something I could call home.

Hook's warm muzzle presses into my hand and I crouch down to scratch him behind the ears. "Thank you for leading me through the Fade. Go off and play, I don't want attention right now." He whines. "I'll whistle for you again," I promise.

Hook sits, insistent.

"Oh, fine. Come along then." I laugh, part nerves and part a joy I didn't expect to know again.

I start running down the staircase, nearly tripping over myself. Luckily, I changed into my trousers so that when I do nearly tumble face-first at the bottom, I don't end up with my skirts around my ears in front of nearby revelers.

"Wait—" an elf woman says "—you just—"

I don't wait for her to finish. I begin sprinting. Hook knows, like always, where I am running toward. He charges through the crowd, barking and howling people out of the way, and I try hopelessly to keep up.

We make it to the tunnel entrance of the castle, blocked off by a row of knights. I skid to a stop before them. Hook rounds my back, keeping the encroaching crowds at bay.

"I…I need…" I wheeze and reach into my satchel. I didn't leave the shop unprepared. I take a swig of fortifying drought I brought and stand straighter, breath caught. "I need to see the king."

"You're—"

"But you're a—"

"Aren't you?"

All the guards seem to talk amongst themselves at once. They're silenced by a familiar voice.

"Let me through!" Rinni barks, pushing her way forward. She stops, blinking at me until a sly grin works its way across her cheeks. "You're almost late."

"Sorry to keep you waiting." I smile. "I lost track of time on the other side of the Fade. Did I miss the coronation?"

"Not yet." Rinni guides me into the tunnel. I hear the rumbling of a mass of people on the other side of the castle doors. Rinni opens them with a flash of her eyes.

I step into the castle and, for the first time, I see color. Tapestries of bright blues and vibrant greens stretch from ceiling to floor, hung along the wide columns that support the large entryway. More garlands of flowers are hung from the railings of the mezzanine.

Vases of flowers line the great hall behind the gathered crowd. Men and women of all colors and shapes are here and all their eyes swing from where the Elf King stands on the stairs—presumably having just been giving a speech—to land on me.

But his eyes are the only ones I focus on. His mouth is slightly agape. Shock has shattered his usual mask and he stares in a stunned silence.

I know there are important people here—lords and ladies. People of his kingdom, *our kingdom*, if he'll let me share it with him. I know I've come before them with dirty knees and in what they'd consider pauper's clothing. I know that I had one chance to make this first impression count and I ruined it. I have ruined Eldas's years of planning, sacrifice, and suffering leading up to this moment. None of this has gone according to plan.

I didn't even think of what I was going to say. So I open my mouth and say the first thing that comes to mind. I let my words echo to the top of the hall.

"King Eldas, I love you!"

thirty-nine

THE SILENCE IS DEAFENING. I could hear a cherry blossom petal land it's so quiet. I don't know what everyone's reactions are. The only person I'm focused on is Eldas. The only person whose opinion even remotely matters to me here is him.

His shock fades into something I'd dare say is warm. After the initial horror at my outburst—at how *none* of this is in line with his traditions—fades away. There are the eyes I recognize. Eyes I fell in love with and have been longing to see while back in the Natural World.

"And I love you," he says, finally.

Four words, and things click into place. I have a lot I need to figure out here. There are a lot of unknowns surrounding what I will be to this world now that a Human Queen is no longer needed to make the seasons turn. But I'll figure everything out, because the man standing before me is every possibility I want to embrace.

"If—" Eldas clears his throat "—if you will all excuse the queen and I for a moment." Eldas holds out his hand and I cross the room to him, trying my best to glide and hold my head high.

I might not look like the queens they know. But maybe in time they'll embrace the different sort of queen I already am. I slowly ascend the stairs and Eldas's fingers curl around mine. My magic calls out to his and invisible sparks fly between our skin, leaving me breathless.

He escorts me up the stairs and into a side room, closing the door quickly behind us.

Eldas rounds on me. I might have expected him to be slightly cross for how I handled things, but there's a fire in his eyes that isn't angry in the slightest. His hands are on my face, cupping my cheeks. "Say it again," he whispers like a sigh of relief he's been holding ever since I left.

"I love you," I repeat from earlier, but this time only for him. "I've loved you since the cottage. Since…I don't know when. Somewhere along the way I fell in love with you. You and I…these circumstances we met under have been a bit of a mess. But I love you despite them all."

"Then why did you stay away?" he whispers. "Why didn't you tell me before you left?"

"Because I was a coward," I admit aloud for my sake and his. "I was afraid that I only thought I loved you because I had little other option. I thought the love was fabricated for my own survival, since I thought there was no other way out—that I would be stuck here forever. I was afraid of a love that came from a lack of choice. I was afraid I didn't even know what love was because I don't think I've ever felt it before."

"But when you had your way out…when you had the choice you desired…you came back." Eldas trails his eyes over me now and I tingle with delight. A look has never been more intimate. I'm stripped with a gaze alone.

"I *had* to come back. I found my answer while I was in Capton—I love you for all you are and all we are together. It is not my imagination; it isn't survival. Yes, Eldas, I had freedom and choice and I *choose* you. I know none of this came about in a conventional way, but it's genuine. And I thought that, maybe, we could give this another try."

"A try?" He arches his dark eyebrows and I laugh softly.

"We went about this backwards, you know. We got married, tumbled into bed, fell in love. Usually it's the other way around."

"I liked how we went about this," Eldas says. His voice is

auditory silk. It brushes over my skin and my body tenses. "Because it led me to you."

"I think I can agree with that," I breathe.

He crushes his lips against mine with a restless kiss of pent-up desire and longing caresses. He presses me against the door, groping at my rear, pulling at my hair. For the first time in my life, I hate that I wore trousers.

I kiss him with equal fervor. I run my fingers through his raven hair, shamelessly spilling it over his shoulders and curtaining it around our faces. I caress his cheek as his mouth moves against mine. I taste his tongue over and over and hope it is merely the *first* taste of many I get of him today.

And when he pulls away, I am weak in the knees and relying on the door behind me for support. I am ready to tumble on the floor with him naked. I am ready for that whole room to hear my cries of ecstasy so long as it means I would have him moving within me once more.

"So what now?" I breathe, glancing between him, the floor, and the door behind me.

Eldas pulls me to him and his other arm slips back around my waist.

"Now," he growls over my lips. His fingers have slipped into my hair and I tilt my head back to give him full access. "Now, my queen, my *wife*, I will take you to bed."

"But the people—"

"Let them wait. We are the king and queen, after all. Our coronation will occur when it is meant to."

Two days slip through my fingers like the ease of Eldas's fingers through my hair when we're in bed. The outburst has been the talk of the town and speculation has been firing left and right about why the Human Queen came rushing in, what it had to do with Eldas's announcement about the seasons, and why the Human Queen was wearing such plain clothing. There's even been some speculation that our love itself was what broke the cycle of the Human Queens.

That is a history I will be certain to rewrite. Love is powerful, but so is the hard work Eldas and I have put in. The hard work we will continue to do to be good rulers for this land.

If it were up to me, we would've stayed in his chambers for eternity. But duty calls eventually. Sooner rather than later the coronation must happen. We could stall for a day or two, but any more would blow past scandalous into lewd behavior.

We stand before the main entry to the throne room. I have Eldas's hand in mine with a white-knuckled grip.

"Don't be nervous," he whispers.

"Easy for you to say," I reply and try to smooth out invisible wrinkles in my skirts. The gown the seamstress made for me is breathtaking. Layers of chiffon shaped like leaves almost have a scale-like appearance when I'm stationary. But when I move, it looks like leaves departing late summer trees on a gale. It would've been such a shame to see this wearable art go to waste if I hadn't returned.

"All you have to do is sit."

"You know that's one of the first things you said to me, more or less." I grin up at him and he chuckles. But worry quickly gnaws at my levity. "We should have tried the throne beforehand just to be sure it won't try to siphon from me."

"We were occupied." Eldas smirks. I give a yank on his hand and steal the expression with a kiss. My husband can't look that handsome without ending up with my lips on his.

"After this, let's be *less* occupied. I want to know what's going on."

"Going on? About what?"

"Everything," I say. "I'm here to rule alongside you, after all. I'm more than just a pretty face now that the seasons are fine without me."

He gives me a small smile and is about to say something when Harrow and Sevenna enter. Harrow still looks thin, and a little paler than I'd like. But his eyes are bright and sharp. His movements are strong.

My hand falls from Eldas's and, ignoring Sevenna entirely, I cross to Harrow and sweep him up in my arms.

"Good gods, she's hugging me," I hear Harrow murmur. But he's relaxed in my arms. A hand even pats my shoulder lightly.

"I was so worried about you." I release him and pull away. Eldas had sneaked in an update on Harrow's condition between sessions under the sheets—we had to eat sometime—but this is the first time I've seen him.

"It seems I worried everyone." He looks guiltily between Eldas and Sevenna. I can tell there are still some discussions to be had about Harrow's tangle with glimmer and Aria. But there's time for that. And I'm here now. So I can at least make sure Eldas doesn't come down too heavily with punishment on the young man's shoulders.

"We're just glad you're all right." I confidently speak for everyone in the room.

"Harrow, go and speak with your brother," Sevenna commands icily. "I'd like a word with the Human Queen."

He obliges, glancing between his mother and me before leaving. Even though Eldas and Harrow quietly talk between themselves, they glance back over regularly. Sevenna ignores her sons.

"Harrow told me what you did for him," she begrudgingly admits. Her hands are folded before her—white knuckled. "And I think half the kingdom knows about your declaration for my eldest boy."

"I know it's not traditional—"

"Oh I think you made tradition with that," she says curtly. I can't tell if she's pleased, proud, cross, or upset, so I try and keep my face blank. Sevenna sighs. "However, Eldas wrote and gave me context. He informed me of your choice."

"My choice?"

"That you had freedom, and you came back. You chose my son and your oath to him as a wife." I watch her throat constrict as she swallows hard. Sevenna forces the next two words out almost violently. "Thank you."

I barely resist asking her how hard that was to say. But I'm too floored that she said it at all. Plus, this is the mother of my husband and the man I love. It's time to begin smoothing over the rough edges in our relationship for everyone's sake.

"You're welcome." Even though this woman makes me more

nervous than anyone, I can speak calmly and plainly when it comes to my feelings for Eldas. "I love your son. And I want to love Harrow like a brother, if he'll let me. Same with Drestin and Carcina." I glance over my shoulder and see Harrow looking our way. He no doubt heard his name.

Sevenna snorts softly. "Good luck with that. My youngest is wild."

"Don't I know it?"

We share a smile that almost seems like camaraderie. There's more work to be done here and more layers to Sevenna. But I'll have time to peel them back.

I'll have the rest of my life in Midscape.

My husband's hand slips into my own as the doors open. Trumpets blare and a rain of petals cascades down from the ceiling magically at our entry. Eldas's walk is as rigid as his crown, his face severe. But I can't help smiling in wonder as I take in the room.

The same mass of people is here as before. Earlier, they had arrived for an announcement. But now they are here for a coronation—the *last* coronation of a Human Queen. The room is filled with wild magic and all the creatures who wield it. In it, I see my home—a place where I belong and nothing is missing. It's the home I have chosen.

Eldas escorts me to my throne and then faces the room.

"The Human Queen has returned." His voice echoes to the highest beams of the ceiling. "The cycle begins anew. But this cycle we begin now shall be eternal." He accepts a crown of gold-gilded redwood leaves off a pillow held by Willow. The young man's eyes shine with tears of joy. "All hail Queen Luella. The last queen of spring."

"All hail Queen Luella," the room echoes as Eldas settles the crown on my brow.

Together, Eldas and I sit on our thrones and the room erupts in cheers. I finally relax in my seat. There's nothing more than the quiet whisper of magic on my skin, humming from across the Fade—a magic that reminds me of where I've come from, as I look out on where I am.

I can finally relax here. I hold out my hand and Eldas takes it with a smile. Everything is in balance, and all is right with the world.

How about a bonus scene?

Not ready to say goodbye to Luella and Eldas? Want a glimpse of the elves spring celebrations? A bit of marital bliss? Head over to my webiste to learn how you can get a special bonus scene that takes place over a year after the end of the book. It will also give you a hint to what you can expect from the next book in the Married to Magic universe: A DANCE WITH THE FAE PRINCE.

Learn how you can get the bonus scene for FREE at:

http://elisekova.com/a-deal-with-the-elf-king/

Do you want more?

Married to Magic is not a series, but a world. Each stand alone novel set in this universe will be championed by its own heroine who encounters magic, romance, and marriage before reaching her ultimate happy ending. If you enjoyed *A Deal with the Elf King* and want more, then check out the next **Married to Magic** novel...

a DANCE
with the
FAE PRINCE

a MARRIED TO MAGIC novel

Learn more at

http://elisekova.com/a-dance-with-the-fae-prince/

A Dance with the Fae Prince was initially titled "A Dance with the Fae Rogue." The title changed a few months before its release and, as a result, some earlier printings might mention its former title.

About the Author

ELISE KOVA has always had a profound love of fantastical worlds. Somehow, she managed to focus on the real world long enough to graduate with a Master's in Business Administration before crawling back under her favorite writing blanket to conceptualize her next magic system. She currently lives in St. Petersburg, Florida, and when she is not writing can be found playing video games, watching anime, or talking with readers on social media.

She invites readers to get first looks, giveaways, and more by subscribing to her newsletter at:
http://elisekova.com/subscribe

Visit her on the web at:
http://elisekova.com/
https://twitter.com/EliseKova
https://www.facebook.com/AuthorEliseKova/
https://www.instagram.com/elise.kova/

See all of Elise's titles on her Amazon page:
http://author.to/EliseKova

THE
AIR AWAKENS
SERIES

A young adult, high-fantasy filled with romance and elemental magic

A library apprentice, a sorcerer prince, and an unbreakable magic bond. . .

The Solaris Empire is one conquest away from uniting the continent, and the rare elemental magic sleeping in seventeen-year-old library apprentice Vhalla Yarl could shift the tides of war.

Vhalla has always been taught to fear the Tower of Sorcerers, a mysterious magic society, and has been happy in her quiet

world of books. But after she unknowingly saves the life of one of the most powerful sorcerers of them all—the Crown Prince Aldrik--she finds herself enticed into his world. Now she must decide her future: Embrace her sorcery and leave the life she's known, or eradicate her magic and remain as she's always been. And with powerful forces lurking in the shadows, Vhalla's indecision could cost her more than she ever imagined.

Learn more at:

http://elisekova.com/air-awakens-book-one/

AIR AWAKENS:

VORTEX CHRONICLES
THE COMPLETE SERIES

A sweeping magical adventure, filled with royals, romance, family bonds, and sacrifice. Perfect for fans of Sarah J. Maas and Holly Black!

Vi Solaris is expected to rule an Empire she's barely seen... but her biggest problem is the dangerous magic that's awakening within her.

Now, alongside her royal studies, she's training in secret with a sorcerer from another land. From his pointed ears to enchanting eyes, he's nothing like anyone she's ever met before. She should fear him. But he is the only one who knows what's happening to her.

As Vi fights to get her magic under control, the Empire falters from political infighting and a deadly plague. The Empire needs a ruler, and all eyes are on her as Vi must make the hardest choice of her life: Play by the rules and claim her throne. Or, break them and save the world.

This coming of age, epic fantasy is a story of family, sacrifice, sorcerers, slow-burn romance, wrapped up in a magical adventure that will ultimately take readers to places they never imagined.

Learn more at:

http://elisekova.com/vortex-visions-air-awak-ens-vortex-chronicles-1/

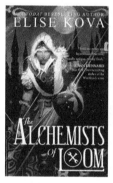  

Acknowledgements

Amy Braun—without you picking apart this manuscript it wouldn't be anywhere near what it is now. Thank you so, so much for working with me, for being patient with me, and for nitpicking everything. I can't tell you how appreciated you are.

Miranda Honfleur—you helped me so much on getting my first few chapters right and (let's face it) that's one of the most important parts of a manuscript. I appreciate your critique and hope we can work together in the future.

Alisha Klapheke—even when you had so much going on, you took the time to help me and, for that, I'm eternally grateful. Thank you for helping this book put its best foot forward.

Melissa Wright—just so you know, I still don't regret you pushing me to get critique partners. As you can see above... it was one of the best things I've ever done. Also, sorry my feedback for you took so long. You can blame this book.

Danielle Jensen—fantasy romance *queen*, I can never say thank you enough for how amazing you are. You inspire me. You let me vent. You're incredible and I'm so very lucky to be your friend. Here's to many more years as friends and many more books!

Lux Karpov-Kinrade—thank you for being such an early cheerleader for this book and sticking with me throughout. You've helped me stay the course and keep a level head even when I was filled with nothing but doubt. Thank you so much for your kindness and friendship.

Marcela Medeiros—I so enjoyed working with you on this project. Thank you for your patience and hard work in bringing my characters to life. The cover is more incredible than I could've dreamed.

Kate Anderson—your enthusiasm is always so motivating. Thank you for cheering me on and for giving this book a look at when it was in its early stages. I so appreciate your feedback.

Rebecca Heyman—thank you for encouraging me to trim the first act of this story dramatically. It certainly needed the haircut.

Melissa Frain—this might be the first manuscript we worked together on, but here's to many, many more in our future.

The Man—your love is my muse. Here's to our own love story now and over the years to come.

My Dear Tower Guard—thank you all for your help every step of the way. I can't tell you how much it means to me to have you all on my journey.

The turtles—thank you, ladies, for keeping me m otivated, for being so supportive, and for having an entire channel dedicated to wine. I needed *all* of that this year.

Every Instagrammer, Facebook Expert, Twitter Maven, Blogger, and other influencer who helped spread the word—you all are the champions of the book world. I am so lucky to have worked with each and every one of you for the release and promotion of *A Deal with the Elf King*. Words cannot express my gratitude.

CPSIA information can be obtained
at www.ICGtesting.com
Printed in the USA
BVHW081047050522
636220BV00006B/91

9 781949 694284